THE FALL OF THE
FOUR

ADAM W. SHAHAN

THE FALL OF THE
FOUR

Tate Publishing & *Enterprises*

The Fall of the Four
Copyright © 2010 by Adam W. Shahan. All rights reserved.

No part of this publication may be reproduced, stored in a retrieval system or transmitted in any way by any means, electronic, mechanical, photocopy, recording or otherwise without the prior permission of the author except as provided by USA copyright law.

This novel is a work of fiction. Names, descriptions, entities, and incidents included in the story are products of the author's imagination. Any resemblance to actual persons, events, and entities is entirely coincidental.

The opinions expressed by the author are not necessarily those of Tate Publishing, LLC.

Published by Tate Publishing & Enterprises, LLC
127 E. Trade Center Terrace | Mustang, Oklahoma 73064 USA
1.888.361.9473 | www.tatepublishing.com

Tate Publishing is committed to excellence in the publishing industry. The company reflects the philosophy established by the founders, based on Psalm 68:11,
"The Lord gave the word and great was the company of those who published it."

Book design copyright © 2010 by Tate Publishing, LLC. All rights reserved.
Cover design by Kandi Evans
Interior design by Stephanie Woloszyn

Published in the United States of America

ISBN: 978-1-61566-586-0
Fiction / Science Fiction / Military
10.02.18

To my wonderful grandparents, Nana and Papa.

Nana, I will see you again soon—you were my best friend. Papa, without your help I could not have gotten this book published. I love you both.

CHAPTER 1

A young boy looked out from the single window of his family's soot-covered lean-to. It was a conglomeration of scrap, trash, and neglect of those who lived above them in the towering circular residential building. Steam-powered airships sailed through the night air, a vestige of his current circumstance, a reminder of why his father was now jobless. Fuel recovery sites all across the Seven Provinces were shutting down as Oronus Bretton and Omni Revival Technologies continued in their quest to excavate the ruins of the civilization that went on before them and to achieve "the prosperity of the Ancients." It seemed as though every time O.R.T. discovered a new technology, some new group of people lost their jobs.

His belly growled at him in hungry annoyance, and he shuffled across the room to gaze into the empty pantry for the hundredth time.

A nobleman's airship sailed through the night air, and he gazed down at Harrah, the capital city of his province. On a pilgrimage to the holiest site in all of the Seven Provinces, The Basilica of the Four, he began reciting praises to the Four he had learned from childhood in anticipation of his audience with the High Priest. In his worshipful state, he did not notice the airship sail eastward out of O.R.T.'s hangar bay.

In the sleeping quarters of O.R.T., a small alarm went off at the captain's bedside—someone had entered the hangar bay and taken an airship. He leapt from his bed and grabbed his emerald cape, banging on the door that led to Anna's quarters.

"Honey, wake up!"

She met him at the door, and they sprinted up the bridgeway to the hangar.

Oronus came out of the hangar director's office with a scowl on his face. "Whoever did this downloaded the map to the final house. This is getting more serious by the second. Who would do such a thing?"

Aaron let the airship hover over a grassy hummock on the eastern side of the Great House. There was a stretch of water that wrapped itself around the eastern wall; a great bridge arched over it and up to the entryway. He slid down a large rope, his kit slung across his shoulder, and walked away from the just-rising sun and toward the Great House. This was it. This was the last one. There was a rush of adrenaline inside him that was almost euphoric as he approached the stone bridge. He would return with the mysteries that this arcane dwelling contained—or he would not return.

He examined the entry of the bridge very carefully, which was made more difficult by the time of day—the sun had barely broken the edge of the horizon. As soon as O.R.T. began its daily routine, though, they would know what happened, and they would come for him.

He did not see any visible signs of an enchantment or a barrier, and so he cautiously crossed the threshold and stepped onto the stone bridge. To his great surprise, there were no traps or enchantments all the way to the spacious landing and the entryway doors. This was very unusual to Aaron—it almost seemed *too* easy to approach the house.

Walking cautiously toward the doors, he removed a long, silver knife from his kit, slipped it into the keyhole, and began delicately twisting it back and forth. He heard and felt the doors unlock and stepped quickly aside as the right entryway door opened outwardly.

His heart was almost beating out of his chest; he was incredibly frightened, yet excited about the prospect of entering this place. It was the *last* one—they had excavated all the others. The prosperity of the Ancients would be fully realized after today, and he was there to usher in a renewed age of technological convenience. It was selfish, and he knew this. However, it was something that, if done correctly, could open up all kinds of opportunities for advancement for him; he could be a department head, the youngest ever! How could Oronus say no? Better yet, how could Anna? He stepped confidently over the threshold and into the Great Room.

The floors were covered with dark green marble, and a faint blue light pulsed through the hair-thin cracks that covered it. The walls were paneled with ornate woodwork, and an immense, layered chandelier was hung from the vaulted ceiling. To his left was an archway into the western wing; to his right was the eastern wing. Before him was the Great Room with its elaborate furniture and honorific statues of the Four. Paintings of a landscape Aaron's generation would never see were displayed in magnificent frames. He forewent the eastern and western wings on the first floor and chose to first ascend the spiral stairway ahead of him. The second floor, he knew from experience, would contain the bulk of the rooms and artifacts. Aaron wondered how the Ancients lived here; he felt as though it was more of a tomb they had built to bury their advancements than a *house,* as it had come to be called.

He removed a thick pair of gloves from his kit and prepared to climb the spiral staircase.

As he approached the first step, his eyes were drawn to a long-legged table sitting against the side of the first few stairs. On this table was a medium-sized chest with a glass top and skilled woodwork along the sides. The corners held talon-like feet and there were looped iron handles on each end. Inside was what looked like four glass spheres resting on a velvety surface of midnight blue. He lingered at the foot of the stairs and gazed at the chest, wondering what its purpose was. He resolved that on his way out he would make this chest the last thing he took from the Great House. The steps themselves showed no sign of enchantment, so he reserved his greatest precautions for the threshold to the second floor that awaited him.

When he reached the top of the stairs, he found a closed door that had no handle or hinges—it was as if this section of the wall were simply made of a different kind of wood than the rest. He removed a pair of pliers from his kit and approached the door. He slipped the head of the pliers into the thin space between the door and the rest of the wall. With calm, quiet force, Aaron gripped the pliers and began to pull the panel away from the wall. After a few tries in different places, he was able to pull the panel away to reveal the hidden doorway. There was no sign of the Raujj, so he crept forward into the massive hallway. There were several rooms on each side.

He soon discovered that all of these doors were open and that none of them were protected by any barrier or enchantment. Furthermore, every room he entered held no artwork, no machines, and no new technologies—*nothing!* He became increasingly frustrated as he passed through room after room and had nothing to show for his exploits.

This was the strangest thing Aaron had ever experienced. In every other Great House they searched, they *always* found devices or machines, sometimes still functioning, and pieces of artwork. This Great House was *empty,* and Aaron became concerned that someone had already been here. This emptiness meant that, not only would Aaron be in a great deal of trouble for coming alone, but he would also have nothing to show for it.

In dejected silence, Aaron made his way back down the stairs. He explored the shorter, less-occupied eastern and western wings on the first floor but to no avail.

It was when he walked back into the Great Room that he remembered the chest on the table. He reasoned that, after seeing that the chest was the only thing in the Great House anyway, Oronus would *have* to commend him for retrieving the only artifact in the place. He walked back toward the table. Approaching it, he looked down through the glass top. He leaned in to look more closely at the gray, lifeless spheres, and as he did so, the breath from his nostrils fogged two sections of the glass. It was when he breathed on the chest that the spheres began to take on color and to spin. Aaron's eyes widened with excitement at the sight of this, and he placed his hands on either side of the chest as he looked on.

Immediately after touching the chest, there was an awful sound, loud and long and deep, that roared all around him. The spheres began to whirl against the velvet inlay, and Aaron jumped back and covered his ears with his hands. The entire Great House began to shake, and Aaron looked up just in time to see the chandelier snap from the ceiling and fall with a *crash* that caused pieces of crystal to fly in every direction. The shaking had become so violent that Aaron could barely keep his balance, and as he turned back to grab the chest he noticed that the archway to the eastern wing was collapsing.

In a state of panic, he grabbed the chest and sprinted around the fallen chandelier for the doors. As he ran forward, it seemed as though the ceiling above him was making every effort to *flatten* him, and when he turned back as he reached the entryway door he saw that most everything was beginning to crumble and collapse. With great effort, Aaron slung back one of the doors and sprinted toward the bridge. Hearing a loud *crack*, he looked back to see the roof of the Great House collapse to the ground, sending a cloud of debris toward him. Not wanting to dive into the water, but having nowhere else to go, he gripped one of the iron handles of the chest and hopped over the side of the bridge, gripping the bridge's railings with his free hand. It was not long before he began to lose his grip. He fought desperately to hang on until the chaos subsided. The noise from the collapse soon ceased, and the dust clouds were clearing when Aaron felt his grip on the chest's handle and on the ledge both slipping. Sweat began dripping down his arm, and it was making it increasingly difficult to have a good hold on the chest. In anguish, he had to finally choose either losing the artifact and saving himself or trying to save the artifact and possibly losing it *and* his life. It was too late, however—the chest slipped out of his hands.

"*No!*" he shouted as, in a reflex, he brought his other hand down to grab the chest. Eyes closed and teeth clenched, he prepared himself to meet with the surface of the water. However, he did not feel the sensation of falling, nor a rush of wind. He slowly opened his eyes, fearing that he was trapped in some enchantment or barrier, but he simply gazed out toward the level and stationary horizon. It was then that he noticed the increased pressure on his ribs and under his arms, and he looked up to see Captain Oronus Breton's face glaring down at him.

The captain pulled Aaron up and over the ledge and dropped him on the ground. Ashamed and guilty as he was, he still felt a twinge of anger and annoyance for the way in which Oronus let him go. The captain stared down at him, his fists on his hips and Anna beside him. Despite the enormity of what was going on, he was still taken by her high cheekbones and long, silky hair. Oronus's words snapped him back into reality.

"Aaron Ravenhall, for being the person I might choose to succeed me, you certainly aren't living up to the title! This is the most irresponsible, arrogant, and negligent thing that has ever happened under my direction! What in the name of the Four were you *thinking?*"

"I just—"

"You may have just destroyed *countless* technologies that we will never know of! You could have destroyed artifacts that could have been given to the basilica and the high priest—more importantly, you could have gotten yourself *killed!*"

"I thought—"

"You thought!" Anna added with a sarcastic guffaw. "Thinking was definitely not a part of this, Aaron. Do you know what you've done?"

At this point, Aaron had decided not to respond, knowing that he would simply be interrupted and scolded even more.

Oronus raised his eyebrows. "Well?"

Aaron set the strange artifact down and stood up, dusting himself off and facing the two interrogators, who were swiftly becoming prosecutors. "I thought if I took a Great House on by myself and showed you that I was ready, that I was the *best,* that you would finalize your plans for me to succeed you over Dardus or Parrus or anyone else."

"Fool!" Anna shouted, and Oronus snapped a warning glance at her to signal silence. Aaron appreciated this.

When Oronus turned from looking at her and surveying the damage Aaron had caused, he turned back to Aaron and looked down by his feet. He was about to press Aaron even harder to account for his actions, but as he continued examining the strange chest he lost all thoughts of Aaron. He approached the chest and gently motioned for Aaron to move. The captain bent low and began to examine it—its markings, its language, its contents. Anna stepped forward and peered over her father's shoulder.

"What is it, Daddy?"

Oronus spoke to Aaron without looking at him.

"Where did you get this?" He remained in his position, bent over the chest. "Where, Aaron?"

"In the Great Room, on a table, next to a set of stairs."

"Was there an enchantment around it?"

"No. Actually, it was the only artifact in the whole Great House. There were no enchantments at all, and the whole place was empty except for that chest."

Oronus nodded in silence and continued to stare at the chest.

Anna's eyes widened, and she scowled. "That's convenient! I would say I saved the only artifact in the whole house too if I were in his place!"

"Silence, Anna—I believe him. Aaron, did the Great House begin to collapse before or after you touched the chest?"

"After."

Oronus stood slowly, bringing the chest up with him as he did so. Oronus was pale faced and grim.

"Daddy?"

Oronus spoke softly. "I think this is the Chest of Worlds."

"The Chest of Worlds? You mean, it's real?" Anna asked.

"What is it, Captain?" Aaron puzzled. He had never heard of such a thing.

Oronus shook his head and turned. "We've no time for questions—we must leave immediately and tell no one what has happened or what we have found. I fear that this is going to change things, and I don't know that it will be for the better. We'll have time to talk later, but first," he said, turning to Aaron, "you must board the craft you stole from my hangar and return to O.R.T. Every action has a consequence, Aaron."

"Yes, Captain." Aaron began walking back to the personal craft, slowly becoming more and more anxious about the magnitude of his consequence, but he was stopped.

"Oh, you're not going alone—Anna, accompany Aaron to O.R.T."

With that, they left the resting place of the final House of Ancients, the final Great House, and headed for Harrah, the capital city of the fifth province.

CHAPTER 2

As the airship Aaron had commandeered, the *Auspicious,* passed down through the clouds, he marveled at the beauty of Harrah from the sky, in spite of the sinking feeling in his stomach. The circular ports that rested above Harrah's majestic, old buildings were a comforting sight. Some closed and became clocks, others great mirrors, and still others paintings of ivory structures laced with ivy. People in other provinces might not agree, but Aaron insisted to himself that Harrah was the most beautiful capital city of all.

The network of buildings that made up Oronus's headquarters held a different beauty, however. Located almost in the center of Harrah, this network of buildings held a *raw* beauty. Six octagonal buildings surrounded a connectional system that ran all the way to a hangar resting at the top.

Anna and her engineers and cartographers were experimenting with new transportation and charting the expansive skies. Oronus's scientists constantly struggled to understand and reconstruct the artifacts that his excavators recovered. Philosophers and artists immersed themselves in the books and paintings written in a language and created with media that they worked to decipher and re-create. Scholars and mages worked on books and scrolls of the Raujj constantly.

The Raujj was not usable or even revived in this age, and it was for that reason that Oronus's family had maintained a monopoly on the existing texts: so that it could not be manipulated and used for wrongdoing. Oronus constantly acted as ex-officio to all the departments that were at work in his forefathers' complex, their dream and his. It was a place devoted to rediscover the world that had gone on so many years ago, the time of the Ancients and their Great Houses, and their mastery of the mind and the senses that was the Raujj.

"Whoever discovers its key," Oronus often said, "needs to be devoted to the good in people or at least as devoted as humanity will allow."

CHAPTER 3

Anna waited as Oronus and a thin man with a constantly spinning and adjusting monocle and a long, handlebar mustache rounded the corner of the bridgeway leading to the hangar. Aaron had just descended from the *Auspicious* using the hydraulic ramp that had come to rest on the hangar floor.

Oronus and Anna made quite a pair, Aaron thought. Oronus was a tall man with broad shoulders and thick sideburns that ran down to his jawbones. Every outfit he had ever worn, at least as long as Aaron had known him, was offset by a flowing emerald green cloak with a golden ruby clasp that rested above his collarbone. Anna had a long, golden-blond ponytail and she always wore a black O.R.T. riding suit with shiny, metallic pauldrons and riding boots.

Aaron had never seen the third man before, though he knew that the monocle he wore had to have come from one of Oronus's departments, spinning and adjusting seemingly on its own accord. He wore a white, military-looking suit with a mandarin collar and a dark green cape. Aaron thought it looked far too short for him.

"Aaron."

Oronus's voice was deep and concerned, and his bright blue eyes, eyes his daughter had inherited, looked soft and saddened. This hurt Aaron even more than the response he was expecting, which was some severe punishment.

"Aaron, what were you thinking? As far as we know now, this was our *last* Ancient's Home to excavate. What made you think you could even make it past the front grounds without the Raujj that was present claiming you? You are as bullheaded as you father was, Aaron. Do you know what you've done?"

Aaron stepped back at the mention of his father. So many horrible feelings coursed through him: shame, embarrassment, and a kind of unwarranted defensiveness against this trio that stood before him.

"I thought I was ready. I thought this would show you I was ready," he resigned, embarrassed.

"Ready? For what, your own death? You *fool!*" Anna shouted.

"That's enough, Daughter." Oronus stepped forward. "Aaron, I want you to tell me what happened."

Aaron began to tell the trio about his passage across the front grounds of the Great House, his entry and exploration, and, finally, the salvation of the chest and the collapse of the Great House.

Anna looked away, Oronus looked amazed, and Aaron thought the tall, thin man looked as if he might vomit.

Oronus spoke again. "You do not realize the potential importance of the artifact you recovered, and for that you have our thanks, but—"

"But," said the tall, thin man as he brushed past Oronus, "you have destroyed ze final Great House, idiot! Ze fact zat you saved zis artifact does not excuse your actions! Ze ozher provincial directors and I vill see zat zis entire complex is shut down before you rob us entirely of ze Ancient's Raujj!"

His fist was raised, and spit flew from his mouth as he shouted in Aaron's face. At this point Oronus lost his concern and candor and bent toward the man's face.

"Aaron! Meet Jacques Aevier, the director of the sixth province, who will be stepping outside for the time being!" He was now standing between Aaron and the director.

"Bah! Gods knew zat zis vas inevitable, Oronus. If ze ozher directors saw through you as I do, zhey vould have never let you take zis *peasant* on at ze level of apprentice! And now look at vat he has done!"

At this comment, Aaron turned and ran back to the airship, closing the ramp behind him. As far as Anna knew, Aaron was as high in the nobility as she was. She knew nothing of his upbringing, and this embarrassed him a great deal.

Oronus took Jacques by the shoulders, forced him to turn around, and marched him into the nearest office; he was, after all, a much larger man than Jacques. When they were both inside, he shut the door and turned to face Jacques.

"You listen to me, Aevier. That boy is as gifted as they come, and I will not fire him. I have raised him like one of my own ever since his father died. Also, I can assure you that this complex will remain in operation and that Aaron will continue on his path to succeed me. You know that it takes extraordinary talent to enter a Great House *alone*. There should have been five of my people with at least twenty years more experience to tackle the final house! Jacques"—he loosened his grip and calmed a little—"you seem to be forgetting that my buildings are *packed* with technologies and artifacts from the other known Great Houses, all of which are *still* standing, mind you. Also, he may have saved the actual Chest of Worlds! It was not intentional, and he broke several of our rules by entering a Great House alone, but we may have the divine artifact in our hands now. We don't want to jump to any conclusions, obviously, but this could be a breakthrough."

At this statement, the anger melted away from Jacques as he considered Oronus's words. If it turned out to be real, if he were the one that delivered the Chest of Worlds to the high priest, he would be greatly rewarded.

"You are right, Oronus—zis could be ze real thing. I vill back down for now. However," he added, regaining some of his greed for the power of the Raujj, "I expect zis to be ze greatest year of turnout your teams have ever experienced. You need to redeem yourself…or me and ze ozher directors vill take control of zis facility!"

Oronus opened the door and gestured to Director Aevier. "We'll see about that, Jacques. Good day."

The director gathered up what little he could from his undersized cloak, draped it over his left arm, and marched out of the office and down the bridgeway without looking at anyone as he left.

"Gods." Oronus sighed and placed both his hands down on a desk, lowering his head. "I've got to do something, or Aevier will take the study of the Raujj in a direction it shouldn't go."

He sat down at the desk and began writing a letter to Richard Alden, director of the fifth province and longtime friend of his. Oronus needed to start gathering allies in the other provinces before Jacques could begin his molestation of the Ancients' crafts. After all, there was no binding pact that kept the study of the Raujj within the halls of Oronus's fathers. His safest haven was the ignorance of the people in the provinces, and Jacques had a loose tongue.

CHAPTER 4

Anna called to one of the crew members of her own airship, the *Regalus*, and asked him to lower the ramp of the *Auspicious* manually. Anna was very worried about Aaron. She knew that she was the reason for his embarrassment, and even if she told him that she cared not for his status, she doubted he would believe her. Like it or not, familial placement in the provinces was very important, and Anna had turned down many sons of directors and nobles in her day.

"Ramp's down, marm." The old geezer had been working for Oronus since she was born, yet she didn't even know his name.

"What is your name?"

"Edgar, marm," he said with some pride.

"Thank you, Edgar. You may go about your business," she said. She straightened the hat on his fuzzy, old head and smiled.

"Thanks, marm," he said sheepishly and walked away with a bounce in his step. As she walked up the ramp of the *Auspicious*, she turned down the hallway to the central room, where she assumed Aaron would be. He was not there; not in the captain's quarters; not in mess; and not in crewmembers' quarters or medical. She knew he would not be in the engine room of the airship—the steam that the ship's blimp pumped into its bowels made the machinery far too hot to be around even hours after use. As Anna came back toward the ramp, she heard a noise above her. She turned and saw that the hallway's hatch to the deck was slightly open. She climbed the ladder and found Aaron sitting at the helm, where the crooks of the port and starboard railings met and beneath the wonderful metallic glowing statue *The Auspicious Woman*. Oronus had recovered it from a Great House outside the seventh province for Anna so long ago; it rested there and glowed even more as the sun passed through the still-open porthole.

"Go away."

"Aaron..."

"Leave me, Anna. I might as well just pack my things and go look for work in the Market District. I am a peasant and a failure."

"Aaron, you are not a failure, an idiot maybe, but—"

"See what I mean?" Aaron threw his hands up. He stood up and turned to face *The Auspicious Woman* and the setting sun.

"I was only joking, Aaron!" Anna said this laughingly and walked toward Aaron, placing her hand on his shoulder.

"When Mother was still alive, on the night of the christening of Daddy's flagship, *Orion*, I wanted to impress her and show her how ladylike I could be. I used her makeup and put on her evening gown and gloves and ran to our courtyard where she was. I ran on the ends of the dress all the way there and tore its edges. I began to dance around her, showing her how graceful I could be in an evening gown and heels. As I spun, I tripped and knocked over a row of candles on stands. They fell on me and caught the dress on fire. Look."

Aaron turned, and she lifted part of the black, soft cuirass to expose a scar above her right hip bone.

"From the candles," she said. "See? Many people do something with the best of intentions in mind, but it doesn't turn out the way they had planned. They end up hurting themselves or the ones they love."

Aaron began to laugh. He laughed so hard that Anna took offense.

"Why are you laughing at me?"

"Thank you, Anna," he said. "That hardly matches what I have done this week, but I appreciate your care and effort!" He continued to laugh.

"Aaron!" She playfully punched him in the side, and in her playfulness, laid too hard a punch.

"Oops. Sorry," she said, and they both laughed together there, under the careful gaze of *The Auspicious Woman*.

"Aaron?"

"Yes?"

"Tell me about your father."

People in the Residential District of the fifth province's capital city ran out of their homes on all levels and out onto their decks as the *Orion* passed between the rows of great buildings leading up to the director's mansion. It was quite a remarkable sight. The *Orion* looked as though it were made of pure silver and turquoise. Yet this beautiful airship could be used just as easily for a battle as a formal visit to a director's mansion.

As Oronus approached, a great clock face opened at the top of the enormous estate to expose the docking bay where the *Orion* would come to rest. Oronus always loved visiting Richard Alden—it was he, after all, who convinced the other directors, including Jacques Aevier, to turn the excavation of the remaining Great Houses over entirely to Oronus and provided the funding needed for such a venture. The study of the Raujj had always been in their family, but technically anyone could come and go from the Houses of the Ancients. Besides that, they had been friends for at least twenty years. Rachel, who was Oronus's wife, and Gwen Alden, Richard's wife, had also gone to school together.

The *Orion* gracefully came to rest in the director's hangar. Oronus swung off the deck of the *Orion* and landed gracefully in the director's docking bay.

"Hello, Gwen!" he shouted as he strode toward her and embraced her warmly.

"Good to see you, Oronus! Welcome!" Gwen pulled Oronus away from her, hands on his shoulders, as if to take in an old friend. "How have you been? You will have to excuse my appearance; I have just come from my lab. Richard told me Aaron was almost killed!" Oronus took her hand and walked with her toward the entrance to the main stair, reassuring her along the way.

"You always did enjoy alchemy more than I thought was healthy!" He chuckled. "No, he is just fine, Gwen, and so am I. Aaron was very foolish in his actions this week, but he also saved something very important. What are you working on in that little lab of yours?"

Gwen smiled and said, "Oh, you know me, Oronus. I'm always looking for ways to improve life for my Richard. I'm working on an augment to an engine that could possibly make airships go even faster and with less steam power!"

Oronus chuckled at this. "But with more of whatever chemical you're using, I'd wager." Gwen frowned and elbowed Oronus in the chest. "Oronus! You always spoil my fun. I may just have to put it on Richard's personal craft just to prove you wrong!" They both laughed for a time, and then Oronus changed subjects.

"Anyway, are you ready for this, Gwen? Aaron recovered the Chest of Worlds." Gwen stopped and turned to him.

"The Chest of Worlds is real? How is this possible?" The Chest of Worlds had come up in the tales of all of the Seven Provinces for ages.

"Yes, Gwen, and I am having it closely guarded, though I'm not sure I believe in the stories that have been spun around it."

Gwen opened the doors to the main stair, and they descended to the rest of the house. Gwen led him down the massive staircase to the third floor, where Richard no doubt "snoozed dutifully in his study," she had told him in passing. Portraits of past directors lined the staircase. As they reached the third floor, a hovering machine with an ovular shape and robotic arms, hands, and fingers came from down the hall and greeted them.

"Good evening, madam. Director Alden is in the study. May I take your cloak, Master Oronus?"

"Yes, thank you, Max." Oronus handed Max the cloak, and it sped down the Great Stair, bent on some other duty. "I had forgotten how polite O.R.T.'s teabots were; I never see them when they're on." Oronus chuckled as they walked toward the study.

Sure enough, there rested Richard Alden in a high-backed chair behind a large, oaken desk. A glass of scotch was tilted slightly in his hand over the chair's arm, and a cigar sat smoldering on a small, golden tray in front of him. There was no light in the room save the small lamp on his desk. Gwen smiled and walked over to him, pulling the scotch out of his hand and putting the cigar out. She kissed him on the forehead and whispered into his ear.

"Honey, Oronus is here to see you." No response.

Oronus grinned, walked over to a bookshelf, and grabbed a large, leather-bound book. He walked to the front of the desk and held it out with both hands. Gwen smiled and moved the scotch glass as Oronus dropped the book, and it fell with a loud *bang*. Richard jumped up out of his chair with a shout and looked at Oronus, bewildered at the disturbance and disoriented from a nap he did not need.

"Gods! Well, Oronus! Good to see you!" he said as he rounded the desk to shake Oronus's hand.

"We'll have none of that, Alden!" Oronus proclaimed as he bypassed the handshake for a hug.

"You've caused quite a disturbance in the provinces, old

friend! Gods know I like things a little shaken up occasionally, though destroying the last remaining House of Ancients is heavy business. Gwen, dear, could you pull us up some chairs? We have much to discuss."

"Of course, dear. Would you like a fresh drink?" Gwen was happy to have Oronus with them. Since Rachel's death, his visits to the director's mansion were rare.

"Excellent idea, sweetheart, that is just what I was thinking! Oronus, would you like a drink?"

"Nothing strong for me, thank you. Though, I would enjoy a nice glass of iced tea."

"Max will bring them in shortly. You two try and stay out of trouble. I'll be in the lab if you need me."

Gwen closed the door to the study, turning on the lights and the ceiling fans as she left.

"Gwen and her alchemy... Never cared for the stuff, but I will go along with whatever keeps her happy. She is the best thing that has ever happened to me. Now, Oronus, about this Great House business, for the longest time I had the other six directors convinced that all of the crap that goes on behind your walls in regards to recovered technologies should be isolated from the eye of the Council of Directors and centralized to your staff and equipment."

Oronus chuckled. "Yes, and the provinces have been quite pleased with the product of this decision, I think. Max is in homes in most of the provinces, they are opening new schools of art in *all* of the provinces, airships have increased the efficiency of travel and trade, and my new steam-powered ships have made the harvesting of fuels obsolete! Richard, with these revivifications, we are beginning to realize the prosperity of the Ancients."

"Yes, Oronus, I agree. As uncharted as the things you are dealing with are, I see it as a blessing that the excavation and revivification of these artifacts turned out the way it did, but—"

Just then, the door opened, and Max floated in carrying a

glass of scotch in one hand and a glass of iced tea in the other. "Here you are, Director Alden, Master Oronus."

"Thank you, Max," said Richard, and Max floated back out of the room. Oronus took a long, slow drink from the glass and set it on the floor beside his chair.

"Delicious! I had forgotten that Gwen made such excellent tea. You were saying?"

"Where was I? Oh yes, *but* the provinces being governed by this oligarchy somewhat limits my abilities to control those who do not listen to my persuasions."

"Aevier?" Oronus knowingly guessed.

"Of course Aevier! Who else? You know as well as I do that he wants the restoration of the Ancient's language and the Raujj to be governed by the council, meaning *he* wants to govern its restoration."

"Yes, and with my staff leading 'ze vay!' Pompous rat." At this impersonation, Alden choked on a sip of scotch and, half laughing, half coughing, set down his glass and regained his composure.

"Well, pompous rat or not, Jacques Aevier may become more of a threat than you realize. He is not the same sniveling twit that he was when he came onto the council twelve years ago, Oronus, though his disposition when he became director of the sixth province played out in his favor. It was me, after all, who placed him as head of the Industrial Districts, hoping he would continue to be more concerned with his newfound position of power and its perks, which would keep his nose out of your business."

"And I thank you for that, Richard. The autonomy you have given O.R.T. has saved us on more than one occasion."

Richard nodded at this and shifted in his seat. "Yes, Oronus, but as overseer of all Industrial Districts, he has access to all files and information that pass through any of the seven mainframes. They all link to his personal office and his office at the council's headquarters in the fourth province. All this time, Oronus, we assumed Aevier had his attention elsewhere. His inaction in the community and his approval of amendments in the districts without a passing glance seemed to prove it." Alden had lost some of his cheerfulness at this and became more solemn, looking directly at Oronus.

"So what is the point you are trying to make, Richard? Yes, Aevier is a lazy fool who is riding on the coattails of the council. So what?"

"Let me present to you a theory, Oronus. A *theory*, mind you. Remember that." Oronus shook his head and reached for his glass.

"Every time Anna and her engineers went out on expedition, every time they located one of the Great Houses, every time a new artifact was discovered and revived or recreated, it was logged into your server. Any new industrial happening in any of the seven facilities, particularly yours, is logged specifically for Aevier's viewing."

Oronus gave an annoyed sigh. "Yes, thanks to Jacques every time I *cough* I have to log it for him. It is his way of pretending he actually does things for the districts."

"Yes, Oronus, that is how it seems. Melinda Stockstill and I are in charge of appointing department heads, and when we do, we hire them administrative assistants. The catch, though, is that these assistants also answer to Melinda and me, and we have them fill out monthly reports on each head's activity."

Oronus's eyes widened at this. "So you have spies, then? You rascal! What would the other directors say if they knew you knew what they knew?"

Richard chuckled at this and shrugged. "Sometimes an oligarchy is a dirty business, Oronus. Anyway, Aevier has been much more active than you may have guessed. Melinda oversees the reports from the Industrial Districts and only recently came to me with a pattern she discovered in Aevier's logs in the main server. Aevier's viewing of the other six Industrial Districts' goings-on was a mere once every quarter. Yours, however, was quite a bit different. The mainframe at the headquarters of the council resets at the turn of every year for maintenance purposes, and Aevier's logs onto your system seemed to be syncing up with these resets. In other words, it looked like Jacques only looked at your files once a year. This was comforting to both of us and seemed to support my appointment of him to the Industrial Districts. When Melinda and I met last month, she told me that she met with Aevier in the sixth province at his request. Apparently Aevier invited all of the directors, excluding me, of course, to his mansion to discuss the language of the Ancients and the excavation of Great Houses."

"What?" Oronus edged to the end of his chair.

"I didn't think it was a big deal. He has invited them to his province for the same reason after every one of the council's meetings. Anyway, he stepped out of his office for a piss break during his meeting with Melinda, and while he was out she stepped behind his desk to look around. She saw the screen on his desk, the one that connects to the mainframe, and saw O.R.T.'s file open on his screen.

"That's not so odd, Alden. O.R.T. was why she was there, was it not?"

Richard nodded. "Yes, but that's not everything. Melinda used a code that is installed in the mainframe to bring up previously viewed files and the length of time they were accessed. What she discovered was that O.R.T.'s file had been open for *months*."

Oronus slid back in his chair. "What does this mean, Alden?"

"Well, I think that ever since he had access to the mainframe, meaning *twelve* years ago, he has had your file open at all times. This is why it only appeared that he checked your progress once a year; he had to reopen O.R.T.'s file after the mainframe reset for maintenance."

Oronus stood and walked toward the bookshelf by the door, the one he had taken the book from to wake up Alden. He ran his fingers along the spines of the books.

"Why would he do this?"

"That is where my theory comes into play. I believe that Aevier knows *far* more about the Ancients than he lets on. I think he has been internalizing the information that you and your men have logged for the past twelve years. And I think he wants to use this knowledge to start a slow takeover of the study of the Ancients and, eventually, the Raujj."

"That's impossible, Richard. O.R.T.'s logs are not detailed enough for Aevier to train himself or anyone to enter a Great House alone or study the Ancient language adequately. I may appease Aevier's wishes when he persists, but I am not stupid."

"Maybe, Oronus, but the fact remains that this particular snake is proving to be far more slippery than anyone anticipated. He may not be able to train himself, but he could definitely compile a valid argument to take to the council to assume control of such a dangerous business as this."

"What are you saying, Alden?"

"I am saying that the majority of the directors are devoted to the prosperity of the provinces and the welfare of the people. If Jacques can manage to convince them that this independent study of yours is potentially damaging to the provinces, it could fall into his powers to assume control of O.R.T. We also can't rule out the possibility that he is sharing this information with an outside source."

At this, Oronus hammered his fist down on one of the shelves.

"Why?"

CHAPTER 5

Aevier stepped up to the deck of his airship and headed for the helm. He was always nauseous when he sailed, and the purpose of this particular flight helped little. He approached the helmsman. "Ve have almost reached our destination?"

"Yes, sir. We will be able to land within the hour."

"Very vell. As you vere."

He walked to port and gripped the railings. He always hated reporting to Eleazer. The man made his skin crawl. He also knew that there was no way out of the allegiance he had made to him. The Raujj at work within Aevier's will was too strong to break; he was completely immersed in the throes of servitude. The only thing that kept Jacques sane was the promise Eleazer had made, training in the art of the Raujj in exchange for services rendered. It seemed almost too good to be true, but Aevier had shunned that thought from his mind a long time ago. He would be as loyal to the high priest as he needed to be until he learned the ancient art, and then he would turn on him.

"How crushed and miserable Oronus vill be when I become strong enough to take control of ze provinces and ze minds of ze people. I vill force Oronus himself to hand me ze texts he has guarded for so long and bow at my feet!"

The thought of this dictatorship and his soon-to-be ability to tap into the ancient Raujj sent chills down his spine. He looked down through the clouds, feeling the cool, crisp night air fill his lungs, and watched as they passed into the seventh province.

"Soon zhere vill be no borders to speak of, only one empire. I vill usher in a new order and reign, and my qveen shall be ze indomitable Raujj."

"Sir, we have reached Astonne. We can be ready to land at the Basilica of the Four in twenty minutes."

"Very good, helmsman. Do not make preparations to shut down ze ship; I am hoping zat zis task vill not keep me indefinitely."

The airship lowered a great deal, hovering thirty feet above the ground in front of the basilica's massive sandstone courtyard. It was riddled with bushes and small, winding trees, and the Four Representations made a square around a giant fountain centered in the courtyard. Aevier motioned to the crew on deck to lower a great, knotted rope over the side of the airship. He slid down awkwardly, his fear of heights and of falling causing him to regain his previous nausea. He landed on the stone pathway to the courtyard bottom first, his monocle slipping off his face and the air in his lungs escaping him all at once. He quickly rose and dusted himself off, furious at the laughter he could hear over the sounds of the engine and propellers.

"Just you vait!"

He stormed down the pathway and entered the courtyard. In spite of his fear of Eleazer Graff, high priest of the Basilica of the Four, he could not help but feel a little peace pass over him when he saw the Four Representations, and he paused briefly and kneeled. He never quite ascribed to the Teachings of the Four, but he came with his parents as a child and recited a praise almost out of habit:

"Visdom for myself and for our leaders; Justice for ze oppressed and forgotten; Mercy upon zhose whom ve don't vish to show it; Grace for us fools who need to be penitent. Ze Awesome quartet of Visdom, Justice, Mercy, and Grace be praised."

He stood up, brushed the sandstone residue from his knees, and continued forward through a great archway leading to the entrance of the basilica. He entered through the main door and found himself in a grand entryway. Murals and statues lined the walls, telling the stories of the world's beginning.

The ceiling was at least fifty feet above him, and massive chandeliers with candles hung down from it, making the shadows of the statues dance along the walls. He walked forward through another sandstone archway and found himself in the Sanctum of the Four.

Four enormous, colorful windows were the first thing Jacques noticed, two in the front, two on the sides. The second thing he noticed was Graff. He stood at the front of the sanctum in his dark red and black robes with silver stole and a great, oaken serpentine staff in his left hand; the bottom of the staff was pulsing with blue light. Above his right hand floated a large, ancient-looking book, and Jacques could not understand what Eleazer seemed to be muttering under his breath. Aevier wondered how old Graff really was. He had flowing, silver hair and leaned heavily on the staff, yet in his face he looked no more than forty.

Except for his eyes, Jacques thought to himself, *his eyes look as old as ze Ancients.*

"Good evening, High Priest." Aevier bowed low.

"Ah. A fine evening it is, indeed, my little puppet. Tell me, have you brought me news from the provinces? Has the council assumed control of Oronus's facility yet?"

"No, sir. Ze council still vishes for control to remain in ze hands of Oronus. As far as new business, I know zat Oronus had a little visit vist Alden. Also, ze Chest of Vorlds is being held at O.R.T. presently. Ze brat survived the collapse of ze Great House, I am afraid. But ozher zhan zat…"

"What of the second and third provinces, Aevier? Have they joined sides with you, as I asked you to see done?"

Aevier dropped his head. "N-no, sir. Oronus intervened in zat process through Alden. I am sorry, High Priest. He got zhere first."

"Oh my. This is troublesome, indeed. Such a simple task as this..."

"It is not like I didn't try! I have been faithful to zis cause of yours since ze beginning, High Priest."

"Hmm. I suppose you are right, puppet. No matter, I think you will find my previous plans obsolete when you hear what I have to say. Follow."

The book slammed, causing Aevier to jump and let out a shrill squeak. Graff rolled his eyes and walked forward, thrusting the book into Jacques' hands.

"Hold this, o loyal servant, and follow. Quickly now, there is much ground to cover." Aevier looked at the book that had been thrown to him. It was black and had four silver symbols on the cover that he did not recognize.

"Are ve leaving ze Basilica? I thought zis meeting vould be short."

"Follow. Quickly now..." The voice caused Aevier to shudder yet obey wholeheartedly. Graff pulled back part of a giant tapestry that hung between the two great windows in the front of the sanctum to expose a dank, dark hallway.

"You first, humble puppet."

Aevier walked forward, unaware of his surroundings in the thick blackness of the foreign hallway. They walked for what seemed like ages, the only light seen being the gentle pulse of Graff's serpentine staff. The hallway began to slope upward, and they came to a large opening that led still to a larger courtyard on the other side of the basilica. It was much higher than the front courtyard, and a stone pathway wound through the middle. At its end, there was a steep drop off.

"Come, puppet." Graff strode past Aevier toward the edge of the courtyard where the cliff lay. "Oh my puppet, I have discovered a revolutionary key in my little study of the Four. I believe I have the solution to retrieving from Oronus what you say belongs to the council."

"Ze texts of ze Raujj…" Aevier straightened a little, and his monocle span and adjusted faster than usual.

"Oh my puppet, you seem to be even greedier for its treasures than last we met. Yes, you are correct. You see, I am now glad that I did not send you after Aaron on that last excavation. He has made things far easier than I thought. Do not misunderstand, puppet. I am grateful for your scavenging of those houses after Oronus and his teams left. What you have found has been very useful to me. However"—Eleazer pointed the end of the staff to the openness below the cliff and muttered something inaudible to Jacques—"recent findings have made further inquiry on your part unnecessary for me, puppet."

Just then, a bolt of lightning shot upwards from below the edge of the cliff, sending Aevier sprawling behind a nearby bush.

"Stand and take account, puppet!"

Aevier got up and moved to stand beside High Priest Graff. What he saw amazed him. It seemed as though all air and matter had split open in midair, exposing a pulsing blue sphere that rotated and looked electrified.

"By ze Four…"

"Not Four, my troubled puppet—One."

"Vat are you talking about? Vat is zis devilry?"

"Hmm. Perhaps some explanation is in order before the end."

Aevier stepped backwards, tripping over a stone and hitting his head hard on the sandstone floor of the courtyard. Eleazer glided forward and aimed the glowing end of his serpentine staff just above Aevier's frantically spinning and adjusting monocle.

"Oh my, little puppet. I would not advise any more movement. Rest your legs here for a while. Oh my, where to begin? Ah, yes, the concept of the Four Representations, the awesome and mighty quartet, the rulers of Justice, Wisdom, Grace, and Mercy was created by the Ancients and called into reality through the power of the Raujj over two thousand years ago. Do you feel cheated? Angry? Imagine where I stand, puppet, as leader of the grandest farce in history. Oh my...I have discovered through my little study of the Ancients and the Four that the Chest of Worlds was paramount in this creation. Four spheres, four keys, one impenetrable Chest of Worlds. Do you need a minute to soak this harsh reality in?"

At this point Aevier was letting out shrill cries every few seconds, squirming yet too afraid to move his head from its place below the pulsating blue end of the staff.

"No? Oh my, very well. Puppet of mine, were I to achieve the opening of this chest, and through my study of the ancient Raujj, I could shatter the false reality of Ever-Watchful Four."

"Puppet—"

Aevier froze in horror at the sound of his voice.

"I will be God."

Aevier began screaming and crying. He tried to roll out from under the gaze of the staff when Eleazer struck him in the temple and placed one foot on his chest. Aevier continued screaming. Eleazer cackled and spoke over the horrified noise.

"Oh my, puppet. Your excavations have been quite useful to me, yet your actions on the council as of late have been less than fruitful. I need someone with a little more political shrewdness than I think you can muster! Yet, you must still fill this role. Quite paradoxical, isn't it?"

Aevier froze, silent.

"I am no longer in need of a puppet. I need an elegant marionette to dance under my graces. Welcome to the Void, puppet. You shall emerge a marionette, and I will hold the strings!"

Silently, Graff bent low and delicately removed Aevier's monocle, kissing him gently on the forehead. Rising up, he thrust the end of the staff through the newly exposed eye. He lifted the now-lifeless body and flung him over the edge of the cliff and into the pulsating blue sphere. It closed around the fallen, limp body and shot up another great bolt of lightning causing a shroud of smoke to emerge. Eleazer began to mutter as the staff pulsed brighter and more violently with every inaudible word. The smoke cleared.

CHAPTER 6

Aaron pierced Anna with an offended gaze. He then looked away, wavering between the thought that she meant no harm and deserved to know the truth and the realization that telling her would reopen a long-closed wound—one that had never healed properly. "I need a moment to gather my thoughts."

"It's okay if you can't, Aaron. I won't press you—"

"No, it's fine. I just need a minute."

"I'll go close the portholes and come back." Anna squeezed Aaron's forearm, walked across the deck, and disappeared under the lid of the hatch.

"Gods..." Where to begin? Aaron heard the gears used to close the portholes beginning to turn. He knew he had about ten more minutes of solitude before Anna returned.

By this time, it was well into the early morning hours. As the porthole for the *Auspicious* closed, the moonlight was blocked from the hangar, and Aaron was left in the dark. He walked to the hatch, climbed down a few rungs on the ladder, then closed the hatch and sealed it. He hopped down and walked to the control room, where there would be adequate lighting and comfortable seating for the story he was preparing to tell. He saw that the map boards were still on and decided to erase the coordinates he had stolen from the terminal and return the map chip to Oronus's office, but as he started to do so, he discovered that someone had already done just that.

"Anna. Don't you trust me? Can't you just trust me?" He walked toward a table and sat down, facing the wall of the cabin.

"I do trust you, Aaron."

He turned to face Anna, who had come in without him noticing.

"But you have to realize that something like this shook all of our trust. If we're supposed to be a family at O.R.T., then you stole something precious from your family." She walked over to the table and sat down across from him. "I'm sorry, Aaron. I just need to get past this. Families also forgive each other, right?"

"Yeah, I suppose so."

"Then let's agree that what's done is done, all right?"

"All right."

Anna leaned back in her chair, crossed her legs, and put her boots on the table. Aaron stood up and walked over to the blank map board, running his hand over its wire-ribbed surface.

"Before we start, how did Osiris die?"

Anna took her feet off the table and leaned forward, palms and forearms on the table's surface. She looked sideways, away from him, her ponytail resting on the table between her forearms.

"Well, I think he's alive, if you want to call that living."

Aaron turned to face her. "What?"

Anna sighed and stood from her chair. "Oh, about eighteen years ago he conducted the first-ever practical experiment with the Raujj that O.R.T had ever made. Oronus is focused on the technological discoveries we make, but Grandfather spent most of his time with the mages and scholars. One of them volunteered to let Grandfather enter his mind using an enchantment. It happened in the auditorium of O.R.T.'s Re-Creation department—

everyone in every department came to watch. Even some of the directors were present. Jacques Aevier was there too, though he was not yet a director, and so was Eleazer Graff, though Nicodemus was still the high priest at that time."

She paused and stared off into space, as though remembering the event, even though she was not present.

"What happened?" This had peaked Aaron's interest.

Anna sat back down. "Well, the volunteer died instantly, and Grandfather lost his mind. He took a prototype hovering craft Daddy and Dardus Hale were working on that was intended to be lowered from an airship fifty feet above the ground. He drove it off of the hangar." Aaron's eyes widened.

"How could anyone survive a fall from so high? Even if he did, it's too dangerous to live on the ground-level, especially alone."

Anna nodded her head. "That is precisely what we thought too. However, when we went to look for debris and his body at the base level of O.R.T., we found nothing. No broken craft, no body."

Daddy finally resigned to the thought that he was dead. Since then, he has been in command and has forbidden further experimentation, only study."

Aaron was amazed. "So why not just destroy the texts so no one can ever revive the Raujj?"

Anna laughed. "Don't think we haven't thought about it, Aaron. The problem is that many of the technologies we revive for the provinces are infused with the Raujj. Many of the scholars use that as a practical example of how the Raujj could very well have manifested itself in other forms over time."

"It evolves?" This was almost too much for him.

"Possibly. In other words, even if we destroy the texts, the revival of the Enchantments is not out of reach to the determined and the able. Daddy strongly believes that the Raujj must be eliminated internally in this great, manifested presence, and the only way to do that is to learn how to use it."

Aaron walked over and sat on the edge of the table. He scratched his head, and they sat in silence for a while.

"Now, Aaron, what about your father. What happened to him?" Anna asked.

Aaron stood up again and began pacing.

"While you were still at school, Oronus offered my father work as a mechanic; he had originally been a recoverer of fuel at the ground level in the first province. We had been struggling a great deal financially, so he decided to come here while my mom stayed at home and worked in the Market District. I, of course, was supposed to stay, but I snuck into the cargo hold of the airship that took him to Harrah. When he got off, I jumped out and surprised him, but he was far angrier than he was surprised. He wanted me to go back, but I wasn't in school and didn't have a job at the time. He agreed to let me stay for a month.

"I went to work with him every day, and that is how I met your father. Oronus showed me around O.R.T. and told me many things about the revival of art and literature of the Ancients, as well as the technological artifacts they excavated. He showed me the airships and the hangar, telling me how they were made and of his desire to move away from fuel to a new resource: steam, moisture from the world around us that would be pushed through the ship by the great blimp and out again through the center of the propellers. It was a marvelous idea, and Oronus made possible the re-beautification of what little inhabitable land was left at the ground level.

"However, as Oronus began production of these steam-powered ships, the people in the first province began to suffer. Thousands of men and boys were out of work all at once, and the province buckled under the financial strain.

"Oronus sent out one of his new steam-powered airships to the first province that was *packed* with food, clothes, and great barrels of water; when it landed in Restivar, a large group of angry and out-of-work fuel recoverers boarded the ship and killed everyone inside. They burned the goods and made it their headquarters. Oronus was outraged, but the council managed to calm him down and convince him not to retaliate.

"Luckily, the basilica sent aid immediately after this happened, and the province accepted. They are still in the recovery process, trying to find work in the Market and Industrial Districts for the unemployed and the hungry. Even to this day, a group of people has remained on Oronus's ship. No one knows why they are there, though many think that they are plotting an attack on O.R.T. My Father, Cebran, became their inside man at O.R.T. He couldn't stand the fact that he was helping produce the thing that was destroying his home. And so, one night as he left, he ducked back in and snuck up to the hangar.

"Very early in the morning, Cebran opened one of the portholes and let in a group of men from the first province who had flown a fuel-powered cargo ship. They flew in low and scaled the building to the hangar. They had explosives. I guess they wanted to blow up the hangar. After the men were inside, Cebran had them board the *Regalus,* one of the nicer, newer steam-powered ships. He planned on flying away in that and detonating the fuel-powered ship in the hangar on their escape. Only, as my father began placing explosives around the final ships, the lights came on, and Cebran found himself and the *Regalus* surrounded by O.R.T. guards. Cebran ran around to the other side of the ship, dodging pistol fire. As he rounded the *Regalus,* however, he was met by your father's poleaxe. The men were captured and taken to Council Headquarters in the fourth province for sentencing, and I was sent home to tell Mother about Cebran."

Aaron inhaled long and deep and then exhaled.

"And that's who my father was."

He walked back to the table and sat down, gazing at everything and nothing. Anna dropped her head.

"I'm so sorry, Aaron. I had no idea that that your father was killed. How can you work here under the man that killed your father?" He looked at her with a combination of sorrowful tears and a bitter smile.

"Oh, my father was not himself that day. I mean, when I was sent home I truly hated Oronus for a long time, but I knew that my father's actions didn't have to reflect on myself and that my passion had become learning all of those strange, wonderful things from Oronus. I devoted myself to O.R.T. and to bettering the provinces. I came back after three months, and Oronus welcomed me into his excavation team. One year and nine months later, you arrived." Anna looked at Aaron in amazement.

"Wow. All this time and I had no idea." She walked over to Aaron and hugged him. "You may not be a noble, Aaron, but your words and actions are."

They stayed like that in silence until sunrise.

Chapter 7

There at the edge of the cliff stood Jacques Aevier. His body was rigid and erect and his eyes and mouth were closed. No injuries were on his body. His eye socket was perfectly normal.

"Oh my..."

Eleazer glided forward, leaned toward the seemingly lifeless body's ear, whispered to the monocle cupped in his hand and placed it back on Jacques' face. This new Jacques Aevier opened his eyes and looked directly at Graff. Graff was amazed; he began adjusting to the fact that he now saw with two sets of eyes. The paradox of looking at Aevier and staring back at himself was almost maddening, but he quickly shut himself off from this newfound ability and spoke to Jacques.

"Hello, my graceful marionette. Are you ready to dance for me?"

"I am ever villing to serve ze One God."

Eleazer's eyes rolled in the back of his head and he shuddered. "Oh my. God. I do like the sound of that. Follow, servant, we've much ground to cover."

This new Aevier picked up the ancient book his predecessor

had dropped and followed High Priest Graff back into the dank, dark hallway.

"Oh my..."

Graff was in the lead on the way back to the sanctum. As they walked in the glow of Eleazer's staff, he began issuing his divine orders.

"Oh my, servant, I seem to remember that the first province tried to mount a resistance against O.R.T. some years ago..."

"True, my Lord. Oronus infuriated ze province vist ze construction of ze steam-powered ships."

"Very good, servant. Apparently your predecessor was willing to pull his head out of his puppet's hind quarters to take account of some things..."

"I do not understand, my Lord."

"And you never will, servant, so take no mind. Now, do you remember who it was that sent aid to the province after they obliterated Oronus's little gift and his crew?"

"Ze Basilica of ze Four, my Lord."

They reached the end of the hallway, and Eleazer pushed up one corner of the great tapestry as they found themselves once again in the Sanctum of the Four.

"Oh my, servant, you are correct. I did send aid to the first province to help sustain its welfare. Now, servant, are you aware if this group is still functioning on that ship in Restivar?"

"I know not, my Lord. Only, I seem to recall zat ze ship still remains on ze outskirts of Restivar at ze ground level. Gods know if it is still intact."

Eleazer turned on Aevier and struck him in the neck with the serpentine staff, forcing him into a kneeling position.

"Who knows if it is still intact? Who, o loyal servant?"

"If anyone is avare of its status, it is you, my Lord."

"Very good, servant. You would do well to remember that the Ancients created the Four to ruin us."

He took the book from Aevier, helped him to his feet, and

smiled. He walked forward, placing the book on a glass stand that pulsated with blue light.

"Three men loyal to the basilica have maintained that ship and have been smuggling explosives and arms for eight years. One works for O.R.T., and the other two are Basilical Missionaries who report directly to me. They are the ones who supervised the distribution of goods in the first province so long ago. I intend to honor their loyalty.

"Servant, you will spend your time and energy on the Council of Directors building goodwill in the Seven Provinces. You will reform the Industrial Districts in the name of unity concerning how we as a people travel and transfer our goods. This will force Oronus to share some of the monopoly he has created in the districts. You will act kindly in council matters and concede to its will where you otherwise would not have. In this way, you will begin breaking down the wall your predecessor created with Richard Alden.

"After enough time has passed, you will begin your real work. Richard Alden is a liability and a potential usurper of my cause. Kill him. Then go to Restivar in the name of this Basilica and inspire revolt in the province against O.R.T.'s injustices—the beauty of the Ancient's treachery is that the Four were often in favor of war. The following months are crucial to my... our success. All that you do in the watchful eye of the community, do so in the name of the Basilica and the Four. I will see what you see, servant. Treachery on your part will result in an eternal visit to the Void. Lastly, you will rediscover your interest in the Basilica of the Four. You will make open, monthly visits to the basilica for praise and for penance. This will be the easiest method of maintaining contact. Go now, servant, and do my bidding."

"Yes, my Lord."

With this, Aevier walked out of the sanctum, through the great archways, and back to the airship that still hovered in the air. With confidence he grabbed a hold of the rope, secured his feet above a large knot, and motioned for the men to begin pulling him up to the deck. When he was close enough, Aevier gripped the railings and hopped over them to the deck with some ease.

"Raise ze rope, helmsman. Ve leave immediately for Oronus's headquarters in Harrah." Aevier stood there as the men stared at him. Never before had Jacques sounded so sure of himself. "Now!"

They sprang into action. Jacques went below deck to the control room, where he stayed in silent preparation until they reached the fifth province.

~

Aaron and Anna walked down the ramp of the *Auspicious* as the sun rose and shined through the already opened portholes of O.R.T.'s hangar. Even at this early hour, it was alive with activity. They stood there, in the middle of the hangar, as the realization of duties came to them both.

"Thank you for your honesty, Aaron. I feel like we have come away better friends than when we boarded."

Aaron hid the sting of this statement with a smile and a pat on the shoulder.

"Yeah, I think so, too. Hey, I'd better go check in with Oronus."

Anna's eyes widened and her mouth hung agape. "Oh, I was already supposed to be down in Navigation! Bye, Aaron." She kissed him on the cheek and hurried off down the bridgeway.

He paused for a few seconds. What a bittersweet kiss! Would she ever take notice of him in a way other than friendship? He pondered this thought as he walked down the bridgeway to the Re-Creation Department, where he assumed Oronus would be working with engineers in the experimental craft production facility.

As he moved into the new building, he was immediately in the midst of great tables and workbenches, engineers crowded all around examining, reexamining, and tinkering with all manner of tools and ancient machines. How devoted they all were. Many looked as if they had come on to O.R.T. when Osiris was Oronus's age.

He wandered around the mass of tables and workbenches until he came to the area where experimental crafts were held. He strode down a sloped walkway as the ceiling climbed higher, and there, in the midst of a flurry of activity, stood Oronus. Aaron walked to him and stood beside him for quite a while without Oronus's notice.

"Oh, Aaron! Come with me, we've much to discuss!" He touched the small of Aaron's back and ushered him out of the area. Aaron kept looking back over his shoulder as they left. It looked as though they were working on something he had never seen.

"Oronus, what was that—"

"Never mind that, my boy, not right now." They strode back up the walkway and into one of the narrow hallways of Re-Creation. Aaron lingered briefly as they passed a strange obsidian slab resting on its side—he thought he saw a soft glow on its surface, but it faded as quickly as he had looked at it.

They walked past rows of offices with walls of glass where men in white coats and gloves were placing flattened, ancient scrolls between slabs of glass. They came to the end of the hall, and Oronus opened a large sliding door to reveal an elevator.

"Right in here, Aaron."

"Where exactly are we going, Oronus?"

He smiled. "Well, you recovered the chest in such a rush, I thought I would let you take a good look at it and hear a story or two concerning it."

Aaron hid the excitement that was mounting in him. "I would like that very much, Oronus."

"Ah, here we are," Oronus said as the elevator came to a rather abrupt stop. "We are actually at ground level, Aaron. I have taken extra precaution to make sure the chest stays safe."

They walked down a metallic-looking hallway to another

sliding door. Oronus opened it, and they found themselves in a bright, seemingly empty room. Aaron was puzzled.

"Why are we here? Where is the chest?"

Oronus smiled and laughed. "It's right in front of us, my boy! Carlson, turn the switch!" Aaron thought Oronus had gone mad.

"Oronus, what are you…" Aaron began his question, and it was answered as thirty armed men, the Chest of Worlds, and the table it rested on wavered into view. Aaron jumped back with excitement. "What is this?"

Oronus guffawed again. "Aaron, say hello to our newest revival: a machine that disrupts wavelengths and particles to make objects blend in with their surroundings! We have only been able to hide this small number of objects, but one day we will be able to mask airships! Think of it, Aaron!"

Aaron was not as overjoyed with the thought. The only reason he could think of for masking an airship would be to take someone or something by surprise and then only to hurt them, but he did not voice this thought.

"Would you like to see it? Let's go." They walked across the room to where the Chest of Worlds rested on a small wooden table. Aaron approached it and felt as though he had never seen it before. When he was escaping the Great House, he didn't have much time to examine the wooden and glass casing or the midnight-blue felt that covered the bottom. There were four spheres that rested there, all four gray and perfectly still. Aaron remembered how frantically the spheres span and how many colors they emitted, and he was confused.

"Oronus, when I was leaving the Great House, these spheres were multicolored and in constant motion. What has happened?"

Oronus shrugged and moved to stand beside Aaron. "I wish I could tell you. Our people believe the Chest of Worlds was aware of the Great House collapsing around it. Being aware of its deteriorating surroundings also means it sensed *you*. It knew you were trying to escape, so it wanted to escape with you." Aaron suddenly felt uneasy in the chest's presence.

"So ... is it aware of us ... now?"

Oronus shrugged again. "I have no idea, Aaron. The Artifacts division of Re-Creation thinks that it is still aware but that it senses its safety for the time being and is therefore dormant."

Aaron leaned in close to the Chest of Worlds. All this trouble over one chest and four spheres. What did this all mean? Aaron sat down in front of the table and looked up at Oronus.

"What is this thing, Oronus? What would you have me know?"

Oronus scooped his emerald green cape from behind him and sat down beside Aaron. He smiled at him and then gazed at the far end of the room.

"You see, Aaron, for many, many years, stories of a treasure such as this filled the provinces. People knew very little about it; I mean, there were those who went out in search of the Chest of Worlds, but if they didn't come back empty handed, they didn't come back at all. Of those who came back, some were honest and told the truth; either they couldn't find a Great House to explore, or they were turned back by the Raujj that enchanted the grounds, or they were simply too afraid to risk their lives. Others spun wild tales about imaginary foes who halted their progress and turned them away. Aside from this, there was very little information about the chest. It is mentioned once in the *Book of the Four*. Something like 'Four spheres, four keys, one impenetrable Chest of Worlds.' Of course, no one really knows what that means. There aren't even keyholes on the thing, and we have found no keys in any of the Great Houses. That is why Aevier, one of the more religious sorts, who knew of your recovery and the destruction of the Great House, was outraged; you have potentially destroyed the hiding place of the four keys."

Aaron looked downward at this, feeling a little nauseated at the thought of having more people turn against him for destroying something mentioned in the *Book of the Four*. Oronus seemed to notice his downtrodden state.

"Oh, don't worry, my boy! That is purely speculation on their part! Besides, if there were four keys, I doubt they would all be in the same place with the chest. Like I said before, there aren't even any keyholes on it!"

Aaron felt a little better at Oronus's reassurance.

"Anyway, there are three prominent schools of thought concerning this chest, all of which are based on little solid evidence. The first is that this is a Divine Artifact, meaning that because it was deliberately mentioned in the *Book of the Four* that the Four actually created it, though for what purpose no one knows. The second theory is that the Ancients created it, and that they enchanted the chest and the spheres heavily with the Raujj. At this point, proponents of this theory go one of two ways: either they believe that the opening of the chest by one or four who are worthy will bring knowledge and prosperity, or they believe that the opening of the chest will bring the destruction of the provinces. The third theory is that the *Chest of Worlds* came into being alongside the Four, that the chest is as old as the Four dating back to our genesis. Personally, Aaron, I tend to think that it is just another artifact of the Ancients. Don't get me wrong. I am firmly convinced that it is heavily saturated with the Raujj and that opening it would be a bad idea at this point, ergo the guards and the secrecy, but I don't think that this is a product of the Four or was co-created with the Four. The safest bet then is to keep it safe in a place conducive to the discovery of its purpose. Shall we head back to the elevator?"

They stood and made their way out of the room and down the hall. Aaron looked back as they entered the elevator and watched as the contents of the room wavered back out of sight. The elevator returned once again to the main floor of Re-Creation.

"Follow me, Aaron." Oronus led Aaron up the bridgeway

and into the Navigation building. The main room of Navigation looked like the largest airship control room Aaron had ever seen in his life. He was astonished; he probably hadn't seen this room since Oronus showed it to him years ago. At the center of the room was a round conference table with a large screen, where all of the department heads and Anna sat. Oronus approached the table, and they all stood.

"We'll have none of that, please," he said almost in passing, and they all sat down together.

"Now," said Anna, "I'm sure you are all aware that we are in the final stages of our newest craft, a hovering craft that has been modified and improved from the one that Osiris destroyed some time before I arrived at O.R.T."

Oronus shifted in his seat.

"This hovering craft has an engine that brings in air and pushes it through fifteen holes on its underbelly, supporting it six feet above ground when functioning at one hundred percent capacity. The control area also consists of main and auxiliary steering systems, a monitor connection that is synced up with the airship that drops her, and a map board that can upload schematics to the airship from the ground level and display our existing coordinates. The hatch leads to a one level area beneath the deck, which is split into three sections. The farthest section is the engine room, the middle section is mess and bedding for a maximum of four bodies, and the front section is storage for supplies and a shower. With the benefit of steam power, our airships can fly farther away from the provinces without the fear of running out of fuel. Our hope is to be able to send out teams that can stay on the ground level in these hovering crafts for a duration of at least two months, all the while maintaining contact with the airship she is dropped from. With this new development, it is feasible to increase our maps to two times their size in two years time. We believe we have found—and Aaron has destroyed—the final Great House, but now we can be sure, and who knows what else we can potentially uncover in the process?"

Anna had been passing the schematics for the hovering craft around the table as she spoke. "Now, what questions do you have for me?"

Parrus Vademe, head of Communications stood and voiced his opposition. "I have a question for you: do you recall that we have already found the remains of a destroyed civilization down there? Do you actually think it is safe to separate small groups of people from the protection of an airship down there? Are you mad?"

Oronus looked over at the department head. "Sit down, Parrus. You already know that these crafts have the ability to remain in constant contact with an airship, and if there are any difficulties, the airship will reach them in no time! Also, if there *were* a civilization down there, we all know that it was probably destroyed by the abuse of the Raujj, and keys for its use are safely behind the walls of O.R.T."

"My apologies," Parrus muttered as he took his seat. Oronus interlaced his fingers and leaned forward on the table.

"Now, are there any more constructive questions to ask that do not question the sanity of my daughter?" Aaron smirked as Parrus's cheeks turned red.

"I do, Daddy." Anna moved from conducting the meeting to asking the questions.

"Yes, Anna?"

"Given this new advancement, I think it would be safe and appropriate to search for Grandfather."

Everyone at the table fell into an uncomfortable silence.

"No."

"Why not, Daddy?"

"No, Anna. He is dead."

"You don't know that. We didn't find his body or the craft!"

"I said no, Anna, and I forbid any action to be taken in that direction."

"Yes, you seem to do that a lot these days," Anna muttered.

"What is that supposed to mean?" Oronus demanded.

"Look around you! The scholars have nothing to do with the language you are having them decipher, and the mages have mostly sat on their hands since Osiris left. The only thing you really care about is reviving your stupid toys!"

Oronus stood from the table. "That is quite enough! I am restricting certain progress in order to protect the welfare of the provinces. It has been a tactic of this family for one hundred and fifty years! It was a tactic that only your grandfather managed to break, and that resulted in his committing murder and then suicide!"

"You don't know that he's dead! You don't know that!" Anna stormed out of the Navigation building. She bumped into Aevier as she passed, tears streaming down her face. Seeing Jacques Aevier walking through the door, Oronus resigned that this meeting was definitely over.

"Ladies and gentlemen, it would seem as though our meeting is adjourned for the time being," Oronus said before walking toward Jacques and his crew.

"Director Aevier, I must say this is a surprise."

"Good morning, Oronus. Yes, my plans have ... *altered* ... a little as of late, and I have something I vish to discuss vist you."

Oronus felt a little indignant, remembering Aevier's previous threats in the office area of the hangar. "What's the matter, Jacques? Are my people not *crapping* out new technologies fast enough for your grubby little hands to get a hold of? Don't think I don't know about your meetings with the other directors about shutting me down—I am not a stupid man, Jacques."

"Razher, Alden is not a stupid man, you should say, and I'm afraid I vill not be sent avay crying as easily as zat daughter of yours, Oronus."

Oronus flushed at the comment.

"Please, Oronus, I am not here to fight vist you. Please ask ze board to take zheir seats back at ze conference table." Oronus looked from his department heads to Aaron back to Aevier. What brought on this new sense of authority in Jacques? Whatever the reason, he conceded to trust Alden's advice to play nice for the time being. He motioned to his department heads to sit down. Aaron began to sit, but Oronus stopped him.

"Not you, Aaron. I'm sorry, but you can't be here for this. Would you please try to find Anna for me and calm her down?"

Aaron nodded and walked out of the building and to the bridgeway. He cursed when he was out of earshot of the meeting. "Well, I suppose spending time with Anna is a good consolation."

He passed through the bridgeway and back into Re-Creation. He also planned on using this time to take a peek at whatever those engineers and mechanics were working on, though he assumed it was the hovering craft. Regardless, he knew he had to find out. When he had passed the tables and workbenches, he was astonished to see Anna pulling back the large sheet that was covering the experimental hovering craft. "Anna, what in the name of the Four are you doing?"

Anna's tears were replaced with anger and resolve. "I am going to go find my grandfather. I *know* he's alive, Aaron. I know he is. I know he is. I know he is…" She continued saying this as she boarded and began to prep the hovering craft. Aaron ran forward and shouted up at Anna.

"You can't do this, Anna! You haven't even flown this thing yet! Besides, Oronus forbade you to go!"

"Well that didn't stop you from destroying the last remaining House of Ancients *ever,* now did it?"

"I thought friends forgave each other, hmm? As a *friend,* I'm trying to talk some sense into you! Don't do this! It's too dangerous and besides, you don't even have another person to go with you—"

"I can fly it myself!"

"Then who is going to fly the airship to the ground level for you? Surely you're not going to just drive off the edge like your grandfather?"

Anna was as curt and resolute as ever. "No, Aaron Ravenhall, I am not. I have asked someone from the hangar to prep the *Regalus* for flight and to lower it down for me, and he has graciously agreed."

"How did you manage to do that?"

"I simply told him that I decided to advance our schedule and field test the hovering craft today."

"This is madness, Anna. Please come down and let's talk about this!"

"Well, technically I *am* doing a field test. Rather, *we* are."

"What?"

"You have two options, Aaron. You can go with me and help me find him, or you can stay behind and explain how you let me get away."

"Are you crazy? Oronus would kill me after all the trouble I've already caused!"

"It's your choice." She hopped into the driver's seat and made preparations to lift off.

"You haven't even packed the craft yet, and now we need supplies for two of us!"

"That's not a big deal, Aaron. We can gather our supplies when we get this thing up to the hangar. Now stay and face my father's anger, or come with me, keep me safe, and help me bring back his father, who no one has seen in eight years!"

This put things a little more into perspective for Aaron, and he hopped on to the deck of the craft with Anna. The hovering craft was engaged, the fifteen jets of air lifted it off the ground, and they drove up a spiraling ramp that led to the hangar. They arrived and found the *Regalus* already prepped and ready for flight.

"Who did you ask to do this, again?"

"Oh, a new friend of mine named Edgar." She waved up at him. "Thank you, Edgar!"

He waved back over the railing of the *Regalus*. "Not a problem, marm. Not a problem in the world!"

They got out and brought two months of standard supply boxes for two people, loaded the craft, and hovered directly beside the airship where two large clamps on the airship's side were parallel to the craft. Edgar and three other men threw two great chains over the railings and past the hovering craft.

"Aaron, hook these chains to the outside railings while I clamp the inside railings to the ship."

He did as he was told, still in shock about the decision he had made to disobey Oronus once again. When everything was secure, Anna waved back up to Edgar.

"All set here, Edgar. We're ready to go!"

"Wonderful, marm! Please take a seat so we don't throw ya!"

"Come on, Aaron!" Anna shouted over the roar of the propellers and the preliminary engines.

They sat down in the control area of the deck and strapped themselves in as Anna brought the glass shell over them.

"I hope you know what you're doing, Anna."

"Oh, Aaron, shut up and enjoy the ride!" Anna laughed, almost hysterically. Aaron thought she was going crazy.

They sailed through the porthole, and the *Regalus* began its descent to the ground level. When they were about seventy feet above the ground, Edgar ceased the *Regalus's* descent. The abrupt halt caused the hovering craft to shake and the chains to shift. Anna and Aaron looked at each other with some confusion. Anna lowered the glass shell.

"I hope nothing is wrong. Stay here, Aaron." She got out of her seat and looked up toward the *Regalus'* deck. Edgar was leaning over the railings wearing the same, sheepish smile he always wore. "Is something wrong, Edgar? We need to descend another twenty feet to drop safely!"

"Sorry, marm! Jus' followin' me orders!"

"Edgar? What are you talking about?"

"Sorry, marm! Maybe your father should have thought about

the consequences o' these steam-powered contraptions before he built 'em!"

"Edgar, you traitor!"

"Sorry, marm! Boys, release our extra cargo!"

The hovering craft lurched as the first chain was released from the deck of the *Regalus* and fell over the edge, pulling the craft with it. Anna fell and rolled toward the edge of the hovering craft. Aaron unstrapped himself, jumped toward Anna, and caught her, hugging her against him and falling backwards. He rolled them to the side and toward the control area as the second chain slammed into the deck and the craft was ripped away from the *Regalus*. They were close enough now to get back into their seats and strap in; the second chain, though it put a hole in the deck, had counter-balanced the weight of the chain that had fallen port-side.

"Quickly, Anna, get that engine started!"

"I'm trying, Aaron!"

Back on the *Regalus*, Edgar pulled out a pistol and shot the three men who were with him. "Thanks for the help, boys, but I'm headed for Restivar by me self!"

CHAPTER 8

Oronus and the department heads reclaimed their seats at the conference table as Aevier made his way to join them. He turned to his men. "Please vait out on ze bridgevay." They nodded and walked out of Navigation. Aevier took a seat beside Oronus and smiled at all of them.

"Thank you for having me on such short notice; I know zat O.R.T. is a busy place vist much to do."

The only one to return the smile was Oronus, though it appeared that he was smiling at the opposing wall.

"Vell, I am sure zat you are all vondering vhy I am here. As you are already avare, I have been placed over all seven Industrial Districts in ze provinces. As such, I vas given ze task of ensuring ze velfare and advancement of each district." Murmurs were heard from around the table.

Oronus turned toward Jacques. "Well, well, Director, that seems to be a task you have *diligently* chosen to ignore." There was more murmuring from the department heads, and Brevard Thoreau, head of Re-Creation, chuckled out loud. Aevier's eye twitched, his monocle spinning and adjusting very quickly as he fought back the urge to shout at Oronus. He managed a faint smile.

"Yes, Oronus, I am afraid zat I have fallen down on ze job somevhat. In all truthfulness, zat is precisely vhy I am here. O.R.T. has been leading ze vay in Industrial progress since before I vas born. Being part of ze fifth province has placed zis Industrial District vell above ze ozhers. All of ze districts do, of course, share ze load of travel, transportation, and maintenance, but O.R.T., under ze careful vatch of Oronus and his predecessors, has cornered ze market in craft production and technology—I do not, of course, factor ze study of ze Ancient's language into zis equation."

Oronus was cursing Jacques profusely in his mind at this statement; of course Jacques meant the Ancient's language ... and the Raujj.

Oronus fought to maintain a calm demeanor. "And all under the approving eye of the council, mind you. The council approved our excavation of the Great Houses, it approved our expanding of the map, and it approved our production of the steam-powered ships."

"Ah, but it did not unanimously approve ze production of those ships, Oronus, and you know it. Melinda Stockstill is *still* fighting for a return to stability for her people. You know as vell as I do zat ze majority of fuels ve used for airship travel came from ze first province."

Oronus remained in his defense of O.R.T. "Come on, Jacques, you have to think long term on this! We are coming closer to realizing the prosperity of the Ancients every day. I admit that we have caused a setback in the first province, but we *did* send a ship packed with supplies there with the intention of repeating this action until they decided to kill my men and burn the supplies!"

Aevier nodded. "Yes, Oronus, perhaps zat vas not ze best course of action for ze first province or rather ze group of disgruntled fuel workers zat decided to commit such an action.

However, you did send ze supplies in on ze very thing zat took their jobs from zhem, a symbol of zheir suffering."

Oronus guffawed. "Aevier! In the long run, things will be fine for all of us..."

"It is hard, Oronus, to think zat far down ze road vhen your family is hungry."

Oronus was filled with both sorrow and anger at this. "I did not produce these ships to starve people, Jacques, and you would do well to remember it. Gods know I tried to help them!"

"Yes, Oronus, you are right. And Gods know that ze basilica vas ready to pick up vhere you left off." Nods and soft agreement were seen and heard around the table. "I thank the Four for yours and ze basilica's villingness to serve. To zis day, ze basilica still sends aid to ze first province."

"As do we, Jacques. We don't send food or clothing for *obvious* reasons, but Melinda has received a quarterly monetary gift from O.R.T. since the fallout of fuel recovery in her province."

"And I'm sure she is very grateful for your assistance. O.R.T. is a shining example for ze ozher districts, and zat is vhy I am here. I vish to schedule a tour of zis facility for ze Industrial District managers of ze ozher six provinces, so zat zhey may analyze O.R.T. and discover vays to improve zheir own vork. I realize zat not every district can excavate a Great House while sneaking past enchantments, but I do think zat zhey could learn something."

Oronus sighed. If that was all Jacques wanted, it was a good day.

"Also—"

Oronus's hopes dropped a little.

"I vould like to discuss vist Oronus ze possibility of sharing ze load of certain productions vist ze ozher districts, particularly ze Industrial District of ze first province."

There's the catch, Oronus thought.

"But ve can do zat later. Above all"—Aevier stood and pushed in his chair—"it is time zat I start thanking ze Four for ze blessing of my position, and it is time zat O.R.T. starts showing a little more 'universal' support from ze vorkmens' perspective. Good day."

Jacques draped his undersized cape over his left arm, as usual, and left Navigation. Oronus followed Jacques out onto the bridgeway. "Jacques, we have done nothing out of line as far as the council or the laws of the provinces have been concerned. I mean, the third province is making personal crafts for families and small businesses, the second province deals with *all* the provinces for water; they all have a purpose. We have done nothing wrong."

Aevier turned to face Oronus. "No, but you have raised many interesting questions vistin ze council. I can eisher continue following zis course of action, or I can pursue ze shutdown of O.R.T., vhich I vould razher not do, Oronus. I leave you vist ze blessings of ze Four."

With that, Aevier and his men walked up the bridgeway to the hangar—Oronus marched back into Navigation. "Ladies and gentlemen! It seems as though our esteemed *overseer* has found his faith and his sense of duty overnight. Personally, I smell a rat! Now, in the eventuality that a large group of people comes for a tour of this facility, there are some things you must prepare your departments for. The first thing to remember is that with Aevier in the lead, the 'tour' will most likely be a scouring of O.R.T. As such, there are some obvious things that are for our eyes only. We have to be ready move anything that has any connection to the Raujj to a secure holding place until Aevier is gone. The other district heads might not notice, but I fear Jacques would. Secondly, anything that has to do with the Ancient's language must be removed. The works we have been releasing are obviously in our tongue. As such, no one is familiar with the language of the Ancients, but you all know as well as I do that the Ancient's language does play a part in the use of the Raujj. Obviously, speaking it alone holds no power, but it does play a part, and we must therefore keep it hidden from Aevier. You will go now to each of your buildings and inform everyone about this tour. Do not ramble on as I have to you about the Raujj, but let them know there are some things that only we should see. You are dismissed."

~

"Aaron. Aaron. Aaron, please wake up." Anna sat by Aaron, whom she had placed in the remaining bed (the other had been smashed by the chain). "It's no use."

Anna got up and began her cleanup job once again. She had managed to drag most of the broken pieces of the deck that had fallen below out onto the ground by herself, but moving that chain and cleaning the chunks of earth out of the air holes on the underside were not one-person jobs. If they did not get the craft up and running soon, she knew that a lot of their supplies that needed cooling would spoil, and Gods knew how they were going to get back. If only she hadn't designed the communication system to link up solely with the ship that dropped the craft; she realized only too late that the line of communication should have gone directly to O.R.T.

Aaron stirred and opened one squinted eye. "Gods...what happened? My head is killing me." Aaron sat up in bed with much effort. "Anna, are you okay?"

She dropped a piece of wood from the deck and walked over. "Yes, Aaron, I'm fine. Much more so than you, I'm afraid. You took a nasty bump to the head on our way down." Aaron lifted his hand and felt the cloth that she had wrapped around his head.

"That explains this massive headache, then. How long have I been unconscious?"

"A few hours. I have managed to clear out a lot of debris from the top, but we are going to have to get this chain out of here and clean out the air holes if we want to lift off."

Aaron lay back down with a thud. "How are we going to clean out the air holes if we are on the ground?"

Anna laughed. "Well we're not fully on the ground, Aaron.

Our land favored port side. If we can clean out the holes that are exposed, then when we turn the engines over the air should push out the remaining earth from the other holes."

Aaron looked over at her. "What if it doesn't?"

"Well, if it doesn't, the air that should have been released through the other holes will be concentrated solely on the ones that we cleaned out."

"So?"

"So...we'll flip the craft over and be stuck inside until our supplies run out and we starve to death...but I don't think that will happen."

"Gods..." Aaron pulled the sheet over his head and turned onto his stomach with his arms tucked beneath him.

"Hiding under the covers will not save you from helping me move this chain, Aaron Ravenhall, or from our forty percent chance of dying when we try to lift off."

"Well, since you put it that way!" He shouted from under the covers and slid off the bed. "Let's get to work."

Anna and Aaron spent the rest of the day and part of the night clearing the ship of debris, unhooking the chains, and putting things back in order. A new sun was rising when they had finished scooping out earth from the last air hole. They stood together, panting in the light of dawn. Aaron spoke up. "Maybe we should rest."

"We can't. By midmorning they'll send a team down to search for us. We have to get moving."

"You mean you still want to do this now that we have *no* airship support or connection to O.R.T.? We should just wait for them to find us! We won't have achieved our goal, but at least we'll be alive!"

At this, Anna dropped the piece of wood she had been using to scrape the earth out from the air holes and climbed up to the deck. "I'm leaving, Aaron. With or without you, I'm leaving."

"Gods, you are impossible!" He climbed up and sat next to

her in the control area. Aaron began strapping himself in when Anna stopped him.

"No, Aaron. If the ship flips, we have to be ready to jump."

"Great…"

Anna rolled her eyes and started the engine. It started with ease, but the craft began shaking violently. Aaron and Anna looked at each other frantically.

"What does this mean, Anna?"

"I don't know!"

Just then, the starboard side began to lift off the ground, and they felt the jets of air expelling the debris they couldn't dislodge. However, the port side stayed on the ground.

"What do we do, Anna?"

"Wait." A few seconds later, something that sounded like an explosion erupted portside and made the craft jump. This temporarily caused the whole of the craft to be off of the ground, and it provided just enough time for the jets of air to do their work. Several more of these eruptions occurred in rapid succession, and when they ceased, Aaron and Anna found themselves floating steadily in the craft.

"Yes!" Anna shouted and slapped Aaron hard on the back. Aaron was so excited that he returned the slap and caused Anna to bump her head on the monitor in front of her. "Anna! Sorry! Are you okay?"

"Way to kill the moment, Aaron." She laughed. "I'm fine, so let's get out of here."

"Where are we going?" Aaron asked.

"Well, the only other place that has ever had access to the texts of the Ancients or the study of the Raujj has been the Basilica of the Four, which is east of here in the seventh province. Obviously, Grandfather didn't make it that far, so maybe he's living somewhere between here and border of the sixth province."

"The Basilica has studied the Raujj? I had no idea."

"No one does, except for Oronus and the council. A long

time ago, the high priest accused Oronus of withholding materials that could be essential to the productivity of the basilica and the work of the Four. The council unanimously agreed to have Daddy share any of the Ancient texts with him that had anything to do with the Four. All right, Aaron, let's get going."

~

Edgar left the *Regalus* floating just outside Restivar and next to the steam-powered airship Oronus had sent so long ago that had become their headquarters. He swung down off of the deck and walked toward the other ship. He shouted up toward the opposing deck.

"Simon! Thacker! Getcher act together and lemme in!" Almost immediately the ramp lowered to the ground. At the entrance stood Simon Gardner and Thacker Wallace. Simon was tall, thin, and young, sporting long, blond hair and lanky-looking arms and legs. At seventy-eight, Thacker was older than Edgar and had been with Cebran when they tried to blow up the hangar of O.R.T. He had sold out explosives dealers in the second and third provinces for a shorter punishment. He was about five feet tall and was beginning to show the signs of his old age.

"Fortune smiles on us today, boys! I have brought a gift from O.R.T.—the *Regalus!*"

"Great! A new ship for the cause!" Simon was excited but not as emotional as Thacker had become.

"Gods, it's the *Regalus*. Cebran..." A tear rolled down his cheek. He quickly brushed it away. "Boy, you know naught of this vessel, but the founder of our cause died trying to steal her straight from the hangar of O.R.T. some time ago. Now we have it." It was almost too much for the old man.

"Speaking of Cebran, guess who I had to dump off? Aaron, his boy! He's been working for 'em ever since Oronus killed Cebran! I even got to dump Oronus's daughter!" Edgar shouted.

Thacker was taken aback. "How did you manage all of that, Edgar? These are things we were planning for some time now, and you did it all at once!"

Edgar smiled his sheepish smile. "Oh, well, it was nothing but pure fortune. The girl came to me with a request to lower them to ground level for a field test of a new craft. I saw that she talked the boy into comin,' so I knew it was the time! We stopped about thirty feet 'afore we should've to lower the craft, and dumped 'em! I took care of the men I talked into helpin' me out and headed home!"

Thacker cackled. "That sure is some fortune, Edgar. Well, I suppose we should pay a visit to the basilica for some praise and penance, if you follow me!"

Edgar nodded. "Just what I was thinkin'! Simon, mind the ship while we report to the high priest!"

～

"Sir!" Dardus Hale rushed into Oronus's office in the engineering section of Re-Creation. Oronus was finishing up another letter bound for Alden's.

"What is it, Dardus?"

"Sir, the hovering craft and the *Regalus* are gone!"

Oronus set down his pen and closed his eyes. "Where is Anna?" He already knew what had happened—Aaron hadn't found Anna in time, and she left to find Osiris.

"We don't know, sir. Anna, Aaron, Edgar, and three other men from the hangar are missing as well."

Eyes still closed, fists clenched, Oronus said, "Tell me what you know."

"Our teams have discovered broken pieces of wood and two large chains at the base of O.R.T. We have no idea where the *Regalus* is."

Oronus got to his feet. "Dardus, my daughter and Aaron have

taken the hovering craft and are currently searching for my father. I can only hope that Edgar is searching for them as we speak."

"Sir, we tried to make contact with the *Regalus*, and it seems as though communication with O.R.T. was deliberately severed from their end." Oronus fought to maintain a level head for a little while longer.

"If this is true, Dardus, then there are only two options. The first is that Edgar and whoever is with him are helping Anna and Aaron in their search. The second is that Edgar has taken the *Regalus*. The only other person to attempt that was Cebran. If these two instances are connected, then it is possible Edgar is allied with the group in Restivar. We could not move against them without the approval of the council, but we can be ready. Go to the hangar and create two teams who are appropriately equipped to deal with both scenarios."

"Yes, sir."

Oronus crumpled up the letter and stuffed it into his pocket. "This had better be another personal visit."

He donned his emerald-green cape and left for the hangar.

CHAPTER 9

Aevier's ship floated once again in front of the basilica.

"Zis vill be short, gentlemen. I simply seek to engage in ze rite of praise and penance, vhich vill not take too long."

They dropped the large rope, and he slid down with much more ease than his last descent there. He walked through the courtyard and knelt once again at the statues of the Four Representations.

"Ze awesome quartet of Visdom, Justice, Grace, and Mercy be praised."

He rose and continued toward the sanctum. As he entered the sanctum, he saw Graff standing at the front and reading aloud from a very old book.

"Oh my. Do you have news for me, marionette? I saw that you have met with Oronus and his little friends. What transpired?"

"Master, I have arranged a tour of O.R.T. for ze ozher district heads. During zis time, I plan on having Oronus give me a *personal* tour, as I am sure zhere vill be things zat he takes great pains to hide from me. Many of his department heads showed much affinity for my mentioning ze basilica and ze Four. Your plan is vorking, my Lord."

"I have much to tell you, faithful one. My men in Restivar have notified me that they dumped the girl and the brat at ground level with a broken hovering craft and left them for dead. What's more, they have stolen one of Oronus's ships. What fortune, what chance! I will eventually smile down on all of this from my place in the heavens. This little event has perhaps forwarded our plans, loyal one. I want you to call an emergency meeting of the council and inform them of your decision to hold a tour of O.R.T. Also, set forth a vote for legislation that would break up the power play O.R.T. is pulling on the other provinces. Richard, and surprisingly Melinda, will be against it, but the other four will no doubt agree to this course of action. You will then hold some sort of 'inter-province' gatherings at your estate. You will slowly worm your ideas into their minds. Whether our original two years has passed or not, when you feel that you have gotten a hold of the council's reigns in the name of the Four, kill Alden as you see fit. He will be our last obstacle, as I believe you will be able to break Melinda through some means. Remember, servant, I see what you see. You must continue to tell me what you hear, regardless of our confidence in this plan. Go now and do my bidding."

"Yes, my Lord."

Aevier bowed low and made his way back to the airship. After being raised to the deck by the crew, he issued his swift commands.

"I vill need someone in my chambers immediately to dictate. Ve leave for ze council headquarters in ze fourth province. Vhen I arrive, make a trip to Restivar and ensure zat ze high priest's men take no action and remain under ze radar. Move." The crew took their places, and they flew west toward the fourth province.

Aevier summoned one of the crew members, and they went below deck to the control room. "Are you ready? Good, let's begin.

With a measure of authority, Jacques dictated a directorial

order that called for the creation of a new aircraft production facility and a turnover of any and all materials associated with the Raujj to the Basilica of the Four.

The crew member folded the manuscript, placed it in a leather-bound sleeve, and handed it to Aevier. "Very good. You are dismissed." The crew member bowed and went back up to the deck.

"Oronus, my friend, I hope you are prepared for some company."

Oronus was doing just that. He ascended to the hangar and walked toward Dardus, who was orchestrating the creation of a tactical offensive team and a recovery team. He was shouting orders and waving his arms, vainly attempting to control the commotion that came with these operations. He saw Oronus approaching, pointed toward his office door, and then continued his rant. Oronus made his way into Dardus Hale's office and took a seat. A few minutes later, Dardus came in and leaned on the door, forehead on the glass window, as he closed it.

"Gods, Oronus, I'm glad that's over. We have some good news regarding Anna and Aaron."

"Go on."

"Well, Anna originally designed the hovering crafts to link solely with the airship that they were dropped from. If they needed to make contact with O.R.T., then it would have to have been done by the airship."

"What is your point, Dardus?"

"Well, Captain, when Edgar intentionally cut his link with the hangar, it produced a side effect I don't think he anticipated. Communications believes that we will be able to connect directly with the hovering craft."

"Excellent, Dardus! How will this be done?"

"Edgar's severing his connection essentially cut out the middle man between Anna and O.R.T. We believe that we will have direct contact with Anna and Aaron, Captain."

"What's the catch, Dardus?"

"Captain, this will only work if they are within a certain distance from the base of O.R.T. Airships have no problem maintaining a connection in the air, but keeping one on the ground is much more difficult. We think that this is why Anna chose to confine the hovering craft's connection to an airship. It could maintain a decent range with the craft on the ground and still be able to ascend to an elevation suitable for contact with headquarters."

"Very well, Dardus. Continue your preparations and keep me updated on the connection. I am leaving for Director Alden's immediately."

"Yes, Captain," Dardus got up from his chair and opened the door for Oronus. "I'll send some men to prep the *Orion*.'"

"Thank you, Dardus. Keep me posted."

CHAPTER 10

They hovered over rough, wilted terrain and passed large bases of buildings that towered so high above them they couldn't see their tops. There was little grass, and there were very few hills or elevation of any sort as they made their way east to the border of the sixth province.

Anna and Aaron studied their surroundings as they traveled east, occasionally looking at the radar screen for signs of life. Aside from the sea life that lay within the Faereth Sea and the Achibar Strait and the few wild beasts that managed to survive on hunting each other and what little edible vegetation remained, there was *nothing* down there. The disaster that was sent on the Ancients so long ago, the disaster that was the response to the Raujj being used to end life, the disaster mentioned in the story of creation, had destroyed most of the beauty and usefulness of the land. Fuel remained to be extracted, fish, birds, and a few beasts lived, but any sign of human existence on the ground level disappeared long before they were born.

Aaron was first to speak. "How can we be sure about where Osiris is? I mean, we may have passed him already on this course."

"If Grandfather was headed for the basilica in a busted craft, I think it's safe to assume that he took the most direct route out of the province."

Aaron looked out from his side of the glass dome. "Maybe, but if we don't find him on this route, when do you plan on turning around? We don't have enough food and water to search the entire ground level of the fifth province."

"When I feel like it, Aaron. When I'm satisfied that we have to extend our search or stop searching altogether, so go along or get out."

"Gods, you're grumpy!" Aaron folded his arms and leaned back in his seat. He situated himself for a few seconds, preparing for a nap to escape what he saw as unnecessary complaining, but he saw something on the plain to the north of them that caught his eye.

"Smoke."

"What?"

"Smoke, Anna. Look!" She turned and saw a single, thin, winding column of smoke in the distance.

"Aaron, that could be Grandfather! Let's go!" She turned north and headed for the smoke.

"No, Anna, not like this! If whatever is causing this smoke isn't friendly, I don't want us zooming in unannounced."

"I'll take my chances."

Aaron closed his eyes in frustration. "At least let's drop the craft behind a building and walk when we get closer."

"Have it your way, Aaron, but know that we could very well be attacked between here and there if we walk."

Aaron shrugged. "The chances of us getting hurt by a wild beast are far less than that of whoever caused that smoke hurting us, and we still have a little daylight to work with."

Anna veered west around the great circumference of a looming building and lowered the craft. "Aaron, check the outside for anything that needs to be repaired that we can handle. I'll go below and pack up some supplies."

Aaron nodded and hopped down off the deck and began his inspection. The chains had left some long, deep scratches in the sides of the craft and had ripped off part of the portside railings, but other than these large-scale issues Anna had done a good job patching it up, considering their position. He turned and looked out at the surrounding area: charred earth, dead grass, *lots* of sand, and no water in sight. He was not entirely comfortable with being outside of the protection of the hovering craft, and it was because of this disposition of his that Aaron jumped as he heard the craft's small ramp lower to the ground. Anna smiled and handed him a leather bag with food, water and bandages inside. He hung it over his shoulder and tried to regain a normal heartbeat.

"Scared, Aaron Ravenhall?"

He let out an awkward laugh that made him cough. "Scared? No, I just … I didn't expect the ramp to come down right next to me is all." Anna smiled wider.

"Sure, Aaron, or did you think a wild beast was about to pounce?" She laughed.

"That's a serious concern, I think!"

"Oh, that reminds me! Hold on, Aaron." Anna went back inside the craft, came out with a short pole axe, and handed it to Aaron. "Let's be prepared for anything out here." Aaron took the pole axe and studied it, tossing it from hand to hand.

"Well, let's hope I don't have to use this. I've been through excavation training and fitness training with Oronus, but there were always guards who accompanied us to Great Houses." The ramp closed, and they began walking back around the great building to head north toward the smoke.

"Well, if it comes down to it, pure adrenalin will save a novice in a fight with a wild beast or a wild person, but I've got some combat experience too."

They rounded the building as the sun began to set. There was little grass and no other vegetation in sight, just charred, dead earth.

"If this is what the Raujj is capable of, no wonder Oronus wants to destroy it."

Anna nodded. "Yes, the disaster that took place here is mentioned in the creation story handed down by the Ancients. Are you familiar with it?"

Aaron laughed as he stepped over a mound of earth and rock. "Me? No, my family was never that religious."

Anna nodded again. "Okay, so then you do not know that the same text also tells us that the Four took the ability to use the Raujj away from the Ancients after this disaster."

Aaron was confused. "Then why is Oronus trying to destroy it? He never mentioned this to me."

Anna smiled. "Well, Daddy is not all that religious either, Aaron. I do not think he places much stock in our recorded genesis. However, if the story is true and the Four did remove our ability and if anyone actually did use the Raujj successfully..."

"What? What?"

"Nothing. I guess sometimes I think Daddy is delving into something that may run deeper than he thinks—all the way to the Four."

This sent chills down Aaron's spine: a course of action that would bring one into the physical presence of the Gods... how fascinating and fearful a notion.

"Gods, this camp is farther away than I thought. I assumed we would be much closer by now."

Aaron nodded. "Yes, whoever is there will probably be asleep by the time we reach the camp. We have to be careful—this may not be a friendly encounter."

They continued to walk in silence, contemplating what awaited them. Half an hour later, they came upon what Aaron thought to be just another pile of rock and earth. Anna stopped, squinting.

"It can't be..."

She walked forward to the dark mass and found it to be a

long-since abandoned hovering craft primitive to Anna's design, a predecessor to the craft they rode in on.

"Grandfather. He's alive, Aaron. I'll bet anything that that is his camp out there. Grandfather!"

She began running toward the camp, and Aaron took off to catch up with her. They ran for about twenty minutes and reached the outskirts of the campsite. A single makeshift tent rested beside the fire pit that had led them there. The tent seemed to be made of animal hides and wooden and metal pieces dismantled from the hovering craft; in fact, most of the seating, housing, and materials heaped about the camp were parts from the hovering craft.

Aaron whispered, "Whoever lives here must have recently gone to bed. Let's check the tent quietly and see if it's really him." Anna nodded and started for the tent, but Aaron grabbed her arm and pulled her back to him, still whispering.

"Anna, you need to be prepared for the fact that your grandfather might not recognize you or that he may be hostile... or dead. Just because Osiris built this campsite doesn't mean he still inhabits it."

Anna gave another solemn nod. They crept forward to the tent, whose doorway was covered by a large, broken piece of plank. They lifted it as quietly as they could and moved it slowly to the side a few inches. There, amidst a heap of blankets, rested Osiris. Anna smiled and started inside, but Aaron pulled her back once again.

"No, Anna! He's not expecting us. If you wake him, he may strike out at you or worse. Who knows what he's been doing with his time out here—he could have continued his attempts at using the Raujj in a demented state."

He pulled her away from the tent but not without her struggling.

"He's right there, Aaron!"

"I know, I know. But we need to at least wait until morning to approach him." Anna resigned to Aaron's suggestion, and they started back the other way when a voice froze them in their tracks.

"Do not move young ones! You just stepped into one of my hieroglyphs! One more step and you'll be visiting the Void!"

"Grandfather, it's me, Anna! We've come to get you!" Osiris hobbled forward and rounded the two in order to see their faces.

"Tricks of the Four, or of the Ancients, I should say! My actions come back to haunt me once again. But you weren't there, no. This is odd. But then again *I* am very odd! *He* was there, though. He let me touch his mind with my own. He's dead! Dead, and yet he visits me still." He rushed forward at them, entering the ring. "And he screams! I hear his screaming even now! The texts are too powerful, the treachery runs too deep! You have no idea of the death that awaits us! And we ushered it in! The Ancient's fooled us into this fall, and fall we did!"

Anna was crying, and Aaron was pale faced. This was not the man Anna remembered. He had been living out here for eight years, his only company being the madness that gripped him.

"Osiris! It's Anna, your granddaughter! We are here to help you!" Osiris pushed Anna down and bent down over her.

"I don't need your help! The only assistance I need is to enter the Void to escape this demon!"

He raised his arm to strike her, and Aaron reached his left arm around Osiris's neck, pulling him back and choking him at the same time.

"Don't step too far, now! The Void awaits the one who steps outside this glyph of mine!"

Aaron had a thought. "Well, you are in here with us, old man, and regardless of who made this I bet we'll all be killed!"

"Matters not to me, peon! I would gladly take death over his screaming!" Aaron thought he would at least test the man's word.

"All right, then," Aaron said and made it seem as though he would leave the ring.

"Wait! No, child!" Aaron smirked and tightened his hold.

"Then I suggest you undo whatever curse you placed on this ground before I send us all into this Void of yours!"

Osiris nodded violently and wriggled his way out of Aaron's grip. He slowly began making characters over the existing symbols with his finger, muttering inaudibly as he did so.

After he did this a bright ring of pulsating blue light shone around them and then faded. Osiris's markings were gone from the ground around them. Anna stood up and Osiris pushed past them both and ran back into his tent. Aaron walked forward and spoke to the mouth of the tent and the blackness that lay beyond it.

"Osiris."

He whispered back, as though he was completely exhausted. "What do you want from me?"

"We need you to come back to O.R.T. with us. I have recovered the Chest of Worlds, and with its secrets, we may finally be able to destroy the Raujj."

Osiris's now-disfigured, pale, and vein-ridden face appeared from the shadows. He sounded even more exhausted than before. Aaron stepped back, and Anna gasped. "The Chest of Worlds ... but how could you ... if he were to gain control of it ... You delve into terrible secrets, children ... One God ... never the Four ..." He coughed and gasped. "Beware the high priest ..."

Osiris slumped over onto the ground outside of the tent. He was completely white, and his skin was riddled with dark, purple veins. Anna rushed forward and picked him up in her arms. "Grandfather ..." she said as tears rolled down her face. Aaron put his hand on her shoulder, disappointed that they were too late, but as he looked down, he saw that Osiris's chest was moving ever so slowly.

"Anna, he's still breathing! We have to get him back to O.R.T.! Let's go!"

She smiled, kissed Osiris's forehead, and they began running back toward the hovering craft.

Oronus sat in a small office off of the hangar, studying the layout of Anna's communications system. He desperately wanted to expedite this process, so he had begun his own research alongside Dardus's team. Seeing that Dardus was within shouting distance, he called to him.

"Dardus! I need you for a moment!"

Dardus turned and gave a quick nod, then finished his delegation to a small group of mechanics bunched together in front of him. They nodded and scattered as Dardus turned to enter the office. He closed the door and took a seat in a padded chair in front of the desk. Oronus continued reading over the specifications of the craft and addressed Dardus without looking up.

"Any new developments, Dardus?"

"Yes, Captain. We are extremely close to making audio contact with Anna and Aaron. Our team has discovered a way to bypass the severed connection between the *Regalus* and O.R.T., as we discussed earlier. We will be hearing from them soon, Captain."

Oronus looked up from his research and smiled, pleased at the news Hale had delivered. "Very good, very good."

Oronus smiled at Hale, and when he was alone once again, he walked to the window of the office. The hangar was a flurry of activity, with the area being committed to many preparations and tasks at one time. A team was preparing for the eventual defense of O.R.T. against the rouge group in the first province; another was prepped and ready for the rescue of Aaron and Anna; yet another ran constantly from workstations in the hangar to Navigation and Logistics, struggling to gain contact with and extract coordinates from the hovering craft.

"Just come home, honey. Please." Oronus pulled the shade down and turned off the light to the office, then sat down and closed his eyes.

CHAPTER 11

Six of the seven portholes that lined the executive side of the council's headquarters were occupied as Jacques's ship made its way to the docking bay. He smiled and walked to the hatch.

"Inform me vhen ve are about to land, helmsman," he said as he lifted the hatch and began descending the rungs to the control room. He sat down at the far end of the room and crossed his legs. "Soon Alden vill be dead, and Oronus vill lose much of his production to ze first province. O.R.T ... humph ... zhey vill soon be losing some of zheir steam." Twenty minutes later, one of Jacques's crewmembers came to inform him of their arrival.

Aevier rose and nodded. "Thank you."

He went back up to the deck and watched as the ship passed through the remaining porthole. They docked, and Aevier's secretary greeted him.

"The other six directors are all waiting, sir. I have passed out your proposals, and they have been talking amongst themselves."

"Thank you, Stephanie. You have been most helpful. I vill call on you soon."

Stephanie nodded and accompanied Jacques as he entered

the elevator. "I'll be in my office should you need anything, Director Aevier."

The doors slid open, and Jacques found himself on the directors' floor that actually rested *above* the hangar. Circular in shape and nearly half of a mile in diameter, this new floor was added on six years before Aevier came onto the council. One hundred feet of metal alloys separated the place from the hangar. The layout was almost like a pie; seven triangular sections were designated to split up the administrative goings-on of each province (because of this odd number, the sixth and seventh provinces had half as much space, but Jacques was hardly ever here anyway, so he didn't mind).

All seven of these 'pie pieces' led to a circular conference room used for executive meetings. Aevier entered, and the discussion ceased.

"Hello, everyone!" Aevier said through a smile as he took his seat at the table. There were rumblings of salutation across the group.

Alden was the first to address the council. "Before we address this proposal by Director Aevier, I think that it would be beneficial for us to give progress reports from within our respective provinces. It would be good to hear what we've all been up to for the past few months. Is that agreeable?"

Alden's request was greeted with a unanimous aye, so he continued. "Well, then let's start with Melinda and work our way up, shall we?"

Melinda Stockstill scooted forward and opened a folder, smoothing its pages out. "As you are all aware, the first province and Restivar, but, more specifically, the smaller cities on the outskirts of the province, have suffered much in recent years due to our miraculous progress in travel and trade. As such, we are still engaging in humanitarian outreach to the smaller cities, as well as shifting out-of-work fuel recoverers to merchant, shipment, and mechanical posts in the other districts. The basilica and O.R.T. have been very generous in their giving, though I do not make it widely known that O.R.T. is supporting the province, as there is still much resentment toward them in the minds of the people. In fact, that brings me to my next point—I have been occasionally sending high-flying personal crafts out of Restivar to keep watch on the rebellious group of fuel recoverers that tried to attack O.R.T. a few years ago. I received word four days ago that they now have *two* airships, and their newest addition has been identified as the *Regalus*, a large airship out of Oronus's fleet. I have sent messengers to O.R.T. to inform Oronus of this occurrence, and I have no idea why it is there. It is odd to me that Oronus has taken no action in the situation…"

"Well, Melinda, that's not entirely accurate."

Alden hadn't been sure before the meeting if this would even come up, but he had prepared to handle it if it did.

"He had planned on meeting with me today to talk about engaging in negotiations with the group or engaging in reconnaissance to retrieve the vessel. Obviously, I cancelled to honor this emergency meeting. However, this information is essential to what is happening at O.R.T. right now. The short version is this: Oronus's daughter and his apprentice are stranded on the ground level and are so because of the actions of whoever took the *Regalus*. Oronus didn't know if the *Regalus* was simply looking for the two or if it was taken, because communications have been severed. If you'll excuse me, I must make immediate contact with Oronus." Michael Reath, director of the second province, stood. "Alden, we don't need a war right now, and you know it! I support Oronus, but we all know that those nut jobs have explosives!"

Estelle Nichols of the fourth province was quick to retort. "Michael, if they are growing, and given the fact that one of their men was on the inside of O.R.T., Oronus needs to put an end to this thing before it starts!"

Aevier spoke next. "Vell, if O.R.T. hadn't crippled ze first province, zhen maybe zhey could handle zis on zheir own!"

"What? How dare you, Jacques! Oronus has been wonderful

to us. You simply can't see past your own nose to envision the long-term result of steam power!" Aevier's monocle spun outrageously faster than normal.

"If you vould pull back your vision a little, Melinda, you would see all of ze poor and hungry you left in ze dust for ze basilica to care for!" Soon the entire table erupted in disagreement. Alden shouted over them. "Quiet! All of you!" He may have been small in stature and slightly overweight, but Richard Alden knew how to command the attention of the council when he needed to. "These people apparently have *only* two ships. Much of their leadership is still in prison or is deceased, and they are aggressing against the man with the largest number of aircraft in all of the Seven Provinces. Now, please calm yourselves and continue the reports. We have all compromised something to be here on such short notice, so let's not waste this time trying to win a shouting match. I will return shortly."

The anger ebbed a little with Alden's reassurances, and the directors reclaimed their seats at the table. Michael Reath had begun his report concerning the increased sales of personal crafts to families as the door closed, and Richard quickly made his way for the fifth province section of the council offices. Luckily, the directors' offices were closest to the conference room, so he didn't have far to go. He entered his office and sat down at his comm panel. "Oronus. Oronus, it's Richard. Can you hear me?"

~

"Sir! We have an incoming transmission from Director Alden." Oronus's eyes widened.

"Divert one of the panels we are using to connect with the hovering craft and put him through."

"Oronus. Oronus, it's Richard. Can you hear me?"

"Yes, Alden. What news do you have for me?"

"Oronus, Melinda's men have found the *Regalus* in Restivar. Whoever took Anna and Aaron to the ground is friendly to the resistance that is mounting against you."

Oronus was livid. "Gods curse the traitors! Do you know anything else?"

"Yes, Oronus. I've just recently seen the proposal that delayed our meeting today, and it involves a scale-back of O.R.T. in favor of the first province. I have to get back to the meeting, Oronus."

"Wait! Alden, do I have your approval to take my ship back?"

"Not until you have returned those two kids safely, Oronus, that is the topmost priority. Make sure that they're safe. Then we can talk about possible courses of action."

Oronus felt ashamed at this. "Of course, Alden, how silly of me."

"Good-bye, Oronus. I will pay a visit when this is over."

Oronus stood on a nearby workbench and shouted, "I need your attention, please! Attention!"

Most of the hustle ceased as Oronus began his address.

"Ladies and gentlemen! I have received confirmation that the *Regalus* is in the hands of the disgruntled group in Restivar and that Edgar and a few others from O.R.T. deliberately stranded Anna and Aaron to steal the ship! I know that there are two teams right now preparing for different scenarios, but I want all attention focused on returning those two to safety! You will spiral search the area using O.R.T. as the center point! Do not stop until you have located Aaron and Anna! Get to work!"

Immediately, the team that was already prepared for this task lifted off, six ships in all. The other team, who had been prepping four WASPs, or weapons-activated sentry prototypes, now diverted their focus to four cargo ships that were close by. Oronus went back to the area of the hangar that was the temporary branch of Communications and Logistics.

"Are there any new developments, men?"

"Yes, sir! We have managed to locate a delayed signal from the craft; apparently, they tried to make contact at some point. They may not be at this location anymore, but it could very well lead us in the right direction. The coordinates lie north and east of here."

"Good work, men! Load these coordinates into all of the map boards. Let's bring these two back home!"

As the first ship prepared to leave, Oronus ran forward, waving his arms. "Wait! Wait!" One of the crew members on deck spotted Oronus and motioned to the helmsman. The hydraulic ramp was lowered, and Oronus quickly made his way to the deck.

"I'll take it from here, helmsman!"

~

Alden returned to the conference room just as the director of the seventh province, Raulph Hartsfield, finished his report. As Raulph finished, Aevier rose to address the council.

"Thank you all for honoring the calling of zis special meeting. I realize zat you are all very busy vistin your own provinces. However, zis is a matter zat concerns us all. As you know, I oversee ze Industrial Districts in ze Seven Provinces." Aevier paused at the sound of murmuring and chuckling. "And I *realize* zat I have not been as attentive as I should have been over the past few years. Zat is vhy I have placed zis proposal in front of you. O.R.T. has been a shining example for ze ozher districts for a long time now. Zheir increasing rate of success and production, however, is having an adverse effect on ze ozher provinces. I feel zat it vould be beneficial, zherefore, for ze council and ze district heads from each province to take a tour of O.R.T. and see how zhey function so successfully. Hopefully zis vill give ideas to ze ozher provinces and encourage zhem to engage in new endeavors."

Reath spoke out. "Obviously, Jacques, we can't all have teams that excavate Raujj-enchanted buildings and revive enchanted and long-dead machinery. That is an art that is unique to Oronus's family line, and the council is okay with this uniqueness." Ayes sounded from around the table.

"Very true, Michael, but vat about ze texts zat are recovered, hmm? Perhaps texts zat could be used by the basilica? I feel as zhough High Priest Graff has ze right to examine ze texts O.R.T. has on hand. Also, steam power is quickly becoming ze most popular means of travel, yet O.R.T. is ze only facility creating such transportation. If zis continues, zhen ze ozher districts vill simply have to cease production of crafts, and O.R.T. vill hold a monopoly over one more aspect of our lives.

"Ze second and third districts have zheir personal craft production; ze fourth has the Council Headquarters and ze only vaste disposal facility; O.R.T. is in ze fifth province; ze sixth province specialises in ze acquiring of fish, fowl, fruits, and vegetables for ze Market Districts; and ze seventh province has ze Basilica of ze Four. The first province has *nothing!*" Aevier slammed a fist down on the table next to Alden, and everyone jumped.

"Zis brings me to ze final point of my bringing you all here. If O.R.T.'s craft production was scaled back, no one vould suffer greatly. Zhey are already involved in reviving texts and technologies, as vell as charting uncharted areas of ze Seven Provinces and ze outlying areas. I believe zat ze first province should be home to a new, council-sanctioned craft production facility specialising in travel and trade between ze provinces. Zis is a vay in vhich O.R.T. becomes less of a threat to communal velfare, and at ze same time ze first province has plenty of vork for its people once again."

Aevier sat down, gazing at everyone around the table.

Alden spoke quietly. "What about the mechanics and crew members at O.R.T. that would lose *their* jobs because of this?"

Aevier responded quickly. "They vould still have ozher jobs to take part in at O.R.T., and those zat vished not to stay could move to ze first province to train and supervise."

Alden didn't know what to say. He obviously couldn't refute the tour of O.R.T. That would make it seem as though there was something behind its walls that he didn't want them to see. It would also be difficult to persuade anyone out of this scale-back. Melinda was practically salivating at the idea of the boost that would come from this new addition to her province. He was also surprised about the texts. He was so sure that Aevier was preparing to propose the takeover of the Ancient's language by the council—instead he wanted the texts reviewed by the basilica. He, and the rest of them, he assumed, were so used to Jacques's inaction and apathy that this move caught them completely off guard.

He knew that there was no way to get a majority vote against any of these proposals. "Well, Jacques, if the only scale-back is going to come from O.R.T.'s hangar and work areas for aircraft, then I propose that the tour be only of the hangar and those work areas. If the other Industrial Districts will not be engaging in the technological aspect of O.R.T.'s business, then we needn't waste our time analyzing those areas."

Melinda agreed with Alden. "Yes, I think that this is an appropriate suggestion given the nature of the proposed scale-back."

Aevier frowned.

Melinda continued. "Furthermore, I believe that the scholars within O.R.T. should file reports with Oronus when they come across a text that may have something to do with the Four. Then Oronus can gather the texts and take them to the basilica. I see no reason why the high priest should be allowed complete access to the texts at O.R.T. We have all agreed on many different occasions that the knowledge of the Raujj is best kept behind closed doors."

Reath and Hartsfield answered with an aye. Alden also sounded in agreement. Aevier was angry. This was not how he saw the meeting panning out.

At least ve will be taking ze tour and zhey have warmed up slightly to ze idea of ze high priest taking part.

Aevier rose. "Very vell. All in favor of a tour of O.R.T.'s production facilities?"

"Aye."

"All in favor of an investigation into immediate scale-back of O.R.T.'s production facilities?"

"Aye."

"All in favor of ze *sharing* of religious texts, vhen found, vist ze basilica and High Priest Eleazer Graff?"

"Aye."

The other six directors rose.

Alden spoke. "All right then. In one month's time, we will gather at O.R.T. in the fifth province; I will send out details to your offices. After the tour is completed, we will compile our thoughts on the scale-back. Also, while we are there, we can inform Oronus of our desire for his teams to check through their newly recovered texts for anything the basilica could use."

The seven directors collected their things and began making their way back to their respective office wings or provinces.

Alden approached Aevier on his way out. "I trust that this text business is honorable, Aevier? You seem to have had a change of heart regarding the books and scrolls of the Ancients."

Aevier looked at Alden. "Ze use of ze Raujj is not as important as discovering ze texts regarding ze Four. Zhey could contain vital information to our spiritual velfare, Richard. Nothing more, nothing less."

Aevier walked past Richard, who continued questioning him.

"But surely you realize, Jacques, that the high priest must have already come into contact with the power of the Raujj through his previous appeal to the council for texts. Is it not dangerous for one person to know so much more about such a delicate subject than anyone else?"

Aevier stopped without turning. "Are you insinuating something, Dick?"

Alden chuckled at this. "You have become very *faithful* as of late, Jacques, that's all. I just want to ensure that your newfound source of sustenance is being used honorably and not for a private gain."

Aevier smiled, back still turned to Alden. "Blessings of ze Four upon you and your household, Richard. Good-bye." Aevier made for the elevator When he arrived, his airship was already prepped for flight.

"Have you made ze appropriate modifications to Alden's craft, helmsman?"

"Yes, sir."

"Vere you spotted?"

"No, sir."

"Good. Get us into ze air. Zhere are things I must discuss vist all of you."

~

"What do you make of this, Melinda?" What do you make of our new saint?"

Melinda giggled. "Well, he certainly has had a change of heart, though I don't know how honorable it was. Regardless, Richard, this move could be the enhancement that the first province is looking for. I'm going to play along, and you should too."

"Well, I guess you're right. We were able to reduce the magnitude of those proposals a little with our suggestions. Anyway, just let me know if Stephanie reports anything new to you."

"All right. I think I'm going to stop by my office for a little while. I'll contact you if anything happens."

He nodded and they parted ways. Alden entered the elevator and got out at the hangar. He boarded his smaller, personal aircraft and got into the control area with the three crew members who waited with the ship.

"Let's go to O.R.T. I have to see Oronus in person."

CHAPTER 12

Aaron drove the hovering craft as Anna cared for Osiris down below. Osiris was still breathing slowly, but he was getting very hot. Anna poured some of her water onto a cloth and placed it on his forehead. She sat down on the floor beside the bed and shut her eyes. Removing that enchantment must have been more than he could handle, but at least he was alive.

Aaron was beginning to lose his focus and started to doze off when he heard loud crackling and muffled voices. He jumped and looked around him, fixing his gaze on the speaker beside the small map board.

"Hello? Hello?"

Aaron saw a button beside the speaker, and a knob. He pushed the button, and it began blinking green.

"Anna. Anna. This is O.R.T. Can you respond?"

"Yes, this is Aaron! We hear you, O.R.T.! We are heading your way right now!"

"Wonderful, Aaron. Are either of you injured?"

"We've got some bumps and bruises, but we are doing well, considering. Also, we found Osiris. He is with us right now."

"Gods! *They've found Captain Osiris! He's alive!* Aaron, is he all right?"

"No. He is very weak right now, and I fear that he is near death. He needs immediate attention."

"All right, Aaron. Listen, we have airships coming out to look for you. You should be in one of their fields of vision soon. How far out are you?"

"I would guess that we still have four days until we are close to O.R.T."

"Aaron, the airships will cover ground much faster than you can. Can you tell me where you are in relation to O.R.T.?"

"All I know is that we are north and east of O.R.T."

"Thank you, Aaron. I will contact the ships in the air and send them in that direction. You should be spotted sometime in the next couple of days. Also, we have received word from the first province that Edgar has taken the *Regalus* to Restivar, so he must be in league with the group that is unfriendly to O.R.T. there. Just keep your eyes open, Aaron. Hang in there."

Aaron slowed the craft and left it hovering so that he could tell Anna the news. When he came below, Anna was a little irritated and was rubbing her head.

"What just happened, Aaron? Why did you jerk the craft so violently?"

He smiled. "Sorry about that. Anna, I just talked to someone from O.R.T.! They have airships headed our way right now!"

Anna breathed a sigh of relief. "Thank the Four. Do they know about Grandfather?"

"Yes, Anna. I told them he needs immediate attention."

"Very good. All right, Aaron, let's get moving."

∽

One of the crew members of the *Bismarck* rushed to Oronus, who was on deck at the helm. "Sir! O.R.T. has made contact with Anna and Aaron. They are safe!"

"Gods! Wonderful news! Do we know where they are?"

"All they know is that they are northeast of O.R.T. At least four days by way of hovering craft."

"All right. I want you to get a hold of Dardus. Tell him to call back all airships. Have them move all the communications equipment they can back to Communications. Prep five of our WASPs for the retrieval of the *Regalus*—that ship may be heavily guarded. Also, have Parrus Vademe contact Director Alden, and have him come to O.R.T. as soon as he can. The *Bismarck* will change course to go find Aaron and Anna. Get moving."

"Sir?"

"What is it?"

"They have Osiris with them. He is alive." With that, the crew member left to begin his list of duties. Oronus was pale faced.

"Father... you fool. Helmsman, resume your post! Turn starboard one hundred and sixty-four degrees bearing northeast. Have spotters ready to locate the hovering craft. It could be today, perhaps tomorrow early on."

Oronus walked to the hatch and made his way to the control room, finding one of the officers.

"Officer, find a free panel and contact O.R.T. See if they can replace the *Regalus*'s severed connection to the hovering craft with our own. Contact me as soon as something happens. I'll be in my quarters."

"Yes, sir."

Oronus made his way back to the captain's quarters. He entered and lay down on the bed, staring at the ceiling.

"Father..."

"Dardus, someone is approaching O.R.T."

"I know, Wells. I've just called back six of the seven airships that were out there searching."

"No, sir. It is a personal craft. Not one of ours."

"Is it close enough to link a signal with?"

"Yes, sir."

"Then find out who it is! You don't need my permission for that—we're trying to get back into order here, Wells, so take some initiative!"

"Sorry, sir. I'll find the signal."

"Good. Call me when you do."

"Yes, sir."

Dardus left the makeshift communications area in the hangar and walked toward the docking bays. Two of the ships had already returned, and the crew members were awaiting orders.

"All right! We will begin prepping five WASPs for the retrieval of the *Regalus*. If you run out of things to do, maintenance could always use assistance. Move out!"

As Dardus returned to the Communications area, he found that they were already moving equipment back to its department. "Good, men! Let's get the panels up and running in Communications as soon as possible."

Wells came running from the bridgeway and found Dardus. "Sir, Parrus Vademe has notified me that the personal craft is Director Alden's. Oronus has requested his presence here."

Dardus nodded. "All right, Wells. Go down below and open one of the smaller portholes for the director. When he gets here, send him to Parrus."

Dardus sighed. *It's still a frenzy around here, but at least some order is returning,* he thought to himself.

In the Communications building, Parrus was working on connecting the *Bismarck* with the hovering craft. "Stephens, can't we just reconfigure the *Bismarck*'s uplink to be compatible with the new configuration Anna used for the hovering craft?"

"It's not that easy, sir. Anna's new configuration isn't a part of O.R.T.'s overall communication capabilities yet. It's just an experimental system. However, we were able to connect with the craft from *here*. I can send a sustained signal to the hovering craft and the *Bismarck* at the same time. They could, theoretically, make contact over O.R.T.'s system, like a conference call."

Parrus sat down at a free panel. "Okay. Start the sustained signal to the crafts."

Wells entered as he was doing so. "Parrus, Director Alden will be docking soon with O.R.T."

"Very well, let's go to the docking bay. Stephens, take it from here. Good work on this."

"Thank you, sir."

With that, Parrus and Wells went to the hangar to greet Director Alden. As they entered, the remaining ships that were searching for the hovering craft had returned and docked.

"What was Alden riding in, Wells?"

"His personal craft, sir. We have opened a porthole for him down below."

"All right, then. Let's go."

Back in Communications, Oronus made contact with O.R.T. "Parrus, it's done. Patch us through."

"This is Stephens, sir. Parrus has gone to greet Director Alden. I will try to patch you through."

"Very good, Stephens. Alden arrived sooner than I expected him to."

Stephens called Anna's craft and the *Bismarck* simultaneously.

"Anna or Aaron, this is O.R.T. Oronus, this is O.R.T. Can you both hear me?"

"Aye, Stephens."

"Yes! This is Anna, O.R.T.!"

"Anna!" Oronus shouted.

"Daddy! Where are you?"

"I'm headed your way, honey. Are you all right?"

"I'm fine. Daddy, I have Osiris. He's alive! I told you he would be!" Anna's voice gained a little edge with the final statement.

"I'm sorry, Anna. We can reconcile this matter later, though. I just want you to be safe."

"I love you, Daddy."

"I love you, little one. Keep heading for O.R.T. We should be spotting you soon. Take shifts with Aaron."

"I am, Daddy."

"How are you on food and water?"

"We're rationing appropriately on the off chance that Grandfather wakes up."

"And your injuries aren't severe?"

"Daddy! We're fine!"

"Sorry, honey. Contact me if anything changes."

"All right, Daddy."

Anna smiled as she continued her flight back to O.R.T. That conversation brought a peace over her that she had not felt in some time. She slowed and left the craft hovering. It was Aaron's turn to drive.

Aevier's ship floated high in the seventh province, above the Basilica of the Four. He had paid his men a great deal of money to remain so loyal to his plans, to the high priest's plans. However, they knew nothing about the who and why of their actions of late. It was time to let them into the inner circle. Those who refused to capitulate would simply be eliminated.

"Helmsman, assemble ze entire crew on ze deck. It is high time zat ve discuss some things."

"Yes, sir." Within ten minutes, all twenty-five provincial crew members were on deck awaiting Aevier's address. He stood on the steps that led to the helm.

"You have all been quite loyal to my requests and have acted more often zhan not vistout asking questions. Loyalty zat is paid for is still loyalty, is it not? Still, I know *ve* have come to a point vhere some things must be revealed. Vhen I am finished, if you still feel ze same loyalty, you vill be velcomed varmly. If not, zhen you have ze choice to leave, no questions asked. It is apparent zat my trips to ze basilica have become more frequent, and zat my actions vistin ze council and in ze province have made a substantial turn. Zis is because I have come upon a knowledge zat vill change ze lives of everyone from zis day forward. High Priest Graff has uncovered knowledge zat ze Four Representations are actually a ruse created by ze Ancients and called into 'being' through ze power of ze Raujj, vhich is no longer readily usable by humans. He is creating a course of action zat vill promote ze physical, mental, and spiritual velfare of all ze provinces. You have put in extra hours, you have helped me track Oronus's teams, you have even assisted me vist the assassination of Director Richard Alden. Zhese are all important pieces in a greater puzzle."

Parrus and Wells entered the lower half of the hangar just as Alden approached landing distance. "Ah. Here he comes now. Wells, I think I'm going to go check in on Stephens. I trust him. I just want to ensure that contact is made. Bring Alden to Communications, and I will show him to an office."

"Yes, sir."

"Vhen he lands, ze device you planted vill begin vorking. Vhen ze engine shuts off completely and begins to cool, his craft vill explode. Zis also ties in vist ze humanitarian injustices created by O.R.T. in places like ze first province. You all know of zis. Some of you have come to me as a result of fuel layoffs.

"Oronus! We are picking up a large, moving object on our screens. It must be Anna! She is approximately one hundred miles to the northeast."

"Gods! Hah! They are closer than they thought. This is wonderful!"

〜

"Ze devastation to O.R.T.'s hangar zat ze explosion vill cause, along vist ze death of ze man who has safeguarded O.R.T. to ze council for *years,* give us time and vill furzher my cause for ze initiating of a council-sanctioned scale-back of O.R.T.'s facility. A large portion of zeir craft production vill be relocated to Restivar. Oronus, having just lost ze *Regalus,* vill more zhan likely assume zat ze explosion vas an act of terrorism by ze rogue group in ze first province. Vist Alden gone, he vill more zhan likely act on his own accord by launching an attack against ze group. Ze basilica, and zherefore ze high priest, re-enters ze equation."

〜

Alden's personal craft landed smoothly in the lower docking bay, and Wells stood at the ready to receive the director. He hopped out of the control area and stood on the deck as the other crew members began shutting off the ship and its systems.

"Geoffrey! How are you?"

"Hello, Director. I am fine. It has been a while, eh?"

"Yes, perhaps too long. I do love coming here."

"Captain Oronus has not returned yet, but I can take you to Parrus Vademe, who has prepared an office for you."

〜

"Anna or Aaron? This is Oronus. Can you hear me?"

"This is Aaron. Oronus, I'm so sorry about this. I know I've already screwed up once and—"

"Shut up about that. Look, I know you can't see us yet through the darkness, but we'll be meeting sooner than we guessed. You must have never stopped! Anyway, I want you to stop and send up a sustained signal to verify that what we have on our screens really is you. Prepare Osiris to be transported. We can't take the craft, though. The *Bismarck* is not equipped to carry auxiliary vessels. I'll see you soon."

"I'll tell Anna. We'll stop here."

Oronus switched over to Stephens at O.R.T. "Stephens, we have located the craft and are preparing for immediate retrieval. Has Alden arrived safely?"

"Yes, sir. He just landed. Dardus has prep—"

Oronus was puzzled by the sudden silence. "Stephens? Stephens, can you hear me?"

The conversation was interrupted by a loud noise and then silence. Oronus walked over to the leading officer in the control room.

"Officer, have we had any other malfunctions with the communications equipment? I've suddenly lost contact with O.R.T."

❧

Wells turned in shock and surprise as the engine on the personal craft began to spark violently.

"I thought this was a steam-powered ship!" Alden shouted as he brushed away a spark that singed his jacket.

"Director, come away from there! Please, hurry!" Wells shouted, but it was too late. A section of the engine exploded, killing Director Alden and his crew members instantly. The blast knocked him to the floor, and he lived long enough to hear the rest of the engine explode and see a large chunk of ceiling fall toward him. As the blast ripped through the metallic ceiling, it exploded into the top part of the hangar above the smaller porthole. Shrapnel-like debris and intense flames killed dozens of mechanics and engineers who were located close to the blast. As the flames shot upward, they made contact with one of the

WASPs being prepped for the retrieval mission. Dardus got to his feet, dizzy from being thrown into a nearby wall, and began shouting orders.

"Get away! Down the bridgeway! Down the bridgeway! Get water in the air! We need to dump it on those flames! No! Get away from those—"

The ship exploded, sending chunks of the corresponding wall and porthole panels flying in all directions. The broken rubble that flew outward fell to the ground level; the inward debris killed Dardus and several from Communications instantly. Two ships that already contained large barrels of water were lifting as the wall exploded. One was high enough to remain unscathed, but the other sustained a ruptured blimp and nosedived for the ground level. Many had escaped this blast and its aftermath by running down the bridgeway, but they were now trapped, and the horrific chain explosions of the other three WASPs ensued.

These massive explosions decimated the northern wall of the hangar. The terrible force of these blasts even caused parts of the floor around some docking bays to crash below to the lower half of the hangar. If any mechanics or engineers were down there, they were dead. A virtual quake was felt in Communications, Logistics, Navigation, and Re-Creation, sending texts, devices, scholars, mages, artists, philosophers, linguists, and engineers tumbling.

The electrical system was blown; communications were disrupted. One hundred and thirty died in the hangar, including Dardus Hale, Alden, Wells, and the other three crew members in the lower half. Eighty-five were secure but trapped on the bridgeway, several of the retrieved machines in the revival process were shattered, and much of the portable communications equipment that was brought into the hangar was destroyed. Many were now trapped within the flaming wreckage of the northern half of the hangar, with little hope of survival. The forty that had run down the tunnel that led to the experimental craft area were overtaken by a jet stream of flame.

Another explosion of undetermined delay finished the job. It sent the northern half of the eastern wall careening for the Navigation building. The ruins hammered into Navigation, some passing through great windows on Navigation's western side. The officers on the top floor that weren't killed by the flying debris were crushed by the collapsing ceiling. Parrus Vademe sat in the bridgeway between the hangar and Navigation, blood from a cut on his head mixing with tears. He was in shock. The explosions had happened so suddenly.

"Alden, Wells, Dardus, all of my head officers in the top floor... If I hadn't left when I did..." He began sobbing. "If I hadn't left..."

The officers in the ship that was now floating over the hangar debated on what to do. "We can't just drop the barrels! We'll kill even more people that way!"

"We don't have a choice! It'll take too long to pry them open and dump it out! Dump the barrels!"

Soon several barrels filled with water were thrown over the edge of the ship, with the hopes that they would land on the largest area of the flames. Several hit the mark, but others fell to the ground level, and others unfortunately landed in other areas of the hangar, killing mechanics as they were escaping. The officers surveyed the damage in sorrow and grief. Some ships and offices remained. In fact, everything on the southern and western side of the hangar was relatively intact. The northern wall, though, was devastated.

"What are we going to do?"

"There's an open porthole! Land! We need to help!"

～

The officer was stumped. "I don't know, sir. Everything is fine on our end. Perhaps the patched link has failed on their end."

Oronus sighed. "Very well. We will improve on these methods on our return. Let's just get my kids home."

"Yes, sir."

"Anna, we're stopping here. Oronus just made contact, and he's almost to us. We need to do what we can to give Osiris a comfortable transition. We'll be raised on one of the ropes, I assume."

She stood over him, caressing his face with the cool, damp cloth. "I just don't know how much longer he'll hold on, Aaron."

He walked forward and placed his hand on her shoulder, looking down at Osiris. "It's just so amazing to me how he survived for *eight* years on the ground level. Where did he get water? Where did he get food?"

Osiris stirred and opened one eye a little. "It's easy to... get food... when all you have to... do is... *think* at something... to kill it... The water came... from him..."

This unsettled Aaron a great deal. "Who is him? And entering minds... isn't that what twisted you in the first place?"

Osiris cackled and went into a coughing fit. "Ironic... and cruel, yes?" Osiris gasped and lapsed back into unconsciousness.

"Aaron! Don't press him! He's very weak right now. You know that."

He left the bedside. "I know. I'm sorry. But who did he get water from? There was no one else at the site; no tent, no sign of life other than Osiris."

Anna prioritized things in a way Aaron hadn't. "Let's just make sure that we can sustain his life. Then, when he's *stable*, we can ask the tough questions."

Aaron and Anna sat in silence for a moment, and then Aaron returned to the deck.

"Sir, we think we can still see the craft on our radar. It didn't blend in with the geography of the ground level. The mark is still unique enough to make a distinction."

Oronus nodded. "Very good. I am going up to the deck. Notify me when we are close."

"I guess we'll just have to wait here. Surely they'll find us," Aaron told himself as he stared out into the blackness.

Anna sat with Osiris below deck as his fever steadily rose. "Hurry, Daddy."

≈

"Sir! We are approaching the craft. We can start our descent in fifteen minutes." Oronus stood at the very front of the deck, hands gripping the rails. "Very good."

≈

Aaron sat in the control room. His forehead met with the shell and he sighed. As Aaron lifted his head, he saw something in the sky, in the distance, approaching fast. He continued watching, and now that his eyes had adjusted to the darkness Aaron could make out the front of a large blimp.

"Oronus! Yes!"

Aaron stood up from his seat in excitement and hit his head hard on the shell. He sat back down in the chair and rubbed his head.

"Gods, I'm ready to be out of here!"

He sat and watched as the *Bismarck* approached and, hovering far above their heads, began a slow descent. Anna already had Osiris wrapped tightly in a blanket with a cool rag on his forehead. She had packed up each of their bags.

"They're here, Anna! Let's go!" Aaron hurried to collect Osiris as Anna slung each of their bags over her shoulders. They made their way up to the deck and watched as the lit-up airship hovered above them.

Anna cursed as she looked up. "This ship isn't built to hold auxiliary craft! I'll have to start all over again! She sighed in frustration as they watched a great rope descend from the *Bismarck*.

It came to a stop and a large knot rested before them, as well as a sort of sling that hung from the rope. Aaron and Anna looped Osiris into the sling and made sure that he was steady. They then stood on either side of the knot face-to-face. Anna held onto the rope with both hands, Aaron wrapped an arm around her, and the rope began its ascent. When they were parallel with the railings, a group of crew members retrieved Osiris from the sling and took him immediately below deck to the medical room. The rope was raised once again, and Aaron and Anna were helped onto the deck. Anna watched as Oronus held the hatch open for the men who were carrying his father. She could not read his emotions.

He closed the hatch and ran to Anna, picking her up and swinging her around. "My little girl! You're safe!"

"Look, there will be time to discuss this little adventure of yours later. Right now, I want you down in medical. The same goes for you, Aaron." He walked forward and hugged him. "Thank you for keeping my daughter safe."

Aaron and Anna went below together, leaving Oronus with the deck hands. "All right! Raise the rope and raise the ship! Let's go back to O.R.T.!"

Oronus went below and made his way for the medical room. Aaron sat on a table opposite Anna.

Oronus walked to Anna and sat down on a nearby stool. "Honey, did you find Osiris unconscious, or did he pass out while you two were there?"

"He was awake. We walked into something he called a hieroglyph, something written on the ground that he said would have killed us. Aaron pulled him inside the glyph, though, and threatened to kill him and us by leaving the glyph and setting off the Raujj enchantment. Grandfather stopped him and undid the enchantment, but afterward he went straight into his tent. He passed out soon after that."

Oronus looked down, sighed, and shook his head. "Did he say anything... odd? Unusual? Out of place, maybe?"

Anna closed her eyes and tried to relive the happening in her mind's eye. "Yes. The last thing he said before he went unconscious was odd, something about 'one God' instead of the Four. Then he told us to beware the high priest."

Oronus shrugged. "Well, it could have been the fever. Anyway, we won't know for sure unless he wakes up. Did he say anything else?"

Anna nodded. "Aaron asked him how he got food and water all those eight years. He essentially said that he killed for meat the same way he killed the scholar at O.R.T., but he said the water came from 'him.'"

"Who's *him?*"

"We never found out. He passed out again shortly thereafter. That was also around the time that his fever started rising." She stood up and they walked over to Aaron's table together. Oronus put his hand on Aaron's shoulder and hugged Anna with his other arm.

"You two... I can't say I wasn't angry, and I'm still a little hurt that you would blatantly disobey me and put your lives in danger. I know he's your grandfather, Anna, but he could have killed you. Both of you. I'm not even comfortable having him on the ship." He stopped and clenched his jaw, pursing his lips together and inhaling deeply. He was consciously redirecting the path his emotions were taking. "The important thing, though, is that you are safe. I'm going back up to the deck, and you should probably get some sleep."

He smiled and walked out of the medical room. "Gods... I *hate* that!" Anna said as she plopped her forehead down on Aaron's shoulder. A rush of excited nervousness swept over him at her touch.

"What do you hate?"

"When I would mess up a project or a class at university, Mother would never get angry. She would simply say, 'I'm not mad, Anna, I'm just disappointed.' I *hate* that! I would rather be beaten."

Aaron laughed. "Well, I would take that over a beating any time. Now let's go take a nap. I'm exhausted." They walked off together to the crew members' quarters.

CHAPTER 13

Oronus took in the cool night air, no longer afraid that those he cared about were stuck within the mysterious blackness on the ground level. He knew, though, that as soon as they returned to O.R.T., Osiris would be restrained and would be as heavily guarded and cloaked as the Chest of Worlds itself. He loved the man dearly, but his hatred of the Raujj was just as palpable, and though he knew now that his father lived, *he* had lived with a very different idea for eight years now. This would take some getting used to. He walked to the front of the ship and looked toward home. To his surprise, Oronus could see a bright orange dot on the horizon in the direction of O.R.T., and he strained his eyes to try and make out what it was. He turned and thought for a moment, then went back down to the control room.

"Officer, have we regained a connection with O.R.T. yet?"

"No, sir, we're still trying, but we aren't picking up *anything* from their end." Oronus looked up at the ceiling, contemplating things. He then turned and went back up the hatch and straight to the front of the ship again.

"What *is* that?"

Parrus Vademe stood before a disheveled group of mechanics, engineers, and crew members, along with hundreds of scholars, mages, artists, philosophers, and linguists from the undamaged buildings. They gathered in the southwestern corner of the hangar. Standing next to Parrus was Kline Stephens, the officer who had discovered how to connect to the hovering craft. Many more mechanics, crew members, maintenance, and janitorial staff were behind them in the northeastern half of the hangar fighting a raging fire that had engulfed many airships and now spilled out of the gaping holes in the walls and rose to the sky. Others worked in areas where the fire had been put out, moving debris, rushing those caught and still alive to the medical wing, and laying out the corpses.

Beside Parrus lay Dardus Hale. Next to them was a closed crate that, to the best of their knowledge, housed the unrecognizable remains of Provincial Director Richard Alden and communications technician Geoffrey Wells. Alden's crew members were not recovered. Parrus stared at the group of department heads, officers, and seasoned employees. Some were angry, others heartbroken, others still in a state of disbelief. He struggled with what he could possibly say to them. He had already made the trip personally to the bowels of Re-Creation to ensure the safety of the Chest of Worlds, and now there were matters that needed to be addressed. With Oronus and Dardus gone, Parrus knew he had to momentarily take the reins.

"O.R.T.!" he shouted. "Can I have your attention? Will everyone please direct your attention to me?" The noise of so many individual conversations slowly subsided and was replaced by workers shouting in the distance behind him, a fire being fought and rubble and remains being moved, and the quiet sobbing in front of him.

"Everyone! I am not before you to crush you further or to take our many losses lightly, but O.R.T. needs you right now. You are here because you have survived, and because you are the best now at what you do here. I do not wish to treat the matter coolly, but there are some things that we need to accomplish before we stop to grieve over our terrible losses today. Our maintenance team has already transferred O.R.T. to its reserve power source, but communications are still down, the medical room is short staffed and underequipped, and Oronus, Anna, Aaron, and the rest of the crew are still out there on the *Bismarck* and are headed for a docking bay in which they cannot safely land. These matters *must* be addressed before we take time for ceremony and sorrow.

I want all of you to split up into three teams. One team for the re-establishment of communications, one team to assist in medical and to take the overflow to CentrePointe in the fourth province, and one to assist our ongoing cleanup of areas where the fire has subsided. If Oronus gets back before we are able to contact him, then we need an operable docking bay ready. You all know your affinities and skills, so group up accordingly.

In spite of Oronus's absence, I am taking the momentary authority to place Kline Stephens in charge of Communications. He is just as good, or better, than me. I will lead in the hangar until Oronus gets back and appoints a new department head. Also, for your comfort, there is a small group of men and women in Re-Creation that are contacting families and making arrangements for a memorial ceremony. The sooner these tasks are completed, the sooner we can address matters most close to our hearts right now. Go!"

Parrus looked down at Dardus, his face miraculously untouched by the flying debris that killed him. "I'll never replace you, old friend. No one will. No one can."

He pulled the sheet up over his face, then turned and went up a small flight of stairs and into Dardus's office, where he surveyed the action from behind its glass walls.

The crew members of Aevier's ship stood before him on the deck. Some were talking amongst themselves, others were yelling at him, and some just stood in silent contemplation. He smirked and stepped forward, some took simultaneous steps backward as he did so.

"Silence, please. *Silence!*" They stopped, staring at a man whom they had never taken seriously before these last few weeks. He addressed them all once again. "You have been given your options, ladies and gentlemen. I vould ask zat all of zhose who vish to support ze cause and ze basilica step forward at zis time."

There was uniform hesitation and uncertainty. Finally one of the crew, a woman named Antalya, stepped forward. He winked at her, and she smiled. Three other women and two men stepped forward. Another. Another. This continued for several minutes. Eventually, thirty-six of the forty-five on deck had stepped forward. Aevier smiled.

"Very vell. I vould ask zat you all get back to vork, so zat ze ozhers can leave. Ve should fly a little to ze east, I think. I don't vant to be directly over ze basilica."

They nodded and went about their duties while nine crew members stood awkwardly before him.

"All right, zhen. You are free to leave. Go."

They stood there, frozen, staring at him. One of them laughed very loudly out of nervousness and confusion. Another spoke up.

"All right boys, let's go pack our things and—"

"Oh, I vouldn't vorry about zat. I vill send zhem after you. You may leave. Now."

All relief, humor, and nervousness were replaced by a disoriented terror.

"Is something wrong? Perhaps you need assistance? Ah, yes. Antalya! Please gather some of ze crew to escort zhese few off of ze ship. Zhey are heretics and cannot be trusted."

One of the nine took off toward the hatch, but as he did so,

Aevier pulled a small pistol from inside his jacket and shot the man in the back of the head. Aevier loved this little artifact Oronus had discovered, the power that it gave him. He had voted a hearty yes when it was brought before the council whether or not these contraptions should be given to all the directors for protection. Almost every guard unit in every province had them by now, but they were not for commercial sale or use and probably never would be.

"All right, let's be reasonable here. Ze high priest can offer complete absolution. Join ze cause right now, and you vill be forgiven of zis heresy."

Five of the eight still alive stepped forward. "Good choice, disciples of ze High Priest. Go below and join ze ozhers."

With that he pulled the pistol out once more and shot the remaining three men who refused to change their minds.

"Someone please help zhese three to ze door, and zhen clean up ze mess. Ve need to make a short visit. It is time for praise and penance once again."

He placed the pistol back into his jacket pocket and watched as the ship turned and flew west once again, lowering to that very familiar sandstone court. He was lowered on one of the great ropes, and he walked through the courtyard, passing by the Four Representations for the first time in his life without kneeling; they meant nothing to him now, and if he felt anything toward them, it was anger. He walked through the two great archways and was about to enter the sanctum when he heard Graff's voice.

"This way, my little marionette. I am through with the sanctum for today. Let us talk in my chambers."

Aevier nodded and turned right, heading through the long breezeway that housed depictions of Creation and the Four on its walls. He came to a winding stair and saw Eleazer standing there in the unlit case.

"Right this way." He continued climbing the stair, with the high priest leading the way, until they came to a small wooden door. "Ah, here we are."

Graff opened the door, and Aevier found himself in a large room of dark green granite or marble that seemed to be pulsing a gentle blue light. The floorboard, corners, and edges were accentuated by ornate woodworking, and all of the furniture was glass and some dark material, like obsidian or onyx. Eleazer went to the end of the room, walked up a short set of semicircle steps that spanned the length of the room and sat down at a large, glass desk with a dark marble inset and smiled at Jacques. An enormous window was behind the desk, and the great black curtains had been pulled back, exposing the mountainous and arid region that was the seventh province. The topsoil was carried through the air by constant wind. It was unsettling to Aevier, and this milieu did not help the anxiousness of standing before the potential God. He continued forward, looking left and right as he did so. Each wall housed great oaken double doors. The left led to what appeared from his distance to be a bedroom. The other looked like a study. His gaze was fixed on this would-be study. He spotted artifacts crafted by the Ancients, artifacts that he had recovered and brought to the basilica, but these artifacts were revived. Had the high priest done this? Eleazer must have noticed Aevier's awe.

"Oh my...beautiful, aren't they? The silver-tongued Ancients made many great and awesome things amidst the spinning of their lies, marionette. Please have a seat. Perhaps we can discuss their uses later, for I have found great uses for them."

Aevier nervously sat before Eleazer in the icy obsidian chair. "My Lord. Ze meeting vas a success. Ze tour and ze scale-back are both agreed upon. Also, my men planted ze explosive device on Alden's ship. He and whoever greets him at O.R.T. vill be dead."

Eleazer stood and walked to the window. "Oh my...yes indeed. In fact, I just received message from O.R.T. that they want to conduct a memorial service for their fallen friends. How touching. This little explosive of ours did far more damage than you guessed, marionette. Currently, O.R.T.'s large-scale communications are down, and several of their craft are destroyed. Our next moves now fall so readily into place. Oh my..."

Graff stood and walked to the window, folding his arms behind his back, his hands sliding into opposite robe cuffs, respectively.

"O.R.T. is in no state for a tour and won't be for months. We will use this to our advantage. You will approach the council and suggest an amended showing of the facility. Instead of district heads and the entire council, you will suggest that only yourself and District Head Thomas view O.R.T. with Oronus. My original intent was to have Thomas go along with Dardus Hale, leaving you to try and 'uncover' any information on the chest that you could but, oh my, it seems as though Hale met his end during the explosion. Pity."

Aevier looked confused. "Vhy just Thomas and myself? Vill Oronus allow us to even come to O.R.T. at zis point?"

Graff spun around and glided to his desk, grabbing the serpentine staff. "Oh my... I have previously warned you, marionette, not to question my judgment. I fear I am not willing to warn you again."

Aevier shifted in his chair. "I am sorry, my Lord. I—"

"Enough. If you must know, the devastation to O.R.T.'s hangar was quite significant. This only adds an increased appeal to set up a business-class aircraft production facility in Restivar. Obviously, I will give my approval of this plan to Melinda and promise monetary support from the basilica. On the outside, it will appear that the council and the basilica are engaging in a dual effort to support the economy of the first province as well as to come to O.R.T.'s aid. This also shows promise for our little rogue group outside of the capital. I will arrange a meeting with District Head Thomas to take his eyes, but you'll need to bring him to me for that. You have work to do, marionette, and remember, as always, that I see what you see. Go now, and do my bidding."

Aevier stood and bowed. "Yes, my Lord. I shall have Thomas brought to ze Basilica, and I vill be in immediate contact vist ze council."

High Priest Graff smiled his twisted smile and returned to his desk. Aevier watched as light reflected off of Graff's face. The surface of the obsidian inset had lit up. Graff waved his hand, and the light faded as he looked at Aevier.

"I seem to remember dismissing you."

Aevier gave a quick nod and briskly walked out without saying a word. Graff looked back down at the surface of the inset and smiled as he watched some of the artisans in O.R.T.'s Re-Creation department. The stone Aaron had passed that lay on its side, Graff discovered, was somehow connected with this one and could see what it saw. Oronus must have assumed during excavation that they were two identical pieces, which left one for Aevier to find. If Oronus only knew what had passed by that surface on its way to the bowels of Re-Creation. Graff knew where the Chest of Worlds lay. He had decided to keep it to himself for now, but the time would come when the fortuitous placement of that stone and the watchful eyes of Aevier would serve him well.

"Oh my... keep up the good work, men."

Aevier heard his chilling laugh as he descended the winding staircase and proceeded to quicken his step. When he had reached the ship and was raised to the deck, the helmsman was already prepared for direction. They had all realized now that they had a new task and location every time Aevier returned from the basilica.

"Helmsman, ve leave immediately for ze Industrial District in Restivar."

"Yes, sir."

Jacques turned and addressed the remainder of the deck hands. "I am not to be disturbed until ve reach our destination."

"Yes, sir!" They responded unanimously.

"You'd better come up here," Aaron said to Anna as he pulled her out of the bunk she had chosen for her nap in crewmembers' quarters and continued pulling her into the hallway. She started to resist and was feeling quite irritable, being rudely roused from a rest that was too long to be a nap and too short to do any real good.

"What? What are you doing, Aaron? Where are we going?" Aaron knew that nothing he could say would be any more effective than her seeing it with her own eyes. They passed through the control room, and Anna noticed that it was alive with activity and that officers at their communications panels were contacting more than just O.R.T. technicians.

"Aaron, what..."

He shook his head without turning to face her as they approached the already opened hatch that lead to the deck. He motioned for her to go up first and followed closely behind her.

"Aaron, I don't understand! If you'd just—"

All mental and physical disorientation ceased as she broke eye level with the deck of the *Bismarck*. There, one hundred yards from their helm, stood a smoldering O.R.T. hangar. She rushed forward to the helm. Oronus grabbed her and pulled her to him, eyes still fixed on the destruction in front of him. She sobbed gently into his chest. She looked up at him. He noticed this, but continued looking at the hangar and the part of Navigation he could see from this angle.

"What happened, Daddy? What is going on?"

He made no movements. "I don't know, sweetheart. I just don't know." His gaze was broken when one of the officers approached and reported.

"Sir!"

He turned. "What of Director Alden?"

"We cannot locate him, sir. He is no longer in CentrePointe, and Lady Alden has seen no sign of him."

"Thank you. Notify me if this changes."

"Yes, sir."

Oronus, now broken from his trance, turned to Aaron. "Watch her for me, Aaron; I need to go below deck."

"All right," Aaron said as he walked toward Anna and stood beside her, saddened and angered by the destruction that lay before them. However, as he looked upon the mess, he saw a porthole to the northwest of them beginning to open. When it had, they saw many people jumping up and down and waving.

Aaron shouted to Oronus as he was descending the ladder. "Oronus, I think we're being waved in!"

Oronus stopped abruptly and looked in the direction that Aaron was pointing. "Gods... Helmsman! We land immediately!" He looked down below him and shouted to those below deck. "Make landing preparations! Now!"

He climbed back up the ladder and came to where Aaron and Anna stood at the front of the ship. "Aaron, go down to medical and have them prep Osiris for transfer." He nodded and left. "Anna, honey, I need you to be ready for this. This looks bad, and I can only assume that many were hurt or killed. If we walk into a state of disarray, people will be looking to us for guidance."

She nodded and looked up at him with swollen eyes.

"That's my girl," he said, smiling. "Besides, I'm sure Dardus took a handle on things." They stood at the helm together as the *Bismarck* docked in O.R.T.'s hangar. "Gods, who did this..." Oronus gazed upon the devastation.

Almost half of the cargo ships were destroyed. The five WASPs in prep stage when he left were still smoking, huge piles of rubble were everywhere, and bodies lay side-by-side between them. Isolated fires were scattered throughout. Hundreds of people were running around frantically, yet Oronus noticed a sort-of determined nature behind all of their actions.

He turned to Anna. "Go below. Tell everyone to stay on the ship until I give the word. Go now, sweetie. I hear the ramp opening."

Anna nodded; her crying had begun again at the sight of the bodies. Oronus grabbed one of the ropes and swung down from the deck to begin his search for Dardus Hale. He walked in the direction of Hale's office, and those that he passed barely even recognized his presence. He stopped at the table just outside Hale's office—a body lay on it, covered by a sheet that was stained with blood, and a large crate sat next to that. He looked up at the long window that made the outside wall to Hale's office and saw Parrus looking down at him. He looked back, confused, and then looked down at the sheet. With much hesitation, he pulled it back and saw the face he feared he would see. Hale's face was fine and looked peaceful, but his chest was crushed and soaked with blood.

"Gods be with you, old friend." He replaced the sheet and went up to Hale's office to see Parrus. He entered and embraced Parrus.

"Oronus, I'm so glad you've returned," Parrus said.

Oronus walked to the window and surveyed the damage. "Tell me everything you know, Parrus. Everything."

Parrus sat down in one of the chairs and ran his fingers through what little hair he had left. "Right after we received word that you were returning, we also received word that Director Alden was coming to O.R.T."

"Gods! I forgot about Richard! Where is he?"

Parrus shook his head and looked down at the floor. "He's dead, Oronus."

Oronus closed his eyes and sat down in a nearby chair. As much as he wanted to lose his control in rage and mourning, he knew that he must keep a cool head. "Go on."

Parrus related all he knew of what transpired to Oronus, and followed with a status report. "We are on reserve power. Communications are at fifteen percent capacity. I took the liberty, in your absence, of appointing Stephens to command Communications. I also created several teams to help with the tasks at hand. We have two ships on their way to CentrePointe with wounded as we speak. I am sorry, Oronus."

The almost robotic way that Parrus responded sent chills down Oronus's spine. *No one should have to be desensitized to this,* he thought.

"Are families being notified?" he asked as he rose from his chair.

"Yes. We have a small group that is contacting them now, and they have also contacted the basilica in hopes of having a memorial service here. And, Oronus, we haven't notified Gwen. I thought that you might want to do that." Oronus shuddered at the thought. He had already lost Rachel, and Gwen had been so kind to him after her passing. He hated the thought of being the messenger but knew it was the right thing to do.

"Yes. Thank you, Parrus, for your thoughtfulness. I also want to commend you for stepping up in leadership in mine and Dardus's absence. You have conjured determination out of these downtrodden men, and organization arose from apparent chaos. Well done."

Tears streamed from Parrus's eyes. Oronus was almost glad that his robotic air was waning. "Thank you, sir."

"I need to see all of the department heads immediately. There is much to discuss. We will meet in Re-Creation."

"But, Oronus, that part of the bridgeway is covered by debris right now."

"Have it cleared then. There is a reason I want them all there."

Parrus's eyes widened. "The chest? You don't think—"

"I don't know what to think, Parrus, but it's time everyone knows about the chest. We have to move it immediately. O.R.T. is not safe right now. I don't know who did this or why, but we can't rule out that the chest was a motive behind this."

"I'm not following you, Captain. A ship malfunctioned."

"No, Parrus, it didn't. I built Richard's personal craft myself. It was not large enough to do that. I sense foul play. Get to it, Parrus."

"Yes, sir."

Oronus walked to Dardus's communications panel that connected to the other departments and called the medical wing.

"Medical."

"This is Oronus. I need to speak with Dorothea."

"One moment, sir."

"Oronus! Thank the Four you are all right!"

"Thank you, Dorothea. Listen, I have an important task for you."

"What is it? We are terribly overrun right now, as you can imagine."

"I know, but something must be done quickly, and it must be you."

"Oronus, I am the director of this facility! I can't leave now!"

"My father is currently in the medical bay of the *Bismarck*."

"Osiris is alive?"

"Yes, but barely. He is slipping in and out of consciousness, and, he is potentially a threat to everyone at O.R.T. He must be taken to a secure room below Re-Creation, and I want you to set up a room for him there. We need him alive, but right now we need him sedated."

"All right. Just let me go and finish up with one of my—"

"Dorothea! I need you to do this now! With each passing second, our hopes of uncovering paramount truths are dwindling. Gather a team. Go to Re-Creation. Now."

Oronus turned and addressed Parrus on his way out of the office.

"Gather the heads, Vademe. Do it now."

Oronus went down the small flight of steps and past Hale's body once again. It was almost too much to handle. He shouted to a deck hand on the *Bismarck* as he reached the docking bay.

"Lower the ramp!"

When the ramp came to a stop, Oronus saw Anna, Aaron,

and Osiris, wrapped in a blanket and laying on a rolling table. It was his father.

"Anna, Aaron, have Osiris sent to Re-Creation. I need you two to come with me."

Aaron ran back into the ship and summoned an officer. After Aaron, Anna, and Osiris were off the ship, all of the deck hands and officers immediately left the *Bismarck* to assist in the hangar. Oronus pulled the two aside and spoke to them as quietly as he could, without being drowned out by the sounds of the relief effort.

"I am sending Osiris down with the chest. A medical team will be waiting for him when he gets there. I have important jobs for the both of you." He turned to Anna. "I need you to relieve Parrus in Dardus's office. I have sent him to collect the other department heads, and then he needs to be on the hangar floor. At this point, the people that did this may call us, and I wouldn't rule out a visit from Director Aevier either. I need you to be ready to relay information between the hangar and the other departments. If Aevier shows up and wants to do anything but help with recovery, stall him."

"So you think that someone caused Director Alden's ship to explode?" she asked, horrified.

"Yes. I do."

Then he quickly turned to Aaron. "You are going down with Osiris. I am having him sedated, but when he wakes up I want you there to talk to him." Aaron was taken aback by this request.

"Me? Why do you want me to do that? I don't even know what to say!"

Oronus stepped closer to Aaron and spoke again with a more determined air. "Aaron, listen to me. You know about the Great Houses, and you know a little about the Raujj. More importantly, you were the first to talk to him in eight years, and he knows who you are. I just need you to keep him talking." He stepped back and looked at both of them.

Aaron knew that he was probably *not* the first to talk to Osiris, if this "him" Osiris mentioned was actually real. "This was not an accident. I built that personal craft for Alden myself, and I know that it was in good condition. I have to go and deliver the news to Gwen. I will return as soon as I can and will join you, Aaron. Go."

They both nodded. Oronus turned and headed for the other end of the hangar. The open ramp to the lower half of the hangar was at the far end, and he hoped that at least one of the craft was left functioning. As he rounded a row of cargo ships, though, his eyes fell on a saddening sight. There sat the *Orion*, his flagship, the symbol of O.R.T.'s fleet. Piercing its middle was a large chunk of one of the walls, and the blimp was broken and tilting upwards. The craft farthest from Alden's, the first one he came upon, was relatively unharmed. Two of the other craft had fallen against it and damaged its side, but they had also shielded it from the blast. He opened the porthole and lifted off, shirking the leaning crafts aside as he did so. There, in the solitude of his flight, he wept.

※

Aaron walked ahead of Dorothea and her small team and took them through Re-Creation to the elevator. The many tables and workbenches that were so recently packed with engineers and scientists were now mostly deserted, save the few who remained to clean up what the blast's tremors had knocked over. He led them through that familiar narrow hallway, and they entered the small elevator.

"I still can't believe he's alive," Dorothea said to Aaron.

"Yeah. I tried so hard to talk Anna out of going, but now that he's here he could help us get closer to understanding the Raujj. I just hope he pulls through."

The elevator stopped, and they came upon the dark hallway that led to the safe room. Aaron opened the door at the end of the hall and entered the bright, white room. Dorothea and her team of three entered with Osiris, and they stopped and surveyed their surroundings.

Aaron spoke. "It's okay. We're here on Oronus's orders."

"What? Aaron, who are you talking to?" Dorothea said and gasped as several armed men and what seemed to be a large chest appeared out of thin air. "What's going on, Aaron?"

"I don't know if I can tell you. Just worry about keeping Osiris sustained and sedated. When Oronus gets back, he can fill you in."

Aaron walked forward to the Chest of Worlds and stared down at it. He watched as the four spheres spun lazily inside their glass case and recounted the scene at the Great House that had occurred months ago, though it seemed as if it had happened yesterday. There was so much mystery behind it, so much he did not understand. If Alden's death wasn't an accident, then were the secrets of the chest behind his assassination? These thoughts angered and confused him, and he knew that the best way to find out for himself would be to learn how to read the language of the Ancients. A silent commitment was made to start his own private investigation. He turned and walked to the corner of the room where Dorothea had sectioned off part of the room with paper dividers. Aaron approached one of the guards.

"Do you know how to make all of us invisible at will?"

"Yes, sir."

"Be ready, then. This man is to be treated in the same regard as the chest, and we all need to disappear if something happens. We're going to be down here for a while."

"Yes, sir."

Aaron turned. "Dorothea, let me know when Osiris wakes up. I'm going to rest now."

"All right, Aaron. I'll get you if anything happens."

Aaron went back to the chest and sat beside it, then leaned back and closed his eyes. He began to drift in and out of consciousness and was almost asleep when he heard glass shatter and people shouting. Aaron jumped up and ran toward the group of guards that was now forming around Osiris and the nurses. Osiris was awake.

"Aaron! Aaron, get over here!" Dorothea and one of the nurses struggled to keep Osiris's arms and legs down, while the other tilted his head back and placed a foam wedge into his mouth. "Aaron! Go to my cart and grab the blue syringe! He is having a massive seizure! Hurry!"

Aaron ran to the cart. His hands were clumsy as he fumbled through the cart's contents. He found the syringe and ran back to the table, reaching over Osiris to hand it to Dorothea.

"No, Aaron! I need you to do this! Jab the syringe into his chest!"

Aaron turned pale. "What? I can't do that!"

Dorothea snapped back at him. "Aaron, the Four help you if you don't do it right now! *Do it!*"

Aaron looked from his hand to the convulsing body on the table and closed his eyes. He screamed and jabbed the needle into Osiris's chest, then hammered down on the top with his thumb to release its contents into his body. He pulled it out and tossed it aside, watching as Osiris's convulsions slowed and his body stilled. For a moment he thought Osiris had died, but he sighed in relief as he saw Osiris' chest beginning to rise and fall.

CHAPTER 14

Oronus approached the director's mansion and the great clock face opened to receive him. He docked and headed for the great stair, and was greeted by Max at the door.

"Hello, Master Oronus. Lady Alden is currently in the director's study. Would you like me to take you to her?"

"Yes, Max. Thank you."

"May I take your cloak, Master Oronus?"

"No, thank you, Max. I am pressed for time and must make this short. Please take me to Gwen."

"As you wish."

Oronus's heart sank with each step he took toward the study. Max opened the door, and Gwen stood at the window that Richard had always left the curtains pulled over. She turned at Max's address. "Lady Alden, Master Oronus is here to see you."

She went to Oronus and greeted him. "Oronus! How are you? I'm glad you stopped by. I simply cannot seem to contact Richard. I'm starting to get worried, Oronus. He should have been back from the fourth province three days ago."

A knot formed in Oronus's throat as she hugged him. "Gwen, sit down with me." She looked puzzled as they sat down.

"What's wrong, Oronus?"

He looked at her and then immediately looked away. She pressed again. "Oronus, what's wrong? Is this about Richard?" Still no answer. "Oronus! Answer me right now!"

He looked back at her, face sullen. His voice cracked as he answered her query. "He's dead, Gwen. He died yesterday. I'm so sorry, Gwen."

"What? How can this be? Surely you are mistaken. How do you know this, Oronus?"

He looked into her eyes, feeling as though she was piercing him with her maddened gaze. "His ship exploded at O.R.T. He died in the explosion."

She slung his hands from her own and stood up, tears streaming down her face, and walked briskly back to the window. He heard her quiet weeping and stayed in his chair, his back to hers. "What happened, Oronus? I have to know." Oronus told her of the events at O.R.T., starting with the explosion and ending with Osiris's presence at O.R.T.

"I'm so sorry. I'm so sorry, Gwen." Oronus began to sob into his hands. After a time, he regained composure and walked to her. He put his hand on her shoulder, and she shirked his touch. "Gwen, I—"

"Was it a malfunction?"

"I don't think so. I built his personal craft myself."

"Then who did this?"

"I have no idea."

"It would be very easy to blame *you*, Oronus. Richard made most of his enemies in the provinces by supporting O.R.T. and keeping all of your stupid secrets!"

Oronus backed away. He felt the sting of her words pierce through him. Gwen immediately realized what she had said and apologized, tears still streaming down her face.

"Oronus, forgive me. I didn't mean that." She quickly embraced him and began weeping. They stood there for a few minutes, Oronus doing his best to comfort her. She pulled away and looked at him; her maddened expression returned.

"Oronus, promise me that you'll get to the bottom of this. I want whoever did this to be punished, and I don't care if it is inside or outside of the council's rules. Do you understand me?"

He nodded. "Gwen, I have to return to O.R.T. There are things that must be done. I promise you that we'll find out who did this. I promise."

With that, he left. Gwen slumped down into a chair and buried her face in her handkerchief. As Oronus headed back down the hallway to the great stair, Max hovered to him from the opposing hallway.

"Master Oronus, will you be leaving?"

He continued walking. "Yes, Max. Listen, I believe Richard has been murdered. Gwen is in a bad way right now, and though I would like to stay, I must return to O.R.T. Please see that she is taken care of."

"Yes, Master Oronus." He opened the door to the docking bay.

"Gods. This isn't happening." Oronus boarded his craft and left for O.R.T.

※

Parrus set off to call the department heads to gather in Re-Creation. The fact that they were gathering there, Parrus knew, was to travel to the safe room, where the chest and now Osiris waited. An hour after Parrus left the hangar, Anna watched as the department heads passed by in the bridgeway.

"What is going on, Parrus? This must me rather important for us to be drawn away from our duties in this dark hour." Victoria sighed at Vademe as they walked briskly down the bridgeway. She was an eccentric old woman, with a fashion sense that matched her personality. Her hair was short and spiked on the top with tight curls on the side that clung to her skull. She wore a large blue cloak with embroidered birds around the collar and edges and a flowing blue and green scarf. How she was keeping up with him down the bridgeway Parrus could not understand, for he knew that she had been in Linguistics since Osiris was Oronus's age.

"I can assure you, Victoria, that this is not a waste of time and you will not be disappointed." They entered Re-Creation from the bridgeway and Brevard greeted them.

"Hello, all! Please join me in a side conference room."

He was balding on the top with long, curly hair on the sides and sported the black work suit of Re-Creation but with a bright pink shirt and a long black cape. He led them into the conference room, and they all sat down together.

Brevard spoke first. "So, any news on the explosion? Was this merely a malfunction, or are we suspecting a foul hand in all of this mess?"

"Oronus does not believe it was a malfunction, Brevard," Parrus said as he reached for the pitcher, "and neither do I."

"Well, *I* think it was those scallywags from Restivar! They've already stolen one ship, attempted to strand—maybe even *kill*—Oronus's daughter and apprentice at ground level, and I *know* that some of us around this table are old enough to remember Cebran's treachery!"

Parrus spoke again. "Calm, yourself, Brevard. A cool head is what everyone needs right now, and we know that Director Alden was coming from the council headquarters in CentrePointe. You know as well as I do that Cebran's group hasn't left the first province for years."

Brevard raised his eyebrows. "No? Then how do you explain Edgar, hmm? They had an insider in this facility since Osiris took the reins from Olan. Parrus, who knows what *they* know about our secret projects!"

There was much murmuring around the table at this.

"Secrets? What are we talking about here?" Stephens had no idea what was going on. He was, after all, new to leadership at O.R.T., coming from his previous post as a communications technician. Until now, he hadn't needed to know about some of the quieter works of Re-Creation and Linguistics, and he knew nothing of the Chest of Worlds.

Victoria was quick to pre-empt a response from Brevard. "You will receive information as it becomes imperative to your knowing. We don't have time to give you the history of the Ancients, much less the history of O.R.T. Just know, young one, that O.R.T. is housing the most important and ancient artifact that the Ancients ever created, if indeed it was they who created it and not the Four."

Stephens choked on a mouthful of water.

"Ah, now you see the importance of security and safety at present." Victoria smiled at Kline and turned to face Parrus. "Where is Oronus? This is no time to sit and discuss things at a table."

Oronus had walked in as she said this, and he placed his hands on the top of her chair. "Well then, why don't we walk? Please follow me. I hope you don't mind if we continue our discussion, Victoria." Everyone rose from their chairs and began filing out of the conference room.

Brevard patted Oronus on the shoulder as he walked past. "Where were you, Captain?"

"I felt the need to deliver the news of the director's passing to Lady Alden personally."

"And that," said Brevard as he smiled and continued walking, "is why you will be one of the most remembered of your line, Captain."

Oronus smiled and walked to the front of the group. "That, and I'm trying to destroy the power of the Ancients. Hah! But you're right, Brevard. My father was never one for common courtesy. Speaking of Osiris, let's all go see him, shall we?"

Victoria's face lit up. "What? Oronus, have you gone mad?" Oronus put a finger up to his lips. "No, Victoria, but I'm afraid that he might have. Just follow me."

He led them through the narrow hallway to the elevator. They descended low into Re-Creation and came upon the dark hallway. They stopped just short of the safe room door.

"I can't see anything. Where are we, Oronus?" Kline asked nervously.

"Don't worry, Kline. I assure you we are safe. Everyone, we are about to enter a room that has been a secret reserved only for myself and my fathers before me, as well as those we choose to—or must—reveal it to. Inside is the Chest of Worlds and something that is potentially of equal importance, my father. Anna and Aaron recovered him a little over a week ago, and he was brought here immediately after the *Bismarck* landed. From what Anna and Aaron have told me, he had placed hieroglyphs around the camp."

Victoria gasped in surprise, and Brevard gave a shout. "What? Only through the power of the Raujj could he have achieved this! I thought, from his attempts previously—"

"That the Raujj could no longer be used by humans? Yes, and so all of us thought, Victoria. The truth is that Osiris stewed in his madness and his knowledge of the Raujj for eight years, knowledge that was just broad enough to be dangerous. If we can get him to talk to us, then hopefully we can find out more about the Raujj than we ever have from any one source"—he paused, thinking—"and then undo it."

Kline spoke up again. "Undo what, Oronus?"

Brevard turned and scoffed. "Why, the very Raujj itself, my boy! If we can prevent it from ever being fully restored, then we can prevent another War of the Ancients. After all, we have already been forced to move outward, and after upward, we've been left with little else."

Oronus stepped in. "This is a very important conversation to be had, but I'm afraid we must move on. There are things we must give our immediate attention to." He turned and opened the door, and the group filed in to the bright white room. Oronus spoke to the seemingly empty, white room. "It's okay. Lower the field."

The group watched in amazement as the armed guards, the Chest of Worlds, and a clustered group of people in a far corner wavered into view. Brevard laughed heartily and clapped. "Yes, sir! I knew it would work! Genius, Captain, pure genius. Think of the possibilities!"

Oronus smiled and patted Thoreau on the back. "Couldn't have done it without you and your knowledge of the Ancient's artifacts, Brevard." He turned to face the group. "You may now go and examine the chest for yourselves. Please feel free to continue your earlier discussion. I need to go and see Osiris."

He headed for the paper dividers across the room. Dorothea was the only one awake. She looked up at him with tired eyes as she wiped Osiris's brow with a damp rag. "I was wondering when you would get here. We almost lost him a couple of times."

Oronus looked at the pale old man that was strapped to the bed and remembered the days when his father was in charge and he was in Aaron's shoes as an apprentice. He had had the same thick sideburns, the same rugged features, though he was much shorter than Oronus and a bit heavier. But now, now he was thin and pale. What little hair remained on Osiris's head was white and wispy. What would he say to the fact that Oronus was the only one in their line not to have a son? What would he say to the fact that he was moving leadership out of the family line? What would he say when he discovered that Oronus's primary objective was slowly becoming the destruction of the Raujj?

He grabbed his father's hand. "How is he?"

She smiled at him and walked to the cart. "He's going to make it, Oronus. He'll be fine. It's just a matter of time before he wakes up. However, if he ever tries to use the Raujj again, he *will* die. I don't claim to understand the Ancient's craft, but I saw what it did to him. He won't survive if he tries again."

He nodded. Soon after, Oronus felt Osiris's grip tighten and watched as his eyes slowly opened.

"Aaron! Wake up! He's coming around."

Aaron awoke and jumped up at the sight of Oronus and a now-stirring Osiris. They stood over him as he tried to speak. He pointed at his throat, making queer sign language that Dorothea interpreted as a need for water. She fetched a glass for him and held it to his lips as he drank deeply. He lay back down and let out a satisfying, cool sigh, and his eyes opened fully. It was as though he had been waiting for that drink to fully revive into consciousness.

"Where..." His voice cracked, and his eyes looked from Oronus to Aaron. "Where am I?"

Oronus spoke. "You are in O.R.T., Dad."

Tears rolled silently down Osiris's cheek. "Olan. How ashamed he must be." He looked at Oronus. "I assumed that I was bound for the Void. This is more than I deserve, my son. I never should have returned to this place."

He closed his eyes and shook his head. It was useless to fight back the tears. "I should be dead. I am... tainted."

Oronus looked down at his father in confusion. What did this mean? Oronus turned to face the rest of the room. "Everyone! Please leave me with my father for a time. I will call you back in when I feel ready. Please wait outside."

The department heads, Dorothea and her nurses, and Aaron turned to leave the room. "Not you, Aaron," he said. "You stay here." Aaron nodded and watched as everyone filed out of the safe room. Brevard and Victoria paused at the door, and Oronus watched as they and Osiris shot each other feverish glances. Oronus looked at Brevard and Victoria with suspicion, then turned and looked down at Osiris.

"Dad, you were on the ground level for eight years. How? How did you manage?"

His face saddened again. "It's not hard to obtain food when all you have to do is think at something to kill it, son. I used my perverted skill to rape the life out of things. I am... changed. Unworthy. Unclean. I knew enough about the craft I took to use some of the parts for shelter. Wolves and other beasts always approached my camp. I can understand, though. There is naught down there besides misery. I always thought there was some chance that small groups still lived on the surface—nomads. We all know the stories. I never saw a person though. Eight long years and no human ever crossed paths with me."

"Well, Dad, it's barren. I can understand the lack of—"

"You're lying." Aaron cut off Oronus's statement midway and stepped closer to the bed. "That isn't true."

Osiris narrowed his eyelids and pursed his lips. "What are you talking about boy? You and my granddaughter were the first people I saw, and I almost killed you both! You were the first—"

"Stop *lying!*" Aaron was furious. If the explosion, Alden's death, the Raujj, and what this man knew about it were all connected, then it needed to be made known. "You told me yourself that '*he*' brought you water. He! Who is *he*? You are obviously lying!"

Oronus jumped between their conversation. "Well, Aaron, he was slipping in and out of consciousness, and his mind was clearly not with him."

Aaron grabbed Oronus's shoulder and took him outside of and away from the dividers. "Yes it was, Oronus. I admit that he was acting strange and was probably out of character, but he *did* have lucid moments, and I *know* that that was one of them. He was almost terrified when he said it, when he told me who brought him water. And if he survived that long, then *he* either brought eight years worth of water at once, or he came *back*. How many times? I don't know, but I *do* know that Osiris is hiding something. You're the one that wanted me down here, Oronus. I know I don't know everything that's going on, but I'm tired of everyone getting hurt. Osiris knows something that is connected to all of us."

Aaron walked back into the dividers. He approached Osiris.

"Where is my son?" Osiris shouted.

"He's outside. Now tell me who *he* is! You said no human ever crossed your path when you were—"

"He was not human! He was not a *person!* You are asking all the wrong questions, boy! Where did your skill go? You saved yourself and my granddaughter from my madness with your cunning, not being a slapdash, angry *fool!*"

Aaron looked down, then over his shoulder. Oronus was standing at the entrance to the makeshift room. He looked back into Osiris's eyes. "What kind of being brought you water?"

"An Ancient." Aaron's back straightened, and he felt a chill down his spine.

"How do you know that he was an Ancient?"

"His eyes. Cold and ancient eyes," Osiris said as he closed his own, "and he was able to use the Raujj effortlessly." Aaron's eyes widened, and he looked back to Oronus, who walked to the end of the bed and gripped the railings.

"That's impossible, Dad. Who could know its power as well as you speak. And how could he be an Ancient? The Raujj cannot prolong life. You know this."

Osiris closed his eyes again. "Must I tell you the same thing I told the ignorant boy? Use your *reasoning*, Son! What? That's the question! What organization has had access to our findings since the beginning?" Oronus and Aaron were both thinking the same thing: the Basilica of the Four.

Aaron spoke. "'Beware the high priest.' You said it just before you passed out."

Osiris nodded grimly. "I see you found the 'who.' That was the next question. Yes, boy. High Priest Eleazer Graff frequented my campsite. He first came when he heard the rumor that I was living on the ground level. He came because he heard that I had gotten close to using the Raujj. How he found out about this is another story entirely, and one that you would do well to research, Oronus. This was a secret not kept lightly.

His first few visits were few and far between—months would pass before he would return. He simply came with simple questions, and my price was, tragically, as simple: water. Water and knowledge of what the basilica had claimed from O.R.T. The latter, though, was secondary. I needed to quench my thirst. It was driving me mad. He asked me things like, 'What did it feel like? Could you see with your eyes *and* with his eyes? What was your routine of meditation to reach out spiritually?' These questions were easy enough, and I knew that telling him would harm no one. Then he came seeking new knowledge. He told me that his comprehension of the Ancient language was incomplete, and that he wished to learn more to benefit the 'furtherment' of the Four. He seemed genuine, so I obliged.

During this period, I became a little saner. I had water, and I was taking my mind off of what I did to that scholar. I know that all you saw was the exterior, and he looked as though he died of natural causes, but, Oronus..." He felt tears and sorrow flooding back to him. "I *destroyed* him. On the inside. In his mind, in his heart. Our souls touched, Oronus, and it was the most wonderful feeling I have ever felt besides hearing your mother say yes to me. But then it went away so quickly, and the warmth in me was replaced with cold. I still feel the cold, Oronus. I can't get rid of it. I *destroyed* him."

Aaron and Oronus stood in silence.

Osiris recovered enough to continue his discussion of the high priest. "However, his visits became more and more frequent, and every time he returned he was angrier than last I saw him. His questions were aggressive and complex. I couldn't answer most of them. He tortured me, both physically and mentally. He used the Raujj in dark, perverted ways, but I did not appease him. More often than not, I couldn't! But he still pressed me. One day, the pain in my mind was so great that I passed out. When I woke up, there was a small machine near the camp. When I approached the machine and looked down into its core, I saw water. I fetched some dry skins I had fashioned into containers and filled them with the stuff. It was cool and clear and refreshing. When I had drained the core of water, I returned to the camp. When I awoke the next morning, I heard a noise, one that I had not heard in my few years in the spot. I turned and saw that it was coming from the machine. This time, the machine had a fine mist around it that was slowly entering the core. I approached it, and to my amazement there was water in the core again! I knew that it had not rained, just as I knew that drinking rain water through the fuel-ridden sky would be unwise. This machine was pulling water out of the air for me! Only he could have left it there. I never understood it though. He cursed me, hated me with every inch of his being, yet"—he reached for the cup and took a sip of water— "he tried to spare me. I may never understand."

Osiris was quiet then. Oronus and Aaron looked at each other.

Aaron shrugged and turned back to Osiris. "Thank you and forgive me for being so harsh with you."

Osiris looked up at him. "It matters not, boy. Do not tarry upon it. If you would, please take this cup and fill it with water for me. I am thirsty."

Aaron nodded and took the cup out of the room, not knowing where a faucet was, but knowing the direction Dorothea had walked.

When he had gone, Osiris spoke again to Oronus. "Son, I have not yet revealed to you the most shocking revelation of my encounters. Sit down."

Oronus placed his hand on his father's and sat down next to him. Osiris's words were slow and deliberate.

"The Four don't exist. The Ancients created them to cover up their misdeeds. The Ancients abused their privileges. Stewards of the planet, they used their knowledge and their power to *consume*, to gain. The Four never existed. Generations of people have worshipped divine beings of nonexistence."

Oronus was dumbfounded. He searched for the right thing to ask. "Then how did you use the Raujj? How did Graff harness it? You must be in tune with the Four to be capable of enchantment."

Osiris smiled. "You must be looking for the *'what'* again. Very good, my son. Only this time, it's the what, the who, the when, the where, *and* the how. I'm talking about God, Son. God. A single God. I never actually used the Raujj. I tried to use it and reaped what the Ancients sowed so long ago for those who would try: death and madness. Graff uses it because he knows. He knows of God. Mind you, he is not acting on the will or by the authority of this God, not anymore anyway. When Graff became a student of Nicodemus and the basilica, he was not who he has now become. Anger and revulsion at the worship of the Four threw him into disillusionment."

Oronus looked concerned. He was not concerned for the same reasons as his father though. He was concerned that the news of this revelation did not affect him as he felt it should. He had removed himself so far from this aspect of life that the news fell on numbed ears and a numbed heart.

"What does this mean, Dad? What will the provinces say?"

Osiris was quick to respond. "Nothing, because the provinces don't need to know! We could potentially send the continent into mass religious hysteria! And then the 'who' comes back into play. Who started the mess? Who revealed the awful truth behind the broken lie? *You* did. Who again! *Who* do the faithful and the frightened rally under to regain stability, to increase religiosity? *Graff.* No one should know for now, Son. For how long they should not know, well, that is not within my *own* knowing. But I *do* know this: Graff wants the Chest of Worlds, though why you have it and why the Source House was destroyed is still a mystery to me. What happened?"

Oronus looked down with furrowed eyebrows. *Source House?* he thought to himself. "Since Anna was attending university and had no real desire to take over for me when I step down, I picked Aaron Ravenhall to take my place. He is very gifted, Dad, more so I think than many of my excavators that were here when you were. He foolishly attempted to search the Great House by himself to impress me. He barely escaped but did *and* with the Chest of Worlds. When the House sensed him, it collapsed around him, and if I hadn't shown up when I did, the chest might have been lost. Why did you call this Great House the Source House? What does that mean?"

Osiris's eyes widened. "You don't know? Why, it's the first Key! The first of the four Keys to unlock the Chest of Worlds! By the Four!"

The latter exclamation seemed silly to them now, but old habits die hard. Oronus looked at his father. "Well, that explains why the genesis accounts speak of 'keys,' yet we have found no keyholes on the chest."

Osiris nodded as Aaron returned with a glass of water. Oronus jumped back into questioning. "Then do you know what the remaining three keys are?"

Osiris shook his head. "No, my son, I do not. That knowledge rests in Graff's hands."

"When did you find this out? Why didn't you tell anyone?"

Osiris's voice fell. "I discovered the book in our archives just before I left. It was fascinating! The *Codicil* it was called: I don't know how we missed it. Anyway, I took the text with me. It was in a bag strapped across my chest when I jumped. After Graff had tortured me into unconsciousness, I awoke to find the book missing. Son, the reason that the Source House collapsed was not because it sensed a threat to itself but rather a threat to the chest. That's the job of the first key, Son. In its own way, the first key was set in place to *prevent* the chest from being opened. I'm sure that if you return to the location of the Source House, you would find it missing, vanished. The Source House was built to send the Chest of Worlds back into the Void. If Aaron hadn't stumbled upon it, the chest would have vanished from our existence. Ironically enough, the only way that Graff can see the fruition of his evil ends is to obtain it. You both need the chest, Son."

Oronus turned. "Evil ends? What are you talking about?"

"As I said before, he must've thought that he killed me. At the beginning of my interrogation, Graff simply caused my mind pain when I did not respond to a question, but by the end I was floating in the air and I felt as though all of my bones would break. He moved from attempting to obtain knowledge from me to simply torturing me. Before I slipped out of consciousness, though, I heard him shout something."

Osiris paused and drained his glass of water. "I need more of this, Son. I am still thirsty."

"In a minute, Dad. Tell me what the high priest said."

Osiris gave a longing look at his empty glass but continued.

"He said that he would reconcile everything when *he* became God."

"What?" Oronus and Aaron asked unanimously.

"He wants to become God, and in the sense that the Ancients created the Four, he could very well achieve this. Son...this has moved passed the goals of this facility. It is, however, this facility that is equipped and knowledgeable enough to address the task of keeping Graff in check. You have a lot of information to share with your teams and with the board. Once everyone is on the same page, it will be time to start planning."

"Planning for what?"

"I don't know. The hiding of the chest, spying on Graff, revisiting the Source House, combing through all of our texts and artifacts—that is for you to decide. But I will say this: Graff wants the Chest of Worlds, and I don't think it is wise to keep it here."

Oronus sat down in the chair next to his father's bed as reality sank into him. His past focus on airship production and technological revivification was gone. His future was, for the first time in a long time, unclear. He stood and walked out of the room.

"I need water, Son! Water!"

He ignored this and continued to the entrance of the safe room. He opened the door to find the company standing in a semicircle around someone. He couldn't recognize any of them in the dark.

"Daddy," said the figure, "Director Aevier is just outside the hangar. He wants to dock."

CHAPTER 15

"Is Communications well enough for me to contact Aevier on his ship?" Oronus asked Kline Stephens as he, Kline, Parrus, and Anna made their way to the hangar. Oronus had ordered the department heads back to their offices and asked Aaron to stay with Osiris.

"As far as I know, Captain. If he is that close to the facility, then there should be no trouble making contact."

"Good. This is not exactly the best time for visitors. Parrus, Anna, go to Parrus's office. Kline, take me to Comm."

They dispersed, and when Kline and Oronus had passed the bridgeway and entered Communications, they immediately went to work.

"Kline, patch me through to Aevier's ship."

"Yes, sir."

Oronus sat down in front of a screen that rested in the center of the control room and awaited the face of Aevier or one of his officers. After a short time, a woman with blond, closely shaved hair came into view on the screen.

"This is Oronus. I need to speak with Director Aevier."

"The director is engaged presently. You may deal with me. I am chief officer Antalya Greigovich."

This angered Oronus a little. After so much had happened, he had no desire to jump through hoops to entertain impromptu guests.

"If the director is so busy that he cannot speak to me, after arriving unannounced, then you may leave at once. You can tell him I said that. If he decides to speak with me, then I will gladly *consider* his docking. As I'm sure you can see from your position, we have suffered great losses as of late. However, if his stance does not change, then under our current state we will consider your ship a hostile craft, and I will be forced to escort you back to CentrePointe. You can tell him I said that too."

Oronus motioned to Kline, and the screen flashed off. Oronus stood and walked to Kline's station. "If his position changes let me know. I don't have time for this."

He then turned with the intention of returning to the hangar, but one of the officers stopped him.

"Captain! Director Aevier requests a conference with you." Oronus sighed and returned to his seat in front of the screen.

"Hello, Jacques. What can I do for you? As you can see we are in a state of recovery after horrible losses occurred in recent days."

"And for zat you have my deepest sympathies. Ze council has been following ze reports vist great concern. However, recent events have increased ze need for ze tour of O.R.T."

Oronus laughed loudly. "Are you serious, Jacques? *Right* now? I can assure you that we are not ready for this to happen. All our attention is focused on recovery. Besides, the hangar is in a state of disarray! Wasn't that your primary reason for coming, to see the hangar?"

Aevier nodded grimly. "Yes, Oronus, it vas. And for all intents and purposes, it still is vhy I am here. Know, however, zat I amended ze terms of zis tour greatly vist ze approval of ze council. Ze only people you vill show zis facility to are Joseph Thomas, Industrial director from Restivar, and myself. Ze council and ze ozher Industrial directors are not here. It is ze intention of ze council to create an airship production facility in ze first province. In light of your recent mishap, I fear zat ve must accelerate our plans."

Oronus stood and walked toward the screen. "Mishap? How dare you speak so lightly of the death and destruction that we just experienced! I can *assure* you that this was no *mishap!* I built Alden's aircraft myself. There was nothing wrong with its engine! For the sake of the Four, Jacques, it ran on *water!*"

"But not entirely on vater, Oronus. Takeoff procedures on all of your crafts require a small amount of fuel, yes? I think zat your imagination is running ahead of your reason. Don't create an enemy zat isn't zhere."

"Isn't there? I'm sure you are aware that Cebran's organization in Restivar *stole* one of my ships and tried to kill my daughter and my apprentice! An enemy *is* there, Jacques, and though I am not accusing them, *yet,* of the explosion, the board and I *all* agree that there is foul play involved."

"Regardless, I must see ze facility. Vhezer I do it vist your permission or by ze permission of ze Council of Directors is up to you."

Oronus was fuming, but he did not show it to Jacques. "You may dock in bay six once I have word that it has been cleared of debris and *dead bodies.* Welcome to O.R.T."

He walked away from the screen and out of Communications without waiting for the screen to shut off and without speaking to anyone. He stopped in the bridgeway and waited. He knew that he must regain his composure before Jacques landed.

⌇

Graff stood over his desk in his chambers, staring intently into the surface of the obsidian inset *and* seeing the airship dock through

Aevier's eyes. Swirling cyclones of eroded earth spun past the great window behind him as he smiled and glared through the glass desk into the glow of the inset's surface.

Oh my. This is extraordinary. Soon three sets of eyes shall become one. I sincerely hope that I am able to maintain my sanity. The Chest of Worlds. Soon it will be mine. The fallacies of the Four shall pale and fade in the light of my majesty.

～

Jacques descended from the deck through the hatch and found Joseph Thomas waiting patiently in front of the ramp. He looked down the narrow hallway to the engineer who was preparing to lower the ramp and held out his index finger.

"Give me a moment." He turned to face Joseph. "You know vhy ve are here, and you know who sent us. A successful mission is ze only acceptable outcome. Ve must appease ze Lord. Do you understand?"

Joseph stared into Aevier's eyes, recounting the gruesome threats hurled at him by Graff should he fail to do Graff's bidding.

"Yes," he said gravely, "I understand."

"Good. Lower ze ramp!"

Anna and Parrus were waiting for Director Aevier and Joseph Thomas when they reached the bottom of the ramp.

"Ah! Anna Bretton, Parrus Vademe! It is good to see zat you are both unharmed! Zis truly is a blessing, but vhere is Oronus? I vas expecting to see him here." Parrus shook hands with both of them.

"Oronus will be here shortly. Please come with me to my office. We can all wait for him there."

They began walking, and Aevier and Joseph looked intently around the room, surveying the damage and the recovery effort.

"By the Four..." Joseph said, sickened by using the phrase.

He was glad that the high priest could not hear his voice too. "This is awful."

Aevier grunted in agreement and shook his head. "Zis *is* terrible. Who could have predicted zat an accident vist one craft could cause such exponential damage."

"This was not an accident, Director. This was a violent and intentional act against this facility." Anna was calm yet resolute in her statement.

"My dear, ve mustn't jump to such conclusions in a stressful time such as zis! Discussion and investigation are in order before zhese vild accuzations are made."

"Wild accus—"

Parrus shot a warning gaze at Anna. "I suppose you are right, Director."

"Yes, my dear. Parrus, is zis your office? I thought zat Dardus Hale officed here." As they reached the steps, Parrus pulled back the sheet to reveal Dardus's face and continued right up the steps without hesitation or a backward glance.

"Dardus is dead." He walked in and left the door open as Aevier, Joseph, and finally Anna entered the room.

"I know zat our presence here is less than velcome right now, and I assure you zat ve both understand completely. I hope, zhough, zat you realize ze necessity of zis tour for ze vell being of ze provinces *and* O.R.T."

"Frankly, Director, I don't know what to think right now. This has been quite a shock to us all."

Aevier nodded and looked out the window of the office. He spotted Oronus coming up the bridgeway and stood. "Ah, zhere he is. Joseph, let us go down and meet vist Oronus."

Parrus stood to object, but they were already out the door and making their way down the steps. They stood next to Dardus's table as Oronus approached them.

"Oronus, I am glad zat you chose to allow zis visit. I can

assure you zat ve are here for ze benefit of ze provinces and of O.R.T. itself."

Oronus gave a curt nod. "With all due respect, Director Aevier, I feel that it would be better for both of us if we begin immediately and continue until the facility has been viewed in its entirety. If you would both follow me, please." Aevier spoke as Oronus turned.

"Actually, Oronus, I think I can make zis simpler. It vill only be necessary for us to view ze hangar, board some of your ships, and visit ze Re-Creation building. Zis vill prove, I believe, to be a much shorter and much more efficient course, and vill allow you to return to your duties much sooner."

"Why does Joseph need to see Re-Creation, Jacques? That department has nothing to do with craft production. If you'll just follow me, then we can begin the tour of the hangar."

"I thought, Oronus, zat Re-Creation vas vhere you tinkered vist experimental crafts?"

Oronus nodded. "Yes, it is. However, I do not recall you mentioning that this business-class cargo ship facility you suggested would be having an experimental branch."

"No, Oronus, I did not. I do not plan on mentioning it eisher. However, I feel zat it vould be beneficial to see your mechanics and engineers in zheir element. Please make zis easy on both of us, Oronus."

Oronus knew that by that he meant "without council interference," so he nodded and turned to face the rest of the hangar. "Well, gentlemen, this is the hangar. It is divided into three sections. The first section, which we are currently in, contains all of our offices and docking bays, as well as several small maintenance stations that make small repairs to ships after they dock. Every porthole on this level is as large as our largest ship requires, so any and every ship that comes through O.R.T. is able to fit. What we are passing now, where there are still docking bays and intact portions of wall, are a varied mix of the types of airships that are created here. This is one of our only remaining WASPs, or Weapons Activated Sentry Prototypes. Three of these exploded after the initial blast, which was the main reason for the destruction up here. Next, we have a business-class ship, which is used for travel and trade within the provinces. It has the same basic layout of our cargo ships, but they are much more spacious and comfortable to travel in. Here we have a line of cargo ships, which are used primarily for bulk trade between provinces. Mechanics and engineers are constantly moving from the maintenance stations to the ships in order to maintain maximum efficiency. They are all either trained by a master mechanic or are teaching the art to apprentices presently. You can see, as we move along, that every ship, though housing fundamental structural similarities, are all built slightly different. This is a strong point for our line, and on a lighter note it is a kind of reward to our builders, whom we struggle to keep out of the throws of monotony."

They continued along and wove between piles of rock and ship fragments and soon found themselves at the bridgeway on the opposite side of the hangar next to a cargo ship that was unscathed from the blast. "Let's board this vessel, shall we?"

Aevier nodded and watched as crew members lowered the ramp to the ship. They entered, and Oronus began his discussion.

Oronus quickly rushed Aeiver and Stephens through a cargo airship, and on their exit intentionally walked the two past a row of bodies and debris.

Aevier fought for a civil way to express his annoyance at the briskness of the tour. "Zis is all, vell, vague. I know zat you are rushed, but I feel as zhough zis is not very helpful, Oronus."

"I will pretend, Jacques," he said as they began their walk back across the hangar, "that you did not just say that. If you must come back again with enforcement from the council, then do it. I don't have time for this *unannounced* visit as it is, so I would very much appreciate your silent cooperation."

Aevier's monocle spun and adjusted extremely quickly as he

fought back his urge to be outwardly angry at Oronus's reprimand. "All right, I vill."

Oronus assumed that his latter statement applied more to council enforcement than remaining quiet, and he chuckled softly at this thought. They reached the other end of the bridgeway and found themselves at the entrance to Re-Creation. "This, gentlemen, is O.R.T.'s Re-Creation building. It is here that all artifacts discovered in our excavations are brought for examination and revivification. It is also where we experiment with new ideas for airships and smaller craft in our experimental production facility."

They walked in and passed through a large room of men and women surrounding several tables and workbenches, focused intently on the different artifacts that lay before them. After they passed through the room, they came to an area with a large descending ramp, and next to that a narrow hallway. Several large sacks rested against the sides of the hallway, and Aevier noticed a large black piece of stone that looked incredibly familiar. Oronus noticed Aevier staring intently down the hallway. This was too close for comfort. "This way to the production area, Jacques."

This seemed to snap Jacques out of staring at the large stone. "Yes, sorry. Please continue."

Oronus stood in the center of the large room with Jacques and Joseph. "This is where creativity and imagination meet engineering and mechanics. We do most of our best work in this room. As you can see, there are some older ships here that we are using for parts and experimentation. There are a set of engineers whose sole responsibility is to stay in this part of the hangar and Re-Creation and focus on new ways to transport and travel."

All three turned as a mechanic came running toward them. "Captain! Captain! Something's wrong with the director's ship! It is smoking violently! We can't stand another explosion! Please come, Captain!"

Oronus turned back to the two. "Do you know anything about this, Jacques? Has this happened before?"

"No, Oronus. Zis is new to me."

"Jacques, we may have to cut this short. I need to go up there."

"Do not vorry. Ve vill follow you. After all, ve cannot leave unless it is fixed. Vould you mind if I used an office to call my secretary? I vill need alternate traveling arrangements made if ze ship is unable to fly."

Oronus nodded. "Of course. If you go back up the walkway, you will find a set of offices. Use any one you wish."

He then turned and jogged away with the mechanic.

"You know vat to do, Joseph." Joseph nodded and ran off in the direction of Oronus and the mechanic.

Aevier walked back up to the hallway and looked around. He knew he didn't have much time, and he didn't really know the precise location of the chest. All he knew was that it would be in a very secure place and that it passed by the large stone, the one that matched that glowing inset he had seen in Graff's office. He walked down the hallway and passed the obsidian stone. The face of the stone was at an odd angle. It faced the corner where the wall of the hallway met the wall of the main Re-Creation room. Jacques knew that the only way the chest could have gone directly past it was through the hallway. He looked down the hall to see if there were any secured doorways or barricaded turns, but he could see none. He strolled down the hallway casually, looking in at offices and observing the large room with glass walls where scientists were working diligently to preserve ancient scrolls and books. However, when he reached the end of the hall, he found an elevator that matched the walls surrounding it. Oronus, in his rush to send Jacques away, had forgotten to slide the covering to the door back over the doors of the elevator. He slid the doors open and entered the elevator. He pressed the lowest button. "Zis seems secure, indeed. I guess I'll start at ze bottom." The elevator stopped after a time, and the door slid open, revealing a dimly lit metallic hallway leading to another door, which was silhouetted at the bottom from the light that lay beyond it. Jacques walked forward and stood close to the door. He placed his ear to it and listened: no sound. He carefully cracked the door and peered into the room. It was very bright, with white walls and a white ceiling. He opened the door all the way and walked inside. "Zis is a strange place." Jacques had no idea that thirty armed guards, Osiris, and Aaron were watching him in silence as he walked to the middle of the room.

"Zhere are too many buttons on zat panel for me to check every one of zhem!" Aevier turned to leave the room. Aaron had already gone to the door, and when Aevier got close enough he slammed the door.

"Agh! Vat is zis?" He turned to face a room that was no longer empty. All of the guards had their guns pointed at Aevier, and Aaron and six of the guards stood in front of the chest, blocking it from Aevier's vision.

"Hello, Director. Can I help you with something? You look lost! Did you get separated from your party?"

Aevier glared at Aaron. Were it just the two of them, Jacques told himself, the brat would already have a bullet in his head. "Aaron, ve meet again. No, I am not lost. Oronus vas called avay to ze hangar, so I thought zat I vould look around at ze place. Zhen again, I could ask you ze same question. Vat vould bring you down here vhen ze hangar needs all of O.R.T.'s attention at ze moment?"

"Nothing important, Director Aevier. If you'd like, I can show you back to the elevator. I don't remember this room being on schedule for a tour."

"Nothing important, eh? I have never seen something be so unimportant *and* guarded by a group of armed men before. How strange. Perhaps something rests on zat table behind you? Is zat it?" Aaron smiled and remained in front of the table.

"I don't know what you mean, Director. We are simply engaging in some training exercises to deal with the eventuality of infiltrators and thieves. I'm sure you understand."

Aevier's eye twitched, and he forced a grotesque smile onto his face.

"My apologies, mister Ravenhall. I shall find ze vay back to ze elevator myself. Good luck vist your... training."

As Aevier turned to leave, he spied an old man lying in a bed in the corner of the room that was sectioned off by makeshift walls. He paused curiously and then left the room.

~

"*What? He's alive? No!*" Graff turned, serpentine staff in hand, and in a flash of blue light decapitated a statue of the Representation of Grace that stood behind his desk.

"*A time is coming when* fortune *will not smile on the weak and the wounded!*" He screamed in rage and shut off the obsidian stone with a wave of his hand.

Observing all of this were Edgar and Thacker Wallace—Simon Gardner was on his way to CentrePointe. Graff glided down the semicircle steps to the place where they stood. He stopped in front of them, closed his eyes, and exhaled.

"Oh my. It seems as though we must go back to our original plan. We wait for the craft production facility to be completed, and we start 'skimming off of the top,' as Edgar so affectionately worded it. You will bring them here. No one goes beyond the basilica, and there are places in those little mountains that would be ideal for hiding ships. Just keep collecting those explosives, children. I assure you that, unlike the Artificial Four, I shall actually reward you for your loyalty. Simon, my faithful missioner, has taken a special letter to Council Headquarters. Aevier will contact him. He will either tell him take the letter immediately to Michael Reath, director of the second province, or to return immediately to the basilica. Go now, and do my bidding."

The two left without question or hesitation. Eleazer turned

to face the great window. For the first time since he had possession of the book, he felt insecure.

Oh my. I... told him... everything. Surely he will die soon or at least slip back into madness. The foolish old man will never quench his thirst again. If I am lucky, and with the terrible goings on at O.R.T., subtleties such as these will continue to go unnoticed until it is too late and I am God!

∾

Oronus came out of the engine room and made his way back down the ramp of Aevier's ship. He was covered in soot and smelled of smoke. He approached Joseph Thomas and dusted off his hand to shake the district director's. "I have no idea what happened. The good thing is that I found nothing wrong with the ship—it should fly without any problems. However, I would suggest having it looked at by professionals in the hangar at council headquarters when you have more time on your hands." He looked around, hoping to see Aevier nearby, but he was nowhere to be seen.

"Where is Jacques? Surely his call did not take an hour."

Joseph shrugged and thrust his hands into his pockets. "I have no idea, Oronus. I assumed that he was right behind me when we ran up here. Maybe his call wasn't returned, and he needed to wait close to a comm panel."

Oronus sighed. "Let's go back down the bridgeway. Maybe he is simply waiting for us." They traveled back down the bridgeway and through Re-Creation. They came to the walkway just as Aevier was coming down the hallway from the elevator.

"I hope you didn't send for someone, Jacques. I have no idea why the engine room smoked like that, but everything appears to be fine. If you don't mind, I think that this is a good note to end on. I have pressing matters to attend to."

Aevier smiled and moved to stand by Joseph. "No one is coming, not to vorry. Thank you for your villingness to stop and assist me in zis stressful time. I'm sure zat ze council vill be in touch vist you. Oh! I almost forgot." Jacques pulled a folded set of papers from inside his military coat and handed them to Oronus. He was instructed to give these to him if the original plan of stealing the Chest of Worlds failed. "Blessings of ze Four on you."

Oronus took the papers and started to ask what they were, but Aevier and Thomas were already on their way back to the ship.

He shouted at them. "Aevier! What are these?"

He answered without stopping or turning. "Just read zhem, Oronus. You vill find zhem to be self-explanatory, I am sure."

Oronus went into his office and closed the door, checking the room out of his suspicion of Jacques. He found nothing, and nothing that was there looked as if it had been moved or tampered with. He sat down at his desk, turned the folded pages over to where they were sealed, and was taken by surprise. What he expected to be the seal of the Council of Directors was actually the seal of the Basilica of the Four. "Gods. Why is Aevier delivering the high priest's messages?" After this unexpected arrival and Osiris's revelation to Oronus, he was very suspicious about anything connected to Eleazer Graff or the basilica. He snapped the seal and unfolded the papers. A note fell out into his lap that looked as if it had been written by Jacques. It read:

Oronus,

By now my tour of your facility is at a successful close, my ship is repaired, and I am on my way back to CentrePointe. I feel obliged to inform you that High Priest Eleazer Graff of the Basilica of the Four has received word that O.R.T. is currently in possession of the Divine Artifact, the Chest of Worlds. A formal request from the basilica for possession of the Divine Artifact is being read at council headquarters even as you read this. The Chest of Worlds, crafted by the Four, belongs in the hands of those who seek to further the spiritual well-being of the prov-

inces, Oronus. The High Priest simply wants the chest to help uncover new revelations, new evidence of the role of the Four in our lives.

We are exploring the necessary changes that need to be made regarding the artifacts and texts you now possess. I am sure that you will hear from the council soon—perhaps you will hear from the high priest as well.

Blessings of the Four upon you,
Jacques

Oronus set the note down on top of the formal request and closed his eyes; there was no need to continue reading. It was clear that Aevier's allegiance lay in more than one place. He had never felt threatened, truly threatened, by Aevier, the council, or the basilica, but this time was different: Alden was dead, O.R.T. was severely damaged, and Aevier was in league with the high priest. Had he always been? It didn't matter at this point. All that mattered was that Jacques told the high priest that the Chest of Worlds was here. The only solace Oronus found was in the fact that the chest was hidden. He stood, grabbed the note, and walked out of his office.

Aevier and the priest may know I have the chest, but they don't know exactly where it is. Besides, it will take the council quite a while to agree on anything drastic that has to do with the Raujj. He was coming up the walkway just as Aaron exploded out of the hall. Oronus jumped. "Hey! Aaron, are you all right?"

Aaron leaned against the wall, his casted arm hanging at his side. "He knows, Oronus. He found the safe room. He knows where the chest is."

Oronus's jaw tightened as a look of indignation swept across his face. In his rush to read through the pages, he had paid no attention to the line "my ship is repaired." *"He wasn't calling his secretary—he was snooping around! I should have known!"*

Aaron looked confused. "Oronus what are you—" Oronus handed him the note. Aaron read it and looked up at Oronus.

"Aevier. He's in league with Graff. What do we do, Oronus?"

Oronus pointed down the hallway. "We go talk to my father again. Let's go."

They went to the elevator and reached the safe room without speaking to each other. When they opened the door, Osiris called out to them.

"Son, bring me water... I need water..."

Oronus looked at Aaron. "Do you mind?"

Aaron nodded his head and went to get a glass of water for the old man. Oronus walked up to the sectioned-off space as everyone and everything wavered back into view.

"Dad, did you see a lanky bald man with a big mustache, a monocle, and a ridiculously small cape come in here?" Osiris answered with one hand wrapped around his throat.

"Yes." He forced out the word. He was constantly trying to swallow and work up saliva in his mouth.

"Dad, what's wrong with you? Do I need to get Dorothea again?"

Osiris shook his head and answered, "Water..." Oronus furrowed his eyebrows in concern and confusion. Oronus shouted Aaron's name when his father began making odd guttural noises.

"Aaron! Hurry up! Bring that water, son!" Aaron came from the opposite end of the room with a quickened step. He had found a larger glass and filled it all the way to the top. He passed it to Osiris, who snatched it greedily from Aaron's hands, slopping some of the water across the bed. He drank in long, slow gulps until the glass was drained.

"What's wrong with you?" Aaron shouted as he wiped his wet hands on his shirt. Osiris looked up at him, embarrassed.

"I am sorry. I am ashamed of myself. Sit down, both of you." They both took a seat in the chairs that sat beside his bed. "I don't know what's happening to me, but I'm starting to feel that way I felt when I tried to enter minds *all* the time. The satisfaction of a full stomach and a refreshing drink leave me; physical warmth and the warmth of love and friendship subsides, and my ability to control my own emotions goes with it. Graff has done something to me."

He instinctively reached for his glass and raised it to his lips, then closed his eyes when nothing came. After a few seconds, his eyes shot open, and he rose up in the bed. "Of course! It makes so much sense!"

Aaron edged forward in his seat. "What are you saying, Osiris?"

"The machine. The machine he left me. I never understood why he did all of those horrible things to my mind and body and then left me a source of life. Like all things we've studied here, son, I can only assume that it was infused with the Ancient Raujj. He poisoned me. He's killing me. My God…"

Oronus and Aaron looked at each other and then back to Osiris. "Are you serious, Dad? Do you really believe this?"

Osiris nodded gravely. "Think of the whys, Son. He told me secrets that he wanted to die with me on the ground level. It was his assurance, his reserve plan in the event that I recovered from his torture."

"Is there anything we can do? Do you want more water?"

Osiris smiled and handed the glass to Aaron. "The only time I feel normal or safe is when I'm drinking the water. Yes, please."

Aaron took the glass and hurried off to fill it up. Oronus turned to face his father. "Can we keep this from happening? Dad, you already died once! I don't want you to die again! What can I do?"

Osiris placed his hand on his son's arm. "Yours is a love that I don't deserve, my son."

Oronus stood and looked down at him. "Why do you always *say* that? Why do you keep putting yourself down? You can't change the past, Dad. You can't live in it."

Osiris inhaled deeply. "It's the 'who' again, my son. Who completed Graff's knowledge of the Ancient's language? Who supplied him with the sensory knowledge required to meditate properly? *I* did, Son. *I* did. I am just as much a part of this as Graff. I also killed a man in the name of something that you seek to halt—reviving the Raujj. I am a fool. I deserve this death."

Oronus shook his head, put his hands on his hips, and paced back and forth in silence. He was still pacing when Aaron returned. This time, however, Aaron came with a cart filled with glasses of water. He parked it on the side of Osiris's bed opposite the chairs. Osiris laughed long and hard.

Aaron looked hurt. "I thought this would be easier."

Osiris raised his hand. "I'm not laughing at *you*, boy! In fact, this is marvelous! I simply laugh at the futility of the matter and, I suppose, the irony. My unquenchable thirst for this forbidden knowledge has given me an actual, unquenchable thirst. How sickeningly appropriate."

Nevertheless, after he finished speaking, Osiris turned and quickly drained the first glass. Then the next. Then the next.

"Whoa, Dad. Slow down, okay? You'll make yourself sick."

"I don't care!" he snapped as he continued drinking.

Aaron reached for the handle of the cart to pull it away, but Osiris snapped at him, as well. "Leave it, boy! Isn't that why you brought it—to leave it for me?"

Aaron fought his anger and forced himself to remember that this was not Osiris's fault. This was Graff's fault.

"Osiris, please listen to us. You need to pace yourself." This time Oronus walked over and grabbed the cart. As he was pulling it away, however, Osiris reached out with his arm and grabbed the other handle facing him. "Leave it! I need this!"

"No, Dad! Just let me put the cart over here. It'll be better for you this way. Please let go."

Osiris closed his eyes and reached into Oronus's mind. His skin paled, and the veins running through his cheeks and forehead became more pronounced. Oronus put his hands over his face and stumbled backward. He backed into one of the paper dividers and fell through it. Aaron stood between them, shocked and unsure of what to do as a group of guards rushed forward with their guns pointed at Osiris.

"Shall I shoot him, sir?" This did not register to Aaron. He simply looked back and forth between Osiris and Oronus, who was screaming at this point.

"Sir? Shall I shoot him? Sir!"

Aaron reacted without thinking. He didn't want Osiris killed, but he didn't want Oronus to die either. "Shoot him in the arm!"

"Sir?"

"Do it!" Aaron screamed.

"Yes, sir!" The guard aimed and put a single bullet through Osiris's left arm. He screamed in pain and reached for the wound with his opposite hand and rocked back and forth. Oronus lay on the ground, and Aaron rushed to him and knelt beside him.

"Oronus, are you okay?" Oronus slowly opened his eyes and looked up at him.

"I...think so..." That was enough for Aaron. He sprinted out of the room and to the elevator; the drawback to the safe room was that there was no communications panel. He sprinted down the long hallway and into the first office he came to and called the medical wing.

"Medical bay?"

"Yes, I need to speak with Dorothea immediately. This is an emergency."

"Hold on."

"What is it, Aaron? Is something wrong with Osiris?"

"He tried to hurt Oronus, Dorothea. I had him shot in the arm to break his concentration. He's bleeding a lot and Oronus's head is in a lot of pain. You need to come back down here."

"By the Four! Hold on, Aaron. I'm coming right now."

Chapter 16

At Council Headquarters in CentrePointe, five of the seven provincial directors sat in the central conference room in silence. Michael Reath sat next to Melinda Stockstill, patting her on the back; she was still very upset about Alden's death.

She looked up at the group and spoke to them. "Everyone, I know that it is hard to focus on business at times like this, but we have to remember that there are people counting on us today. O.R.T. is in bad shape, which serves to speed up our plans for production in the first province. Richard"—she stopped to fight back her emotions—"has passed on and left a very important post vacant, and now we are faced with one of the high priest's most aggressive proposals. What have we done and what do we do?"

Michael spoke. "The second province is preparing a ship of supplies and volunteers from across the province. They should be leaving sometime tomorrow."

Estelle Nichols, director of the fourth province, was next. "We have sectioned off an entire wing at Nurenhanzer for blast victims. We are also planning to send nurses and supplies to the medical bay at O.R.T. once we know they can dock extra ships."

Raulph Hartsfield of the seventh province was next. "The High Priest is preparing a monetary gift for all families of blast victims and has offered to cover the costs of the memorial ceremony. Also, the people of Astonne have put together a volunteer force to assist with the recovery effort at O.R.T."

Johannes Addlebrecht was the last to speak. "It is the wish of the people of the third province to send volunteers to O.R.T. if they are needed."

Michael seemed pleased with the reports. "Good. We're all on the same page, then. Now, as for the production facility in the first province, there are some important factors we need to discuss."

He bent down, pulled a set of packets out of his bag, and set them on the table in front of him. As he was doing this, a woman of medium height and build with a tight-fitting blouse, tight pants, and shoulder-length blond hair pulled into a ponytail walked into the council chambers. She stood at the front of the table and surveyed the group. Max was floating beside her, holding her jacket.

"Gwen! This is a pleasant surprise. Welcome." Melinda stood and walked over to Gwen Alden to greet her with a hug. When they embraced, though, Melinda lost control again.

"I'm so *sorry!*" she sobbed into Gwen's shoulder.

Gwen patted her on the back and consoled her. "There, there, Melinda. Everything will be fine. Let's sit down."

It seemed odd to Michael to observe Gwen consoling Melinda on the loss of her own husband. What was more, she was no longer the soft-spoken, long-haired, dress-wearing sweetheart that she once seemed to be. Her hair was cut, her voice was firm and confident, and she had abandoned her usual dress for something entirely different.

"I know that this is not on your schedules, but I wish to address the council." Everyone voiced their respective agreements at the same time. She nodded her head in thanks. "Well, as you all know, Richard was very dear to me. We found it difficult to be apart from each other for long periods of time, and we shared *everything* with each other. I tell you this because he probably, at some point, told me things that were supposed to be confined to the ears of the council. He shared his policy with me; he asked my opinion on a lot of issues. He also allowed me to do a lot of work around Harrah and the smaller cities. I will never go a day again without sadness creeping into my heart and mind. He was ripped from life, from *me,* far too soon. The reason I am here is because I wish to step into his place. I want to help the council and help the fifth province by continuing the flow of service and leadership that came from Richard. Allow me to help to continue that flow. Let me join the council."

Michael looked at Melinda, then at Estelle, then at Raulph, and finally Johannes—nods of approval from all of them. "Gwen, this is unexpected, though not unwelcome. Obviously we cannot make this decision right now because the whole council isn't here and there are procedures to go though and a fixed progression of actions to take. We'll have to address the fifth province as a whole as well. It is a slow and deliberate process, you know this. However," he smiled at her, "I don't see why we can't, in this emergency, elect some temporary leadership. Because of your closeness with your husband and your obvious knowledge of what goes on here, I would feel, and I'm sure the council would feel, good about granting you the title of interim provincial director of the fifth province until we have time to devote to the selection of a new one. All in favor?"

"Aye." It was unanimous.

Michael grabbed the packets, took one, and passed them down the table. He opened his and flipped through the first couple of pages. "All right, everyone. Join me on page four, and I will walk you through some of the particulars of the new production facility." They were all opening their packets and turning the pages as Jacques walked in, slightly out of breath. He had seen a ship docked in the hangar with a great number five on its bow and had apparently rushed in to see who was here from the director's mansion. His eyes fell immediately on Gwen, and he smiled at her.

"Lady Alden, vat a privilege it is for ze council to host your presence. I am sure zat it has already been stated, but ve are terribly sorry for your loss and vish you comfort in zis time of need." He walked around the table and sat between Michael and Gwen. "Have I missed, perhaps, an address or statement from ze fifth province made by you, Gven?"

Michael shook his head. "No, Jacques, nothing of the sort."

Aevier nodded and smiled again. "Very good, very good. Lady Alden, I mean no disrespect, but I am about to address ze council on my tour of O.R.T. and vill say some things zat only ze council needs to hear, so if you could just—"

"Actually, Jacques, we decided to allow Gwen to step in for Richard until we select a new provincial director."

Jacques tapped his fingers on the table and let out an awkward, high-pitched sigh. He had not foreseen this eventuality at all, and he shot a glare at Director Heartsfield. "Ah, vell, are you sure zat you are fit for zis? Ve vant you to be able to have recuperated fully from Richard's death, Lady Alden."

Gwen turned to look at Jacques. "I don't think I would have it any other way, Director. This is where I need to be."

This didn't please him at all. "Vell, did you sanction zis in my absence? I am glad zat my opinion is valued on ze council! Michael, Melinda, zis is not a good idea."

Jacques was silently coming undone. This was not within the high priest's plans—he was supposed to enter Joseph Thomas's name into the nominations. After all, it would make sense for the director of the province with the largest aircraft production facility to supervise the construction of a new one, and in the process, the first and fifth provinces would be reunited. Jacques would be thanked for the plan, and he would in turn attribute it to the high priest. Now a new strategy must be crafted.

"Jacques, positions like this don't require a unanimous vote; we were all here and okay with Gwen coming onto the council. Your being here to say 'nay' wouldn't have changed anything. Now, we have several things to discuss, everyone, so let's get down to business." Michael opened one of the packets to the fourth page and waited for everyone to do the same. He passed one down to Aevier, and when everyone was at the same place, he began discussion. "Okay, the first obstacle of any new building project is cost, and we are in a fortunate and unique position concerning the cost of this facility. O.R.T. is putting forth management and production training for the maintenance of the production facility and the creation of business-class cargo and transport ships *free* of charge. Also, the Basilica of the Four is making a *very* generous contribution to the purchase of materials and the payment of crews for the construction of the actual facility. You have the numbers in front of you, and now you see why I say we are in a fortunate position; what could have been our greatest obstacle is now a mere afterthought by comparison.

All right, the next obstacle is space. If this branch is going to be producing, let's see here, thirty-five percent of the business-class cargo and transport ships that O.R.T. has been responsible for in the past, we are going to need a large space. Melinda has been exploring different possibilities for locations, so I'll let her take over from here."

She nodded and continued. "Obviously, we needn't build a facility that is as grandiose as O.R.T., but it is going to need to have the room to create parts, move them, and construct them in docking bays. Add to this space requirement for storage of materials, offices, bathrooms, and perhaps a kitchen or some sleeping quarters, and we are looking at a large area for building—approximately a half mile in length and two-thirds of that in width. A base needs to be built that is at least seventy feet above the ground level, and then the actual construction can take place. We want it to happen in the eastern part of the province between Restivar and a neighboring city called Reavene. There is a long-since dry fuel site there that spans much farther than that. The schematics you all have are a modified version of a set I procured from O.R.T. some time ago. It should be relatively easy to just scale back the figures for a smaller building based on these schematics. I think it would be a good idea to let Jacques talk to us about his trip to O.R.T. now, since we're on the subject of the building. How was the tour?"

Jacques smiled at Melinda and decided now was as good a time as any to discuss the chest. "Vell, ve all know zat O.R.T.'s hangar is in terrible condition at ze moment, and everyone's attention is on recovering qvickly and caring for ze vounded and ze dead. However, Oronus found a short time to allow Industrial Director Thomas and I to view ze hangar, a couple of airships, and zheir Re-Creation building. He sent ze particulars, files, and schematics to my office at CentrePointe because of ze brevity of ze tour. Vhen I have reviewed ze files and schematics, I vill draft a formal report to bring to ze council. Vhile I vas zhere, my ship began smoking. Obviously, ve all panicked—zheir have already been enough accidental explosions zhese past few days."

Aevier assumed even the council had ideas that this was not an accident, because when he said this all of them either looked down, away, squinted their eyes, or shuffled papers around. But he didn't care. He gained pleasure from their uneasiness. They should prove it if they thought it was intentional.

"Vell, I searched from a communications panel to contact Stephanie, and vhile doing so I happened upon a strange elevator. I vas curious, and already touring ze building, so I decided to see vhere it vent. Vat I found, to a lesser extent, could change how ze council, O.R.T., and ze basilica handle artifacts. To a greater extent it could change ze lives of everyone on ze continent."

Everyone was looking from Aevier to each other and back, trying to figure out what he was talking about, and not realizing that the conversation had strayed away from the tour and the new building.

"That's a very strong statement, Jacques, especially for someone who was snooping around while Oronus's back was turned. I'm not even sure if it's morally acceptable to bring it up in this setting," Gwen said with concern in her voice.

Aevier turned and was preparing to rip into her, but Michael stepped in. "An overly dramatic statement is what it was, Director, unless you can back it up. Please continue."

"Oronus has ze Chest of Vorlds. He holds ze divine artifact in ze depths of O.R.T. It is real, and he has it."

"Preposterous!" Johannes laughed. "The chest is a story told by the basilica to small children. Nothing more. For all we know, the genesis account of the chest could be completely metaphorical, symbolic." Ayes were heard around the table.

Michael shifted in his seat. He had the letters from Jacques and the high priest in his hands; this was not something that could be passed off, and he knew that they *all* knew this fact.

"Actually, Johannes, the high priest feels the same way Jacques does, and though we can't move forward until we prove this to be true, there is a real possibility that it *does* exist. Unfortunately, the only person Oronus told was Jacques, based only on what Jacques has told me. That alone is not enough to proceed yet, I'm afraid."

"*Vat? Vat are you saying?*" Aevier was standing now. "Quit speaking as zhough you vere ze voice of ze whole council, Reath! Vat in ze name of ze Four gives you ze right to simply *ignore* zis?"

"Sit *down*, Jacques. Don't think that the council hasn't noticed your 'evolving' relationship with the basilica and High Priest Gaff as of late. I understand that you have rediscovered that part of your life, but we can't rule out that your bias is interfering with your work *here*. If he had told someone else as well, then I don't think there would be a problem, but until we bring in Oronus to talk to the council, I don't think we should address the issue."

"He told Richard! He told Richard *everything*. You all know zis!"

Gwen turned. "Well, let's call him up, shall we, and ask him a few questions!"

"Calm down, everyone. We're not here to fight. And though she spoke out of anger, she's right, Jacques. Richard is gone." Michael grabbed the arm of Jacques' chair and scooted it closer to him. Jacques sighed and sat down.

Michael looked down the table at Gwen. "Did Richard or Oronus ever say anything to you about the chest, Gwen? Anything at all?" She thought back and struggled with how she should respond. After convincing herself that no one could prove otherwise, she responded:

"No. Neither of them ever spoke to me about anything like that."

Michael nodded. "Yes, I thought as much. Well, if he does have it, then I don't think we can stand in the way of the basilica claiming ownership. We need Oronus, and I don't think we should summon him until O.R.T. is functioning again."

Aevier stood and gathered his things. "I don't think zat anyone here truly comprehends ze gravity of ze situation. Zis Chest of Vorlds vas created by ze Four for ze people. Ve are all engaging in ze vorship of something ve can't begin to understand. Ze chest could hold ze key to our understanding ze Four, ze Ancients, and ze Raujj. Zis is bigger zhan any of us. If you cannot grasp ze seriousness of ze matter, zhen I vill simply bring ze high priest here to tell you all himself." He walked around the table and stopped at the door. "Zis vill not be pleasant for any of us. I am sorry to force ze issue, but if you are going to judge me and refute ze importance of our religion, I vill not stand by and vatch." With that, he turned and walked out the door.

"Jacques, wait!" Estelle shouted as she leaned forward over the table. Outside the door, Jacques smirked and turned around. She leaned in and whispered to them. "This will *not* end well for any of us if the high priest shows up under the impression that we are discriminating people for their religion." Aevier returned and stood in the doorway.

Michael looked over at Estelle disapprovingly and then spoke to Jacques. "Jacques, please sit down. Perhaps we were a little insensitive. *Perhaps.* Let's try and talk through this." Jacques walked around the table silently and took his seat once again. He sat in silence with wide eyes and linked fingers, waiting for someone to say something.

"Two things need to be understood," said Johannes. "The first is that this council never has and never will discriminate against the people's faith or against the faith of those on the council. If your time spent with the high priest and in the basilica is overtaking your time spent with the sixth province and in the council and if we notice that and say something, that is *not* discrimination. The second is this: devoted followers of the Four have been worshipping for generations without the basilica's possession of the chest. If it does exist, if it does hold any significance, and if Oronus *truly* has the genuine Chest of Worlds, then a few more months without it aren't going to crush the Way of the Four. Now, we have already determined that when we find out the answers to these questions, the basilica has the authority to claim ownership. This, to me, seems sufficient. Thoughts?"

"I agree completely, Johannes. Well said," Melinda added.

Estelle nodded. "Yes, very good."

Aevier knew that there was no way around capitulation, so he conceded. Now, then, was the time to win hearts, a time that the high priest had promised him would come.

"I must confess zat my zealousness has increased somevhat as of late. You have to understand zat I have been coming to ze realization zat over ze past two years I have done virtually nothing for ze provinces. Vhen Oronus's apprentice found ze Chest of Vorlds, I snapped into reality. Our provinces are divided, some are entirely vealthy, and ozhers are struggling to survive. I have done very little to assist vist ze Industrial Districts. I apologize. I simply overcompensated. Perhaps zis new facility and, tragically, ze explosion at O.R.T vill bring us togezher once again. If I have assurances zat ze chest is ze rightful property of ze basilica, zhen ve can move forward."

"In the twelve years that you have been on the council, you have never said anything like that. Perhaps you *are* changing," Melinda said.

Gwen was also moved by Jacques's sentiment. "I agree wholeheartedly with Director Aevier. We have a wonderful chance to achieve a unity that we have not felt for years. That being said, there is a related matter that ties into the new facility, O.R.T., and provincial unity. Before anything happens with Oronus or O.R.T., I think we should conduct an investigation into the cause of the explosion. Examination of the site of the explosion could tell us if someone did this on purpose or not. If this was an intentional act by an individual or a group, then the Council of Directors has to act against them before they are able to do something like this again."

"*Zhem*, eh? Sounds like you already have a group in mind, Lady Alden."

"I am merely reminding everyone that there is a group in the first province that tried this once before. Also, they have taken the ship *Regalus* from Oronus's fleet. This, if you recall, is the same ship that Cebran tried to steal the first time around. Though these may be simple coincidences, I think that they warrant investigation. I have brought with me a proposal for an interprovincial investigatory team comprised of two people, one director, and one randomly selected citizen from each province to assist with the gathering of evidence and interrogation."

She handed them around the table. Jacques scoffed. "By doing zis, Gven, ve vould risk furzher alienation of ze people in Restivar, vhich vould be detrimental to our ozher objectives. I vill not support zis."

Melinda looked at Gwen reassuringly. "Gwen, I think this is a good idea. This could unite us and make the provinces feel equally responsible in keeping each other safe."

Aevier shook his head and scoffed again, adjusting his monocle and straightening his papers. Gwen looked at Jacques and then turned to face the others. "I don't think that it would be wise to continue our efforts until we know with full certainty that what we promise and what we build won't be destroyed in a similar manner."

Michael nodded. He knew he needed to find middle ground. "Aevier would be correct if the investigation involved the whole of Restivar. However, it only involves a small group operating on its outskirts. Melinda's thoughts could very well transpire if we do this, and Gwen is doing right by her concern for safety and efficiency. Given our current circumstances, though, I think it is a good idea to start building as soon as possible. The people of the first province need the work desperately, and their new work will be affecting all of the provinces."

Johannes nodded in agreement. "We could launch the investigation, the building project, and the relief effort to the fifth province all at once. The whole of the provinces will be devoted to its restoration for a time, and I think that that is just what we need. If I may backtrack a little, though, the revelation of the chest (if it does exist) would be better received after we slow back down and have more order."

Discussion continued within the council for some time, and culminated with a reexamination of building particulars and construction timelines and the new facility, the interrogation and the true possession of the chest were decided upon. They rose to go back to their respective duties, and everyone, excepting Jacques, greeted Gwen and applauded her courage and ideas. Michael and Johannes were complimented by Melinda and Estelle for picking up so efficiently where Richard had left off.

Before they left, Jacques made an announcement to them all.

"Everyone! Before ve depart, I must invite you all and any guests you vish to bring to a gazhering at my home. Zhere vill be food and refreshments and ve vill be discussing vays to connect each ozher provincially. Next month, everyone. Immediately following our meeting. Please come!" With that, he walked out of the room, weaving in between everyone to be the first out of the room.

Melinda smiled. "I really feel like he's turning around." Michael rolled his eyes and patted Melinda on the back. "I wish I was as accepting as you." He chuckled and they dispersed. Melinda walked down the familiar hallway to her office, and Gwen caught up with her.

"Follow me."

Gwen pulled her into a side hallway, and they stood there, sides against the wall. A tear rolled down Melinda's cheek. "What's wrong, dear?"

Melinda laughed and brushed away the single tear. "Oh, nothing really. It's just that Richard did the same thing right before he left, pulled me into this hallway, and we leaned against this very wall. I know. It's silly. You two are just so much alike."

Gwen smiled and rubbed her shoulder. "That's not silly at all, Melinda. Those are comforting things to hear and to recall. Listen, I caught up with you because of your final comment. I am going to find out for sure if Jacques is really a changed man. I'm having Max follow him. He's going to sneak onto Aevier's ship and report back to me next month."

Melinda gasped. "Gwen, no! What if he finds out? This will come right back to you!"

Gwen smiled. "Calm down, Melinda. Oronus revived Max for Richard and I a long time ago. It's not like the others, Melinda. This Max has some … extra additions. It shouldn't be a problem. I just can't help it. Richard and Jacques have a checkered history. You know this as well as I do. Let's just make sure that this is all real."

Melinda nodded, and they walked down the hallway.

Max floated directly behind Aevier all the way to his ship. One of the "additions" that Gwen spoke of was the same cloaking device that Oronus used in the safe room. The ramp was lowered, and Aevier and Max boarded. Max immediately hugged the wall of the hallway and followed Jacques into the control room.

"To ze basilica. Hurry."

Jacques turned and headed for his quarters, and Max floated along the opposing wall, following him all the way. Max was almost crushed by the door slamming. Max floated to the far corner near the ceiling and waited, watching, recording. The captain's quarters were small but elaborate. The small bed was adorned with plush silk bedding. There was a small desk of the same dark, polished wood resting beside the bed, and on it were several trinkets, small objects Jacques had taken for himself when he would infiltrate the Great Houses after Oronus and his teams. In the middle of these small trinkets was a large, framed picture of the high priest, wearing his ceremonial red with silver stole and apparently in the middle of some eloquent address to the provinces. On the wall opposing the bed and desk was a large mirror spanning the length of it. On either side were closets. Jacques removed his cape and jacket, placing the pistol and his monocle down on the desk. He hung the cape and jacket in the closet. He then kicked off his boots and lay down on the bed with his hands behind his head, fingers interlaced. He let out a sigh.

"Ze Lord vill not be pleased vist me. Gven Alden is on ze Council of Directors!" He rolled over violently and went to sleep. Max stayed alert.

CHAPTER 17

The large glass room dedicated to the preservation of scrolls and texts had been cleared entirely. The large glass slabs used to seal the scrolls were moved into another area of Re-Creation, along with the scientists dedicated to the work. In their place was a large bed from the medical bay, on which Osiris rested. He was unconscious, and Dorothea had removed the bullet from his arm and had cleaned and bandaged the wound. A small tube ran from his mouth, and a cool, wet cloth rested on his forehead. A whole team of nurses were with him now as well as six armed guards. Oronus, Dorothea, Aaron, and Anna stood near the wall closest to the hallway and spoke in hushed tones.

"What is the tube for, Dorothea?" Oronus asked. His head was still sore from Osiris's attack and was slightly disoriented.

"There is a tiny and constant flow of water entering his system. It is filled with nutrients and minerals so that he can be sustained for a while solely on the water. If what you and Aaron say is true, then this should also keep him from becoming belligerent. It's not taking much to keep him sedated, but we are constantly monitoring his health. Quite frankly, Oronus, I don't know why he's not dead. The exertion required to use the Raujj along with the shock of the bullet should've killed him."

"Well, I'm glad that it didn't kill him and *me* for that matter. We just need to keep him fed and monitored until he is able to wake up again."

Suddenly Parrus was on the comm panel. "Captain, there are groups from CentrePointe and Harrah wishing to land. They say they have volunteers, nurses, and medical supplies for us."

"Excellent, Parrus. However, given the circumstances, we need to send out a couple of ships with some officers to inspect their contents. We can't afford any more damages to this hangar. Notify them of the procedure, apologize in advance for the scrutiny, and send out the welcoming party."

In the hangar, Parrus made preparations to have two docking bays ready and two of their own ships ready to go investigate. As cautious as he knew he needed to be, Parrus was overjoyed with the thought of the other provinces helping them out. O.R.T. staff had been at work for several days by now, and they still hadn't stopped for the memorial ceremony. He found a deck officer and issued his orders. *With any luck,* he thought, *we'll have every injured person in proper care and this hangar cleared and ready for reconstruction much sooner than we thought!*

~

Oronus took Aaron and Anna from the glass room and into his office on the other side of Re-Creation. "Every timeline we had concerning the chest, the Ancients, and the Raujj has been fast-tracked because of this. Aevier shared with me an edict from the high priest claiming ownership of the chest and *any* text that may even have a hint of the Four in them. What I think he secretly means is any text that mentions the Raujj, which is a significant amount. If we want to destroy the Raujj, we have to destroy the chest. The only way to destroy the Raujj is with the chest, and to use the chest, we need to learn how to use it with the texts we have. This is *not* good. Also, the high priest has what was perhaps the most important book we ever owned—the *Codicil*—a text containing the location, use, and purpose of the four keys that open the chest. Osiris told me of this earlier when we were alone. We had no way of knowing, but the Great House that contained the Chest of Worlds was the first key; now Graff knows how to obtain the other three keys *and* is appealing to the council for the chest!

"However, Melinda has talked to me recently about the council's plans to build a craft production facility in the first province to compensate for O.R.T.'s losses and to stimulate their economy and cut their unemployment rate. They also want to launch an investigation into the cause of the explosion on Richard's ship. While all of this is going on, I don't think that they will have any focus on the chest, but if that changes, then the chest will need to go into hiding. Aaron feels certain that Aevier saw the chest while trespassing in the safe room. Because of this, if we have to hide the chest, it will have to be away from O.R.T."

Aaron's eyes widened. "Just show the council the director's note! It proves that he knew about his ship smoking before it actually happened! Anything he says about the chest would lose credibility!"

Oronus shook his head. "I thought of that too, Aaron, but all Jacques would have to say is that he wrote it just before he left, while I was in the hangar. No, but I wish it were that simple. Keep your eyes peeled and talk to no one about Osiris or the chest."

He stood and walked in lazy circles, contemplating things out loud. "How am I going to convince the council of Aevier's motives? How am I going to convince them I don't have the Chest of Worlds? The First Key... Gods, what has that artifact gotten us into?"

He continued pacing as he thought further on the Way of the Four. If it turned out to be wrong, if analysis of history would prove it to be inaccurate, then why was he risking himself and the people around him to preserve it? Not that he could talk to anyone about this, the only people knowing about Graff's true motives being Osiris, Aevier, Aaron, Anna, and himself. Even that, however, was speculation. This was an awkward and risky situation to be in. The provinces were about to be busy with the production of a new airship facility, O.R.T. was fighting to get back on its feet, and Aevier was about to become the face of provincial unity.

Who, then, would believe anything he said? Gwen would, he knew that, but she was new to the council and wasn't even a true member. Melinda was another hope, but her tone concerning Aevier was much different as of late, as though she thought him to be some kind of saint.

"Aaron, the reason the Great House collapsed around you is because it was designed to." Aaron turned and looked as though he didn't understand the language Oronus was using. "The *Book of the Four* mentions the Chest of Worlds this way: 'Four Spheres, Four Keys, One Impenetrable Chest of Worlds.' The collapse of this House of Ancients around you after you touched the chest serves to prove that the *Codicil* is real and accurate. The 'keys' are not conventional keys that one imagines fitting into a keyhole. *These* keys could be anything! The first was the Great House you entered. Its purpose, if Osiris is correct, was to prevent anyone from taking the chest from its place. If the first key was designed to kill, I can only assume that the other three keys also have ill purposes."

∽

At the Basilica of the Four, Aevier waited in the back of the sanctum as affluent pilgrims listened to Graff's words.

"Don't mishear me, however. There are passages that seem to...disagree with themselves. It is out of this disagreement, though, that one can find harmony if he or she looks hard enough. After all, children, the Four emerged in the forms they have now because of disagreement that led to harmony. Not harmonization, mind you, which would only serve to pervert a greater truth, mysterious though it may be. No, I mean harmony. Harmony, children, is the stuff of peace. The provinces are not at peace, children. We know that the fifth province's Industrial District is struggling to get back on its feet. We know that many in the first province are wondering how they will satiate hungry bellies, soothe hurts, and meet needs. I have made painstaking supplication to the Four, children. I would encourage you all to do the same. We are being drenched by a deluge of unanswered prayers. Listen, children, to what happened the last time the people relied on their pedantic manufactured views rather than on the providence of the Four:

"'Certain people had abandoned their innate sense of goodness and manipulated this power for evil. Others used it for good and the advancement of their lives. These two groups clashed, and they began using this power of enchantment to destroy each other. The Ancients named this power of enchantment Raujj. The Four were so distraught with the beings that they pulled the knowledge of the Raujj forcefully from the minds of the beings. People vainly sought to continue its use for personal gain, and for a long time the Ancients turned from the Four. Because of this, the Four sent a great disaster upon the planet to punish them all. Many died, and those who did not die were forced from the place they were living in to find new land. Those that attempted to use it after that point were killed or driven into madness.'

"This is from our creation story, children, our genesis, our origin. Are we the cause of these unanswered prayers? Not even I can say, children. Listen though to a piece of the oft-perverted puzzle that haunts my steps:

"'Eventually, those that had mastered the gift of mathematics and were highly devoted to the worship of the Four found that they could manipulate the world around them when in a heightened state of spiritual sensitivity. The Four did not want this to happen, for fear that the people might become independent from their power.'

"Keep that in mind, children. There's more: 'What the Four could not remove, however, were the writings that the beings had created regarding the Raujj.'

"The Four, it would seem, have the power to destroy, to take away, and to modify things that they have created. The Raujj, children, though discovered by the Ancients, was not a creation of the Ancients. It was a discovery of a part to a greater whole that is the power of the Four. The writings, however, the things that the Ancients created, the Four could not destroy, could not remove, and could not modify."

The devotees shifted uneasily as they stood before the high priest. Was he questioning the power of the Four, or was he simply trying to build confidence within the devotees?

"It is time that we make our own peace! It is time that we attack the opponents of harmony as though they were a disease! It is time to rise up and answer the call of those in need! It is time, children, to make peace happen on our own terms! We can do it in the name of the Four, and if we create the peace, then not even they can take it away from us or ignore our want, no, our need for it!"

His hands were raised in the air as he walked among them, shouting his call for the creation of their own peace. He knew from their applause, from their cries of praise (some to him, some to the Four), that they didn't react at all negatively to his first tug away from the Four. Either they didn't care, didn't notice, or were too confused to react at present. Whatever the case, he returned to his place up the steps and stood before them once again.

"Children, I must go. Please visit the murals, the paintings, the statues. They are as old as the Ancients and tell our story. Write about them, talk about them to your children and your children's children. Go now and do ... what is bid of you."

The latter was too close for comfort. Graff had become so used to the idea of his own deification that he almost ran the risk of destroying his hopes of manipulation early in the game. As the pilgrims filed out of the sanctum, some greeting Aevier as they left, Graff returned to the ancient book that rested on the glass stand. When the last devotee had left, Graff made the *Codicil* hover over his right hand as he often did, and leaned on the serpentine staff with his left. There was scarce a time that Aevier saw the high priest without it and knew that this was not his first time through it; no, he had a feeling that Graff had read that book too many times to count. He walked forward and knelt at the base of the steps. Graff closed the book, and it floated back to its place on the stand.

"What news have you brought me from the council, my graceful marionette?"

"My Lord, ze council has agreed zat only ze basilica has ze authority to claim possession of ze Chest of Vorlds. I could not convince zhem zat Oronus had ze chest, but zhey voted to interrogate him after ze construction of ze new facility begins. Melinda Stockstill, I feel, is coming over to my side. Things are going vell for you, my Lord."

"Oh my. And what of Gwen Alden? There were seven people at your little get-together, yet you told me there would only be six. Did you mention Joseph Thomas for nomination?"

"No, my Lord, zhey had already made Gven a provincial director by ze time I arrived."

"Oh my, marionette. I suppose it wouldn't augur well for us to kill her. You can, however, dance your graceful dance and make her appear unfavorable somehow."

"She did create a proposal to investigate ze cause of ze explosion on ze grounds zat it might have been our men in Restivar."

Eleazer smiled his sickening smile. "Oh my, very good. Perhaps you could dance her into appearing in a vengeful light, or perhaps make it seem as though she tampered with evidence.

Gwen Alden would then have to be removed by the council. A widowed noble, holding just enough power and knowledge to be dangerous. Keep that in mind, marionette. Go now, and do my bidding."

Aevier rose and turned to walk out of the Sanctum of the Four. "One more thing, o loyal servant." Aevier turned to kneel and bumped his head on something, though he saw nothing there. He reached out to cover his face with one hand and swat the air with the other, but he felt nothing.

"What are you doing? Have you gone mad?"

Aevier stopped and knelt at once, feeling foolish and very confused. "No, my Lord."

"Good. Once Gwen has been branded as a manipulator of truths, see what you can do about ensuring that Edgar, Thacker, and Simon end up with jobs in the first province soon. Edgar's name will no doubt be mentioned when the investigation begins, but if Gwen has manipulated evidence, then the council will have its hands tied."

Jacques rose and left the basilica, looking all around him, all the way to the ship. He knew his head hit something. Back in the sanctum, Graff opened the book once again.

"Oh my. I wonder whose little flying machine that was? Though, invisibility narrows my guesses to one person. No matter. I'll be seeing him shortly anyway."

CHAPTER 18

Oronus, Aaron and Anna watched the activity in the hangar as they came up the bridgeway. Many of the piles were gone, and people that didn't even work there were wearing the dark blue of the hangar with the white O.R.T. on the breast. They found Parrus in the midst of the effort, laughing and talking with Estelle Nichols and Johannes Addlebrecht, the directors of the third and fourth provinces.

Oronus walked up with a surprised smile and greeted the bunch. "Well! What is all of this? Estelle, Johannes, great to see you both! What do we have here?"

Johannes clapped Oronus on the back and laughed. "We thought you could use a hand, Oronus! There are volunteers from the third, fourth, and fifth provinces here right now, and after a time, they will ship out, and groups from the second, sixth, and seventh will be arriving. The people of the first province are focused on the new production facility, but Melinda sends her regards."

Oronus smiled. "This is more than we could have hoped for. Thank you all so much." He looked up to Parrus's office to make sure that no one was occupying it. "Let's all talk in private, shall we?" He motioned to Parrus's office, and they walked there together, commenting on the progress that was being made. They entered, and Oronus activated the automatic shutters that closed them off from the eyes of those on the hangar floor below.

"Are we taking any steps to find out who did this? If this act was intentional, then I want to find who did it and ensure that it can never happen to anyone again."

Estelle nodded and spoke. "Gwen wants to head up an investigatory team that would look into the cause of the explosion. The council approved her proposal."

Oronus nodded. "Yes, Melinda told me about that. However, you know better than I do that this does not answer my question. Are we taking any steps to find out who did this? Is anyone watching those *cowards* in Restivar?"

Parrus shifted uncomfortably on his toes.

"Oronus..." Johannes stood from the window ledge he was leaning on behind Oronus. "Calm down. Think through this, Oronus. We cannot single out a particular group from the start. We need to collect evidence, samples, toy with timelines. Also, it would be a bad idea to conduct an investigation so openly in front of volunteers from across the provinces. It could have been anyone, Oronus."

"No, it couldn't have! The only people that *could* have done it were people that would have been around Alden's *personal* ship. That would be anyone and everyone at Council Headquarters in CentrePointe and any and everyone in the director's mansion at Harrah. Richard *never* flew that thing anywhere else, and there are many people who can attest to that. I *guarantee* you that if we look close enough we can connect one of those traitors back to Restivar! The obstinate sluggishness of the council reveals itself when push comes to shove, I see. Gods!" Oronus slammed his fist down and dented a metal table.

Johannes squinted, and his jaw jutted out. "The same council that time and time again saved your hide from Aevier and his agenda? That council? The same council that has granted O.R.T. more autonomy than *any* organization in *any* district in *any* province? That council? Because I'm a little confused here, Oronus!"

"If my grandfather and father hadn't done what they did, who *knows* what could have happened to us! We are *all* in their debt, and I owe it to them to continue their work! There is a threat out there that could change all that! Who knows what could happen?"

"Maybe *nothing*, Oronus! Maybe *nothing* will happen! We're so in the dark on most of what happens with the Ancients' possessions that this could all just be *harmless* information!"

"That's easy to say for someone who hasn't seen their father attempt to use the Raujj and accidentally *kill* a man!"

"Enough. Enough!" Anna had finally broken his silence. "This is getting you nowhere. Just a minute ago, you were down there laughing and talking about hope and prosperity, and now you are fighting like children, so *stop* it. I don't think that any of you realize that we still haven't honored our dead! They're just lined up in rooms in the medical bay, and the people that loved them and worked with them haven't stopped working since the explosion! What does any of this matter if you are so self-absorbed that you can't stop for a simple memorial ceremony? Look at them." Anna activated the automatic shutters, and Oronus looked down on the people in the hangar.

Parrus spoke. "They're from all over. Look at them. There's no distinction now. They're united. They're working tirelessly. I can't even recall how many people came up to me, wondering about the dead and their families and the wounded. We need to honor that, Oronus."

Oronus looked down at the dent in the table. He was ashamed. He had been so caught up with his father and the revelation of Graff's intentions that he forgot about what had happened before that. He walked over to the communications panel and pressed every single call button. "This is Captain Oronus of O.R.T. Please stop what you are doing and listen. As you are all aware, the personal craft of Director Richard Alden exploded in the hangar of O.R.T., killing the director, his crew, and hundreds of engineers, mechanics, cartographers, navigators, and general staff. You all have been hard at work since that time, and many of you have been forced into promotions. Many of you that are here now don't even work at O.R.T. Your resolve gave the other provinces hope, and the provinces' response has bolstered that resolve and prompted our gratitude and thanks. Now, I don't know if this was an accident or if someone intentionally committed this heinous act against O.R.T., the fifth province, the families of those who died, and the family of Richard Alden, but it is evident that they cannot destroy the power of unity and of hope. I want those who have been planning the memorial ceremony and all department heads to meet me in Parrus Vademe's office immediately. As for the rest of you: eat, drink, sleep, share fond memories, and take *showers!* Fellowship is what we need right now. We will send the fallen to their families today and tomorrow. In four days' time, when the arrangements are completed and the high priest has arrived, we will hold a memorial ceremony here in the hangar as the sun is setting. There will be time for mourning as well as the celebration of life, but for now you shall rest."

Just then, Victoria chimed in from Linguistics: "Attention, hangar staff and volunteers! Food and refreshments, courtesy of the people of the fourth and fifth provinces, will be brought out shortly!"

Oronus turned to face Johannes. "Forgive me, Director Addlebrecht."

He stuck out his hand to the wise, old director, thinking to himself that he should follow his own advice and think of all the angles. "Do not even think on it, Oronus. Your words were well received by all."

They shook hands and turned to face Parrus and Estelle.

Estelle smiled and stood from her chair. "I feel much more at ease now. I must return to CentrePointe, though; I am speaking at a charity event for a local community service organization. I will return for the memorial service. Thank you, Oronus."

She left and Johannes chuckled. "She has always been more involved than the rest of us with the individuals of her community. Shames us all. Well, I suppose I must take my leave as well. I'll see you all at sundown in four days."

He walked out, shaking Parrus's hand before he left. Oronus clapped Parrus.

"Thank you, Parrus and Anna. You are truly assets to the leadership of this facility."

Parrus smiled shook Oronus's hand, and Anna hugged him tightly.

Oronus sighed. "Well, I am going to go and check on Dad."

Parrus nodded as Oronus left down the bridgeway to Re-Creation.

Down on the hangar floor, volunteers and O.R.T. staff enjoyed the tastes of baked fish and fowl, with homemade bread and freshly grown carrots, onions, and potatoes. Baskets of fresh apples, grapes, and strawberries were passed around the bunch, and they washed it all down with cool apple cider from the personal stocks of Johannes Addlebrecht himself. Some sat on the broken eastern wall, legs dangling over the edge of the hangar, while others headed to the medical bay to use one of the many showers there. Parrus sat down and smiled. This was a pleasant alternative to the situation they had been in not long ago. Chaos and fear were replaced by organization and fellowship.

∽

Oronus entered the glass room and approached one of the nurses, Dorothea had gone back to the medical bay when the volunteer nurses from Nurenhanzer had arrived. "Nurse, how is he doing?"

"He is stable, and all his vital signs have improved. He still hasn't woken up though."

Oronus sighed and nodded. He needed his father to be awake now more than ever. "Is he still receiving sedatives?"

"Yes. We want to continue administering the sedative until his vitals have reached a certain benchmark that Dorothea set. It shouldn't be too much longer now."

"Thank you, Nurse." He turned and went to sit next to Osiris.

"Come on, Dad. I need you to wake up. We have a lot to discuss."

~

Meanwhile, in Restivar, Melinda Stockstill spoke to a crowd of thousands gathered around communication panels in their homes or in public stores and markets.

"People of Restivar and the first province, I come to you this evening with wonderful news. As you all have heard, the explosion at O.R.T. in the fifth province has left the market of craft production in need. The facility is being restored as I speak to you, but based on some recent decisions by the Council of Directors, it will not resume its former workload. As of the last meeting of the Council of Directors, it has been decided that a new craft production facility will be built east of Restivar over an abandoned fuel-recovery site. The workforce that it will take to build the facility to council-approved specifications and to run the actual facility will be in the thousands. The council has agreed to reserve these positions for the people of the first province! Over time, the facility will boost our economic stability and employ many of those who lost their jobs so long ago and are still struggling today. With the leadership assistance and financial assistance of O.R.T. and the financial assistance of the Basilica of the Four, construction on the airship production facility will begin in two week's time. You need to know that the people of the other provinces and the Council of Directors are excited to bring Restivar and the first province the prosperity and flow of commerce that it deserves! There will be liaisons from my office in every market district of every city and town in the first province beginning in two days' time. This is where you may sign up for work with the construction and maintenance of the facility or full-time employment within the facility. Don't forget to register, don't forget the date of ground breaking, and may the blessings of the Four be upon you all."

People across the first province were celebrating their new-found chance for success. Men and young boys across the province were preparing to travel to Restivar after they had registered. Job security was something they had not experienced in quite some time. It was an anxious and slow-going two days for the people of the first province, but when the time came, almost every able-bodied man not already employed flocked to one of the many liaison sites to register, and from there they found a way (many on cargo ships) to Restivar to become familiar with and find a place to stay in the city that would be their home for the coming months. After the registration, Melinda left for Harrah. In fact, all of the directors, all district heads, and all family members and friends would soon gather there to remember a better time that had so recently and so violently passed into the realm of memories.

"Captain, do you have a moment?" Brevard walked into Oronus's office, black shirt replacing the usual bright pink.

"Of course, Brevard. What can I do for you?"

"Actually, Captain, the question is what can *I* do for *you?*"

"I don't know what you mean, Brevard; I don't suppose I really *need* anything. The memorial service is planned, the high priest has been notified, the volunteers have been fed, and the hangar is being repaired—"

"I'm talking about *you*, Captain. *You.* What do *you* need? You are under a considerable amount of stress, Captain. Simply know this: I have been with this district since the days of Osiris, and I would do anything to see that the legacy continues. Now you know as well as I do that the riffraff from Restivar, those scandalous scalawags, are responsible for this mess. I am in the business of utilizing technology, Captain, and I have been tinkering with a few new toys that I think might help us answer back to those traitors."

Oronus looked at Brevard for a while, thinking. "Brevard, I want nothing more than to fly down there, get my ship, and destroy their camp beyond repair. I want to see Edgar executed at the hands of the council. I want Richard's and Dardus's deaths avenged. I want them to apologize to every man, woman, and child affected by this, and then I want them all to hang."

Thoreau clapped his hands together and scooted forward on his seat. "Then you know what you need! Let me help you. The council will slug through an investigation and nothing will happen! We can take matters into our own hands, Captain! We could wipe them out!"

"No, Brevard, that's what I want. I *want* all of those things. What I *need* is for you to continue confiding in me, for you and the other heads to show hope and resolve in the coming days. I need the love of my daughter, the strength of my son, the good graces of the council, the Chest of Worlds to be destroyed, the Raujj to be erased, the remains of the fallen sent to their families, O.R.T. to function again, the people to understand that this place will never return to the way it was and to keep them here in spite of this, to talk with my daughter about her mother before we forget her, to talk to my father about his son before it's too late, peace, Brevard. I need peace again."

"And that," said Brevard, rising from his seat in admiration and ashamedness, a single tear rolling down his face, "is why you will be remembered as the greatest leader this facility has ever had."

CHAPTER 19

It was autumn then. The hot winds of summer had settled down to cool breezes. The memorial service would not begin until the sun had fully set, yet dozens of airships were already floating at hangar level, waiting. Three of O.R.T.'s airships were going back and forth from these floating guest ships to the hangar, transporting the family and friends of the fallen to O.R.T. Rows and rows of chairs had been set up in the hangar in five great sections. These sections formed a half circle around Parrus's office on the southern wall, where all of the speaking would occur by use of the communications panel. In the days leading up to the service, the bodies of the fallen were cremated and placed in urns, with no urn being exactly the same; there was a name (when the remains were recognizable) on each urn.

This process had been long and difficult, for even though they had the names of everyone who had died, they often couldn't definitively place the names with the remains. These urns lined long, cloth-covered tables below the large window of the office and in front of the chairs. There were 387 in total. People were walking along the tables, some praying, others simply reading the names, and others still placing items of significance by the urns of those who were close to them. A hush fell over the growing crowd as High Priest Eleazer Graff came walking up the bridgeway, garbed in a black robe with silver accents and that same silver stole, relying heavily on the serpentine staff. He was followed by Oronus, dressed in black, but with that same emerald green robe with gold and ruby clasp. Behind Oronus were the department heads of O.R.T. and the Council of Directors. They walked until they were parallel with the first row of the middle section of chairs and the tables of urns.

The last airship was being unloaded of its passengers, and with a signal from the high priest, the council and the department heads walked forward and took their seats on the front row of the middle section. Oronus hated this ceremonial pomp; this was a time to honor the dead, not the council. Graff, Oronus, Brevard, and Victoria walked up the stairs into Parrus's office and remained standing, facing the crowd. The final attendees had either taken their seats or were standing in the back along the docked O.R.T. ships. Graff stepped forward and gestured that everyone should be seated. When silence had been achieved, he spoke.

"Your presence, children, is a living testament of the significance of each person whose lives were so suddenly sprung from the mortal coil. Life throws us into meaningful connections that resonate an emptiness when they are ended. We are here to recognize that newfound emptiness, children, but we are also here to recognize and strengthen meaningful connections with friends and family still with us.

"No one, children, no one is prepared for a day like today or the events that led to this day—indeed we have been caught off guard by grief, anger, and confusion. But just as the Four attempted to counter chaos, hate, injustice, and condemnation with purity, love, justice, and grace, so do we attempt to counter grief, anger, and confusion with peace, appreciation, and understanding. We now understand that over a month ago a ship exploded in this facility, killing hundreds and injuring several more. We also understand that the response was swift, and what once was the scene of death and destruction is now the sanctum from which we honor the dead. We appreciate their contributions to this place and to our society, children, and we appreciate their willingness to share themselves with you all. Through this understanding and appreciation, we are able to experience a peace within our minds and souls, perhaps not at first, but through the healing of time and the providence of the Four, peace can come again to those who lose it."

Brevard and Victoria, now holding two, long candles each, walked ahead of the high priest and down the stairs. The final, faint light of the setting sun caused the hangar to glow a waning orange. They reached the first urn, and Graff turned to face the crowd.

"May the names of these children who have returned to the Void be read in your hearing, that they may not be forgotten but honored in the sight of this community and in the sight of the Four."

He walked to the middle of the long row of urns and turned to face the middle urn.

"Richard Alden." Brevard said the name boldly as Victoria poured wax into a small indentation on the lid of the urn.

High Priest Graff placed a ring on his finger, a signet ring housing one of the symbols of the Four Representations: four ornate circles, interwoven. He pressed the ring into the wax, saying, "May the blessings of the Four be upon you, Richard Alden, now and for eternity."

Oronus looked down from the office at Gwen, who sat in silence, tears rolling down her cheeks. The death of her husband had changed her, and he didn't know whether or not this change was for the better. Victoria spoke next.

"Dardus Hale." Brevard poured the wax, and the high priest repeated the ceremonial rite. This continued until every name had been read, every urn blessed by Graff. The hangar was filled with the sounds of weeping, and Oronus was filling with hatred for whoever caused this. He fought back angry tears and focused once again on the calling of the names. When it was finished, the sun had fully set, and the moon began its course through the black expanse of sky, accented by countless burning stars. Brevard and Victoria began lighting candles along the tables and along the aisles. Person after person continued lighting candles, passing the light from one to the next, and placing them back on their stands. When the final candle was lit, the hangar was glowing with the ebb and flow of warm candlelight. Faces were clearer, shadows were dancing along the walls, and Oronus stood and addressed them all.

"We have come, as the high priest said, to a new understanding in our lives. In the same light, I will relent to you one thing that we will never understand: why this happened. Why anything like this happens. Why innocents die. Why evil overtakes good, if only for a moment. I am fairly certain that no one will ever give us that answer. What I *can* tell you, however, is this: though the winds of gratuitous fate blow against us, though the wanton grasp of death grips us prematurely, though the unjustified acts of the wicked seek to suppress us, we find a way to show our love. Love is the response to the hurt we feel. You see, love created the relationships we once physically shared with these, our family, our friends. A force in this world—call it evil, call it the absence of love, call it the molestation of love—sought to end the love we felt, sought to cause sadness and replace love with fear. It is clear that we are saddened. It is clear that we feel loss. But the folly of those who seek to destroy the love we feel is that we are not responding out of fear but out of the very love we felt! If anything has happened to our love, it is that it has grown because of this! Love will not be taken from us. Love will win the day. At the approval of myself and the department heads of O.R.T., a statue of the Representation of Love will be placed in the center of the hangar. It will rise forty-five feet in the air, and at its base will be the names of every person we honored here tonight."

The crowd burst into applause. Graff stepped forward in the office once again and addressed the crowd.

"Children, as we leave this place, let us never forget those who have gone on before us into the Void. In this new hour, as the new day comes, let us strive toward a day when violent acts cease and when the provinces are united in the spirit of fellowship and well-being. Now, let us rise and honor the fallen with our prayers."

They rose, and each person walked along the tables offering prayers, touching the urns, and singing songs. It was well into the early morning hours when the ceremony had finished, and after the crowd had processed along the tables, family members collected the urns of their loved ones to return them to their home provinces, where individual services would be held in a more intimate setting. O.R.T. crew members were returning guests to their hovering ships as nobles from the provinces, O.R.T. department heads, provincial directors, and the high priest mingled in front of the now empty tables. Oronus was speaking with Johannes and Michael as the high priest approached and greeted them.

"My condolences to the people of your provinces, Directors. And to you, Oronus, again I offer my deepest sympathies for the injustices you have endured of late."

Johannes and Michael shook hands with the high priest and excused themselves from the group. Oronus smiled and nodded at Graff and then turned to leave but felt a cold hand grip his own. Graff pulled Oronus in close and whispered in his ear. Oronus struggled for release to no avail. His whisper was harsh.

"Two things, you ridiculous fool. If you don't want something like this to happen again, then I suggest you pull your little invisible friend off of my disciple. My knowledge of what you toy with here runs deeper than you guess. Also, I believe that you have something of mine, something that I have been searching for for a long time now. No amount of hiding is going to make me believe otherwise. I have also seen more than you guess."

"You..." Oronus struggled again to get away from the high priest's grip.

"Ah! Not so fast now," Graff said as he pulled Oronus in closer amidst the group of people, "I'm not finished yet. How is your father, I wonder? Thirsty? Yes, I thought as much. My sympathies for your impending loss. With Jacques helping me unite the provinces under the banner of the basilica, I should have no trouble demonizing you in their eyes if it becomes necessary."

Oronus smiled at this. "Oh, I'm sure you'll do that whether or not it's necessary, Graff. We might all be in trouble if your 'children' did what you do as well as what you say. I can only hope that the connection between you and that first province scum is exposed in good order; it would seem that all roads of wickedness in the provinces are leading straight to you."

Graff pulled a small, thin blade from the folds of his vestments and struck Oronus in his side so quickly that Oronus thought he was simply being punched. Graff returned the knife just as quickly as he had unsheathed it and pulled Oronus even closer; there was literally a hair's breadth between his mouth and Oronus's ear.

"Oh my...all roads do lead to me, Oronus. Or perhaps I should say all roads will lead to me when the time comes. Do you know who I am, child? I am God. All I need is the Chest of Worlds. Stand in my way, and you shall perish. Stand aside, and I'll only kill those closest to you. Choose, child. The divine hour is approaching when I will be enthroned with the crown of providence, the robe of salvation, yea, the sword of judgment; it falls on you, child."

Graff released Oronus and disappeared into a crowd of guests waiting to board their ships, greeting them and smiling his sickening smile of deception. Oronus began to walk toward the bridgeway. He was angry, and he was afraid; afraid of what he had just heard, afraid of the confirmation that all the events that led to this moment were orchestrated by Graff. The chest had to leave, and soon. He reached the ramp of the bridgeway and felt a hand on his shoulder. He grabbed it, twisting the arm it was connected to and forcing its owner to her knees.

"Anna!" Oronus shouted as he lifted her up off the ground. "I'm so sorry, sweetheart! I thought you were...well, I thought you were someone else." Anna rubbed her wrist and shook her arm around, looking at her father with a strange expression.

"Are you okay, Daddy?" she reached her arms through his cape and hugged his waist. "You seem really tense."

He smiled and hugged her back, kissing her on the forehead. "I'm fine, sweetheart. I'm just ready for this to be over."

"Me too, Daddy." Anna squeezed Oronus. He winced and pulled away from her.

"What's wrong, Daddy?"

"Nothing, honey, I just hit my side earlier. I'll be o—"

His eyes widened as he looked down at Anna's right sleeve; the black and white ceremonial dress she was wearing was now a deep red where she had hugged him. He immediately put his hand where the knife had entered and felt a wet spot. He brought his hand up to his face, and his fingertips were the same dark red as Anna's sleeve.

"Daddy! What happened to you?"

"I'm going to your grandfather's room. Find Dorothea and have her meet me there. Quickly, now." He turned and continued down the bridgeway as Anna stood stationary in complete confusion, staring at her bloody sleeve.

Oronus was now feeling pain every time he breathed, every time he took a step. He reached the platform for Re-Creation and dropped to one knee, taking quick, painful gasps.

"Graff, you fool..."

He woke up. It was dark, and he was lying in a bed next to Osiris in the glass room. He closed his eyes and felt his side; he felt gauze and tape. The cool air from the ventilation system generated for Oronus one of those "comfort sounds" that developed through a childhood spent in the place. He looked over at his father, slumbering contently with the slow trickle of water running down his throat. Across from Osiris, Dorothea was napping in a chair against the glass wall. He rose from the bed and stretched; more pain at his side. He had no idea what time it was. He grabbed his cape from a chair across the room and put it on then headed for the door.

"I see you've been introduced to Graff's little blade."

Oronus turned to look at his father. It was dark, and Osiris looked odd in the dim room, smiling with that tube coming out of his mouth.

"How did you know that?"

Osiris waved him over to the side of the bed. He leaned over as Osiris lifted his shirt to expose several small scars on his sides and on his chest. "The Raujj was not the only method that the high priest used to torture me, Son. Listen to me: with our combined testimonies we could create a case against Graff to the council."

Oronus shook his head. "No, Dad, we can't. It's too late for that. At this point, you couldn't testify that your name is Osiris and have the council believe you, and if I told someone that the high priest of the Basilica of the Four stabbed me in stomach with a hidden knife at a funeral, I would be in the same position you are."

"And what *position* is that?"

"Dad, you drove off the hangar in a hovering craft. Then, you disappeared for eight years. Everyone that knows about it is convinced that you were completely mad before you died. Obviously, you didn't die—"

"And I'm *not* crazy either. Don't try to insinuate it."

Oronus stepped back and lowered his head, showing his palms to Osiris as if to say "all right, you win." He had no idea how their conversation had turned so sour. "I am sorry. That was not my intent." He walked back around and sat down on the edge of his own bed. "The council is already unified on many issues dealing with O.R.T., Dad. They're about to break ground on the new craft production facility in Restivar, start the investigation into the cause of the explosion, and question *me* on the whereabouts of the Chest of Worlds. I think the best thing is to give the council whatever they want on the first two issues, which won't be difficult considering they're headed by Gwen and Melinda. This will allow us to lay low for quite a while. As far as the chest is concerned, though, the minute that they try to even *hint* at forcing it into Graff's hands, I'm sending it away. I fear that it will soon be too dangerous to keep the chest here, though I guess there really is no safe place for it now."

"Yes there is," Osiris smirked as he looked at Oronus's confused expression. "Think of the where, Son, the who, the why. Remember the questions."

Oronus pursed his lips in a half smile, raised his eyebrows, and shrugged.

Osiris rolled his eyes and then pointed a finger at his temple. "Why, in the seventh province, of course!"

CHAPTER 20

Aaron woke up around the same time in the safe room, sprawled out on the steps below the table that housed the Chest of Worlds. He had come here during the memorial ceremony; it was simply too much for him. He rolled up to his knees, stretching and yawning. He stood and stared down at the chest, running his fingers over the foreign markings and thinking back over the past few months. He thought back to the weeks leading up to his decision to enter the House of Ancients alone, how peaceful everything had been, how carefree the atmosphere was. He remembered in anguish the only reason he even wanted to go through with it: jealousy. Dardus Hale had risen faster in the ranks than any employee O.R.T. had ever seen. Oronus had grown up with him, and, aside from Oronus, Dardus knew the most about the goings-on of the place. He knew he was Oronus's apprentice and that Oronus had every intention of naming him successor someday, but jealousy overtook him. If he could please his master more than Dardus ever could, then he would prove himself to be the logical choice. Now Dardus was dead, the Great House had collapsed, and the Chest of Worlds had thrown them all into an alternate fate. He gripped the sides of the chest as though he could will the thing away into the Void with his mind. At that moment, the room dimmed, and Aaron felt an awful sickness creep over him. His muscles were burning, his skin was hot, and his stomach churned. His head pounded fiercely as a series of conversations flashed violently through his head.

"Who are you? Who sent you?"

"Don't be afraid. I mean you no harm. My name is Eleazer. I am a student of the Basilica of the Four. High Priest Nicodemus sends his regards. I was sent here by—"

⌇

"What was it like? I mean, seeing with two sets of eyes? What was it like to enter his mind?"

"Well, young Eleazer, I must confess it was the most mind-blowing experience of my life. I really had to struggle to maintain my sanity."

⌇

"Well, the *Book of the Four* is very ... open ... to interpretation on how one is to achieve metaphysical enlightenment, and the mathematical theorems aren't even addressed—but you are a priest in training. Surely you know this. Why do you ask?"

"I'm just curious. I mean, you weren't even supposed to get as far as you did, Captain. I just want to know the process you went through."

"I don't know, Eleazer. I don't think that I should—"

"Please."

"All right."

⌇

"I just don't understand it enough to get anywhere with these things you've assigned me to collect from O.R.T. My knowledge of the Ancients' language is very basic. High Priest Nicodemus is more concerned with outreach than scholarship—I have nothing to learn from him."

"Well, I don't know about that. Nicodemus has a wonderful way of reaching those that can't make the pilgrimage, young priest."

"Please, Captain Osiris. I just want a more complete knowledge of the language—finish my knowledge."

"All right, young priest. I've never been one to discourage scholarship."

~

"I don't understand, Captain. is obviously wrong."

"Don't get discouraged, Priest Graff. This is just one book's account. Don't place too much stock in it."

"But according to you, this is practically the earliest account. Tell me more about what it contains! This is important!"

"No, not even for you. The knowledge in this book will die with me."

"If the Four aren't real, then why am I even alive? Tell me what the book contains!"

"I am sorry. I cannot."

"I'm so sorry, young priest. High Priest Nicodemus was a true servant of the Four. How did he die?"

"I know not. He was old and frail. I have collected more texts from O.R.T. None of this is adding up, Osiris. Tell me what is in the book."

"I want to help you. I have helped you. Stop asking this of me."

~

"I am now the high priest of the basilica, Captain. I now have access to the archives. I grow increasingly concerned with the dissonance rising from these accounts. Please give me the book."

"No. We've already been through this—"

"What do you know about the Chest of Worlds?"

"Why would you—"

"Answer me, old man. I grow impatient with your prevarications."

"Where is the book? Give it to me, and I will release you."

"Never, High Priest. I have already given you too much."

"That was your last chance. Now I will take your life from you. This will be ... unpleasant."

"No! Please! Agh!"

～

Aaron fell backwards from the chest and collided with the floor. Rolling to his feet, he sprinted from the room in fear and confusion.

The guards chased after him. "Sir! Are you all right?"

"Get back!" he shouted, still in a state of panic. Aaron left the safe room and ran into the dark hallway, where he slid his back down one of the walls and buried his face in his hands. "What is going on?" He remained there for some time, rocking back and forth with the vivid image of the transformation of Graff from a mere student into a monster.

～

Gwen docked at O.R.T. with the other directors and a citizen from each province. She walked down the ramp and was greeted by Parrus and the others who had already gotten off of their respective ships.

"Welcome, council members and gracious citizens of the provinces. I will alert Oronus of your arrival. Please feel free to walk around and view the marvelous improvements we have made, even since the ceremony. We're very excited about reopening. I'll be back shortly." Parrus went to his office to contact Oronus on the communications panel.

Aevier turned and looked at them all. "Zhey have made much progress on zis place. I am impressed."

Johannes nodded in agreement. "Very true, Jacques. Parrus was right—this looks even better than it did during the memorial ceremony."

The group walked around the hangar together noting improvements and was standing around a group of engineers and mechanics who were constructing the enormous Representation of Love in the center of the hangar when Oronus approached them. "Hello, everyone. Welcome back. Please know that we will do whatever we can to ensure that this investigation runs smoothly."

Gwen turned and smiled. "Hello, Oronus. Firstly, we would like to get as close to the site of the explosion as we can, if that's possible."

Oronus nodded. "All right. Some of my men have cleared a path to the remains of the ship while trying to leave it and the area around it untouched. Parrus, please show them to the bridgeway." Parrus nodded and waved the group over to him as Oronus called out to Gwen.

"Gwen, could I have a word with you?" She turned and walked over to him, smiling.

Aevier turned and looked at them both. "Don't be too long, Lady Alden. Remember, you are ze head of zis little endeavor, however futile it may be."

She smiled at Jacques insincerely and addressed Oronus. "Of course, Oronus. What is it?"

"I know what you are doing, Gwen—I know about Max."

She frowned and furrowed her brow. "What are you talking about, Oronus?"

"Please, Gwen. We've known each other for many years; don't lie to me. I know that you have Max tailing Aevier."

She sighed and threw her hands up in the air, walking past him. "How did you know?"

Oronus turned to face her. "Graff told me."

"What? How can this be? How does he know?"

Oronus shook his head. "It doesn't matter how he knows, Gwen. He *knows*. This was foolish of you to do."

She leaned in with a disgusted look on her face. "Don't lecture *me* on what's prudent regarding policy and procedure, Oronus. Besides, this only *proves* that they are in league together."

"No, it doesn't. The only thing it proves is that you are spying on another member of the council, and whether or not Jacques deserves it, which I think he does, the council will fry you if Graff tells Jacques."

"Put yourself in *my* shoes, Oronus! What wouldn't you do to figure out who killed Rachel if *she* was murdered, hmm?" She walked passed him and brushed his shoulder with hers as she headed for the bridgeway.

Oronus walked after her and grabbed her arm. "Gwen, bring Max back. This is not safe at all. I will do everything in my power to help you with this investigation, but if Aevier finds out you're spying on him, it could nullify anything you say or do regarding work within the council's authority, which *includes* this investigation!"

"Fine." She pulled her arm free and continued to the bridgeway. Oronus looked down at his hands and sighed. As the group descended out of sight, Max wavered into view beside him.

"Master Oronus, it seems as though I am now in *your* possession once again."

Oronus looked at Max and smiled. "Max, please come with me. Cloak yourself before we continue."

"Yes, Master Oronus." Oronus led Max to the safe room. When the elevator doors opened to the hallway leading to the safe room, Oronus spotted a large mass in the darkness against the wall. He drew his pistol.

"Identify yourself."

Aaron looked up at Oronus with a maddened expression. "We need to talk."

Oronus nodded. "Max, continue into the room at the end of the hall, please, and await further instructions."

"Yes, Master Oronus." Max glided away as Oronus walked forward and bent down to meet eyes with Aaron. "What's wrong?"

Aaron dropped his hands and stared into Oronus's eyes.

"I..." He shook his head and looked away. Oronus put his hands on Aaron's shoulders.

"It's okay, Aaron. Tell me."

Aaron took a deep breath. "I was in the safe room looking at the chest. I touched it, gripped it with both of my hands. My mind was racing with everything that's happened over the past few months. All of the sudden, I *saw* something. I saw pieces of events. I still don't understand."

Oronus closed his eyes. The divine artifact had to leave O.R.T. That was no longer a question. "What events, Aaron? What pieces?"

"I saw the high priest and Osiris. I saw Graff when he was a student at the basilica. Osiris slowly shared what he knew and taught Graff the Ancients' language. Everything they talked about kept leading to some book, a book that held secrets no other book held. Graff used Osiris's knowledge to learn more and more—Osiris even told Graff certain texts to claim at council meetings from O.R.T. Why would he do that? Then again, the Graff I saw in the first two or three times was different from the Graff we know. Oronus, I think... I think Graff *killed* High Priest Nicodemus. Then Graff learned something, something about the Four, something that wasn't good, as though they weren't even real. After that point, after Osiris continued to deny him the book, Graff decided to kill him. I *watched* him torturing Osiris, Oronus. I *saw* him use the Raujj. It was awful."

Oronus nodded in agreement; he already knew some of what Aaron was telling him. He did not, however, know why Brevard and Victoria would allow a student access to their archives.

"Aaron, did you find out exactly *how* Osiris contacted the high priest?" Aaron shook his head. Oronus nodded. He thought back to their previous conversations with Osiris.

"I think we all need to stay away from the chest for now, unless it becomes necessary. Why don't you go and rest? I'm sorry you had to see that."

Aaron nodded. They rose together, and Oronus patted Aaron on the back. "I have to address a matter down here. Go get some rest."

Aaron nodded again and went to the elevator. Oronus had planned on heading directly for the site of the explosion to keep an eye on Jacques, but now he thought that if he heard what Max may have recorded and could piece it together with what Aaron saw and what Osiris told him that perhaps he could gain some advantage over the high priest. He entered the safe room and looked over at the chest; he hated it more and more every time he saw it, talked about it, thought about it.

"Max. Come here please."

Max glided from a far corner to Oronus, who still stood close to the doorway. "Yes, Master Oronus. What can I do for you?"

"Max, were you able to record anything of significance while following Director Aevier?" Max issued forth several clicking sounds, touching his metallic, jointed fingers with his thumbs. Then:

"Vhy, Antalya, you honor me vist your presence at zis late hour."

"Enough with the formalities, Jacques."

"Ooooh. Far be it from me to deprive you of nature's desires."

"Skip over this, Max. Do you have anything recorded that links Jacques Aevier to High Priest Eleazer Graff?" After more clicking noises, Jacques' voice played.

"What news have you brought me from the council, my graceful marionette? Nothing too bad, I hope for your sake..."

Oronus heard the entire conversation between Graff and Aevier. When he heard that they planned to frame Gwen in the investigation, he closed his eyes and sighed.

"Gods..." Oronus turned and left, heading straight for the investigative party. He only hoped that he would get there in time; Aevier was as slippery as a snake.

~

Meanwhile, on the outskirts of Astonne, Eleazer stood high on the edge of a cliff to the north of the basilica. The hot, red wind was swirling everywhere, and he had a maddened expression on his face.

Edgar was hunkered down behind Graff, covering his face. "Oh, my puppet. Come and see what I've found!"

Edgar slinked his way to the edge, and as he looked into the valley, a tear rolled down his cheek. Graff looked over at him and smiled. "There, there, puppet. Haven't you ever seen a mass of fuel-powered airships before? This isn't a new sight for you, is it, puppet?"

"No, but it's a sight for sore eyes, Lord. I wondered what they did with all of those ships. I mean, they kept some of them for research and experiments and such, but I never—"

"Spare me your trifles, puppet! I care not. This plays incredibly to our favor, puppet. I'm sure Oronus thought he could sweep these airborne beasts under the carpet, but this is no longer the case. Puppet!"

"Yes, Lord!"

"See that you and Thacker start collecting some fuel again. If you know any reliable men, gather their help—men who care not for the system, puppet, men who can be bought. Bring it here for storage. Go now, and do my bidding."

"Yes, Lord."

Edgar ran down off of the great slope to the *Regalus*. When he reached the deck, Thacker was the first to greet him.

"You won't believe what I just saw. Let's fly for Restivar. There's building to do."

~

Oronus descended the cleared path to the lower hangar and watched as the seven directors and the seven citizens debated and searched. Johannes saw Oronus and called him down.

"Ah, Oronus, I am glad you came. We need your opinion on something we found."

Oronus walked down the charred path. Johannes held out some scraps of metal for Oronus to look at.

"What do you make of these?" He dropped the scraps into Oronus's hands. "We found them roughly where the ship's engine would have been. Parrus brought us the plans for a ship the same class as Richard's was, and we want to know where these fall in the list of materials."

Oronus examined the metal. "Well, I can tell you that it's not a part of the materials required. Obviously, you'd need a sample of anything metal in the whole lower level, given the range of the explosion. However, if I had to guess, I'd say these were tiny clamps that held some sort of hollow cylindrical piping. There aren't any pipes that small on *any* class of ship built here, though. But, as I said before, you'd need to collect all the samples you can to be sure."

Aevier smirked and nodded. "Yes, yes, it is as I said before: zis is all pure speculation! Zhere is no clear-cut vay to go about zis!"

Michael stepped in. "Oh, yes there is. We take samples of everything in this place and make sure that every single scrap we find has a reason for being here."

He walked past Aevier and over to where the seven citizens

collected materials off of the ground. Gwen and Parrus walked over to them, and Parrus spoke to Oronus. "Well, we don't have any records of Richard bringing the ship in for checkup or repairs, so I think we can assume that there were no major problems—"

"Speculation!" Everyone ignored Aevier's interjection.

"Well, I know for a fact that he only used it to go from the director's mansion to CentrePointe, so it's not as though he used it every single day," Gwen added. Oronus nodded and walked forward to the spot where the ship was, handing the scraps back to Johannes.

"Well, there are several reasons why the ship could have exploded, but all of them have to do with the engine. Overheating, combustion of the fuel reserve, though, I personally don't think that there was enough fuel to do this kind of damage; malfunctioning parts, like a faulty steam ventilator. When you finish collecting samples, I would like to see them. Perhaps I can categorize the material for you. If you find out what the state the engine was in, then you'll probably know why the ship exploded."

Oronus looked down at what remained of the ship, which was practically nothing, and he looked down the lower hangar at the damage the initial explosion had caused.

"Vell zhen, until ve collect all of zhese samples, I guess zat zhere is nothing ve can do."

"Not true, Director. Not in the slightest. There's still one more issue to deal with today." Oronus pointed at the remains of the ship—scraps of wood and metal—and then pointed down the hangar at the damages. "When the engine exploded, or was *made* to explode, the force of the blast went up and out, but with further examination, I think you'll find that the force was directed far higher than it was wide; the ceiling that used to be above us was my own design, and the council uses it as well. It was designed to prevent penetration of any kind. It would have had to have been projected upward with ridiculous force. Having said that, I don't think that the engine's exploding could have created the *widespread* damage that it did. There was some kind of assistance. Now, if those W.A.S.P.s hadn't been directly above the blast, then the ship would have simply put a large hole in the ceiling, and the upper level would have remained unscathed—"

"Vhich proves zat it vasn't strong enough to do ze damage an explosive device could do."

Oronus shook his head. "Wrong again, Director. Look down the lower level. This hangar reaches as far as the upper level does. It is highly improbable that the explosion would have traveled that far. The ceiling is high and the hangar is wide, which means that the blast funneling is out of the question, and there just weren't enough craft down here to do what those W.A.S.P.s did up there." Oronus stepped back and surveyed the scene.

Aevier scoffed. "Until any of zis can be proved, his testimony is vorthless." Gwen smiled. "You're right about that, Jacques: everyone, collect samples of the ash down here and the ash along the far southern wall in the upper hangar. If we can discover whether or not they hold different properties, then we may be able to discover if an explosive device was used."

Michael spoke. "What if we divided in two? One group could start separating recovered materials with Oronus's help, and the other could get the ash samples and take them to Nurenhanzer; their facilities are better equipped for things like this."

Oronus nodded. "Yes, we have a lab, but it may not be sufficient."

"Good idea," Gwen said. "Let's do that."

Oronus pointed over at the civilian volunteers. "Who are these people?"

"Every director selected a citizen of their province to help with the investigation—objectivity and all that," Johannes said as he walked over to Gwen and Oronus.

Melinda followed. "I'm sorry about this, but I really must be getting back to Restivar. They've already begun construction. Oronus, we need to talk about possible times for training."

"Of course, Melinda. Give me a call, and we'll make arrangements." She smiled and bid them all farewell. Gwen began directing the volunteers. "If you discover anything, please let me know—I'll be in Parrus Vademe's office in the upper level of the hangar." She walked up the ramp as everyone split up and began working.

Oronus waited a few minutes, making sure that Aevier was not paying attention, and then he followed her. He caught up with her and redirected her away from Parrus's office and toward the bridgeway that led to Re-Creation. "What is it now, Oronus?" He took her into Re-Creation, down the ramp, and into his office. He closed the door.

"I listened to what Max recorded." Gwen shot up from the chair she had claimed in front of his desk. "Does it implicate him or the first province? Tell me!"

Oronus shook his head. "Nothing they said directly implicates Aevier or the high priest, and the first province was never mentioned. He said something about it not 'auguring well' for them to kill *you*, but that doesn't prove that they were involved in Richard's death."

Gwen put her hand on her chest. "But it *does* mean that they might be after *me*, Oronus!"

He nodded at her. "Yes, it does. However, everything Max recorded is useless to the council; you are not a full member, nor was it approved. It's worthless to them."

Gwen sat down and sighed. "What do we do then?"

"There's something else you need to know, Gwen. The high priest wants Aevier to frame you for tampering with evidence to make it seem like the first province group attacked O.R.T. He told Aevier to use the angle that you are seeking revenge for Richard's death."

"Well that's not true!"

"No, I don't think it is either. Convincing the council otherwise if Aevier succeeds, though, is the problem. I think you need to step down, Gwen."

"Oronus! The only reason I drafted the investigatory committee was to allow myself to have a direct hand in finding out who did this! I can't leave the committee."

"I don't just mean the committee, Gwen. I think you should step down from the council altogether."

Gwen flexed her jaw muscles and nodded, looking down at the floor. Standing up, she said, "No. I can't do that, Oronus. This is not an option. I will just have to be more careful about what I say and do and document every single thing that happens in this investigation."

"Gwen, Eleazer Graff and Jacques Aevier are horrible people. They'll keep slithering around until Graff has the Chest of Worlds. I'm *worried* about you, Gwen. I'll be the only one left of our group if they kill you. Rachel and Richard are gone. You can still be active in the fifth province without being the director. Please, Gwen. I'm afraid they're going to ruin your life with this investigation."

She walked to the doorway and turned her head. "I'm sorry, Oronus. I have to go." She left Oronus in his office, where he stayed for the next two hours, eyes closed. Gwen returned to the site of the explosion and watched as the first group laid out the pieces and scraps they had found in organized piles on the ground. Unbeknownst to her, Aevier had selected Antalya Greigovich from the sixth province to place something in that pile given to her by Jacques that would soon spark great controversy. When the sun had set, the second group had already taken the samples to Nurenhanzer, and most of the directors had left for their respective provinces. Gwen stopped them in their work.

"All right. Volunteers, thank you so much for your help here today. You will be called upon again at the end of this process when we start the interrogations. What you have collected and sorted today will be analyzed and compared with the materials used to create a craft such as the one Director Alden used. Your cooperation and assistance will hopefully help to lead us to the cause of this mess. Thank you again."

The volunteers were leaving as Estelle, Raulph, and Jacques descended the bridgeway together. Raulph patted Gwen on the shoulder. "Well, Gwen, I think that things are going well. Once those ash samples are analyzed at Nurenhanzer and this evidence is matched up against Oronus's charts, you may very well have a strong case on your hands."

"Oronus asked zat ze evidence be brought up and placed on a table zat he has prepared in ze upper level. Shall ve?"

There were three piles left on the last trip. Gwen went for the middle pile, and Aevier quickly stooped to gather the materials, forcing Gwen to pick up the pieces in the last pile. As Gwen was walking toward the table and looking down curiously at what she held, her heart leapt into her throat. Amidst the tiny wooden and metal mess was a small, cylindrical metal pipe with the letters *G.A.* engraved on its side. She knew exactly what it was. In her private lab, when she dealt with minor amounts of combustible materials, there was a small combustion chamber with a glass casing and a small pipe that led to the metallic chamber where gasses or liquids were able to mix safely. She had no idea why it was there.

Aevier and Estelle placed their materials on the table.

Gwen hesitated and then did the same.

"Vell, I guess ve can leave. I look forward to hearing your report at ze upcoming meeting, Gven."

"I look forward to giving it. It will be good to put all of this behind us."

Aevier nodded and gathered his cape, and he and Estelle turned to leave, laughing and talking as they walked toward their ships. Gwen didn't know what do. *Why is that in there?* "So, Oronus, what are those?" she said while pointing to the schematics on the wall.

"Oh! I forgot something over at ze table. Excuse me, Director Nichols."

~

Oronus looked over at the wall. "These? Well, there are actually two kinds of schematics up here. The first one…"

As Oronus turned to point at the schematics, she grabbed the pipe and put it into her pocket.

"Vat do you think you are doing?" Aevier said.

Gwen turned in complete surprise to face him.

"Jacques! Why… what?" Gwen's heart was racing. *How could I have been so stupid? Why didn't I just leave it there?* She thought back to her conversation with Oronus. *Why didn't I listen to him?*

"Vat did you just take from ze table and put in your pocket?"

"And that is how you can tell the difference in the… What are you talking about, Jacques?" Oronus turned to face them. Estelle had stopped in her tracks and was watching them from a distance.

"I just vatched Lady Alden place something from ze evidence table in her *pocket*. Vat vas it?"

Gwen looked quickly from Jacques to Oronus. "I, well… what do you…"

"Vat did you take?" He stepped forward and reached into her jacket pocket, pulling out the small pipe. "Vat is zis? Vhy did you take it?"

Gwen turned and looked at Oronus, mouthing the words, "I'm sorry." She turned and looked at Jacques. "Well, it belongs to me. It's mine." Oronus walked around the table and stood beside Gwen. "What is it, Gwen? Tell us." She looked at him with sorrowful eyes. "It's a piece from my personal lab at the director's mansion. I don't know why it was down there. I thought I would take it back and—"

"Oh, no, no, no, Lady Alden. You do not simply decide to *take* something from an area under council-sanctioned investigation. Zis vill have to be explained in *great* detail to ze council. Given ze rules of council-sanctioned events operated by inter-province cooperation, I have ze authority to suspend you from ze investigation and ze council until you can clear your name to ze entire council at CentrePointe. Take zis, Oronus."

Aevier placed the pipe in his hands and glared at Gwen. "I don't know vhy you think you are above ze rules in zis instance, Lady Alden, but you are most definitely *not*. Are you trying to cover something up?"

"No! Are you suggesting I had something to do with this?"

"No, but how can I definitively say you *veren't* vhen I caught you stealing evidence?"

"I just didn't understand why it was even there! Why would Richard take that with him?"

"Zis is not ze time for speculation. Oronus, she must be detained by ze council until ve can question her. I must use one of your communications panels to summon the guard at CentrePointe to detain her."

"Well, now, hold on a minute—"

"Oronus, I am sorry. I don't like zis eisher. But ve are dealing vist a council issue zat is out of your range of influence. She must be detained."

Aevier went to Parrus's office. Oronus turned to face her. "Gwen, what were you thinking?"

"I thought that if they found out what that was it would take their attention off of the first province and explosives and focus on an accident caused by Richard or something. I don't know! He hated alchemy anyway! I can't even think of why that would be there. It's part of a small combustion chamber. Those clamps that Johannes found and you identified must have come from it. Oh, Oronus...what have I done?" Oronus looked up as three crew members from Aevier's ship walked toward them; one was Antalya.

Estelle stepped forward to meet her. "I just wanted to thank you for your participation today—"

The three simply walked around her and kept coming. Jacques came down from the office as his crew members approached.

"Do it, Antalya."

She nodded. "Lady Alden, you are to be detained on Director Aevier's ship until the CentrePointe guards arrive to transport you to council headquarters."

Oronus looked at Antalya; he just connected that the person on Aevier's ship that he dealt with on the day of the tour and the woman in the provocative recording were the same person. Had they done this?

"I don't think that will be necessary, Jacques. She's not a criminal."

"Unfortunately, yes it *is* necessary. And until the council can decide whether or not she *is* a criminal, then she must be kept away from the evidence and those analyzing it."

"What about those collecting it? Antalya is one of your officers as well as being one who collected evidence."

"Ah, but she collected *ash* samples, remember? No, I am simply following procedure completely vistin my authority to execute. Take her to ze ship."

She turned to Oronus. "I didn't do anything wrong. I had nothing to do with this. I didn't do anything wrong."

He looked at her with a saddened expression as they moved to either side of her. "I know."

"I am sorry about zis, Oronus. I'm sure zis is all a big misunderstanding—"

Oronus grabbed a handful of Jacques's military jacket and pulled him forward. "You listen to me, pawn. I know that you planned this with the high priest. I know you're his little slave. I know you want the chest as much as he does, but you listen to me:

if you harm her in *any* way, I will bring a firestorm down on you and your little first-province scum. I will go to that mansion and find a way to show that you took that pipe from Gwen's lab. I will *ruin* you. I don't care if I go down, I'll take you with me! Graff will never get away with this. The only thing that will worship either of you will be the maggots that use your bodies for lodging when I fling both of you from my flagship."

He released Aevier, who was wild eyed and surprised. His emotions fell somewhere between rage and a curious fear.

"Vell, sadly you *can't* prove any of zat, and even if you *could*, it vill soon be too late for any kind of action from you or zis place. Face it, Oronus, you *lose*. After ze council questions Gven and voids ze investigation, vhich zhey *vill* do, zhey are coming straight for you and ze Chest of Worlds. Good day." He turned and left.

～

Oronus walked forward after him, then stopped and punched at the air. He shouted and stormed off to his office. Slamming the door and sitting down at his desk, he sighed angrily. "Gwen! Why couldn't you just *leave* it!

He grappled through the night with the fact that their hopes of proving that the explosion was intentional were gone forever. Restivar would have its new facility, Aevier would work toward unprecedented interprovince relations, and Graff would have his way. "But he won't have the chest. I won't let him."

He got up and left for the sleeping quarters that were below the medical bay in Utilities. There he found Aaron and Anna, her head resting on his shoulder as they slept in a large chair in the corner of the room. He shed a tear as he approached them.

"Anna, Aaron. Wake up." He shook them.

"What's wrong?" Aaron said as he looked at Oronus.

"Come with me. We need to talk."

Anna sank back in the chair. "Can't we talk here?"

"No. Please, just come with me to my office."

Anna and Aaron looked at each other with some confusion and concern as they rose and followed an emotionally drained Oronus to his office in Re-Creation. They walked in and sat down together. As Oronus looked at them across the desk, he began crying once again.

"Daddy, what happened? What's wrong?"

He coughed and shook his head a little, trying to regain composure. "There's no easy way to say this to you two, so here it is: Aevier and Graff have just succeeded in implicating Gwen for stealing evidence from the hangar."

Anna was taken aback. "What? How can this be? Is it true?" *That,* Oronus thought to himself, *is a good question.*

"Yes and no. She was probably not taking anything that had to do with the explosion. I believe that Aevier had something significant of Gwen's planted in the evidence piles during the investigation in order to provoke her in some way. It worked, and she responded by taking it. Jacques caught her, and now she is being held at Council Headquarters for questioning."

Aaron leaned forward. "I am in no way trying to make light of this situation, Oronus, but what does this have to do with Anna and me?"

Oronus closed his eyes took a deep breath. "Well, this means that our hopes of proving that the explosion was intentional are virtually impossible. If the council nullifies the investigation because of Gwen's actions, then it will probably be tossed completely. The council was going to wait until the investigation was over to question me about the chest, but now I'm afraid that they will push forward with their questioning. Because Jacques was so involved and was present when you two brought the chest back, even if I lie to the rest of them, Jacques's testimony may be enough to warrant a search of this whole facility. It can't stay here. If Graff were to obtain the chest, then I fear our world would change for the worse and we would all be in danger. I don't see any other way around this: I want you two to take Osiris and the chest and leave indefinitely."

"Why us?" Aaron asked.

"Because you are the two I can trust the most, and you are the two that can leave for a while and not cause suspicion. I just can't leave this task to anyone else. It destroys me that the two that I want to keep closest to me are the two that I must send away, but I don't trust anyone else to do this. I need you two to take Osiris and the chest. Please."

"Where are we taking it?" Aaron asked of him.

Oronus smiled as he remembered the face he had made when Osiris had told him what he was about to tell them. "You're going to the seventh province, in the mountains southeast of the Basilica of the Four."

"What? Are you crazy?" Aaron was out of his chair now. "Why would we do that?"

"Sit down, Aaron. Let me explain—"

"What's there to explain? This is ridiculous!"

Oronus waited in silence for Aaron to calm down. "Graff and Aevier believe the chest is here. Aevier has even *seen* that it is here. The last place that anyone would look would be in the seventh province. It's a move that Osiris and I don't think the high priest will anticipate or entertain."

Aaron crossed his legs and his arms, looking over to Anna to shut Oronus down on this one. She had been staring down at the floor for some time, but then she spoke, still looking at the floor.

"When do we leave?" She looked up at him with a matter-of-fact expression after she had said it. Aaron turned to face her, mouth agape.

"As soon as possible tomorrow morning. Go pack your things. I will have Dorothea prep Osiris for traveling. Listen, I am contacting an inn in Astonne in the morning and reserving a room for you three. I want you to go there and wait for a few days so that if something changes I can contact you to move or come back. I will give you a map that marks where many of O.R.T.'s old fuel-powered ships are resting. The council secretly required the provinces to keep some of these ships in case of emergency. You should stow away in one of those ships. We can talk more about particulars later. Go get ready." They rose and left. Aaron didn't know what to feel. This was still so surreal to him, and he slowly resigned to the fact that they were the best fit for the task. He left in front of Anna, and Oronus stopped her as she was leaving.

"Anna, wait." She turned and he walked forward and hugged her tightly. "I love you, Daughter. More than anything."

She smiled. "I love you, Daddy." He let go, and she turned to leave.

He leaned against the doorframe. "I just killed them. I know I did." He buried his face in his hands in anguish.

CHAPTER 21

In the first province, Melinda Stockstill looked at the construction site from above in her airship. Huge artificial lights illuminated the night shift. She was so pleased with the progress that had been made. Thousands of workers had shown up, and the foundation was halfway completed. Things were looking up for the first province.

In the morning, as the sun peeked through the almost-completely covered northern wall of the hangar, Oronus stood in front of Aaron, Anna, and his father, who was sitting in a wheelchair with a portable tank of nutrient water attached to the back. The fact that he seldom ate solid food was showing physical signs now.

"Anna, your name is Gloria Smith. Aaron, you are Gregory Smith. Dad, your name is still Osiris."

"Well, that's not very exciting." Oronus rolled his eyes as Anna and Aaron laughed at Osiris's comment.

"Okay, okay. Do not say your name or talk to anyone—all they know is that Gloria and Gregory are bringing their grandfather with them. There is no way to tell who is allied with the high priest in Astonne. Listen to me. I am sending armed guards with you to protect you and the chest in case something happens along the way. After you dock at the inn, wait for three days. The guards and the crew will remain on board with the chest during that time. When the time comes, three days if everything goes to plan, I will contact the ship, saying that it is time for you all to move. The ship will take you south of the basilica and drop you off. There are some natural paths in those mountains, and you should be able to travel to the ships by foot.

"Once you are there, find an open ship or break in—I do not care which—and *wait*. You should be all right if you remain hidden. I have left some money on the ship because you will need to buy any perishable goods in the marketplace in Astonne when you get there. One more thing: *your* lives are more important to me than that stupid box. If worse comes to worst, hand it over. Do not die for that thing. Do you have everything you need? Yes? Well, I guess this is good-bye for now."

He walked up and shook Aaron's hand. "Take care of my daughter, Aaron Ravenhall. You are a brave young man." He shook hands firmly with Oronus. "And don't take advantage of the fact that I put you two in the same room!"

"Daddy!" Anna rolled her eyes as Aaron blushed, and he and Osiris chuckled. "I'm sorry, honey. Give me a hug." They embraced, and Oronus's eyes started to cloud up again. He stepped back and shook hands with his father.

"I wish we could have talked more, Dad."

Osiris smiled. "Me too, Son. Me too."

"All right then. Be careful! And don't draw attention to yourselves! If anything happens please contact me!"

He walked them to the *Tortoise*, a ship with a small dome on the deck, below which rested a special safe room for precious cargo. The ramp descended as Anna grabbed the bags and Aaron pushed Osiris into the ship.

"Good luck with the council, Son. Be brave. Protect this place and protect *yourself.* Remember to ask the right questions!"

Oronus waved as the ramp closed and the *Tortoise* sailed out of the dock and into the open air. Oronus felt so empty and sorrowful. The three people he cared about the most had gone on a dangerous mission that could get them killed, and he had helped orchestrate it. He walked over to the Representation of Love in the center of the hangar, which was now completed. Long, flowing hair and a beautiful, warm face looked down on them all now. It had a body of feminine curvature, though even he knew that the Four were supposedly without gender. The engineers and mechanics, with the help of the artists from Linguistics, made it look like it was covered with flowing strips of cloth that were blowing in the wind. She (as Oronus had resigned to call the statue) had her arms opened and curved, as if she was waiting to receive his embrace. He looked down at all the names on the plaque at her base.

"I don't know if you are real or not. I suppose you aren't, or if you are, you are just a greater part of something. I think it's okay that I don't know. If you... if you *hear* me or *see* me, I just sent three people I really love into danger. I don't know if that makes me bad, and I don't know if this even works for someone who isn't even sure of you, but it still remains that I love them very much, and if it is in your power to protect them, please do it. Don't do it for me, but do it for them; do it for the provinces. What they are doing has wide-reaching effects, and it may even affect you, I don't know. Help them if you can."

He looked around, feeling awkward, but was also slightly amused at his sudden drop in diction and maturity when addressing her—it was as though he had become a child again, speaking to an important adult for the first time. Shaking off this feeling, he left for his office to call Melinda about the training for the facility. He needed to act as if nothing was wrong, that nothing had changed. As he entered Re-Creation and headed for the rampway, he stopped and watched as the text preservers moved back into the large glass room where Osiris had been. It was the closure he needed; this was *really* happening, and he still had a job to do. He entered his office and closed the door. Sitting down at his desk, Oronus called Council Headquarters at CentrePointe on his communications panel.

"Council of Directors Headquarters. Would you like me to direct your call to a particular provincial office?"

"Yes. Please transfer me to the office of Melinda Stockstill."

"One moment please..."

"This is the office of Director Stockstill. If this is regarding construction of the new airship facility, I can transfer you directly to the director. If not, please hold, and I will transfer you to one of her aids.'"

"This is Captain Oronus Bretton of O.R.T. regarding mechanical training for the new facility."

"One moment, please, Captain..."

"Oronus!"

"Hello, Melinda. How are things coming?"

"Smoothly. I couldn't ask for better weather conditions or work ethic; these people have been looking for jobs for a long time, and this is just what they needed! We are *five* weeks ahead of schedule, Oronus, *five weeks!*"

"That's wonderful, Melinda. I suppose it's a good time to talk training then."

"I'd say so. There are over five hundred workers who already have the basic training that you requested. Then there are two who are in charge of demolishing surrounding fuel sites that the high priest wants put into management afterward. I think that they used to be missionaries for the basilica. Anyway, there's quite a force ready for your guidance."

"That's quite a large number. You probably won't need more than three hundred full-time mechanics if you're using mass production. Give me a week to settle some things here, and then I'll come to Restivar and bring some of my better engineers to help me."

"Wonderful, Oronus! This is so exciting. A week will be good for me, as well. There's a gathering at Director Aevier's mansion in three days to discuss methods of provincial unity. I guess the face of the provinces is really going to start changing."

"Yes, I think you are very right. Okay, Melinda. Good luck, and I'll see you soon."

"Good-bye, Oronus."

Oronus racked his brain in an attempt to remember ever seeing missionaries from the basilica. Regardless, he could only guess they had been assumed into Graff's treachery. He also hadn't realized how quickly Aevier would begin to "unite" the provinces, whatever that meant, and realized that Graff's demonizing O.R.T. would probably play a part in this "unity." He was just glad that Aaron, Anna, and Osiris were gone with the chest, because after the event at Jacques's mansion, the council would probably summon him. He remained in his office for the next few hours, making plans for his departure.

∽

In all his time spent at O.R.T., Aaron had never set foot on the *Tortoise*. It looked like a cross between a W.A.S.P. and a luxury craft. The hallways ran circles around the safe room, whose circular outer walls were seen in the control room. Aaron walked the circular path that was the control room in an attempt at acclimation. He finally redirected down a side passage that led to crewmembers' quarters, where he found Anna. She was lying on a bed, arms and legs crossed, staring at the ceiling.

"Why, hello, Mrs. Smith," Aaron said smiling as he sat down on the bed across from her. "So, how many people can say that they were able to skip all of the formalities and awkward moments of courting and go straight into *marriage*, hmm?"

"We are not married, Aaron Ravenhall. For all you know, *Mr. Smith*, we are simply brother and sister. Daddy did say that Osiris was *our* grandfather. *Miss* Smith will suit me just fine, thank you."

Aaron rolled his eyes and lay down on the bed. They were silent for several minutes.

"Have you ever been to Astonne, Anna?"

She closed her eyes. "Yes, many times. Daddy never took me. He's never been very religious, but I went on several pilgrimages with Mother. She was *very* devoted to the Four." Aaron smiled and shook his head as she said this. She turned and squinted her eyes.

"What?"

He turned to her, still smiling. "It's nothing. I have only ever heard of wealthy people making pilgrimage, and isn't it *required* for those who follow the Four to make the pilgrimage?"

"Don't lessen the importance of my pilgrimages, Aaron Ravenhall!" He sat up and looked right in her eyes. This had escalated faster and to a greater extent than he had wanted.

"Tell me how the Four could *possibly* approve of wealthy people making countless trips to the basilica while the poor sit in suffering? *My* mother was also very devout, Anna, but we couldn't afford a trip across the continent, let alone our own personal craft!"

"My family has always been charitable to the poor, Aaron. You know this!"

"Yes, but the problem with the Way of the Four is that your case isn't the norm, the average response to suffering."

Anna shook her head. "Where do you think all this money that The Basilica is giving to the first province is coming from, Aaron? The high priest's pocket? No! It's coming from the pockets of the wealthy devout! Is that so wrong?"

They were both standing at this point, between the beds, facing each other. "No, and I never said it was. Instead of flying off to the affluent seventh province to bow down to four ornate pieces of stone, why doesn't anyone go help hurting people that the Four *created*? I mean, it's good to have your own bases covered, but doesn't the *Book of the Four* talk about reaching out to those in need?"

Anna turned from his gaze. "I don't know, really."

"I refuse to accept a religion or a concept of some *divine beings* that created humans and then just stepped back from the picture, Anna! The Four didn't make us to suffer; they made us to help each other! If you are armed with that kind of knowledge and you don't *do* anything with it, then you're worse off than the people who don't even know about it!"

"If you would just—"

"And why is there only one basilica? Why can't there be seven basilicas?"

"It's not just about—"

"And why do people like my parents have to die without ever making pilgrimage and resort to doing bad things just to survive when—"

"Your father was a *terrorist*, Aaron—"

"And *your* father killed him."

She immediately sat down on her bed as if all the air had just gone from her lungs at once and closed her eyes.

"I know. I'm sorry." She began to cry. Ashamedness washed over him. How could he have been so crass? His anger was at the institution behind the Way of the Four, yet he just released it on a precious avenue of its personal administration. He knelt down in front of her.

"I...I'm sorry, Anna. I shouldn't have directed my anger at you. I never wanted to make you feel this way." He hugged her, and she embraced him, crying into his shoulder for a time. She released him, and he wiped her eyes simultaneously with his thumbs. "Tell me about Astonne."

She smiled and nodded as he rose and sat on his bed. She

curled her legs beneath her and pulled her blanket up around her. "Well, the whole city is made out of sandstone. In fact, the buildings of Astonne are some of the shortest in the provinces. There aren't even any portholes on the tops of the buildings."

"Really? So how do they move around?"

"Well, they walk. I know, isn't it strange? The ground is also sandstone, and the city is to the southwest of the basilica with a large, carved path connecting Astonne to the basilica. It's always windy there, so the people wear long robes and cover their faces to protect themselves from the wind and the sand that comes from erosion and the desert region in the mountains northeast of the basilica."

"Huh. I didn't know that there were any people still able to live on the ground level."

She nodded and raised her eyebrows. "They are the only ones. Some say that it's because of the Raujj that was infused in the very stone of the basilica that protects the area from wild animals and the natural disaster that swept the provinces. Also, there is only one *district*, per say, and there are large hangars on the outskirts of the city where people can land and walk from. It's the closest thing to how the Ancients might have lived than any other city in the provinces."

"Well, this whole fate of a religion and the continent thing aside, I'm kind of excited about going there." They laughed for quite a while and continued talking well into the night.

~

"Ze simple fact of ze matter is zat ve have allowed our social ranks, our economic differences, interprovincial trade and council rivalries to separate us further zhan ve have ever been in my twelve years on ze council. As I read my list of noble families, my list of provincial contributors, my eyes vere opened. I had recently turned my desk to face ze vindow zat looks out over zis fine city.

I sat ze papers down, took a sip of hot tea, zhen gripped ze arms of ze magnificent leazher chair I vas sitting in. As I basked in my many creature comforts, I looked out ze vindow; vat I saw changed me forever. I saw a large deck zat vas unloading a transport ship. Families from ze first province poured out along ze deck vist zheir possessions trailing behind zhem. I rose and valked to ze vindow. Looking up at zis marvelous estate and into zat very vindow, vas a little girl. Her hair vas matted, her only covering a large, tattered tunic. At first I simply pitied her and returned to my desk. But as I looked down at ze money I vas about to receive, sitting in my comfortableness, I hated myself to a greater degree zhan I could have ever pitied zat girl. Vhere do ve draw ze line between social order and social outreach? Vhere is ze place zat provincial borders and ostentatious titles fall to ze vayside? Ve are here today to find zat place togezher. Ve are here today, not only for dialogue betveen ze provinces, but also for zat little girl."

The nobles and the council applauded Jacques Aevier as he finished his speech. Jacques waved his arms and shook his head, smiling, as if to say, "No, thank you." He laughed and continued, "But I am not yet finished! In an act zat vill hopefully spark a veritable flood of similar action, I calculated ze cost and *sold* everything in zat study—in zat entire ving of zis place, in fact! Ze money has been given to ze refugees of ze first province zat have come here. Stand vist me, nobles! Give of yourselves for ze greater good! Zhere is more zhan enough betveen us to go around! I have a proposal for you all zat could set ze marker for ze ozher provinces to follow! Togezher ve can bring ze provinces closer and all in the spirit of love and mercy zat is exemplified by ze vay of ze Four! Dare ve turn from its assistance? Dare ve remove ourselves further from its teachings? Join me, nobles; join me in unity and love!"

Less applause followed this portion of Jacques's speech. Several of the nobles in attendance stood to leave in protest as other concerned guests sympathetic to Jacques's view tried to stop them. "No, friends! Let zhem go. Please sit down. If zhey vish to continue subjugating ze less fortunate, let zhem."

When the angry nobles had left and the remaining guests had been seated, Jacques continued. "It is an honor to have ze Council of Directors in my home tonight, save Richard Alden, who has passed away recently. Zhey vill each be giving a short speech regarding ideas zat have been discussed or put into action in zheir respective provinces. Ve velcome zhem now."

In a dark and cluttered room, strapped to a leather chair, Gwen Alden was awakened by erupting applause from above her. She wept aloud in anger and sadness as she remembered how she had arrived in this place, and she felt the throbbing pain from her temple.

"Do you see ze genius behind zis, Lady Alden? Zhey vill valk through zhese empty halls and rooms and believe anyzhing I tell zhem! Ze nobles vill soon be eating from ze hands of ze new God, and since your lies put you here in ze first place, you can rest among mine under ze floor!"

"Don't be ridiculous! You can't get away with this! People will know that I've gone missing! People will realize the absurdity of your religious claims! You won't get away with this!"

"I already have, I'm afraid. You, however, vill soon stand before ze council and have your interim privileges ripped from your hot, little hands for tampering vist evidence in a council-sanctioned investigation. Take her avay."

"You can't do this! The people have always believed in the Four, and they always will! No one is going to believe you!"

"Antalya! Shut her up!"

CHAPTER 22

Oronus stood with his handpicked team of five airship mechanics and five engineers, looking upon the three hundred men, old and young, who were preparing to learn from a master. He had already divided them into ten groups: five specifically for putting the ships together and maintaining parts, five for the actual creation of said parts and the machines that would create the components. With significant donations from across the provinces, he knew that they would not have to worry about running low on materials, and if they did, the basilica would gladly pick up the tab. He never fully put forth his support for this facility—after all, it was limiting the capabilities and potential of O.R.T. significantly—but he had learned long ago not to argue with a unanimous vote from the council. They were in a large, empty warehouse in the Industrial District of Restivar, and Oronus stood before them to call their attention.

"All right! Let's begin!"

His voice reverberated through the empty room, and all talking ceased. "You are here today because you have proved yourselves to have the greatest aptitude for the technical aspect of this operation. Provided none of you *lied*, the training you will receive from me and my men will prove invaluable and will help you a great deal in your newfound positions. You have been divided into groups for a reason, and each of you is in the group you are in for a reason. The five groups to my left will specialize in construction and maintenance; the five to my right will specialize in constructing the actual parts of the ships as well as the machines that create the components for the parts. Each group will be headed by one of my men. We will meet for an hour at a time, breaking for fifteen minutes in between sessions. For the first three weeks, you will be learning the makeup of the two types of ships that will be created here; you'll see examples, learn to read schematics, and learn from the men before you. After three weeks have passed, we will move on to practical field experience. This operation is far simpler than that of O.R.T., gentlemen, and that is why I believe you all have the potential to become proficient very quickly. *However*, if at any point during the training you wish to remove yourself, do it and save us the weakness and burden that will come from your apathy! This is a serious business, gentlemen! There will be people and precious cargo on your ships, and I will accept nothing less than absolute accuracy! Having said that, let's begin. I will call you all back in one hour's time."

With that, the groups separated and began their training; the first session was purely an orientation to the art of airship creation. As Oronus floated amidst the groups, offering encouragement and advice during the orientation, Melinda Stockstill docked and descended into the warehouse with a team of assistants.

"Hello, Oronus! How is the training coming?"

Oronus greeted Melinda with a hug. "Very well, for a start. These men seem ready to learn, and that's good; there's a lot to absorb in the beginning."

Melinda walked around with Oronus and surveyed the mini classes. "Well, this is simply marvelous! I can't express enough to you how pleased I am with your assistance and with the progress being made at the construction site. This is just too good to be true, Oronus! I was received so well at Jacques's gathering. The other provinces are growing more and more confident in this endeavor. Jacques is becoming quite the social advocate, Oronus. I know you two never quite got along, but—"

"Melinda, I need to talk to you about Aevier."

"What about him?"

"Melinda," Oronus said as he led her away from the groups in the empty warehouse, "Aevier is working for the high priest, and the high priest is working against us all."

"I don't know what you're talking about, Oronus. The high priest has been the biggest contributor to Restivar since the introduction of steam power! And Jacques has simply rediscovered his faith in the Four and is acting upon it! This has positive effects for us all, Oronus."

"Is he acting on his faith in the Four or on his loyalty to Graff?"

"Jacques is a *good man*, Oronus! You can't allow your past dealings with him to affect the present. He is a *changed* man."

Oronus struggled to maintain his calm demeanor. "Melinda, I think Aevier *framed* Gwen for tampering with the evidence during the investigation! He wants the Chest of Worlds so he can give it to Graff! You know Gwen had Max tailing him—he found out that they discussed killing her! What more do you need, Melinda?"

Melinda's concern was replaced by indignation and annoyance. "You are simply going to have to come to terms with this metamorphosis, Captain—of Jacques *and* of the provinces. We have accepted the change of your technologies with a heavy cost, and now you must do the same or stand aside. Blessings of the Four upon you."

In all the years that Oronus dealt with the council as director of O.R.T., Melinda had never stood against him on *any* issue, even when it meant the suffering of her people at the advent of steam power. Richard's death had changed all of that, and Oronus was slowly coming to the realization that he was being alienated from the council, not directly, but as a side effect of Aevier's and Graff's actions. What was worse, Oronus knew that this was intentional. To add to this, his ring of support had left him and had taken the one thing that his enemies wanted most. He returned to his rounds, though it was halfhearted and he feigned interest. When the first hour had come and gone, Oronus called their attention once again.

~

The *Tortoise* docked on the northwestern edge of Astonne in a hangar carved out of the existing rock. Anna gathered their things as Aaron helped Osiris into the chair and connected him once again to his water tank. As they gathered in front of the ramp, he addressed one of the guards at the entrance to the safe room.

"Contact the inn immediately if Oronus contacts you. If he doesn't in three days' time, do it anyway, and we'll begin. I don't see how anyone could know about this, but we want to be safe and follow the original plan as closely as circumstances allow."

"Yes, sir."

With that, garbed in their cloaks and face coverings, the trio departed from the hangar and traveled the sloped sandstone path to the ancient city that would be their guise for the time being. Shortly after they had begun their long descent into the city, a large fleet of ships, sailing not for the hangars but instead heading north and east of the slope, passed over them. These were of O.R.T.'s making. They all knew that, and, judging by their appearance, they were no doubt headed for the Basilica of the Four.

Aaron started to criticize them, thought back to his argument with Anna, and decided against it. "Looks like a pilgrimage to see the Four," he added. However, he looked over to see Anna shaking her head.

"No, they aren't. If one wishes to make pilgrimage, Aaron,

they must start from the outskirts of the city and walk their way to the basilica."

He looked down to see Osiris nodding in agreement. "Yes, this much is true, my boy; however, they may still be headed there. When the high priest speaks, you will always find several ships hovering above the basilica. Regardless of his treacherous intent, he is an *excellent* orator."

Aaron stopped pushing Osiris and looked up the northeastern path. "Well, we're here, aren't we? Let's go hear what he has to say."

Anna's eyed widened. "Are you *insane,* Aaron Ravenhall? Why would we want to do that? We'll be caught!"

Aaron shook his head and sighed. "We're treating this like everyone in the provinces knows we're in hiding, Anna—"

"As we should be! It's safe!"

"But they *don't!* No one knows where we are. Osiris, let's go hear what the high priest is up to."

Osiris looked at them both, then up the path. "It may actually be beneficial to hear what he is speaking on. There are a lot of people in that basilica, wealthy, by the looks of those craft. I wouldn't put it past Director Aevier to send a mass of nobles here. We must be careful, and he *mustn't see my face.* We're done for if that happens."

"Grandfather, are you serious? This is ridiculous! We should keep going!"

"Stay blended with the crowd, Aaron. Let's pay a visit to the basilica." Much to Anna's chagrin, they redirected up the path and headed for the basilica.

～

"Imagine, my children, a world in which the realities and prophesies of our most sacred writings came to fruition and failure simultaneously. Imagine a time and a place where those who followed the Four were bolstered and strengthened by the unearthing of a divine piece of mystery that has permeated our culture and enticed our imagination for centuries. Imagine the discovery of a piece of sacred writing that would rival even the Text of the Four! Imagine, my children. Imagine!

"Oh, my children, what if I told you all that I now have the keys to those divine mysteries? What if I told you that our faith, our way of life, was at the stage of celestial transformation? What if I exposed for you a great chasm in the foundations of the Four?

"Behold, children—the Codicil! The divine supplement to the Text of the Four! I have held it in my study for the past eight years, my children. I have validated and revalidated its accuracy and truth! I am preparing, children, to share its divine truth with the provinces! My children, in addition to this unprecedented advance in the study of our faith, I have discovered the existence of the divine artifact, the Chest of Worlds! From the beginning of our history, from the time of the Ancients, the Chest of Worlds has held an elusive place in the minds of the faithful and the irresolute alike. The Codicil in my possession provides the keys to its obtainment!

"And now, after much deliberation, I reveal to you all the reason behind the belatedness of these essential revelations within the way of the Four: my children, over the years, one family has held its grip on the pieces to a greater puzzle. One family has kept these pieces locked away in a tower of secrecy and heresy. One family has hoarded the knowledge of our spiritual past and has therefore hindered the faith of the masses! And now, at the advent of our transformation, one man stands in the face of our way of life: Captain Oronus Bretton, of O.R.T., and his father and grandfather before him.

"Oronus has made it his personal goal to hide the knowledge of the Chest of Worlds and the Codicil from the people of the provinces! He has kept within his walls the books and scrolls that by all rights should rest in these sacred halls! Oronus wishes to convince you all, through his deception, that none of these things exist, that our faith should remain incomplete. My children, my discoveries in accordance with the Codicil and the Chest of Worlds will prove that he is the reason that the Raujj is unusable! He is the reason our knowledge is incomplete! He is the reason our prayers have gone unanswered! He is the reason the people of the first province have suffered for these long years! My children, O.R.T. is the heretical core of our inadequacy! What I will be releasing to the provinces shall prove this to be so!

"I am making a public call to the Council of Directors to utilize their authority and assist O.R.T. in the submission of every scrap of material connected with the Four, including texts on the most ancient Raujj, to the Basilica of the Four for study, interpretation, and immediate implementation! My children, let us rise up as one under my shepherding and claim the advance and transformation we deserve as people of the divine faith! Let us claim what is rightfully ours and return to the faith of the Ancients! Join me in claiming victory over this heresy! Join me!"

Aaron, Anna, and Osiris stood in horror as the high priest basked in an eruption of cascading accolades.

Osiris looked up at Aaron from his chair. "Let's go. Now." The three of them left immediately and headed back down the path. When they had left the sandstone courtyard, they expressed their fears over the now-faint sound of Eleazer's voice.

"Did you see those people?" Aaron was well beyond anxiety at this point. "They ate it up! Every last one of them! What do we do?"

"We tell Daddy! He needs to know that he's just been publicly branded a *heretic* by the high priest! This is awful!"

Osiris raised his hands to silence them both as they continued down the path. "All right, all right, calm yourselves. Anna is right.

We must inform Oronus. Luckily for him, the high priest's message was not heard by everyone. Mark my words, though: these nobles are going to take his message back to their provinces. Soon Oronus and O.R.T. will become universal public enemies of the Four. What worries me the most, however, is how the Council of Directors will respond. They have a history of siding with the people on the heavier issues. I feel that once Graff's demands are met by the council his interrogation will be pursued much more aggressively. Let us find our lodging and contact the *Tortoise* on our arrival."

"Antalya, grab some men and put all of zis stuff back upstairs. Lady Alden, if you would be so kind as to... Lady Alden! Vake up!"

He slapped Gwen across the face, and she regained consciousness with a jerk. "One of my attendants vill be taking you to bathe and freshen yourself before I turn you over to ze council at CentrePointe. I must say, zhough, zat it has been a privilege having you as a guest in my home. Good things must sometimes come to an end zhough, I'm afraid. You must now face ze consequences of your actions. *Jennifer! Get down here!* Jennifer, here, vill be taking care of your needs before ve depart. Zhere is hope, however: I have vord from CentrePointe zat no one has been able to implicate you through ze evidence collected at ze site, including vat you took. I mean, you vill most likely never see ze council chambers again for as long as you live, and I am pushing for banishment to ze ground level, but I think you'll be all right. Take her upstairs, Jennifer."

She walked forward to take Gwen's arm, but after she had helped Gwen out of her seat, Gwen slapped her hand away. "Don't *touch* me! One day the provinces will see you for the refuse you are, Jacques."

"But not today. Good-bye, Lady Alden." Gwen walked out

of the dimly lit room and down the hallway to the great stair, followed closely by her new attendant. When Gwen had reached the great stair, she turned to face Jennifer. "*Well?* I don't know where I'm going. You need to be leading *me*."

"Yes, Lady Alden."

"And do I still have clothes to wear? Or has Jacques 'sold' them to feed the *hungry* as well?"

"Yes, Lady Alden."

"And do you have to be there while I'm *bathing*, as well?"

"Yes, Lady Alden."

"Is that *all* you can say?"

"No, Lady Alden." Gwen grabbed Jennifer's hand, and they both stopped. Gwen sighed.

"I'm sorry. You have nothing to do with this. Forgive me for being so rude."

Jennifer smiled. "Thank you, Lady Alden. No such courtesy has ever been extended to me in this awful place. Come this way. We'll get you cleaned up." They walked side by side until they reached a large bathing room. The walls housed ornamental swords in crisscrossing pairs with intermittent shields. There was a round bathing pool in the center of the room, steaming from the temperature of the water.

Jennifer spoke to Gwen as she walked toward a tall, wooden cabinet to the side of the bathing area. "Lady Alden, go ahead and get in. I will bring you a towel."

Gwen smiled. "Thank you, Jennifer." She removed her tattered shirt and slip and slid into the pool. After a while, Jennifer returned to find Gwen sitting on the steps that led into the pool with small model airships floating around her.

Jennifer burst into laughter. "Director Aevier would kill me if he knew that I forgot to remove those from the pool! I'll just set your things on this table, Lady Alden."

Gwen smiled at Jennifer again. "Thank you, Jennifer. Are you free right now?"

Jennifer looked confused. "Yes, Lady Alden. Well, free to keep an eye on you for the director."

Gwen laughed at this. "Good girl. Jennifer, come over here. Let's talk." Jennifer walked over and knelt by the edge of the pool. "How are you, Jennifer?"

"Oh, I am fine, Lady Alden. The director pays me well, and I am able to send money back to my parents in Restivar."

Gwen shook her head. "How are *you*, Jennifer? How do you *feel?*"

Jennifer looked confused. "About what, Lady Alden?"

Gwen sighed. "Please, call me Gwen. And I'm talking about this, all of this. Do you willingly work for Aevier? Do you know what he's doing? Do you support his efforts?"

Jennifer looked down at her hands. "No, I don't support him, and no, I don't work here willingly. You don't know what a monster he is, Lady Alden, even from what you have seen. He pays well, and as much as I hate it, he is the reason my family can sustain itself, but if it weren't for that I would leave and go to the other members of the council."

Gwen looked up at her. "Then why don't you? If you know of his and the high priest's intents, then why don't you go to them?"

Jennifer laughed hard at this. "Because he has them under his spell, Lady Alden; the council adores him now. Melinda Stockstill has been frequenting the director's mansion recently; this is just one example."

"Can you tell me anything *specific?* Anything I can say when I am interrogated?"

Jennifer reached out for Gwen's hands. "Lady Alden, Director Aevier has been in league with the high priest for his last eight years on the council. He found me as a girl and promised my family that he would take care of me. After I began to mature, though, he began to abuse me."

"Gods. That monster! I'm so sorry, Jennifer, are you okay?"

"Yes. The only thing I can say is that I am now... numb. To everything. I have been taken to the basilica several times to be *healed* internally by the high priest after these abuses. It's not like I didn't try to run away, but the director stopped me. Anyway, I soon made it my vow to collect enough horrible evidence against him to take to the council. The only way to do that, the only way to get close to him while he was with the high priest or was talking about his plans with the high priest, the only way to see just how horribly he treated the staff that weren't in his inner circle was to make myself available to him."

Gwen teared up at this. *How strong this woman must be, how cold.* The saddest part, though, was that she didn't have to be; this didn't have to be her fate.

"Well, this is valuable knowledge! Gods, Jennifer, we have to get you out of here."

Jennifer tightened her grip on Gwen's hands. "Can you? Is there anyone you can contact outside that can help me? Please. Help me. I just want to help."

Gwen smiled and squeezed back. "Of course, dear. Calm yourself. You've made it this far. I just don't understand how you've done it."

Jennifer blushed. "Well, as I said before, it's hard to feel any emotion in this place; I was simply a shell, a receptacle of information collected over eight years. You, though, have shown me kindness, Lady Alden."

"*Gwen*, dear."

"Gwen." She smiled and stood, then turned around to face Jacques, who was holding an ornamental sword. He had been behind them, though Gwen had no idea how long it had been. He walked toward her, and grabbing Jennifer's shoulder with his left hand, he ran the sword through her middle. Gwen watched in horror as a silver tip appeared. He pulled the blade out swiftly, and Jennifer fell backward to the tiled floor. Gwen and Jacques stared at each other in between Jennifer's twitching body. Gwen shook her head and made for the steps; she was speechless. "No, no, Lady Alden," Jacques said calmly as he tossed the sword at her and drew his pistol. She screamed as the sword landed beside her with a splash, and she froze as she heard him pull back the hammer.

She was trapped in the bathing pool, one which now contained the blood of she who held such promise, a would-be heroine of her time, however unsung she might have been. "You ... *monster!* I hate you!" she exclaimed, sobbing. "I hate you ..."

"Save your energy for ze council hearing. Ve're going a little early, zhough—I'm having coffee vist Melinda beforehand. You may not have known zis, but she is actually planning to testify *against* you in my favor. Something about having me followed by an invisible robot; you know, ze one everyone saw you vist ze first time you came to headquarters and no one has seen since. I even had your late husband's estate checked, but I found nothing. I did, however, buy you a new glass combustion chamber. I alvays replace vat I take. Zis girl's blood vill alvays be on *your* hands, Lady Alden. Inspiring revolt and rebellion in a young heart like zat? Shame on you."

∾

Oronus watched from a distance as ten airships were brought into the hangar of the warehouse. He and his men would board each of them personally and create a "problem" that needed to be addressed. Each group of mechanics or engineers would then be assigned a ship to repair. Oronus was confident, from his silent observations, that this exercise would be relatively painless. These men were good at what they did, and their ability to fix a problem would, by virtue, prove their knowledge of how things are put together. Something caught his eye as the ships docked, however. There were eleven ships instead of ten, and the ramp of the final ship immediately lowered to reveal three figures. It was rather dark in the warehouse, and he couldn't make out who they were for a minute or so. He could, however, see that a larger group followed down behind them and formed a line. "What in the world..." He walked forward to meet them. As he got closer, he could see who they were.

"Edgar, you traitor!" Oronus lunged forward and grabbed the old mechanic by his shirt and pulled him up to eye level. He then heard several hammers being pulled back and realized that the line that had formed behind the three mysterious figures were all armed with rifles.

"Put him down, Oronus," Melinda said calmly to him. "*Put. Him. Down!*"

Oronus never broke eye contact with the quivering old man. "Why did you try to kill my daughter and my apprentice? Tell me. Why did you steal one of my ships? Tell me!"

Melinda walked to Oronus's side and shouted up at him; he did not acknowledge her.

"*Tell me!*"

"The penalty for harming someone under the protection of the Basilica of the Four is immediate execution! Release him!"

At this, Oronus grimaced and dropped the old man, who landed on his feet, however clumsily. "Why is this would-be killer protected by the basilica, Melinda? Why have you brought him here?"

She looked at the guards and nodded to Oronus with her head. She spoke as they surrounded him on three sides. "He will be replacing you while you are being interrogated by the council regarding the location of the Chest of Worlds, as well as the documents that you possess concerning the Four and the Raujj. High Priest Graff has insisted that these two men are extremely qualified to be in leadership within this project. They will replace you, and then they will take on greater roles at the production facility."

Oronus became indignant. "Melinda! How could you? You know that I have handed over information every single time it has been asked of me! You know that I am only trying to help the provinces; you *know* this! *And* you must know that this man tried to kill Aaron and Anna *and* stole one of my ships! What would Richard say, Melinda? What would he say about how you are acting and how I am being treated?" It looked to Oronus as though his comments had gotten through to her as she lowered her head and then looked up to the ceiling, eyes watering.

She regained her resolve. "But Richard is not here, Oronus. He is gone. Times have changed. We have much to discuss, Oronus, about you *and* about O.R.T., about your future. Guards, see that Oronus is settled in Captain's quarters. Edgar, Simon," she said as she turned away from Oronus, "take four guards with you and have Oronus's men returned to O.R.T. Once they have been made to leave, you may finish the training that they started."

Edgar grinned and bobbed his head. "Yes, marm. Right away." She turned and followed Oronus and his armed attendants into her ship, where she would reveal to him that he had been convicted of heresy by the high priest himself.

～

"Name?"

Aaron and Anna stood behind Osiris's chair as they addressed the elderly man at the front desk. "Smith."

The man looked at a screen for a few seconds and then addressed them. "Ah, yes. Mr. and Mrs. Gregory Smith." Aaron looked over at Anna and raised his eyebrows, telling her that he was, in fact, correct about their fabricated relationship status that they had discussed back on the *Tortoise*. She smiled, still looking forward, and promptly stepped on his left foot with the heel of her boot. He made an awkward grunting noise, and the keeper of the inn looked up from some paperwork.

"Everything all right, Mr. Smith?" Osiris looked up at Aaron with annoyed confusion.

"Yes, I'm fine."

He nodded and turned to fetch them a key. "Here you are. One of our attendants will show you to your room."

Osiris looked up at innkeeper. "Marcus, are there comm devices in the rooms? I need to contact our airship immediately. It's urgent, Marcus."

Marcus realized from Osiris's tone that he could dispense with any kind of charade. "Best use my personal office, old friend. Come around back, and I'll open it for you."

Osiris nodded. "You two follow the attendant to our room, and I will be there in a little while."

Anna and Aaron went with one of the attendants to their room. The inn housed enough dark green marble and ornate wooden wall accents to remind Aaron of the Ancients' homes. The only difference was that there was no sign of any kind of pulsing light, nor was the light that was present any shade of blue. They followed the silent attendant down a long corridor with paintings of previous high priests lining the walls. They stopped in the middle of the corridor, and as Aaron stopped, he stood face to face with High Priest Nicodemus. The name made him think back to his violent encounter with the Chest of Worlds, one that most likely had never been experienced by anyone before or had simply not been recorded in the annals of history. Aaron assumed that much of that thing's history would remain shrouded from everyone, even Graff. They walked through the door to find a large, round waiting area with couches, tables, and storage space for luggage and supplies. The attendant bowed to them both and left the room.

As they looked around, a voice came from the door behind them. "Anna Elisabeth Bretton. It's been quite a while, hasn't it?"

Anna dropped the bag she was carrying in surprise. She turned to look at the young man who had just entered their room.

"Marcus, Jr.? Marcus!" She ran forward and embraced him

warmly. He laughed and lifted her off of her feet, spinning her around and around."

"Anna Elisabeth! What brings you to Astonne?" Still smiling, she said, "Oh! I'm just here on... business! O.R.T. business! We are here to talk to a wealthy client that lives near the basilica."

"We?"

Aaron walked forward, passed Anna, and stuck out his hand. "Aaron Ravenhall. Pleasure to meet you." Marcus shook his hand, and Aaron remained standing in between them. "How do you know Anna *Elisabeth?*"

"Oh, we were at university at the same time. We even had many of the same professors!"

Anna walked out from behind Aaron, nudging him slightly out of the way. "But we knew each other even before then! Marcus's father has been a friend of our family for years. Our families would always have a large meal together on the Day of the Four. How are you, Marcus?"

"Well, I'm running this place now. Dad turned the business over to me a few months ago. Do you like what I've done?"

"How would she know the difference?" Aaron asked, awkwardly.

Anna gave a confused look to Aaron. "Well, this is where Mother and I would always stay when we would come to Astonne. Marcus's father always let us stay for free."

Marcus reached out and grabbed Anna's hand. "Come on. Let me show you around; a lot's changed since you've last visited."

She looked over her shoulder at Aaron. "I'll be back soon, Aaron." He walked forward.

"Well, Osiris will be back soon, and we should probably—"

"Come and find me if he gets back."

"I don't think that's a good *idea*, Anna. We've got a job to do here."

All three had now stopped in the doorway. Marcus leaned into Anna. "I can come back if it's a problem—"

"You're fine, Marcus. I'm *going*, Aaron. Come and get me if you need me."

He watched as the two left the room holding hands and laughing together. When the door shut he immediately turned and kicked one of the bags. He marched over to a window covered with drapes and ripped them back, putting his hands on his hips He punched the wall next to the window, and immediately shook his hand violently in the air from the pain. He shoved his hands into his pockets and walked around the room angrily. He had hesitated too long. He thought that this was going to be the time and place; off by themselves, and for Gods knew how long. He had blown his chance to share his feelings with any kind of success.

~

"Omni Revival Technologies. May I redirect your link for you?"

"Yes. This is former O.R.T. Director, Captain Osiris Bretton. I need to speak with my son, please."

"One moment, Captain…"

"This is Parrus Vademe."

"Parrus, is Oronus available? This is urgent."

"I'm sorry that you haven't been informed, Captain—we sent word to the *Tortoise*—Oronus has been taken into custody by the council. His efforts in the first province have been halted, and they are considering halting all business done by O.R.T. until the council can interrogate him."

"Does this have anything to do with the high priest?"

"Well, yes, in fact—it has *everything* to with him, actually. How did you know?

"I know that he has accused Oronus of heresy, and that he has demanded access to everything that O.R.T. has excavated. I guess someone needs to know now that Oronus is gone—Anna, Aaron, and I are in Astonne with the Chest of Worlds. Oronus sent us here to hide the chest in the mountains."

"What? Why Astonne? Why so close to the high priest?"

"Because, Parrus, the high priest thinks the Chest of Worlds is still inside O.R.T., and if it moved, he would most likely believe it to be moved farther *west*, don't you think?"

"I suppose you are right. Aside from all of that, what am I supposed to do if the council comes looking for one or more of you three to take part in the interrogation?"

"Call it what you want, Parrus, but this is going to be a *trial*—which means conviction one way or another. If they ask for us, you will simply have to tell them the truth."

"That you are in Astonne?"

"No...that I killed them. Tell them that I killed them and that I then killed myself. I was trying to use the Raujj. I was trying to search their minds for memories of the final Great House. It got out of hand. A pulsing blue light emitted from their eyes and mouth, and they died instantly, so I removed the tube that was offering my life support and died shortly thereafter."

"*What?* What does any of that even *mean*, Captain?"

"Listen to me, Parrus! We cannot allow the high priest to connect the eventual discovery of the chest's absence with our own. Do you understand? Who knows what they might do to my son."

"Captain, the entire council is not working for the high priest! Director Reath, Director Nichols, Joseph Thomas—"

"Joseph Thomas?"

"Yes. He's the newest member of the council. He took Richard's place."

"Where is he from?"

"I think he used to be the industrial supervisor for the first province."

"Well, Parrus, anything that comes from the first province can be considered tainted by the high priest. *Every* high priest before this one has entered into a special agreement with O.R.T. and the Bretton line, that is, if and when we find something relevant to the Way of the Four, we turn it over to the basilica. The exception, though, is that the study of the Raujj remains in our hands. As to that, I believe the Chest of Worlds has more to do with the Raujj than with the Way of the Four, so does the *Codicil*. Graff is getting too close to the matters of the council, and they are *letting* him do it. Combine this with the mystical and revelatory nature of the chest..."

"Frightening."

"You're right about that, Parrus; he is to be feared. Not respected, but feared. All right, I must go. Remember what I said—do not hesitate to use that story if you have to. We must remain hidden with the chest at all costs. Once Graff convinces the provinces and the council that he is more than just a high priest, he will have no problem convincing everyone that he knows the Chest of Worlds is at O.R.T. When it's not there, he is going to be outraged. Stand *firm*, Parrus. Oronus told me about your exemplary leadership in the aftermath of the explosion. Keep up the good work."

"Thank you, Captain. I will."

"Good-bye, Parrus."

Osiris ended the link with O.R.T. "Thank you, Marcus. You've been a great help to us." Marcus opened the door to his office and shook Osiris's hand as he reached the entrance.

"Don't mention it, old friend. If you need anything, *anything* at all, please don't hesitate to ask. Blessings of the Four upon you."

"Thank you, Marcus." With that, Osiris headed for their room.

～

Gwen jumped out of her seat when Oronus entered the conference room behind Melinda and in front of three council guards. "Oronus! Oh, Oronus!"

Melinda raised a hand and pointed to two guards that were behind her. "Sit down, Mrs. Alden." Gwen looked at her and then down at the floor with a hot expression. "Sit *down*."

She backed up to her seat, not breaking eye contact with Melinda. "My apologies, *Director Stockstill*. I had forgotten you abandoned our first-name relationship. I had forgotten the erroneous, egregious policies of this newly corrupted institution. I had forgotten that you must first *screw* Jacques Aevier and then pledge allegiance to that *blasphemer* of a high priest in order to stand on a whim!"

Oronus looked at a shocked Melinda Stockstill with raised eyebrows as he passed by her to sit down at the conference table. She was obviously flustered. "*You ... I ... well ...*"

He sat down next to her, and they both waited for a response. Melinda turned and walked to the door and then turned in the doorway. "Gwen Alden, you will be questioned first by the Council of Directors regarding your blatant disregard for the rules during a council-sanctioned investigation and the subsequent detriment to the discovery of the cause of Director Richard Alden's death that *you* caused. Captain Oronus Bretton, you will be detained until the high priest arrives; he will sit in with the council during your interrogation. As Jacques has already made known to you, Gwen, I plan on testifying against you *personally* today."

Gwen smiled. "I didn't know that the council called upon people to testify during an *interrogation;* that sounds more like a trial. It seems as though I'm not the only one with blatant disregard for the rules."

Melinda clenched her jaw and gave a half-crazed smirk. "The difference between you and me, though, is that *I* am in a position to change rules. Blessings of the Four on you both."

As she left, Oronus called out to her. "Surely you don't believe in the Nonsense of the Four anymore, Melinda! Not after bowing to the New God!" She stopped in her tracks. Then, without turning, she spoke.

"He has offered me release from penance, Oronus. Forever." She left as guards filled her spot in the doorway. Gwen and Oronus immediately got up and hugged each other. One of the guards behind Gwen raised his rifle. "Hey! You know what the director said! Sit down!"

Oronus rolled his eyes. "Well, why don't you shoot us? That would certainly expedite the process, wouldn't it?"

Gwen began to laugh through her tears. "Oh, Oronus, it was awful! I've been at Aevier's since I left O.R.T. He's a madman, Oronus!"

Oronus rubbed her back as they sat back down in their chairs. "What happened, Gwen? Why did he keep you there instead of here?"

Gwen recounted to Oronus her stay, from being bound hand and foot in the dark, damp room to watching Jacques kill Jennifer.

Oronus leaned back in his chair, astounded. "That's awful! I'm so sorry that you had to go through all of that. If only we could prove that any of that happened."

Gwen laughed. "I seriously doubt it, Oronus. Aevier's word is carrying more and more weight nowadays."

Oronus nodded grimly. "Yes, and even more so now that Graff is edging his way into council affairs. When has a high priest ever sat in on a council hearing?"

Gwen shook her head. "Never, if I remember correctly. And offering release from penance?"

Oronus shrugged. "Is that not normal?"

Gwen's eyes widened at his remark. "Of course it isn't! Oronus, penance is one of the two main tenets of the Way and of visiting the basilica—you offer praise to the Four and make penance for misdeeds against self and humanity. Both are necessary in order to become one with the Four in the Void."

"Then what awaits you if you don't do these things?"

"The exact opposite: becoming separated from the Four in the Void."

Oronus hugged himself as he rocked in his chair. "So the high priest has the power to control rites of salvation for everyone?"

Gwen shook her head. "No. At least, not before now. Graff is doing things that are unprecedented within the position historically."

"I know. I'll have to answer to them *and* him when I'm questioned."

Gwen looked over at him. "Yes, why is that? I meant to ask."

"Graff accused me of heresy and of trying to prevent the 'actualisation of the people's faith,' whatever that means, by withholding vital information and artifacts concerning the Raujj and the Four. He publically condemned O.R.T. as well."

"Are you serious? Why would he do something so rash?"

"He wants the Chest of Worlds, Gwen, and he wants to get it and demonize me at the same time. Sadly enough, it seems to be working. They won't stop pressing me until the council is running O.R.T. and I'm forced to hand over the chest."

Gwen reached out her hand to hold his. "I guess all we can do is wait, huh? What would Richard do right now? What would he say about all of this?"

Oronus smiled. "He would go down with us, Gwen. He would fight tooth and nail against Aevier and Graff's attempts at power. He'd be in this room right now, Gwen."

Gwen smiled and squeezed his hand. "He is, Oronus. He's here."

They sat together in silence, awaiting Gwen's time before the council.

CHAPTER 23

Gwen Alden proceeded down the hall that led to the Judgment Hall of the Council of Directors, flanked by council guards. The massive hall connected the main building of Council Headquarters to a smaller building that contained the Judgment Hall and smaller courts, as well as the headquarters for the Council Guard. She had been allowed to send for her favorite black formal dress, at her request. Her hair was now up again, and she wore white heels and a thin, midlength, laced white cape with a golden butterfly clasp.

The council's formal chambers were grandiose, to say the least. The floors and the walls were lined with huge tiles of black marble, held together with an adhesive that was flecked with countless pieces of gold. A stretch of crimson carpet separated two enormous sections of black marble chairs, each housing a crimson cushion. The stretch of carpet ended at her destination: a long table with legs of black marble and a glass surface. The floor in front of the long table led to a massive wall with the same featureless surface. Gwen could not tell when then floor ended and the wall began; she even noticed a slope in the floor toward the wall. Beams of white light broke through the darkness from holes in the ceiling dedicated to natural lighting.

Carved into the massive wall were seven large insets, adorned with crimson drapes and high-backed golden chairs with similar crimson cushions. Dim light shone down on each of the chairs from some source she was unable to see from her vantage point at the table. Gwen wondered why they did not simply choose one of the smaller courts or interrogation rooms; after all, they were in a building dedicated to such, but she assumed that this was simply an addendum to irrational processes of late. There were two guards on either side of the massive wall, a guard at each end of the table, and two guards at all three entrances to the formal chamber.

Gwen looked at the guard to her right. "I don't think I'm in the position to hurt anyone or run. I'm flattered, though, that it's taking twelve of you to contain me." The guard continued looking forward.

"I'm just following the orders that were given me by the council, Mrs. Alden."

Gwen smiled at him. "I suppose I can respect that."

> *Try though she might to save her name*
> *By playing in the council's game*
> *Her pleas fell short of what they knew,*
> *And judgment hammered, hard and true;*
> *The banished harlot staked her claim*
> *Upon the ground in open shame*
> *Where, whilst hid the grand prelates,*
> *The banished harlot found her fate—*
> *Death.*

The words echoed through the Judgment Hall and reverberated in her ears. She turned to see the source of the haunting melody: a tall, thin man with thinning silver hair, a black and silver riding suit, and a deep violet cape with an amethyst clasp was sitting in one of the back rows, smiling at Gwen as she turned. Before she had a chance to say anything, the main doors were thrown open, and High Priest Eleazer Graff walked in, leaning on his staff and carrying the *Codicil*. She stood and took a step forward as the guards on either side of the table ran to block her path to the aisle.

She shouted through them, "What are you doing here? This is not a matter for the basilica to consider, O Highest Priest!"

Graff smiled and took a seat next to the man who had sung the haunting melody. "Oh my. I do favor remaining in the know, my child. Please, sit down before you are detained yet again and the whole process is postponed. This shall prove to be historic."

Gwen frowned at this. Historic? What could he possibly mean? "Who is your friend, High Priest? He seems to think he already knows the outcome of this proceeding." Gwen had heard every word the man had sung: he told of her coming into trial, her judgment, and then banishment to the ground level. The council never condemned anyone to "death," but they did exile people on the ground level with no provisions.

Graff looked over at the man and nodded as though he was sorry that they hadn't been introduced yet. "Ah, yes. I have this man in my employ to record the beginning."

"Of what?" The latter comment had confused her.

Graff smiled and pointed toward the giant wall with one long, thin index finger. "Of the end, my child."

This perplexed her even more, but what she saw as she turned to look in the direction of his pointing ensured that she could not ask him any more about it. The council had arrived; Gwen saw them standing to the right of their seats, all dressed in black and crimson cloaks holding golden staffs. The guard against the massive wall to Gwen's right stepped forward and raised one hand into the air.

"All shall stand in respect for the authority of the Council of Directors! All shall remain standing until the council is seated and prepared to proceed!" Gwen was already standing, so she remained that way, looking up at Melinda Stockstill with a stern gaze. They seated themselves in provincial order, starting from the first province.

The guard stepped forward once again. "All will be seated and will respect the proceedings of the council with their silence!" Gwen sat and crossed her legs, her gaze still fixed on Melinda Stockstill, who shifted uncomfortably in her seat before breaking eye contact with Gwen. Gwen looked away as well, and took note of the man sitting in the chair her husband had sat in in recent years. She did not recognize him. When he had their approval, he spoke.

"Gwen Alden, you are seated before the Council of Directors accused of the attempted theft of evidence in the council-sanctioned investigation concerning the explosion of former Director Richard Alden's personal aircraft at Omni Revival Technologies in Harrah. Those present who can attest to this attempted theft are Director Jacques Aevier, Director Estelle Nichols, and Captain Oronus Bretton. You will be questioned by the members of this council, and if accusations prove true, we will determine the appropriate course of action concerning the judgment that will be given you. Do you have anything to say before we—"

"And if I am innocent? Are there any provisions concerning innocence in council proceedings?"

Michael looked down at his hands. He hated this. He knew what he had to say, but he had always felt in his heart that Gwen was innocent in this matter. He decided to acknowledge her and inform her of her immediate release, were she innocent, but Jacques stepped in.

"I am sure zat you remember, Lady Alden, zat zhere vere vitnesses, on ze *council*, even, who have claimed to catch you in ze act of *more* zhan just tampering vist evidence. Do not interrupt again."

Gwen's jaw muscles flexed, and she breathed hard and heavy. "Yes, Director Aevier." Even she realized that conviction would be serious and punishment would be immediate and harsh. Jacques smiled and leaned to nod at Michael.

He looked up from his hands and started again. "Do you have anything to say in your defense before we proceed?"

Gwen stood and walked in front of the table, meeting all of their eyes before she began.

"Richard Alden was my husband, whom I loved dearly, whom I love to this day. I was extraordinarily active politically and socially within the fifth province and within the council when Richard was still alive, and while I temporarily took his place. I myself brought forth the legislation to form a more intimate and critical investigation of the cause of the explosion at O.R.T., and I myself headed up the interprovince committee that conducted the proceedings.

"I will *not* hide the fact that I removed something from the pile of ash, twisted metal, and splintered wood that constituted our evidence. This was witnessed by Director Jacques Aevier himself. What I will say is this: in the bond of eternal love and friendship that constitutes marriage, certain things that seem insignificant to some can be greatly significant to others. I simply found a fragment of my memories within that pile—a piece of a gift given to me by my husband. I took it in distress and grief that our worldly bond had been broken by an unperceived and unnecessary end. It represented my past, my memories, our love, and our friendship. It represented the places we will never go and the children I will never bear. I took something during the investigation, yes, and perhaps it was out of procedure and against certain policy. However, *every* rule carries with it an exception, and I *implore* you all to see the uniqueness of this instance. He was my husband; he was taken from me. I simply reached out for Richard in the only way I could at the time."

She returned to her seat and surveyed the council members. Melinda looked hurt, hurt and determined at the same time to see her judged. Michael nodded and smiled down at her, and similar reactions came from Johannes and Estelle. Jacques, Raulph, and Joseph, however, appeared unmoved by her words. Even after making the seemingly appealing argument, Gwen felt sick to her stomach. She had meant every word that she said, save the fact that she took that broken piece of her combustion chamber because she feared the very trial that would have occurred had she left it in the pile. It was no secret that she loved alchemy, and she had bragged to Oronus on more than one occasion that she was working on an augment for small engines. If this knowledge had, at any point, found its way into a council meeting by way of Oronus telling Richard and Richard bragging to everyone at Headquarters (as he always did with her), then the explosion could very well be blamed on her.

Jacques spoke again. "How touching. Yes, Richard vas valuable to us all, and ve are all, I am sure, sympathetic to your loss. *However*, you are still guilty, as you yourself have admitted, of a crime, and ve must take action. Raulph, go ahead, please."

Raulph nodded. "Are you aware that you attempted to steal evidence in a council-sanctioned investigation?" This seemed a bit redundant to Gwen, but she knew she had to play along.

"Yes."

"Are you aware of what the evidence was?"

"Yes."

"Please tell us what it was that you attempted to steal."

"It was a broken metal piece of equipment that had my initials on it."

"What exactly was the equipment?"

Gwen sighed. "The piece came from a small glass combustion chamber that Richard bought for me some years ago."

At this point Raulph leaned forward and nodded to Jacques,

who stood and stepped forward. "I stand before ze council as a witness to zis crime." Jacques leaned forward and nodded to Estelle, who stood and spoke.

"I stand before the council as a confidant in Director Aevier's witness of the crime. I saw Director Aevier discover the evidence on Lady Alden's person. Guards, bring him in, please."

A side door opened, and Oronus entered, immediately giving Gwen the same mouthed "I'm sorry" that she had given him when she took the piece of the chamber. Gwen responded with the very same "I know" he had given her. With guards on either side of him, he turned and nodded to the council.

"I stand before the council as a confidant in Director Aevier's witness of the crime. I saw Director Aevier discover the evidence on Lady Alden's person." Oronus left the Judgment Hall without meeting Gwen's eyes. After he had left, Raulph Hartsfield continued.

"And what is the purpose of the glass combustion chamber, Lady Alden?"

She realized that all of her answers were potentially incriminating by nature of alchemy's subject matter. "The chamber is used in experiments to safely mix gasses or liquids without the risk of physical harm."

"Is it still possible, though, to break said chamber if the reaction is too severe?"

"I suppose, but I really have never done anything like—"

"Thank you, Lady Alden. Joseph, you may proceed."

Joseph looked around nervously, and his eyes fell on the high priest. Graff smiled his sickening smile and made circles with his hand in the air as he raised his eyebrows, signifying a need to continue. Joseph shook his head and looked at Gwen.

"The Cou…" He was extremely nervous and extraordinarily afraid of the high priest. "The council has brought a researcher from Nurenhanzer Medical Facilities in CentrePointe, the fourth province, to reveal the results of ash testing that you yourself ordered to be done. Dr. Felding, you may proceed." An older man in a white cloak and spectacles resting on the tip of his nose hobbled in one of the side doors and looked up at the Council of Directors.

"Nurenhanzer Medical Facilities has conducted an analysis and comparison of ash found at the site of the explosion and ash found at the furthest point from the explosion on the upper level. The results were quite dissimilar. When we tested the ash from the blast site, we found traces of Nitro, a ragtag assortment of cheap combustible powders that has been used predominately in the secret explosives rings in the second and third provinces in recent years. The ash collected away from the blast, however, consisted only of the sediments of stone, mortar and dust from other pieces of the building that occurred due to the blast." Dr. Felding nodded to the council and then left out the same side door. Gwen looked up to Raulph to continue his flurry of questions, but it was Johannes who spoke next.

"Lady Alden, am I to assume that you have your very own 'lab' of sorts in your own home?"

"I do."

"And am I also to assume that you have, or your husband has, in the past purchased for you your very own elements to experiment with in your lab, as well as instruments to use?"

"Yes. Richard bought me an assortment of chemicals and my own equipment to experiment with. But if you are going to insinuate that I was in possession of *Nitro*, then I will save you the trouble of asking; I have *never* possessed or used Nitro."

Estelle leaned forward and nodded to Johannes. "Director Nichols, you may proceed."

"Thank you, Director Addlebrecht. Yes, you speak the truth, Lady Alden. Council investigators who searched the director's mansion in the fifth province have confirmed that your lab did not contain any traces of Nitro, nor did any of your equipment. Therefore we must assume that if the combustion chamber was inappropriately used to detonate Nitro, it was not you who did so."

"Or you simply put ze whole thing togezher somevhere else. Vhatever ze case, ve are not in a position to prove eisher scenario fully at zis point. Because of zis fact, ze investigation into your evidence tampering and attempted theft can go no further due to a lack of solid proof. Ze council vill not, zhen, seek to link you vist any of ze deaths or destruction of property zat occurred." Jacques leaned forward to seek the approval of the other six. When he had their nods, he continued. "However, recent events concerning yourself and certain members of ze council need to be addressed vhile ze council in convened and vhile you are here. Normally, zis could not occur. Ze council has never judged anyone of more zhan one crime at ze same time. Zat is vhy I seek ze approval of ze council to do so. I assure all of you zat zis may even have something to do vist ze previous charge. All in favor of prolonging judgment and hearing ze new accusation?" Melinda, Joseph, Jacques, and Raulph leaned forward. "A majority has been achieved. Director Stockstill, you may proceed."

Gwen was extremely confused. She stood and walked in front of the table again. "I am sorry, Directors, but I must confess that I am unsure of what is happening. What of my being accused of attempted theft and tampering with evidence in a council-sanctioned investigation? Will there be judgment passed on that issue? And what of this new accusation? I am sure that the other three members of the council may not feel adequately prepared to entertain an entirely *new* accusation." Michael, Johannes, and Estelle nodded to her statement.

Jacques waved his hand. "I am sorry, Lady Alden, but given the severity of your crimes, and given zat zis new accusation *also* pertains to ze council, ze majority feel secure in continuing zis trial. Director Stockstill, you may *proceed*." Melinda held her hand across her chest, breathing heavily. Her dislike of what was happening and equal desire to see Gwen punished were clashing within her. Jacques had been so good to her as of late, and the high priest had offered her permanent release from Penance. It was too good to pass up.

"I have knowledge of a second offense concerning Gwen Alden that also involves a crime against the Council of Directors. Three months ago, after one of our council meetings *and* while Gwen Alden was still serving as probationary director of the fifth province, she pulled me aside and informed me that she was going to have Director Jacques Aevier spied on for an extended period of time by a teabot of the Max line produced at O.R.T. She said it had the ability to cloak itself from vision. This teabot would then return to her at our next meeting to report on what it saw. However, the director had become aware of this by happy chance, and the teabot apparently broke from its trail the day of the investigation at O.R.T. Spying on another member of the council is also a serious offense and one that must be addressed by the council."

Gwen shifted in her seat. Happy chance? What did that mean? She knew that the high priest had seen it, but for him to reveal that he *had* seen it was also to reveal that he had been toying with the Raujj. Surely he was not ready for this to be revealed. She stood and moved to the front of the table again and spoke.

"Regardless of the spoken words that expressed my intent, there were no other witnesses to vote confidence in the director's knowledge of being trailed, and therefore it is impossible, by council policy, to judge on any grounds other than attempt and intent. As such, I feel as though we should—"

"Ah, but there was a witness, I'm afraid." Chills went down her spine as her fear was confirmed by Graff's voice from behind her. All eyes were fixed on him, and as Gwen turned around she noticed that several nobles had filed in silently during the proceeding and were sitting around him. After a short period of inaction, he said, "Oh! Sorry, how ignorant of me." He stood and cleared his throat, speaking in a matter-of-fact, going-through-the-motions air. "I stand before the council as a confidant to Director Stockstill and Director Aevier's respective witnesses of the crime. I saw the actual teabot floating above the director when he entered the Sanctum of the Four to discuss interprovince relations." Estelle frowned at this.

"High Priest, how is it that you managed to see an invisible teabot?"

Graff nodded to her. "Of course, Director Nichols; how silly of me. Simply put, I saw the teabot because the Raujj used on this teabot was placed with ill-intent. The protective Enchantments placed on the Basilica of the Four from the time of the Ancients prevents its use in that manner." The council erupted in gasps and protests.

Johannes yelled out, "Gwen Alden used the Raujj? Ha! How absurd! This is getting rather ridiculous." Graff rose from his seat and strode down the crimson aisle a little way and stopped, clearing his throat. The council ceased their excited chatter.

"Perhaps I should make myself clearer on this matter. You see, technologies created by the Ancients were always infused with the Raujj. Captain Oronus Bretton of O.R.T. revived this particular teabot with the ability to become invisible, an art that was discovered by the Ancients. The devices that Oronus used to make this happen were more than likely recovered during one of his excavations and are therefore more than likely infused with the Raujj. This proves two things: the first is that, by association, Oronus is also involved in this little offense of Lady Alden's, and the second is that the Raujj has the ability to evolve. At its beginning, the Raujj could not inhabit inanimate objects permanently."

He smiled and sat down, fixing his gaze on Gwen and nodding over at the lyricist and historian Graff had hired. Everything he had said seemed to be happening. She tried to save her name from complete accusations by playing to the council's empathy and relationships with her. Now her pleas *were* falling short of what they knew. She thought back to the chilling verses and remembered what happened next: judgment.

Jacques stood and stepped forward. "After hearing zis, it is apparent zat Gven Alden not only tampered vist evidence in a council-sanctioned investigation, but she also succeeded in *spying* on me for undetermined reasons vist ze intent of gazhering information. Zhese are two charges and offenses against zis very Council of Directors zat cannot be overlooked. Gven Alden, distraught zhough she may have been, committed grievous offenses. Before ve commence vist ze judgment, Lady Alden, vould you mind telling ze council vat you vere spying on me for? Ve are all interested in knowing."

Gwen did not stand this time; she simply looked up at them all from her seat. "I would love to." She was sweating profusely at this point. Her nervousness created a lump in her throat, and her heart beat faster every second. She would reveal what she knew about Jacques, and though four of them would probably think she was crazy, three of them would stop dead in their tracks. This would be her only chance to speak out before they silenced her, perhaps permanently.

"What I discovered was that Jacques Aevier was responsible for the death of Richard Alden and the destruction caused at Omni Revival Technologies; that he has financial links to the rogue group in the first province; and that he planted evidence with my initials at the blast site to cause me to do what I did. All of this was done under the direct supervision of High Priest Eleazer Graff, who ordered the death of my husband and my own sabotage; who wants the shutdown of O.R.T. to further his own power and hold over the Raujj; and who has been an ardent supporter of the first province's rogue group since they formed so many years ago. That is what I learned. This is what I sought to find out. You, Jacques, are a traitor and a coward. You are a liar. You are a murderer. Also, High Priest Graff seeks to destroy the Faith of the Four in order to promote the provinces to worship *him*—"

"Enough!" Jacques was leaning over the edges of his box, monocle spinning, and his face red with fury. Graff sat with an indifferent look on his face. "I don't know vhy you are spinning zhese fanciful tales, Lady Alden, but I can assure you zat zhey are *completely* unbelievable: I am as much a murderer as ze birds zat roost in ze skylights of ze Judgment Hall! And ze High Priest, as ze council has seen and approves of, is only seeking to enhance ze faith of ze provinces and improve our spiritual quality of life! Zat is quite enough *nonsense*, Lady Alden!"

Michael shook his head and strode forward in his box. "Sit *down*, Jacques."

Jacques got an indignant look on his face and continued. "No! I refuse to stand by and listen to zis—"

"*Now*, Jacques!" This time it was Johannes, and Jacques angrily took his seat.

Michael spoke. "We need to pause immediately to discuss what has just been laid before the council by *all* parties involved. We will meet in the Chamber of Deliberation. Now."

Everyone stood and took their golden staves, walking out of the boxes and out of sight. Gwen buried her face in her hands and wept. She knew what was coming: judgment, banishment. Two convicted offenses against the council were more than enough to constitute a ground-level expiation. Exile seemed imminent.

～

"Regardless of vat zat teabot saw or vat she claimed it saw, ze simple fact zat it vas used to spy on me negates anything it could produce to be used against me in ze Judgment Hall! Also, who even *believes* zhese cracked rantings? Zhese are ze desperate defenses of a voman facing judgment! Nothing more!"

Melinda nodded. "I agree with Jacques on this one." Estelle laughed out loud at this.

"And *every* other one, for that matter! Shut up, Melinda! Everyone knows you are Jacques's little lapdog right now. Your opinion is meaningless to me at present."

Johannes nodded. "Very true, Estelle." Melinda scowled at them all, but said nothing.

Raulph leaned forward. "Let us not let Gwen's last comments overshadow what we are here to do. Gwen Alden is guilty of tampering with evidence in a council-sanctioned investigation *and* of spying on Director Aevier. Both offenses are against the council and are serious crimes. I believe that a serious judgment is in order."

Johannes raised an eyebrow. "And what might you have in mind?" Jacques and Raulph both looked toward Joseph, who took a deep breath and said one word: "banishment."

～

The Council of Directors returned after what seemed to Gwen like hours. During their deliberation, even more people had entered the Judgment Hall. The same guard who had announced their entrance stepped forward again. "All will stand out of respect for the authority of the council! All will remain standing until the council is seated and ready to proceed!"

They all sat, and Joseph Thomas spoke. "Gwen Alden, you stand before the Council of Directors guilty of tampering with evidence in a council-sanctioned investigation and of spying on a member of the Council of Directors. Offenses of this grievous nature constitute the judgment of banishment from participation in the provinces. All in favor of the banishment of Gwen Alden will stand at this time."

Melinda, Joseph, Jacques, and Raulph stood. Gwen looked as she did at her husband's funeral: resolute and determined with tears streaming down her face.

When they sat, Joseph continued: "All opposed to banishment in favor of an alternate judgment will stand at this time."

Michael, Estelle, and Johannes stood and looked down at Gwen. Estelle was crying too; Michael looked away immediately. At this point, the entire council stood, and Melinda raised her staff.

"Gwen Alden, stand and face the judgment of the Council of Directors!" Gwen stood, tears still rolling down her cheeks with no sign of stopping. "You are hereby banished from participation within all seven provinces from this moment forth! You will be taken to the ground level of your home province, where you will be released, and from whence you shall never be allowed to interact with society again! Take her away!"

"No! You can't! This is not fair! Director Aevier killed my husband! I had to find out for sure! This is too harsh! Please, reconsider!"

Council guards surrounded Gwen Alden on the floor of the Judgment Hall and swept her away. Her cries continued to fill the Judgment Hall until the doors slammed shut and created a deafening silence. It was soon broken by Estelle's weeping and Michael and Johannes's attempts at consolation.

Melinda stood. "We will adjourn for a short period and will return to the Judgment Hall to begin the interrogation of Captain Oronus Bretton regarding the location of the Chest of Worlds! Unless there is any more business that is immediately pertinent—"

"Oh my, it would seem as though there is." There, as though it had been rehearsed one hundred times over, High Priest Eleazer Graff strode down the crimson aisle of the Judgment Hall, serpentine staff in one hand, the *Codicil* hovering above the other. He walked until he reached the massive wall where the members of the council sat. He turned and raised his hands.

"In light of recent discoveries made by myself in regards to our faith and to the true nature of the Raujj and of the Four, I am forthwith instituting a grand shift in the practice of our faith that will better us as the unified people of the seven provinces.

"Through the knowledge of the *Codicil* and through my study of those who came before us and their Ancient Craft, the Raujj, I have been granted the use of its power and a perpetual communion with the direct, physical nature and will of the Four

Representations. They have named me oracle, my children. I will immediately begin to reveal the prophecies that have been laid before me and the new knowledge of our faith that is contained within the *Codicil*.

"As oracle, and with my divine communion and revelation knowledge, I hereby declare my word to be inerrant and my interpretations of our faith final! It is the power directly given me by the heavens! Those who will pledge their devotion to the Basilica of the Four and to the oracle will be those who advance to the newest stage of our faith. Those who do not will immediately be ripped of the rites of penance and praise and will risk the brand of heresy!

"This decision, reached through my divine encounter, is to ensure the welfare of every man, woman, and child who adheres to the authoritative revelations and interpretations of the divine oracle! The Book of the Four is forthwith banned from use within our faith and will be replaced by the *Codicil* that I now hold in my hand! Messages of our new way will immediately begin their spread across the provinces to ensure immediate obedience to the new order of our faith! The grace and mercy of the heavens will be exercised by the oracle upon those who adhere to the teachings and interpretations of the oracle! My children, we are entering a new age of our faith, an age that will bring us closer to that which created us than we have ever been! Join me in paving the way for our new way of life! Join me in adherence to the basilica and to the oracle!"

~

Oronus had heard every word from the hallway he stood in, awaiting his interrogation. He knew what this meant: Graff had taken his first step toward becoming a deity. He looked over at one of the guards. "What is your name, son?"

"Jonathon, Captain."

"Listen to me, Jonathon. As soon as you can, I need you to

have Estelle Nichols's senior secretary contact Parrus Vademe at Omni Revival Technologies. Tell him about Graff's recent proclamation. Did you hear his words, Jonathon?"

"Yes, Captain."

"Good man. Now, tell him of Graff's proclamation and tell him of the sentence passed on Gwen Alden, do you know it?"

"Yes, Captain."

"Splendid. All right, do those things for me, Jonathon. When my interrogation is over please tell her those results, as well."

"I will do my best, Captain."

～

The hundreds now in attendance that had filed into the Judgment Hall intermittently through Gwen's trial now stood and applauded the oracle. They then filed back out of the Judgment Hall as Graff turned to face the council.

"I would so love a chair for this next part; it would seem that the location of the Chest of Worlds is directly involved in the new path that our faith has taken. I would like to join you in your interrogation."

Michael shook his head. "I don't know if that is a good idea, High Priest—"

"Oracle, my child. I am the oracle."

"Oracle, then. The council has long sought to keep its authority and the authority of the Basilica of the Four distinct and separate."

Graff smiled up at him. "Oh, I don't think that this will have any far-reaching negative effects concerning the council. Also, and as I've already said, the location of the Chest of Worlds has now become paramount in the success of our new order. I would like very much to join you in your interrogation."

Johannes looked down at Estelle, who in turn looked to Michael with an uneasy expression.

"Guards! Bring ze oracle a chair so zat he may sit in vist ze council." As quickly as Aevier spoke, a golden chair with crimson cushion was brought in and placed at the center of the massive wall's base.

Graff took his seat, *Codicil* in hand, and rested his staff against its side. He looked up and behind him, straining his neck as he did so. "Oh my. This is rather inconvenient. With my position on the floor, how am I to recognize the leaning and nodding of the council? Is there an open space for me up above?"

Michael was the first to jump in again. "I'm afraid not, High... Oracle. These spaces have been reserved for the Council of Directors' adjuration since its creation. To allow a basilical authority to be here is to symbolize parallel powers, which is most certainly *not* the case. The Basilica of the Four has no authority in civil matters, Oracle."

Graff made a "click" noise with tongue and cheek as he nodded in agreement. "You are right, Director. My apologies. In that case, would the council mind coming to the floor to sit with me as we interrogate Captain Bretton? This will ensure that I do not interrupt the proceedings or speak out of turn."

Johannes squinted his eyes and curled one side of his lips. "That, *Oracle*, will never happen as long as I sit on the—"

"Guards! Please have our chairs moved to the ground so that we may work most efficiently with the oracle," Melinda pronounced as she, Jacques, Joseph, and Raulph got up to move to the floor.

Estelle remained in her seat. "Oh, come on! This is getting rather ridiculous. This is *not* the Basilica of the Four; this is the Judgment Hall! We are the Council of Directors! This is where we sit!"

The four who had risen, however, did not listen and had made their way down by the time Estelle's protests had ceased. They had left their staves, and, regardless of the action's intentionality, it was another step down for Michael symbolically. With a growl of disapproval, Johannes stood and walked out of his box; Michael and Estelle followed in dejected submission. However, Michael grabbed Estelle's arm as they walked down the stairs and pulled her in close, whispering in a harsh tone: "We won't have to take part in this nonsense if we walk out of here! Let's just go; they'll have to postpone the proceedings!"

Estelle shook her head. "No they won't, Michael. Four to three is acceptable within the Judgment Hall. Those four are all going to side with the oracle. Look, Melinda is in the first province, where Joseph came from. Melinda is sleeping with Jacques, who is sympathetic to Graff. Raulph is from Astonne and has been loyal to Graff for years, Michael. All four of them have a connection to Graff, and now that he is declaring this 'new order' of his, with the obvious support of the nobles, they want to jump at any chance to work side by side with the 'oracle' however they can."

At this point they were stopped in front of a side door that led into the Judgment Hall. Estelle put her hand on Michael's shoulder, shrugged, and walked in; Johannes was already there, seated and visibly disgruntled. He noticed that Graff's chair sat slightly further up on the sloped floor, giving him an appearance of authority. Michael dropped to his knees outside the door, placing his palms on the floor's surface. Tears fell and splashed on the tiled surface.

"Awesome Four of Wisdom, Justice, Grace, and Mercy, I come to you now in a time of need. The Representation of Mercy knew from the creation of all things that we would come before you in times of overwhelming distress; I am in one of those times now. I know not what information the high priest... the oracle has, but I know in my heart of hearts that the Four have been at work in my life. I offer praise to you now and ask that, as the evils of this world seek to suppress the faith of its people, we would still find a way to convey our love."

He rose, dusted off the knees of his robe, and walked into the Judgment Hall. When the final, lagging nobles had finished their conversations and spoken kind words to the oracle, the tall, thin man with the black cloak and amethyst clasp stood again. Twirling into the crimson aisle, he danced a little way down the crimson aisle and bowed low, chanting.

> *The darkened winter of the soul has erupted in a downpour of purest spring;*
>
> *Eternal summer lies in wait; its herald ensures the very thing*
>
> *The truest path of truest salvation has been revealed;*
>
> *Barriers and obstacles now stand to be repealed:*
>
> *The banished harlot, a stalwart captain, the broken, split, and fading seven*
>
> *Old laws, battered and shaken—a Chest of Worlds, unworthily taken!*
>
> *The iridescent glow of the future to come is dimmed only by its incandescent son:*
>
> *Oracle, your time is now!*
>
> *The mighty prophet staked his claim, in Judgment Hall, with noble fame*
>
> *Where, whilst judged the grand prelate*
>
> *The silent Four had found their fate—*
>
> *Death.*

CHAPTER 24

Marcus led Anna through the courtyard that lay in the centre of the inn. He had shown her the entire place and had intentionally made this their last stop. Anna had grown especially beautiful and carried herself well. Marcus knew this, and he also knew that he would not be seeing her again for a very long time if he did not do something. "This is our courtyard. We placed it inside the inn to prevent the harsh winds from damaging the plant life we have brought in recently. I've added new benches as well. Remember the old wooden bench we would sit on when we were kids? I kept that one actually. Here it is."

Anna smiled as they walked down a little sandstone path to the old wooden bench that rested under a shade tree.

"We used to come here and talk about life together." Marcus, Jr., said.

She smiled and nodded as they sat down together.

He grabbed her hand and turned toward her. "That is why I have brought you here, Anna Elisabeth. I brought you here because I can't remember a happier time in my life than those hot summer days. Anna Elisabeth, you have grown into a beautiful woman. I would like you to stay here, in Astonne, so that I may court you, and if the captain approves and you so desire... marry you."

Anna's face blushed, and her breaths became labored. "Marcus, I barely even know you. We shared a few summers, yes, but the rest of those years I spent living in the fifth province."

Marcus shook his head. "But we *do* know each other, Anna Elisabeth—"

"Anna will suffice, Marcus."

"Anna. Sorry. We both come from noble families who are very close to each other. We are both reaching the age where relationships are expected. What happy chance that you should come here. It is a fresh opportunity to rekindle an old friendship—maybe even more. Anna"—Marcus moved his face closer to hers—"let me court you."

Unbeknownst to the both of them, Aaron had been watching them from the window of their room. He had seen enough, and he sank to the floor, covering his head with one of the curtains and sobbing intensely.

Marcus leaned in to kiss her, but Anna backed away and turned her head. "I'm sorry Marcus. I can't."

He let go of her hand. "Forgive me, Anna, for coming on so strong. Let me start over. I really think that—"

"No, Marcus. I can't do this. I'm sorry. We had fun on those summer days, but fun was all I ever saw it as." They stood together.

"Is there someone else?" Marcus, Jr., asked.

Anna closed her eyes and paused for a time, thinking. "Yes.

I think there is. I hadn't fully realized it until now. Good-bye, Marcus."

Anna left him there, standing under the shade tree by the old wooden bench that housed so many memories for them both. Unfortunately, his were significantly more meaningful, and Anna had realized that the person she loved had been right beside her for years.

~

Osiris found their door open and came in to find Aaron sitting by an open window, covered in a drape. From the motion of the drapes across his head, shoulder and chest, he knew that Aaron was crying silently. He pulled the drapes back and looked down at him. Aaron immediately rose up, coughing and wiping his eyes. He shook his head violently and coughed again, absentmindedly fixing his hair and straightening his shirt.

"Osiris. What's going on? Are we leaving?"

"No, son, we've still got some time. Are you all right, Aaron?"

Aaron laughed and nodded. "Yes, yes, I'm fine. I just let my emotions get the best of me for a while. I'll be okay."

Osiris nodded, looking unconvinced. "What's troubling you, boy? Have a seat; let's talk."

Aaron shook his head. "Really, Osiris, I'm fine."

Osiris pushed Aaron, and he fell backward into a chair that rested by the window. "Look, Aaron, we are about to take part in a very dangerous task. We *must* be focused. You *must* have your wits about you! Now if we can talk about this, perhaps while Anna is still out and about, we can try to resolve some things man to man. What about it?"

Aaron dropped his head. "Anna. It's Anna. I've wanted to tell her that I have feelings for her for a long time now, but I've always shied away or she has kept me from saying it somehow. I don't know how to explain it."

Osiris chuckled at this. "You don't have to, Aaron; I've been there. You feel like any time mutual feelings are felt that she hides behind your friendship and steers you both away from your feelings."

Aaron nodded. "Exactly. And now I'm too late, Osiris. I'm too late."

He laughed again. "It's never too late, my boy! Unless, of course, they die... or get married. Hah!"

Aaron shook his head. "It *is* too late! *Marcus, Jr.*, just came in here and swept her off of her feet, and I just saw them in the courtyard holding hands and laughing. I've missed my chance, Osiris! He's rich and good looking! Your families are close friends! I have no chance now!"

Osiris shook his head. "Well, when I passed the courtyard on my way here, I saw her back away from him and leave him in the courtyard."

Aaron's head jolted up at this. "What?"

Osiris smiled. "Yes, boy. Looks like *he* was too late. Now go over to that basin by the mirror and splash your face with some water. She'll no doubt be back soon, and you'll want to look good and have a plan! Go, my boy!"

Aaron was smiling so wide that his face began to hurt. He wasn't too late! He had never felt a hurt like that before, and now it was gone, perhaps forever. The minute that she came back through that door, he knew what he had to do.

∽

As Anna came to the hall that that led to their room, her heart began to pound in her chest. "I hope I'm not too late. What do I say? I wonder if he is even still interested in me. Gods, this is frustrating!"

Aaron was drying his face off with a large towel. After he had dried his bangs and face, he lowered the towel and saw her standing in the doorway. He smiled at her, and she beamed back at him.

"Hi." *Hi?* He had been worrying intensely about his first words to her, and this is what had come out of him. Hi.

"Hi." When she said it back to him, he felt much less embarrassed and regained some of his courage and resolve. He dropped the towel and walked toward her.

"Aaron, we need to talk. I—" It was all that could escape her mouth before he sealed the thought with his lips.

Osiris watched from his chair by the window. "I did *not* see that coming…" Her jaw line fit perfectly into his palms. The frustration and anticipation that fueled this kiss created a passionate bond that neither had experienced before. They released from the embrace, finding that his arms had ended up around her waist, hers around his shoulders as she played with the back of his hair.

"Aaron Ravenhall," she said through what she thought would be a permanent smile, "you continue to surprise me."

He hugged her close to him and sighed deeply. "I thought I had lost you to Marcus. Anna, I've wanted to tell you for so long, but I was never able to."

She smiled, though he did not see it. "I know. I felt it. I was scared, Aaron. I didn't know how to deal with it, so I pretended like it wasn't there. As for Marcus"—she pulled him back and kissed him again, both surprised that it was better than the first—"you needn't worry about him."

They laughed, and he lifted her in his arms, spinning around at the threshold of the room.

Osiris wheeled over to them. "I don't mean to interrupt this long-overdue embrace, but you two have work to do." Aaron set Anna down awkwardly as they turned to face him. "Here, take this money and this list. Go into town and gather our supplies. There's more than enough there, so if you think of something or see something that is not on this list that you think we'll need, go ahead and get it. Remember, though, that *we* are the ones who are going to be carrying it and we may be out there for *months*, so don't buy anything too perishable. Don't be out too late either and remember to cover your faces, as much for the sand as for your own protection. Gwen and Oronus are both probably in the Judgment Hall by now, and who knows what will happen in there or when Graff will return. Be careful."

They nodded, then turned and smiled at each other. "Don't worry, Aaron. I am familiar with this area. We'll be back soon, Grandfather."

"Blessings, child." With that, Aaron and Anna left the inn the way they had come in, only this time they were holding hands. They walked by the front desk, and Marchus, Jr., came from behind it and stood between them and the doorway.

Aaron and Anna looked at each other and then back to Marcus with concern and confusion. "Is he the someone else you mentioned in the courtyard?"

She squeezed Aaron's hand and smiled. "Yes, he is. His name is Aaron Ravenhall, and he is the captain's successor."

Marcus nodded and shook hands with Aaron. "You are a very lucky man, Aaron."

He shook his head. "No, Marcus, I'm not lucky; I am blessed. Thank you for having us—this is a lovely place."

Marcus smiled and opened the door or them. "Thank you very much, Aaron Ravenhall. Going into town, are we?"

Anna smiled and nodded. "Yes, we're going to look at some of the little shops around the base of the hill the basilica sits on. Aaron has never been."

Marcus smiled back at them. "Well, enjoy yourselves. Blessings of the Four."

They waved and walked away from the inn, Marcus still

standing at the door watching them, trying to find resolution within himself. "Hmm. Blessed. Yes, Aaron, you *are* blessed."

Marcus, Sr., came out of his office behind the front desk and called to his son. "Marcus, did Osiris just leave with those two? I have someone on the comm panel for him, says it's urgent."

Marcus, Jr., shook his head. "No. I'll go and get him." He left down one of the halls as Marcus, Sr., went back into his office. He stood back from the comm panel and turned to see Osiris coming in. "Here, old friend." Marcus stepped aside and left, closing the door.

"Parrus, what's the news from the Hall of Judgment?"

"Captain, Gwen has been banished to the ground-level of the fifth province, and Oronus is being interrogated at present on the location of the chest."

Osiris sighed. "Poor girl. She won't survive long down there."

"I'm sure you would know, Captain. Anyway, I'll give you three guesses as to who is sitting in with the council in the Judgment Hall for Oronus's interrogation."

"Oh, I think I'll only need one, Parrus: the high priest."

"No, Osiris: the *oracle*."

"What? What are you talking about, Parrus?"

"Captain, Eleazer Graff is claiming that the Four have appointed him 'oracle.' He has banned the Book of the Four and is claiming that his word is inerrant and his interpretations on our faith are final."

Osiris closed his eyes and sighed deeply. "Then it has started. Listen, Parrus," Osiris said with much remorse, "there are some things I am about to tell you, things that should have been said a long time ago. Gwen's fate is troubling and one that you should work to correct, but Oronus's fate could be just as troubling if he does not give away the location of the chest. Parrus, some time ago, Aaron touched the Chest of Worlds in the safe room—it gave him a series of visions. They were glimpses into the past, Parrus, glimpses of my dealings with Graff during my stay on the ground level."

After a period of silence, Parrus prompted Osiris. "Yes, Captain? Go on."

"No one has ever questioned how Graff found me there, on the ground level, and I have been ever thankful for that. No one has questioned just what transpired between Graff and me from the time he was Nicodemus's student to becoming High Priest, either, and I have been ever thankful for that, as well. But what lies behind these queries is something that Oronus needs to know, Parrus, and at this stage I don't know when I'll see him again. Parrus, what Aaron saw in those visions was me teaching Graff the Ancients' language, how to meditate properly, and, eventually, leading him to specific texts in O.R.T.'s archives that would help him with the language and the Raujj."

"But, Captain, I thought the archives could only be accessed by the high priest, yet you say Graff was a *student* when he came to you. How is this?"

"That's my *point*, Parrus. There would have to be a person on the inside with close ties to the archives to allow that sort of thing. Parrus, the day that I proceeded with the experiment, everyone assumed that the scholar whose mind I tried to enter had died, and that was the story that we worked to spread."

"He did die, Captain. I was there—I saw life leave the man."

"You *thought* you saw life leave him, Parrus, and for all intents and purposes it *did*. However, Brevard and Victoria immediately swept up the body and took it into Victoria's office in Linguistics for... private study."

"What? What about the family, Captain?"

"Logan was an old man, Parrus, he had no other relatives left. For some reason the body preserved, , and they took blood samples and tissue samples and sent them to a close friend at Nurenhanzer, who did a private study of her own. What she found in the blood and tissue was something that she could not identify, so the working theory has been that his body became infused with the Raujj. When I finally stopped running after I left O.R.T., I fell to the ground and cried out an apology to Brevard and Victoria; after all, the three of us were fascinated by the Raujj and by its potential rediscovery, and this was the very thing that Oronus had warned us about time and time again. I knew that he would severely restrict their work. Anyway, I lay there in silence for a moment or two, when I heard Victoria's voice inside my head! I assumed I had further slipped into madness, but she continued to call out my name. I answered."

"How is this possible, Captain?"

"Logan. In my rush to push a field experiment into our plans, I skipped over so many details that should have been given my attention. I succeeded in entering his mind, yes, but the only thing I did was wipe away his existence and essentially make him my mouthpiece. There, in Victoria's office, when I cried out to them, they heard my voice through Logan."

Parrus erupted in anger. "Why didn't they tell anyone? We spent a great deal of time and resources looking for you, and all the while they both knew you were alive? They lied to us all—*you* lied to us all!"

"I know, Parrus, and I can't change what I've done, but I need you to hear the rest of what I have to say so that you may convey it to Oronus."

"Go on."

"We all saw this as a 'continuation' of sorts to the original test. They shared with me that they were hearing my voice through Logan, and I shared with them that I was hearing them in my mind. As Aaron and Anna can attest, though, I was also hearing Logan. He was screaming out from his death-like coma, and his screams still pierce my consciousness."

"How awful, Captain. How do you function?"

"As awful as it is to say, I've gotten used to it. The point, though, is that we could now conduct our own secretive investigations into the Raujj. However, we needed an outside volunteer, a test subject that we would share our knowledge with."

"Graff."

"Yes, Parrus. The three of us were very close with Nicodemus. He was, after all, the high priest that formed the closest and best working relationship between the basilica and the Bretton line. He had just taken Eleazer as a student and offered him up for us to teach. At first, I simply shared with him knowledge of the Ancients' language and other pieces of the Ancients' history that I thought would benefit him in his study of the Four and his preparation for work within the basilica.

As he continued to learn, though, I simply ran out of things to teach, short of showing him what I knew of the Raujj and allowing him to practice on me. After all, everyone thought I was dead—I was the perfect candidate for further study. So I contacted Brevard and Victoria and told them to allow Eleazer unrestricted access to our archives and to allow him to take whatever he needed to further his study. This, of course, led to his increased curiosity about the Raujj. He began pressing me about my own experience using it, so I began to retell the stories I had previously shared but in more detail, recounting the emotions, the physical feelings, the exact method of meditation, and mental preparation.

Graff continued to improve and even entered my mind with no negative results—he simply explored my thoughts and memories and left. It was astounding! All this time, Brevard and Victoria were compiling writings concerning our lessons and experiments in hopes of one day showing Oronus and convincing him to open up O.R.T. for a more critical study of the Raujj once again."

"So Brevard and Victoria have Logan *and* documented accounts today? Here, in O.R.T.?"

"I'm afraid so. Graff killed Nicodemus, for he had devoted the rest of his life to studying under him, who had fueled his belief and trust in the Four. The next time Graff visited me, he was the high priest, and he asked the one question that I never wanted him to ask: he asked me about the *Codicil*."

"You *knew* about the *Codicil?*"

"Yes, Parrus. It was the very book that I took with me when I hurled myself from O.R.T. I had been carrying it with me at all times, because I never wanted it to be read again. It contains the confessions of the Ancients who labored to create the concept of the Four Representations and the *Book of the Four,* as well as the basilica. It also contains the acknowledgment of the Chest of Worlds' existence and the procedure for opening it. Parrus, Graff knew enough about the chest and the *Codicil* at that point to realize that if he could open up the chest, he would become imbued with the true power of the Raujj. He would be the only person with that power, the most powerful individual in the known world—he wanted to become God, Parrus. Graff realized that generations of people had worshipped the Four Representations, who were false. If this was the case, he knew that, with the power of the Raujj, he could convince coming generations of his divinity. What started as an attempt to bring Oronus to see reason ended in the creation of a monster. His actions have ruined any chances to influence the use of the Raujj in the provinces."

"Gods... Captain, I don't know what to say... all this time you, Brevard, and Victoria have been the greatest contributors to the creation of this new 'oracle.'"

"Yes, Parrus. Now you understand my torment."

"What about Nicodemus and the past patriarchs of the Bretton line? Have you all known about the nonexistence of the Four?"

"Yes, though I will say this: the philosophy on our knowledge has always been that, through our devotion to the Four, we *are* worshipping whoever or whatever is responsible for our creation. Through the Way of the Four, lives have been touched, love has been expressed, people in need have been reached, and relationships have been strengthened. We saw no reason to change all that. This, however, is not the time to discuss that philosophy or any others. Parrus, I thank you for hearing me, and I ask that you only share this with Oronus. Do not confront Brevard or Victoria. I'm sure Oronus will be enough.

"Parrus"—Osiris paused and sighed heavily—"tell my son that I am sorry for lying to him for so long. I lied to him before I left, and I continued the lie upon my return. Tell him that I am sorry."

"I will, Captain. Know, though, that you three will come under heavy fire from *all* sides when this plays out. I will never see you in the same light again, Captain."

"So be it, Parrus."

"Good-bye, Captain."

Oronus turned from the communications panel and left Marcus's office. He returned to their room, where he waited in silence for Anna and Aaron's arrival.

Chapter 25

Oronus was pulled out of the dwelling he had temporarily made in the memories of his wife and daughter by one of the council guards assigned to him. "Captain. Captain, they are ready for you."

Oronus took a quick, deep breath and turned to face the guard. "Yes. All right, let's go, gentlemen."

The side doors swung open as Oronus was led to the same glass table Gwen had just been seated at, only Oronus was not brought down the crimson aisle, and when he entered the Council of Directors was already seated.

What Oronus saw when he took his chair, however, surprised him a great deal. The Council of Directors were seated on the floor, not in their boxes, and Eleazer Graff, newly appointed oracle of the people's faith, sat in the middle of the council, noticeably higher on the floor than the rest of the council. The council had been split four and three, with Jacques, Joseph, Melinda, and Raulph seated on the oracle's right, Johannes, Estelle, and Michael on his left. When Oronus had been seated and the side doors had been closed, the guard who had announced the council's presence in Gwen's trial stepped forward once again.

"The Council of Directors will now proceed with the interrogation of Captain Oronus Bretton, director of Omni Revival Technologies, concerning the location of the Chest of Worlds! Guest interrogator seated with the Council of Directors is Eleazer Graff, oracle of the Way of the Four! All present will respect the Council of Directors and the oracle with their silence!"

Oronus immediately stood and walked in front of the glass table, bowing to the council and the oracle. "Before we begin, I have one question. Why is the oracle seated with the council in the Judgment Hall? Is this not a blatant misinterpretation of powers? I humbly ask that the oracle be removed from his seat and be placed in one of the chairs reserved for those who watch the proceedings of the Judgment Hall as they play out."

Jacques laughed. "A noble attempt, Oronus, but sadly not one zat is in your power to enact or even *request* vist any clout, I'm afraid. No, you vill return to your seat and cooperate in your interrogation by ze council *and* ze oracle."

The captain smiled but remained in front of the table. "I thank you for your candor in the matter, Director, and for your clarity. However, I also humbly request that the other *six* Directors be able to express themselves in front of the oracle when he is present. I understand your excitement when standing in the presence of your fondest constituent, as any of us would be, I'm sure, but in a place as authoritative as the Judgment Hall and in the presence of the entire council, I think it only fair to hear everyone's opinion on the matter."

Jacques's monocle went reeling as he tried to respond, but he only managed to sputter out inaudible, fragmented bursts.

Graff patted Jacques's hand with his own, and Jacques calmed a little, though his face was still quite red. "Oh my, the captain speaks a truth that challenges us all. It challenges us to adhere to existing rules while they are still in existence. Let us honor this. If I do not speak out of turn and without stepping on the toes of the council, I think it would be fitting to formally accept or reject my presence here."

They all leaned forward, looking at one another. When all had nodded, Michael stood.

"I do not approve. The authority of the council and the oracle needs to remain distinct and separate. If the oracle wishes to question the captain in regards to the Chest of Worlds, then he needs to do it on his own time and not in the Judgment Hall during a council-sanctioned interrogation."

Estelle was next. "I do not approve." A much shorter affirmation, but effective nonetheless.

Johannes stood. "The reason that the Council of Directors is conducting this hearing at all is to honor the wishes of the former high priest by attempting to discover the whereabouts and condition of the Chest of Worlds. The former high priest does not have to sit on the council to hear the results."

Eleazer smiled and turned his head to face the four that would save his position.

Jacques remained seated and spoke. "I approve of ze oracle's presence vist ze council in zis matter."

"As do I," said Melinda through a forced smile.

"And me as well," Raulph contributed.

However, after a period of silence that had broken the rapidity of Eleazer's saving votes, all eyes turned to Joseph Thomas. He was trembling and sweating profusely. Joseph had been so excited to come on to the Council of Directors, but after Jacques had led him to the basilica and Graff had used the Raujj to share his vision, he had lived in constant fear. He had helped sentence Gwen Alden to eventual death, but he didn't know if he could take any further steps toward putting the chest in Graff's hands and be able to sleep at night and look at himself in the mirror in the morning. He knew that he would be killed if he went against Graff and broke the majority, perhaps even that day, but if it could slow him down in any way possible he was willing to do it. Eleazer nodded at Joseph, prompting him with his sickening smile, warning him.

"I am sure that Directors Aevier, Stockstill, and Hartsfield will inform the oracle of the outcome of this interrogation immediately following this in his office at the basilica of the Four, so I see no reason why he should hold sway in council proceedings now or ever."

Oronus immediately turned to gage Graff's facial expression with a smirk on his face. Graff's right eye twitched, and his smile contorted for a time as his hands gripped the arm rests of his chair without mercy, but then the mood subsided, and he turned to face Oronus with a piercing gaze. Jacques, Melinda, and Raulph all stared at Joseph, visibly outraged at his decision.

Immediately, Michael spoke with a newfound air of confidence. "All in favor of the oracle's removal from this council-sanctioned interrogation will now stand."

Michael, Estelle, Johannes, and finally Joseph Thomas stood. When they had seated themselves, Johannes looked over at the remaining three as though they were rodents that had climbed onto his furniture. "All opposed will now stand."

The three did not even rise all the way out of their chairs before they sat down once again.

Still staring at Oronus, Eleazer spoke once again. "Given the extremely close nature of the council's decision, I think it only fair that I remain here, whether or not I am allowed to question the captain along with the council."

"I'm afraid," said Estelle with a note of humor in her voice, "that a vote of four to three in the Judgment Hall is one of those 'existing' rules you discussed earlier, the very ones that you recommended we honor while they still exist."

"While they still exist, yes." Graff stood and threw his palms out as the serpentine staff and the *Codicil* flew into his hands. He strode past Oronus at his table and up the crimson aisle, motioning to the unknown and mysterious lyricist as he did so. Jutting the staff forward, the guards on either side of the main entrance were pushed violently to the walls, and the massive doors were thrown open. Once outside of them, he turned.

"At the divine word of the oracle, any business dealings with Omni Revival Technologies while the Chest of Worlds remains absent will be branded as heresy and its enactors will therefore fall under the spiritual and civil sentencing of the basilica and the oracle!"

The doors slammed, and Joseph rose from his chair, motioning to one of the guards. "I don't think we'll need this right now, thank you."

He moved from the end of the row and walked to Graff's chair, dragging it back until it was level with the rest of the council. He sat down and smiled at Oronus. "Captain Oronus Bretton, you are seated before the Council of Directors to be interrogated on the location of the Chest of Worlds. Do you understand?"

"Yes."

Melinda shook her head as she looked down at her shoes and then lifted her head. "Let me make this simple, *Captain*. Where is it?"

"Where is what, Director?"

"The blasted *chest*, you fool! Where is it? Save us the 'cutsie' pleasantries and the witty prevarications and just *tell* us where it is!"

Oronus raised his eyebrows and tapped his fingertips on the table. "Oh my. Well, I don't know where it is." Oronus was planning to prod Jacques and Melinda until they revealed knowledge that was only housed in the archives, knowledge they weren't supposed to have.

Melinda rolled her eyes and nodded quickly at Jacques, who stood and addressed the council. "I stand before ze council as a vitness against ze captain's statement. I believe zat I saw ze chest vhile touring O.R.T. some months ago vist Director Joseph Thomas."

Johannes's eyes widened. He had not been expecting this. "Do you have a confidant for your testimony, Director?"

Jacques nodded. "Yes, but you just removed him from ze Judgment Hall."

A moment of awkward silence ensued. What now? They could have removed a potential confidant, *or* Aevier could just be up to no good and trying to stall proceedings.

Joseph spoke, but Oronus noted that he looked at neither Aevier nor anyone, and his eyes appeared slightly opaque. "Without a confidant, I don't believe that the witness can proceed."

Raulph shook his head. "I believe that we can actually proceed with a 'theoretical acceptance,' if you will, given that we removed the witness's confidant ourselves. Also, and given the high status and renown of the confidant, I would feel comfortable taking him at his word and moving forward."

Estelle was next to voice her opinion. "Oronus, we already know that your apprentice, Aaron Ravenhall, recovered a mysterious chest from a Great House. You told this very thing to Director Aevier, did you not? And did we not already discuss this at some length previously?"

"Yes, Director, but in my defense I fear I may have been overly excited about the discovery of a chest that was unable to be opened and housed four spheres. It looked like the Chest of Worlds, but I really don't think that it is. All of the stories surrounding the chest tell of the spheres being brightly colored and in constant motion; however, the spheres in the chest Aaron recovered were stone grey and motionless when the chest you speak of arrived at O.R.T."

Jacques laughed at this. "Vat nonsense. Ze spheres are only active vhen zhey are attempting to use ze Raujj." There were looks of confusion from the other directors, and Oronus smiled; he had done it. "How did you know that, Director? Information of that nature is housed only in the archives of O.R.T., archives that are only accessible by O.R.T. heads, the Bretton line, and the high priest of the Basilica of the Four. You are none of those things, so how is it that you have this knowledge of the Chest of Worlds?"

Jacques laughed again and looked around at the other directors. "Vell, I... surely you don't think... you aren't insinuating..."

"How *did* you know that, Jacques?" Estelle asked inquisitively.

Jacques pursed his lips in frustration. "*I* am not ze one being interrogated right now. *He* is! Ze fact remains zat I *saw* vat I believe to be ze Chest of Vorlds in O.R.T. and zat ze oracle can stand as a confidant to my claims!"

Johannes shook his head and sighed. "This is going nowhere, I see. I move that we postpone this interrogation until a later date when the oracle can come back and stand as a confidant to Director Aevier's witness. Until then, we will assume that the captain does not have the Chest of Worlds. All in favor will stand at this time."

The new majority stood, and Jacques, Melinda, and Raulph were up and moving out of the Judgment Hall before they could be seated.

Joseph looked out over the top of Oronus's head as he spoke to him. "Oronus Bretton, you are released from the custody of the Council of Directors until you are informed otherwise."

He stood and walked forward to Joseph. "Director, your eyes... are you all right?"

Joseph laughed. "Yes, Oronus, thank you. I have had horrible eyesight for a while now, and I seem to have lost it. Thank you for your concern."

"But so quickly, Director, are you sure you're all right?"

"Yes, Oronus. I have had this coming for some time. Please, go on. I'll be fine. Thank you for your concern."

Oronus patted him on the shoulder and stood to face the other three directors who remained. Michael shook his hand. "Oronus, I know we wanted the chest turned over to the basilica before, but this new Graff is proving to be even more ambitious than the old one. I don't know if you have the chest, and quite frankly I don't *want* to, but if I had the Chest of Worlds, I would be hiding the thing right about now."

Oronus smiled and winked at the three. "I'll keep that in mind. Thank you all."

Oronus turned to leave as Estelle, Michael, and Johannes turned to see Joseph struggling to find his way to the door.

"Joseph, are you all right?" Estelle's fading voice of concern was the last voice Oronus would hear in the Hall of Judgment. Oronus went to his holding room, gathered his things, and headed for Estelle's formal council offices, where he would call for an O.R.T. ship to pick him up.

⌇

Back in the Judgment Hall, Michael spoke to the other three. "Listen, if Graff has just claimed precedence over those guilty of heresy, then we need ensure that his ridiculous rules aren't broken. As much as I hate to do this, I fear we may need council guards at O.R.T. to ensure that shutdown occurs."

Estelle sighed and nodded in agreement. "I think you're right, Michael. Oronus is a gifted man, but a *stubborn*, gifted man. He will want to continue as if nothing has happened."

Johannes gave a gruff noise of agreement as he nodded and said, "You two see that Joseph is taken care of while I put through the order to send the guards. I don't like where this is going. O.R.T. will not respond well to this; Oronus will be angry."

Michael nodded. "Yes, but at least Graff won't gain any ground as oracle by engaging in public trials or executions for 'heresy.' All right, Johannes. Joseph, let's get you to Nurenhanzer."

Joseph chuckled. "Oh, I don't think that will be necessary. If you don't mind, I'd simply like to go to my office for now."

⌇

Jacques, Melinda, and Raulph stood on the deck of Jacques's ship as they flew east together, heading for the basilica. Raulph kicked one of the railings. "Well, I hope that little *twit* enjoyed every minute of that, because the oracle will no doubt end him tonight!"

Melinda nodded. "Well, good riddance, I say. He was weak. Anyway, when the people realize that Graff has found the keys to their salvation, they will rejoice, and the transition will be smooth."

Jacques shook his head. "Nothing about zis vill be smooth, Melinda, and you've already seen part of it. devotees of ze Four are going to revolt, and it vill take ze oracle's new authority to judge how he see fits concerning heresy to convince zhem to change; zat is, unless he gets ze chest sooner zhan ve expected."

"Thank you so much. You have both been very helpful, considering how I've been so against you for so long now," Joseph said as they sat him in the large chair behind his desk at Council Headquarters.

"Our pleasure, Joseph. You helped us win a great victory today for the council. Is there anything else we can do for you? We honestly don't understand how it hit you so quickly."

Joseph stuck his hand forward, knowing that Michael or Estelle would understand and shake it. "I know; I didn't think that it would happen that quickly either, to be honest. It's a ... condition ... I've had it since I was young. I've slowly been going blind for years."

Estelle patted him on the shoulder. "I am so impressed with how calm you are being. You are truly an inspiration to us all."

Joseph smiled. "Thank you, Estelle. Could you shut off the lights when you leave; I don't think I'll need them now." He laughed as he said it, and Michael and Estelle picked up on their desired departure.

"All right, Joseph, we will contact your senior secretary if you are needed." They turned off his lights and shut the door. Joseph sat silently in his dark office, tears falling from his blinded eyes.

～

Sitting in an airship cabin, dark as well, Graff closed his eyes and spoke. "Time to die, Joseph. One act of sedition is one too many when dealing with the divine oracle; you, my little marionette, have cut your own strings. Welcome to the Void."

～

Joseph heard the words as his tears slowly turned to blood. There, in the blackness of his office at Council Headquarters, Joseph Thomas became the first martyr in the struggle against the oracle.

CHAPTER 26

Anna and Aaron walked among the little shops at the base of the great road that led to the basilica. "Wow. There are so many people selling religious trinkets down here."

Anna laughed. "Yes, Aaron, and they are aiming at people like *you!*" She laughed as she said this. "All the provinces have them. Did you know that there is actually a man in Harrah who puts out a new toy every time a new flagship is built at O.R.T.? Children all over the seven provinces are playing with miniature *Orions* and *Ontonuses* as we speak."

"I did *not* know that. Hmm."

She picked up on his sarcastic disinterest as he steered her out of the little shop and back toward the bigger stores further out. "Well, what say we get some things from this list? I'm actually kind of excited about it."

Anna nodded. "Why the sudden change of heart? You seemed really worried and *serious* before."

She smiled as he playfully pushed her away from him. "Be quiet. I just mean that it'll be fun to be in the mountains. Think of it as a vacation! Also, it'll be a new feeling to be on the ground level for so long."

"I think I can handle that." They laughed and headed into one of the larger stores to buy dried goods.

They spent the rest of the day purchasing cookware, supplies to start a fire, bed rolls, large tins of water, and the dried vegetables and fruits they would be living on for the next few months. During the day they had slowly gone back and forth between the *Tortoise* and inner Astonne, carrying their supplies little by little. When they had made their last purchases and their final trip to the *Tortoise*, they decided to stay and get a head start on packing their supplies. Anna looked across the massive pile of goods at Aaron, who was intent on fitting a large package of rock salt in a carrying bag that had no room for it. She smiled as she watched him. Had she never noticed his beauty before? Perhaps, but not in the way that she saw it now, now that they had shared their true feelings and she could finally look upon him without putting up a barrier of some kind. She laughed at his stubbornness, and he finally tossed the package aside and closed the bag quickly, tossing it aside as well.

"Aaron," she said, her smile fading, "I'm worried about Daddy."

Aaron stopped what he was doing and looked up at her. He sighed and dropped his hands to his sides. "Anna, your father is one of the smartest people in the Seven Provinces, and he probably knows more about provincial law than some of the directors. He can handle himself in the Judgment Hall."

She paused the packing she had absentmindedly started while he was talking and smiled once again. "Thanks, Aaron, I guess you're right."

They continued packing for almost two hours and headed back for the inn in the moonlight. Even as day settled into blackness, the sand continued to swirl around them in a wind that proved to be constant. They found Osiris asleep in his chair by the window.

Aaron placed his hand on Anna's shoulder as they watched Osiris sleep. "Maybe tomorrow Oronus will be back at O.R.T., and you can talk to him before we leave."

She hugged him. "I hope so. Let's get some rest." Aaron, Anna, and Osiris each slept soundly in their own beds, Anna and Aaron tired from a full day of walking, lifting, and packing, Osiris emotionally exhausted from his revelations to Parrus and his subsequent anxiety about his son's coming response. Though he rested through the night, it was a feverish and uneasy sleep that would become all too common as their journey progressed.

〜

The men that went to CentrePointe to pick up Oronus returned to O.R.T. and docked in the bay that sat next to the *Orion;* Oronus had demanded that it be left there as a sign that even the great and powerful can meet unexpected ends of ruin. As the ramp of the airship lowered, Oronus had expected to see a bustle of activity as Parrus directed the goings-on of the hangar, repairs, remodeling, ship-construction, and the like. What he found happening, though, was the exact opposite: nothing. Oronus heard the heels of his boots on the floor of the hangar for the first time since the silence of the memorial service. Mechanics and engineers alike all stood in complete inaction, surrounded by guards in dark crimson suits and rifles.

Oronus looked up at Parrus's office to see the same; he sat in his chair with two council guards on either side of him. He walked to the closest council guard and stared at him, arms folded, teeth clenched. "What is going on here, son? I would like to know why you stand in the way of my progress."

"We are here by the order of Director Addlebrecht, sir. We are to halt any further progress at O.R.T. until told otherwise."

Oronus laughed. "Well *I* am telling you otherwise. Besides, Johannes wouldn't do something like that. I would like to see some documentation, please."

The guard pointed to Parrus's office. "See Head Vademe. We've already gone through this several times with him."

Oronus nodded. "Don't get comfortable."

He turned and marched up the stairs into Parrus's office. "What's going on, Parrus? This imbecile said that Johannes sent them. That can't possibly be right. Surely he meant Jacques or Melinda or something like that. Let's get them out of here; we have work to do."

Parrus handed him the council order, and Oronus began to read it. Parrus knew by Oronus's perplexed facial expression that he had reached the bottom where Johannes, Estelle, and Michael's signatures all rested.

"Parrus, what is happening? Surely they haven't turned too?"

Parrus shook his head and stood to walk to the window as two council guards followed close behind. "Guard me that close for one more *second*, and it'll be your last assignments."

They stepped backward as Oronus laughed heartily. However, his cheerfulness stopped dead in its tracks when he looked at the guards once again and realized what was happening. "Parrus! Why would they do such a thing to us? I just came from the Judgment Hall. They're the reason we still have the…" He paused, looking at the guards with suspicion. "Why I'm back here."

Parrus turned and pressed a button that closed the massive blinds on the large window. "Well, you were there when the 'oracle' branded dealings with O.R.T. as heresy!"

Oronus silently admired that Parrus never lost his cool in front of the other employees. "Under the act of heresy, Graff can pass any kind of punishment he wants, *any* kind, Oronus, and the council can do nothing about it. My guess is that they want to ensure that Graff can't gain any more ground by punishing you or anyone else for something that has to do with O.R.T."

Oronus sighed and sat down by the communications panel. "Well, I'm going to call Johannes and try to sort this out."

As he did so, one of the young guards stepped forward and pointed his rifle at Oronus. "Under the council order, you are not allowed to use the communications panel for *any* reason."

Oronus jutted out his chin and bottom lip, creating an under bite and scowling. He then stood from the panel, smiled, and punched the guard's face with such force that he was rendered unconscious. The other guard ran forward and raised his rifle as Parrus quickly followed suit; a quick clothesline to the chest brought the guard to the ground.

Parrus pinned his arms with his knees and picked up the rifle, pointing it at his face. "One word…" The guard nodded with eyes closed tight in fear. "*Oronus,*" Parrus hissed at him in a harsh whisper, "*what are you doing?*"

Oronus switched on the comm panel and raised one eyebrow. "What? You did it too. And I'm not pointing a rifle at someone's face. Why are you whispering?"

"*Because I,*" he sighed and dispensed with the whisper, "because you *made* me! That guard was about to strike you in the back of the head with this rifle!" He then realized that he *was* pointing a rifle in his face and set it down.

Oronus shook his head. "I wouldn't do that."

Parrus gave a condescending smile and nod. "And why is that?" No sooner had Parrus said that than the guard threw Parrus's left knee off of his arm with a tremendous push and reached for the rifle. Parrus punched him twice in the face with great force, and waited to ensure that he was also unconscious. He then stood, grabbed the rifles, and set them in a corner away from the guards.

Oronus smiled. "That's much better! Now, come sit down so we can hash this out with Johannes and Michael."

Parrus sat down and shook his head. "This is unwise, Oronus! What if one of the guards comes up here?"

Oronus chuckled. "Well, if they do, why don't you let me handle him? I don't think they will, though—they're guarding all of those unarmed ship mechanics right now."

They both smiled as the voice of Johannes's senior secretary came over the speakers of the comm panel. "This is the council office of Johannes Addlebrecht. How may I direct you?"

"Yes, this is Captain Oronus Bretton of Omni Revival Tech. I need to speak with the director please."

"One moment, Captain…"

"Oronus! How are you *already* using the comm panels? Estelle said that you were stubborn, but this is a little ridiculous!"

"Don't worry, Johannes. Parrus's guards will wake up soon. We just needed to talk to you for a second. I would like you to call back your dogs, please."

"Look, Oronus, we're not doing this as an act *against* you. It's *for* you. If we let Eleazer take action against you or any other parties dealing with you, then the authority of the council could be seriously undermined. I can't allow it."

"How would Graff even *know* if I conducted business from here? There's just no way he could know about it all the way in Astonne!"

"You don't know that, Oronus. You saw him at the Judgment Hall—his staff and that book he always carries with him simply *floated* into his hands! He has some kind of power that we won't ever know about! We can't be sure that he won't know!"

"Oh, come now, Johannes! Omnipotence? Really? Do you *really* believe that ambitious old fart has *that* much power?"

"We can't be sure of it. But what we *can* be sure of is that it is in our power to ensure that Graff can't pass civil Judgment on anyone associated with O.R.T. if O.R.T. is compromised. I have to go. *Don't* get on here again, Oronus, or we'll take coarser measures. I'm sorry. Good-bye."

Oronus punched the metal table that the comm panel was sitting on. He stood up and paced around the office, kicking one of the guards in the side as he stirred on the floor. "This is ridiculous, Parrus. Fear is driving their decisions! It has to stop."

Parrus turned in his chair to face Oronus. "It's not all fear, Oronus. In fact, I have some things that I need to tell you that might shed some light on the council's decision for you—things that Osiris told me before they went into the mountains."

Oronus stopped in his tracks and sat down next to Parrus. "Tell me everything, Parrus." Parrus proceeded to recount everything that Osiris had told him over the comm panel, of Osiris, Brevard, and Victoria's secret dealings with the Raujj, their tutelage of Graff and of the scholar Logan's remaining existence on their plane.

Oronus stood and sat down in another chair away from Parrus, his back turned. He sat in reflective silence for a long time, broken only by his punching a guard that had sat up next to him. Parrus knew not to interrupt, and waited until Oronus finally turned to face him once again. "We need these guards gone, Parrus. We need to be ready."

"For what, Oronus?"

"I don't know. Anything. I don't feel safe not being able to fly out of here if we need to, Parrus—my family and my successor are right under Graff's nose right now; the council is of no use to us at present; the *Regalus* is *still* in Restivar with an angry crew to maintain it; and, worst of all, the Chest of Worlds is out in the open and Graff thinks it's here. I will not be compromised and potentially harmed because of fear, Parrus, and Graff is apparently much more dangerous than I first thought."

They both stood and walked over to a large table. They sat down as Parrus spoke. "We'll need a plan."

"Yes, we will. But first we must speak with Brevard and Victoria. Let's go."

Oronus saw that Parrus's cape was lying on the table, so he grabbed it and began ripping it into long strips.

"My cape! What are you doing?"

Oronus nodded toward the guards. "They have to stay here. Split these strips into two piles and twist them together; we'll need to tie them up. Hide the rifles too."

Parrus did just that, and when they had bound the guards' hands and feet and covered their mouths and eyes, they walked out of the office and headed for the bridgeway.

CHAPTER 27

Anna, Aaron, and Osiris stood in the main lobby of the inn on the morning of their departure. Marcus, Sr. shook hands with Osiris as Marchus, Jr., opened the door for them. "It was wonderful having you and your family here again, Captain. Good luck to you."

Osiris nodded. "Thank you, Marcus. The stay was exceptional, as usual. I pray that I may pass through Astonne again soon."

Aaron pushed Osiris through the doors as Marchus, Jr., nodded to him. "Take care of Anna."

Aaron nodded. "I will. I *am*." He squeezed her hand as he said this.

Anna hugged Marcus as she passed him. "It was good to see you, Marcus. Good-bye."

"Good-bye, Anna."

The three of them left for the *Tortoise*, which would take them to the foothills of the Sandstone Mountains to the north and east of Astonne. They reached the hangar, and the deck guards on duty called down to the control room to lower the ramp. They boarded together, and Aaron and Anna took Osiris into the sleeping quarters, where they had taken their bundles of supplies.

Osiris looked pleased. "Well done, you two. These look well distributed; we shouldn't have too much trouble carrying these bundles."

Anna smiled as she stood side by side with Aaron, scratching his back. "Good! What will we do with the chest, though?"

Osiris thought for a time. "Set it in my lap. Loop my bundle around my shoulders and set the chest in my lap. If travel gets difficult for me, Aaron can always help by pushing me from behind. All right, I am going into the control room to contact O.R.T. If Oronus is there, I'll keep him on for you to talk to, but first get this stuff to the ramp."

Aaron and Anna took the bundles into the hallway that led to the ramp as Osiris made for the control room. He approached one of the officers. "Has Oronus or anyone from O.R.T. contacted us yet?"

"No, Captain. We have also tried contacting them in the past hour and have had no success."

Osiris sighed. "All right. Thank you. Let's make preparations for drop off. If we still can't reach O.R.T. by the time we reach to foothills, then we'll just have to start without notifying them."

"Yes, Captain." Osiris made his way along the rounded corridor to the hallway that led to the ramp and the deck ladder. Aaron and Anna sat there on the ground next to their bundles awaiting their chance to speak with Oronus.

Anna stood up quickly when she saw Osiris. "Can I speak to Daddy now?"

Osiris shook his head. "Sorry, Anna, we can't even make contact with O.R.T. right now. They're trying again now, but if they don't by the time we reach the foothills, we'll just have to start. The crew of the *Tortoise* can fill them in on their return. Get ready; we're lifting off."

As Anna stood to collect the bundle she would be carrying, a feeling crept over Aaron. The feeling was not anxiousness, nor was it the butterflies he received every time an airship lifted for flight. The feeling was fear, and he felt it all the more as he thought back to the brief flashes of memory he had received when he gripped the Chest of Worlds, memories that at one time had not been his own. Anna sensed that something was off from his blank expression, so she kneeled down and put her hands on his bent knees. "Aaron, are you okay? We need to get ready."

"Yes," he said as he thought of Graff and his power, "we do." He stood and picked up his pack, and as Osiris returned to the hallway, he silently looped the pack around him in the chair—he had the Chest of Worlds in his lap.

Much akin to Oronus, this now became very real to Aaron, and he stood with them there in front of the ramp, awaiting the coming trial. Anna slipped her fingers between his, squeezing tightly; it was a comfort the likes of which she would never realize. They stood there for several minutes before they heard and felt the *Tortoise* touch down in a large clearing that was blocked from the view of the basilica.

An officer from the control room reported to Osiris. "Captain, we're here. We should leave quickly to avoid the risk of being spotted by anyone at the basilica."

Osiris breathed a heavy sigh as he accepted the fact that he would not speak with his son before he left. "All right, bring a poleaxe for myself and the boy—be quick!" He turned his attention to his travelling party. "Anna, Aaron, we must be careful and constantly vigilant. The ground level was cleared all those years ago, but no one really knows what is in these mountains. Also, and more obviously, we have the Chest of Worlds, and we're sitting right next to Eleazer Graff. I know that it is a notion that is hard to grasp, but the chest's anonymity is more important than our lives. If it's found, millions are at risk. Pull your scarves up. Let's go! Lower the ramp!"

The party stood together as the ramp lowered to reveal the wind- and sand-swept foothills of the Sandstone Mountains. They walked down the ramp into the clearing and watched as the ramp was raised and the *Tortoise* flew out of sight. Osiris turned in his wheelchair to face the two. "Well, we're here. Best to gain some ground today and get our bearings; when the sun sinks below the western peaks, we'll want to stop."

The clearing they had landed in led to an eastern path into the range. As they began their journey, Osiris looked back at Aaron, who was pushing his chair with Anna walking beside him. "Trust in your companionship; you'll be glad to have it down the line when we've spent countless days alone in this place."

They reached the beginning of the path. There was actually a great deal more grass in the clearing than there was when they had been on the ground level in the fifth province. Aaron assumed that the mountains had protected it, but Osiris knew that the war the Ancients waged had never touched the seventh province. The mountain slopes showed varying shades of red and pink as the sun's light slowly reached them from the east. As always, the wind blew and picked up the harsh and ancient granules of sand; as they entered the path, they soon came to a narrow corridor where the force of this wind and the sting of the sand on any exposed skin were magnified a great deal. It was cool and dark, as the sun's rays did not shine down between its narrow walls. When they had passed through the corridor, they found themselves at the base of several mountains of varying size.

Aaron looked down as Osiris pointed forward. "The most direct eastern path will take us to the airship graveyard. The paths from here on out will not be as smooth or worn, as we are coming upon ground not trodden upon by humans for years. Let's go."

They continued their journey in silence, pausing briefly for a light lunch of carrots, dried apple slices, scones, and drinks from their tins of water.

Anna surveyed her surroundings and spoke between bites.

"It's really beautiful in here. The wind has died down, and the rocks are just gorgeous in the sunlight. I wish more people could see this."

The other two nodded silently, preoccupied with their own thoughts.

They packed up what little they had opened and continued east. The path that they were taking into the eastern part of the range had slowly been turning from smooth, weathered sandstone into a path filled with dead grass and large stones, most of which were hidden. These hidden obstacles served to slow the party down a great deal due to Osiris's condition and his use of the wheelchair; against their protests, he stood and walked when the going was rough, and Aaron carried the chair.

They reached a long, skinny, ascending corridor that would lead them into the actual path through the mountains; somewhere along the way would be the airship graveyard. It was late afternoon, and they paused at the entrance to the corridor. Aaron and Anna momentarily took off their packs and removed Osiris's, along with moving the chest from his lap to the ground beside their bundles. Osiris unhooked his tank of water and stood, stretching long and sighing deeply.

"How are you feeling, Grandfather?" Anna asked.

"Well, my hind quarters hurt, and my lap is sweaty from holding everyone's *favorite* artifact, but other than that I feel all right. What about you two? Aaron, are you fatigued from pushing this old man along the mountainside?"

Aaron shook his head. "No, not at all; we'll probably be travelling a bit slower in the areas with tall grass, and it will take some effort to climb that corridor, but I think we're doing rather well."

Anna nodded and sat down in front of Aaron, resting her back on his bent legs. Osiris looked up at the corridor and then at the fast-setting sun. "Well, I think we should rest here and take that pass in the morning. We'll want daylight when we get up there."

Aaron put his hands on Anna's shoulders and pushed himself up before grabbing her hands and lifting her. "All right, I'll get out the bedrolls, and I think Anna has our little can of fuel and the striking stones. I don't see any wood around here, so we'll need to collect a lot of this tall grass."

Aaron and Anna set to their tasks as Osiris sat and stared at the Chest of Worlds sitting across from him. "You are a bother, to be sure. If only Graff had listened to us. Oronus, I'm so sorry..."

Then, as though it was carried by the wind, Osiris thought he heard the faintest whisper. Its tone was familiar. *"Dad,"* he thought he had heard on the lips of the coming breeze. He took his eyes from the chest and shook his head, as if to shake off the experience. However, he heard the name again, again, and again, growing louder with each repetition. "Impossible!" he blurted out. "Victoria disposed of Logan some time ago!"

∼

Oronus stared at the seemingly lifeless body in eerie surprise as Osiris's voice flowed from Logan's mouth in Victoria's office, which subsequently *also* housed two freshly subdued council guards. He stared into the petrified face, red and white scholar's cap still atop it, red, white, and yellow scholar's robe still dressing him. Logan sat in a high-backed, upholstered wooden chair in one corner of her office, and if Oronus didn't know he was dead (or something like it) he would have thought the man to be in a deep sleep. "No they didn't, Dad. We need to talk."

∼

Osiris buried his face in his hands. "They kept him? They kept Logan? Then they must have also kept the documents. You know now, do you not, the secrets I have kept?"

The voice carried on the wind and into his mind. "Yes, I know everything. And what has become of this? Everything I said about reviving the art did lead to destruction ... didn't it? You are a fool! If the council doesn't make it its personal business to punish you, Brevard, and Victoria, then I will. You'll need to get back safely though and be successful at remaining hidden in those mountains. Stepping back from my anger, how are you three? Have you had any trouble?"

Osiris felt awful for what had happened, but he knew that he, Brevard, and Victoria would never feel remorse for attempting to revive the Raujj—it was a conviction that the coming generations would never understand. Oronus had caught the provinces up in the fascination of new technology to make life easier, and they would never know what had come before that, what preceded and superseded anything Oronus could mass-produce at O.R.T.

"No, Son, we are fine. Tomorrow we will begin the ascent into the mountains and should reach the airship graveyard relatively quickly—three or four days, maybe. We've brought enough to sustain us, and we're rationing for a couple of months time."

The wind seemed to pick up at the same rate of Oronus's anger and disappointment. "Well, don't contact me or anyone else by this method. I feel nauseous even doing this. I can only hope we figure something out before Graff finds out the chest isn't at O.R.T. If something happens, one of your little confidants can contact you—I'll have no part of it. Tell Aaron to be safe and tell my daughter I love her. Good-bye."

The wind passed away with his parting word, and Osiris was left alone with the chest and his own thoughts. Aaron and Anna soon returned with large bundles of the tall grass, and their merriment while preparing the fire and setting out the bedrolls went almost unnoticed by Osiris, who pondered Oronus's words and philosophy of the Raujj, so different from his own and yet proving, for the moment, to triumph over his own. Anna and Aaron boiled some of their water and some spices and threw in chunks of potato, carrots, and onions.

They ate in silence, gazing up at the stars and admiring the purples and blues that the slopes took on in the night, when the stars shone out and the moon governed the shedding of light from the cosmos.

Osiris washed out his bowl and placed it back in his pack. "Thank you, both of you. Not just for the meal, either; you didn't have to say yes to this, and now you sleep in the dangers of the ground level with an old man with seemingly older regrets. I wouldn't envy you."

They both nodded, cuddling on the other side of the fire. "We're in this together, Osiris; this is an important task," Aaron said.

Anna nodded. "Yes, Grandfather, don't get so down on yourself that you forget what we're doing; we're here for you."

Osiris smiled and nodded. "Yes. Yes, you're right. Well, we'd best get some sleep; tomorrow is our longest day. The fire will die out on its own; don't wait up for it. Good night, you two."

Osiris lay down on his bedroll next to his chair, on which sat the Chest of Worlds. Anna and Aaron lay next to each other, bedrolls pushed close, and slowly drifted away as they looked into each other's eyes. Osiris barely slept, his mind racing with thoughts of what was contained in Brevard and Victoria's documentation of their secret experiments and what it could mean for their progress. He also thought of Eleazer Graff and his growing wickedness.

He was the first awake the following morning. He stood, packed his bedroll, and sat down in the chair, placing the chest in his lap once again. "All right, you two! Wake up! Time is wasting away!"

Anna slowly rose and stretched, then punched Aaron in the side as he tried to ignore the wake-up call and roll to his side.

"What's the rush?" he groaned.

Osiris wheeled to his side and looked down at him. "The *rush* is that we need to be hidden before Graff realizes that the chest isn't at O.R.T.!" He kicked Aaron's other side as he attempted to roll the other way and finally conceded to rise.

When they had gathered all of their things, they moved for the corridor. As the sun rose, it shined its light down upon them and through the corridor; the edges of the sandstone walls at the corridor's end were chipped and jagged, so the sun cast rays of light in all directions through the long, narrow path.

"Simply beautiful," Anna said as they approached.

"Yes," agreed Osiris, "this is marvelous, though looking at it may prove to be a far more enjoyable pastime than ascending it. Aaron, carry the chair and the chest, and I'll walk; if you slipped I would go tumbling backward and would take one or both of you with me. Lean your chest and shoulders forward as we ascend, and it will be easier on you. We'll go one at a time to create space between us to avoid interfering with one another's climb. I had better go first so that you can assist me if I fall. Anna, you'll be next and then Aaron. Ready? Let's go."

Osiris hoisted his bundle and tucked the tank into the strap across his chest. Luckily the wind was not blowing through the corridor, as the ground's top layer was loose and would have made it much more dangerous. Osiris began his climb with relatively no difficulty.

After a minute or so, he called down to Anna. "All right, Anna, you can start! Hold the walls with your hands where you can!"

Anna began walking up the steep corridor, careful to heed all of her grandfather's advice. The sand that Osiris had disturbed with his own climb now shined and danced slowly through the many rays that the sun cast through the corridor. It had a musty smell to Anna, as though she were in a long-closed closet full of dusty memories.

Aaron was last to ascend the corridor, and after the steep, dusty climb they found themselves in the actual mountain range; everything before this had been clearings and the foothills. Aaron unfolded the wheelchair and allowed Osiris to sit. Settling the Chest of Worlds in his lap, Osiris pointed forward to a winding pass between two large peaks.

～

Simon Gardner, Thacker Wallace, and Edgar stood before another group of men from the first province outside the production facility in Restivar amidst the thunderous applause of citizens from across the first province.

Melinda Stockstill stood on an enormous platform that had been built just below the portholes on the western side. It was evening, and the platform was lit by great artificial lights on the outside walls.

"Thank you! Thank you all!" She was beaming with pride as she motioned for the crowd to be quiet. "With the introduction of this facility, the first province is now returning to its former prosperity, and our people are regaining their lives and their dignity after a grievous period of loss!" More applause. "This ceremonial flight of our first seven ships from Restivar to Astonne and back will symbolize equality, prosperity, and unity for the provinces in the coming years!"

Her hands were raised as she applauded with the crowd. She turned and raised her arms to the portholes. *"Here they are!"*

Seven portholes opened in unison to reveal the airships: the same size, the same shape, the same color, numbered one through seven in great white numbers against the grey metal. During a new round of thunderous applause, Edgar, Simon, and Thacker addressed the group; they had slowly been calling small groups away to offer them the divine absolution of the oracle for their loyalty and obedience. Money changed hands, oaths were sworn, duties were delegated, and those who did not go along did not go back.

Edgar sent the group back into the facility to board one of the seven ships. "We're in charge o' this little festival, so we get to decide who flies on the ceremony ships. Melinda told me to fly people from every province, but I told 'er t' stuff it! This ain't no victory for the *seven provinces;* this's th' *first* province's victory! We've called on ya t' further the goals o' the oracle, and you've gotten yer eternal reward, gentlemen. You got your assignments; now go, or I'll put ya down."

The men walked in a group back into the facility and began to board the ships with the other men they had already spoken to. The three followed the men back inside and took the first flight of metal stairs in the production area, which led to a surveying platform. They stood and watched as the men slowly created new airships amidst the sparks and churning sounds that the conveyer belts and their engines made.

Edgar shook his head. "This's ... primitive. We went too fast. I was imaginin' a place like O.R.T.'s hangar, or *their* production facilities. This's less than desirable, people're gonna get hurt, young boys most likely; makes me ill."

Thacker spoke from behind him. "How many do you think we've turned, Edgar?"

He smiled and shrugged. "Hundreds, maybe. Enough for a proper fighting machine, I'd say. I don't know why else th' oracle wants all a' these men an' all that fuel. Now, we'd best board th' first province ship and get these boys to the graveyard; we'd best stay a while too t' ensure they won't just sit out there doin' nuthin.'"

Simon glanced back at Edgar; there was noticeable concern on his face and in his voice. "And, our resistance? The *Regalus?* Fighting back the power of steam? Have we abandoned what we originally set out to do?"

Edgar turned on Simon and struck him across the face. Simon fell back as Edgar looked down on him. "*We* get the leftovers o' whatever the oracle uses, got it? Don't you ever question my loyalty t' the cause! *Ever!*"

Simon stood and cowered somewhat. "I'm sorry, Edgar, I meant no offense. Please calm down."

Edgar saw the red mark where he had struck the old man and looked at his right hand, which was pulled back across his body for another backhanded blow. He slowly released it and straightened himself the best he could.

"I'm...sorry, Simon. We're all a little fired up right now, what with th' oracle's business and our own. This *is* the resistance now, Simon. The oracle has set his sights on O.R.T. This *is* the resistance."

Simon followed a step behind as the three boarded the first province ship and walked to the bow, waving down to the enormous crowd with the other men that had boarded. Edgar shouted back.

"Okay! Let's lift off!"

When the first province ship's engines started, the other six started in a waterfall as the sound reached them. *One* lifted off and flew into the night sky, *Two* and *Three* lined up behind it, and *Four, Five, Six,* and *Seven* formed the final row. They turned east together and reformed, then flew over the crowd and the facility heading for Astonne. They would return either the following day or the morning after that, in the light of the sun. Edgar had caught Melinda up in the symbolism and the ceremony so much that he was allowed to move the fuel and men unnoticed to the airship graveyard, a move that only he, Jacques, and the oracle knew about.

〜

Hmmm. Excellent, Edgar. You are fast becoming of more use to me than Jacques Aevier. Continue this streak of efficiency, and you may find yourself at my right hand. Graff shut himself off from all other eyes; he had gotten very good at that as of late.

He moved from his window, watching the Sandstone Mountains and cyclones of sand that formed and disappeared outside of his great window, and returned to his desk. "I wonder what is going on at O.R.T. Nothing too heretical, I hope, unless the captain is caught in the act! I would love nothing more than to end him."

He waved his hand over the black stone, and it revealed the same, limited view of one part of Re-Creation. However, he noticed people there that he was not expecting. "Oh my. Council guards? At O.R.T.? they've halted work there, it seems. Either Jacques and Raulph are trying to help me, or Michael and Johannes are trying to hurt my chances at presiding over a trial for heresy; it is irrelevant to me. If I do not receive the chest from Oronus, he will suffer, along with countless others."

CHAPTER 28

Oronus sat in silence with Parrus, Brevard, and Victoria in Victoria's office in Linguistics. Victoria sat on a brick ledge that housed bookcases full of current authors as well as ancient ones. Next to her was Logan, placed in his high-backed upholstered chair of a dark wood that matched the bookcases. Paintings and statuettes of the Four Representations adorned her walls and her desk. Brevard sat at the desk holding a thick and heavy bundle of papers bound together with leather strips.

Oronus looked at them both for a long while as Parrus watched the door and the guards. "How could you? Gods know I don't play favorites, but you two have exercised an autonomy only rivaled by my *own!*" He punctuated his final word with a kick to Victoria's desk that caused them both to jump.

"Oronus, dear, if you'd just let us talk to Osiris, he can help settle all of this out and..."

"Victoria," Oronus said to her while staring straight at Brevard to second his own point, "if you use *that* to communicate ever again, you can walk."

She gasped quietly and put her hand to her chest. Brevard

set the documents down on the desk and spoke. "Captain, if you will just—"

"Give me those. Now."

"Captain, I don't know if I can."

"As director of O.R.T., and more importantly as a friend, I ask that you turn those over to me immediately."

Victoria stood and reached out a hand to Oronus as she walked forward. "Oronus, honey, we can't afford to lose these. Allow us to keep them safe—"

"I don't have to allow you two *anything*. I am not going to destroy them, though I should! I'm not going to read them either, nor do I want to. You are both partly responsible for making Graff who he is, and I want no part in it. Now, Parrus is going to leave and go back to the hangar to announce that we are allowed to work as long as we have no dealings with the outside. Go now, Parrus."

"Yes, Captain." He handed Oronus the rifles and left. Oronus looked at the unconscious guards.

"I will be working in here until the council guards leave. This way I can coordinate with Parrus in the hangar and make sure that you two don't do anything. I'm sorry; this is the way it has to be for now." He set one of the rifles on the desk and pushed it to Brevard. "Would you help me watch these two while I work, Brevard?"

Brevard picked up the rifle and nodded. "Of course, Captain. I respect you and your position with all that is going on. We won't be an unneeded burden."

Victoria nodded in agreement from her place on the ledge. Oronus smiled and patted Brevard on the back as he walked past. "Thank you, Brevard. I am glad of your friendship."

Oronus scooted up to the desk and turned Victoria's comm panel to face him. He had taken paper and a pen and had begun writing when he heard a hammer click behind him. "Oh, Brevard, I don't think you'll need to do that. They're pretty timid; I don't think they'll try any—"

He turned in his chair to see a rifle pointing not at the guards on the floor but at him. "Victoria, grab the documents. Oronus, one day you will thank us both for taking these. One day, when the Raujj is used universally in homes and in the workplace, when your father's dream finally finds its place over your own—you will thank us. Victoria! Get them please."

Oronus thought about raising his own rifle but was so dejected by Brevard's actions that he decided to simply set it down.

Brevard tightened his grip on his rifle and straightened his aim as he saw Oronus's hands move. "Please don't, Captain. Don't make me use this."

All light in Oronus's air flushed away. "I would never point a weapon at you, Brevard. Never."

He set the rifle on the ground next to him. Brevard closed his eyes in shame and shed a tear at the sting of Oronus's words. "Victo…Victoria, hurry." She hurriedly snatched up the papers crying yet careful not to let her tears touch the pages.

"Do you see what this has done to you, to my father, and to Eleazer Graff? Help me end this," Oronus pleaded.

Brevard backed to the door and motioned to Victoria to open it. "We are going to end it, Oronus—in a way that you could never accept but is, in fact, for the best." Victoria opened the office door as Brevard tossed the rifle to the ground and shouted down the narrow hall.

"Guard! Guard! Come quick!"

Oronus nodded faintly and looked at the ground as Brevard and Victoria were pushed to the opposing wall by three council guards.

They rushed into the room and found Oronus sitting by the two guards with their rifles at his feet. "You are hereby under the custody of the Council of Directors! Detain him!" Oronus made no attempt to struggle; he simply stood and stared at Brevard and Victoria as two guards grabbed his arms and the third struck him across the face with the butt of his rifle.

Victoria burst into tears as Brevard yanked her down the hallway. "We must hide, quickly!" Victoria was in shock at the rapidity of what had transpired. He led her quickly through Linguistics and out onto the bridgeway without being stopped. "We must act calm as we go through Re-Creation. They can't follow us into the elevator."

They made their way into Re-Creation and into the elevator with relative ease. Victoria closed the sliding door, and they both sighed with relief. "Why did we have to treat Oronus that way? Osiris would never have done that! I am so ashamed!"

"Osiris wasn't here; council guards were. With Oronus in charge of those documents, our dreams would *never* be realized."

Victoria shook her head. "Maybe they shouldn't." The doors opened after a time to reveal the hallway that led to the safe room. They entered and placed the documentation of the experiments where the Chest of Worlds had once sat.

Brevard looked around. "He'll thank us when this is over. This is bigger than us or O.R.T. He'll thank us. He will."

Victoria sat on the steps. "Brevard, how long will we have to stay here?"

He looked down at the top page as he caressed it.

"I don't know."

∿

Oronus was led into the hangar. When he entered, he looked to Parrus's office. There, on the stairs, the two guards who had been subdued were now talking to two other guards who had Parrus between them. Oronus shouted up at them.

"Hey! What is going on, here?"

One of the guards who had been assigned to Parrus pointed down at Oronus with excitement. "There he is! There's the other one!"

The guard who had been subdued first looked puzzled. "*Other* one? He was the *only* one!"

They argued back and forth as Oronus and the guards surrounding him walked to the base of the stairs. "One of them is saying that Mr. Vademe was involved; the other says it was just the captain."

Oronus shook his head and called out to them. "Silence! Parrus, thank you for trying to stall for me. They found the other guards I took down in Linguistics; it's over."

Parrus looked at him with much confusion, but when Oronus winked, he knew to play along. He may not have known what was happening, but if Oronus was satisfied then so was he.

"I'm sorry, Captain." Parrus stepped aside as the guard he had clotheslined erupted in protest.

"This is a mistake! The captain was not the only one involved!"

The other guard involved quietly assured him that it happened very fast and he was confused. Oronus addressed Parrus and any other O.R.T. employees who were in earshot.

"We are not allowed to do business with any outside parties, but we are allowed to continue work within O.R.T.! You will take orders from Parrus Vademe! Parrus, go ahead with our plans!"

The guards and O.R.T. employees murmured in hushed conversation as Oronus was loaded onto a council ship and taken away. Parrus knew that he had to issue orders in a way that would not create suspicion with the council guards; for all he knew, Jacques and Melinda had turned some of them.

He walked into his office and addressed the hangar through the comm system: "Everyone! We are not going to sit and rust while the council halts our progress! We must remain sharp and efficient! I want a full-scale prep of the following: W.A.S.P.s for the scenario of council or basilical protection, ships in defensive positions for the protection of O.R.T., as many small craft as we can muster for quick reconnaissance and recovery for the scenario of down ships with survivors! In no way are we to contact *anyone* on the outside of this facility, for doing so would be against the sanctions of the Council of Directors! Get to it!"

The hangar immediately resumed its industrious hustle as council guards stepped back or were pushed aside. Parrus watched as the seasoned mechanics and engineers took leadership on the floor and aided in the preparation of their particular area of expertise.

"Oronus, I don't know what you're doing, but I hope you do."

∽

Osiris woke the same way as he had the past few mornings: sore and exhausted. He stretched his arms and legs, stood, and picked up the Chest of Worlds and then sat down in his chair. Anna and Aaron were already awake, or perhaps they simply hadn't slept. They watched the sun rise above the eastern peaks, sitting by the fire together. Osiris remembered the early days of his time with his true love, Victoria Osborne. They had separated while she was pregnant with Oronus and had kept their relationship secret, which was a hard feat since they worked at the same facility and he was her employer. He delivered Oronus himself, and she gave him over for him to raise, never to learn the truth about his mother. When Oronus was old enough to understand such things, Osiris told him that his mother died giving birth. How Victoria wished to tell him different! She had watched from afar at O.R.T.; silently, secretly conveying a mother's love without revealing the true nature of their relationship. Osiris knew that Oronus might hate him forever if he told him. Too many lies and half truths had been revealed. Anna and Aaron heard the wheels rolling over tiny bits of sandstone as he approached. She kissed him on the cheek as they rose to pack their bundles.

"Good morning, Osiris," Aaron said as he swung his bundle across his back. "How did you sleep?"

Osiris chuckled. "I didn't. I don't think you can call that sleep. I slipped in and out of consciousness, but that doesn't constitute rest."

Aaron picked up Osiris's bundle and slung it across his chest as he sat in the chair.

"Thank you, my boy. Now, we should reach the airship graveyard in the early afternoon. We'll pass between these two mountains, and there will be a gradual slope into the valley where the airships lie. If we push through, we can enjoy a big, late lunch in one of the kitchens."

Anna smiled at the thought of food and a bed. "I like the sound of that. What're we waiting for?"

She pushed Aaron forward, and he almost fell face-first on the ground. They laughed together as they began the day's trek.

The pass between the two mountains was winding and dangerous at times. There came a point where Osiris could no longer travel in his chair due to the rough terrain. He smiled at the two concerned children and falsely reassured them.

"I wanted to walk anyway."

"Are you sure you can do this?" Aaron asked

Osiris shrugged. "I don't have a choice, do I? Anna, you hold the chest."

She nodded, and they continued walking along the winding pass, careful to favor its walled side. After a long while, they came to a rise in the path. Once they had reached the top, they were able to see their destination: the valley containing dozens of fuel-powered airships.

Osiris pointed down at them. "We've found it! Splendid! You can even tell they are fuel ships from here—the frames are so much bigger than the steam ships, the propellers are smaller, and the hulls utilize far less wood. Most of these were built while I was still directing O.R.T. I utilized a signature swooping symbol across the nose of the blimp; your father uses an O.R.T. stamp, Anna…"

Osiris continued his lecture animatedly as they descended into the small valley. The grass where airships did not rest was actually greener than what they had seen before, and wild ferns sprouted here and there amidst the ships. When they reached the valley floor, Osiris was still talking about airships; Anna and Aaron glanced at each other every few minutes, humored by Osiris's continued excitement. They were completely surrounded by tall mountains, and when they were close to the ships, Osiris stopped talking and looked up at them in silent reminiscence.

They were dwarfed by these pieces of history as they walked along the front row. Aaron was the first to speak. "Well, how exactly are we supposed to board one?"

Osiris smiled. "That's easy; we either find a ship with a rope hanging down, or *you* get to scale one."

"Oh," Aaron said, nodding at Osiris's matter-of-factness.

Anna ran her hands along the leaves of the ferns as they came to them. "Wow. We never get to see plants in the ground; everyone has to buy them in market districts."

They turned from walking along the front row of ships and went in between two of them, looking down the aisle they had made for sign of a hanging rope. After maneuvering through the aisles for some time, they finally found a rope.

Osiris laughed with glee, as though he were a child amidst familiar and favored toys. "The *Manifold!* This is marvelous! This was the first ship we built when we truly committed to allowing our engineers and mechanics more artistic freedom to diversify our fleet! Aaron, climb up that rope and go down the hatch; the only difference in lowering the ramp will be that you'll have to find a large, manual lever by the door—this was built before you were born, my boy! It will have a squeeze trigger, and you'll need to squeeze the trigger, pull down the lever, release it, and repeat the process until the ramp is down."

Aaron took off his bundle and sat it on the ground, then turned to face the *Manifold*. "I'll see you soon!" He reached up and began to climb the rope.

When he reached the top, Aaron found two footholds that would allow him to pull himself over using his arms *and* his leg strength. Osiris knew he had reached them and called out. "Isn't that handy! Before the ropes and some of the other components were automatic, crew members often had to pull *themselves* up!"

Aaron laughed as he realized he was quickly becoming as excited as Osiris. "Yes! This is amazing! They should still have these!"

Osiris laughed as Aaron pulled himself onto the deck. "Tell that to Oronus!" Aaron stood on the deck of the *Manifold* and explored the view from his new vantage point. These ships had collected a lot of sand over the years, and Aaron thought them to hold the same kind of beauty he had noted upon returning to O.R.T. in the skies of Harrah after first discovering the chest. It was a raw beauty, accentuated by the swirling and rising of sand that caught the light of the passing sun and caused the great star to reflect off of the tiny grandules. How different he had been not so long ago; how much maturity and wisdom he had gained, maturity and wisdom that had been thrust upon him if he wished to survive in darkening times.

He descended the hatch and found the lever as Osiris had described it. The hallway was dark and extremely hot, and it was a great relief to Aaron as the ramp slowly descended and the breeze rushed in.

As the ramp touched the ground, Aaron walked down to meet them and retrieve his bundle. "We should keep this open for a while—it's really hot in there, *and* it kind of smells."

Osiris laughed. "What did you expect, my boy? These things have been shut off for years! There's been no ventilation, and sand has slowly crept in from the outside with the blowing wind..."

Osiris lost his train of thought as he looked past Aaron and was drawn inside by his memories. Anna and Aaron followed Osiris inside as he walked through the hallway and explored the rooms. "Much of the furnishings were removed before Oronus sent them here. The council wanted to ensure that we would always have some airships to use. It was a plan discussed before my treachery; I was a part of its creation, even though I did not implement the plan." They entered the control room, and Osiris smiled. "See? The ceilings are at angles as they slope to the walls, and the systems panels of the *Manifold* are built into its walls, not at stations. Our productivity increased several-fold when we allowed them more freedom. Let's set down our things in crew-members' quarters." They followed Osiris down a long hallway to the beds. "We can all sleep here. I wouldn't use these sheets though, for obvious reasons!" He laughed as he dropped his bundle down on a bed and dust exploded into the air.

"*Grandfather!*" Anna shouted as they coughed and sneezed.

"Anyway, use your bedrolls. Now we can take our food to the kitchen for storage. Who's hungry?"

They smiled and talked together as they moved their food from their bundles to the kitchen area in a couple of trips. Osiris sat down at one of the tables and sighed heavily.

"You two can make lunch; I need to rest." Through their time of merriment and discussion, Anna and Aaron hadn't noticed Osiris's growing fatigue; walking that far had taken a great deal out of him.

"Grandfather, are you okay?"

"Yes, child. I just need to sit and close my eyes."

She hugged him and kissed him, and then she and Aaron began preparing their meal. Osiris immediately fell into a restful doze that was long overdue and was awoken by the aroma of food in front of him.

He opened his eyes to vegetable and herb soup. Aaron and Anna sat down across from him at the small table and they ate together.

Aaron looked around and then back at Osiris. "So, we're here."

They were all settling into the reality that this was a stay of undetermined duration in a place isolated from society.

"Yes, and for some time, I'd say. Listen, after we finish dinner,

I'd like to go out onto the deck and look around. Would you two like to come with me?"

Anna nodded. "That would be great! We can look at the mountains and watch the sunset!"

Osiris smiled. "Yes, child, and I can take a look at some of my past."

They continued eating in silence, enjoying the comfort of having reached their destination. The three returned to crew members' quarters and Anna strapped Osiris's tank to his back with some of their bandages. Walking back to the hallway that led to the hatch, they climbed up to the deck.

It was late afternoon then, and they were enjoying the last light of the late afternoon. Osiris walked to the helm and grasped the wheel, smiling and feeling youthful again. He left it for the starboard side, caressing the wheel with his fingertips as he left it. He grasped the railings in a similar fashion, smiling and surveying the ships.

"This is stupendous. It's so good to see all of these...no...it can't be."

Aaron turned as he heard this and voiced his concern. "Is everything all right, Osiris?"

He pointed out across the ships in a daze. "The *Ontonus!* My flagship! My personal design...I hadn't realized it was saved out here..."

Anna smiled and walked to the other side of her grandfather. "Let's go see it."

Osiris smiled and nodded. "Yes. Let's go see it! This is wonderful. I don't deserve this!"

He turned and they followed the excited captain across the deck when he stopped abruptly. "Look out west...it's a group of ships."

They paused and looked to the western sky. "It's probably just more nobles headed to see Graff," Aaron assured them.

Osiris shook his head. "Those aren't ships that nobles would purchase for themselves—those are cargo ships."

They watched for a time as the ships grew closer. Osiris squinted his eyes. "Those ships are in formation."

Anna pushed on both of their backs. "Who *cares?* I want to see Grandfather's ship! It's not like they're going to land on top of us! Let's go!"

Osiris shrugged. "I guess she's right. No one comes into these mountains. It's why the secret reserve is here. We should get inside it quick, though, and close the *Manifold's* ramp. Aaron can close it and climb down the rope to meet us."

They walked to the hatch, and Osiris was the last to climb down. As he made to close the hatch, however, he noticed something. The ships had dropped in altitude.

"Those aren't O.R.T. make." He watched as the ships grew closer—their path would place them between the mountains and the basilica in a matter of minutes. He lowered the hatch as low as he could while still watching the ships.

"Aaron," he called down, "close the ramp."

Aaron protested. "Do I have to? If we're going to be sleeping in here, we need all the breeze we can get."

Osiris huffed and shook his head, still captivating by the approaching ships. "I don't think those ships are headed for the basilica... Aaron, close the ramp."

Anna tugged on the hem of his pants. "Grandfather, we're safe here! Let's see the *Ontonus!*"

Osiris's mouth dropped. "What in the world... Aaron, close the ramp! These ships are passing over the mountains!"

They both stood there in a moment of hesitation. Osiris glared at him. "Gods help you if you don't close the ramp right *now!* They'll be here soon!"

Osiris closed the hatch and slid down the rungs. He turned and followed Aaron to the adjacent hallway to close the ramp. Aaron came to the lever, and Osiris stopped him.

"All right, Aaron, to close the ramp, pull the lever down *without* squeezing the trigger. Then squeeze the trigger as you push up."

Aaron did as he was directed, and Osiris watched the ships through the opening as the ramp closed. "Who made those? Gods, they're stopping right over the valley! Hurry, Aaron!"

He quickened his pace as two of the seven ships lowered until they were hovering just above the ground. Osiris watched with anxiousness and confusion as men jumped from their deck to one of the graveyard's adjacent ships. "What are they handing over? Those are fuel barrels!"

Aaron looked up at him with concern. Another one flew low over a ship that was in the row directly behind them. Ropes were lowered, and men slid down onto the deck. "Osiris, the trigger is jammed!"

Osiris looked over and saw Aaron struggling to close the ramp. "Keep trying, Aaron! The ramp is too heavy to hang there for long—its cogs will break under the weight!" After a few seconds of struggling, the lever flew from Aaron's hands as the ramp slammed to the ground. Aaron winced at the tremendous sound it made.

"Oh, no!" Osiris's eyes widened as the men on the ship behind them looked toward the sound, as did the men further down handing over the barrels. "Aaron, we have to hide! Get the chest! Anna, come quick! Anna! Aaron, where is Anna?"

"I don't know! She was already gone by the time you slid down!" Osiris looked out the opening and back at Aaron.

"We *need* to find her, Osiris."

He put his hands on Aaron's shoulders. "This is one of those times I was talking about, Aaron—we need to hide the chest, and it has to be now. Let's get to the engine room." Aaron heard men shouting and heavy footsteps.

"No!" He shouted as they ran through the control room and

into the crew members' quarters to grab the chest. "Who *are* these people, Osiris?"

"I don't know. There's no time for that now, Aaron! We need to hide!" Aaron grabbed the chest and ran back down into the hallway. As he rounded a corner, the end of Edgar's pistol met the side of Aaron's head with tremendous force, and the Chest of Worlds was ripped from his hands as he fell to the floor, unconscious.

~

Aaron awoke with his head throbbing to see Edgar talking to a group of men. "All right; y' did good. We need t' get back t' work, though. Simon and Thacker'll stay here. The boy and th' old man're both bound. Send a ship t' the basilica—alert th' oracle that we have th' chest."

The men who had subdued Aaron and Osiris left, and they were left in the control room of the *Manifold* with Edgar, Simon, and Thacker. "Wake up the captain, Thacker! We need t' talk!" Thacker walked forward and kicked Osiris in the chest.

"Traitor!" Aaron screamed as he tried to free his hands and help Osiris. Thacker laughed as Aaron fell to his side, struggling to get out of the ropes he was in.

Edgar grinned. "Now isn't that sweet? Help the boy up, Thacker."

Thacker laughed and pulled Aaron to a sitting position by his hair. Simon walked forward carrying the Chest of Worlds.

"Good t' see ya again, Captain." Osiris coughed and struggled to focus—there was a kink somewhere in the tube that ran from the tank to his mouth, and the water trickled into his mouth slowly, if at all.

"Hello, Edgar! It *has* been a while! Tell me, Edgar, when did Eleazer Graff begin offering better benefits than O.R.T.? What could he possibly offer you that we could not?"

Edgar spit on the ground at Osiris's feet. "Maybe you forgot that O.R.T. was the cause o' the sufferin' and poverty in th' first province. Maybe you didn't realize that my parents lost their home cause a' steam-powered ships! Th' oracle's given me quite a bit, Captain: security for m' family, money, and supplies for th' resistance, and—are you ready—absolution and a release from penance! He can do that now, ya know."

Edgar looked over at Thacker. "Go check for anyone that's hidin' from me, Thack. Start up on deck and work your way t' th' engine room." Thacker left as Edgar motioned to Simon to place the chest on a nearby table.

"Hadn't seen this before! This thing's had th' oracle in a tiff with you boys and the council for a while now—quite a tiff. He'll be excited to have it! I'm not sure why he wants it, but I know he's gonna set us up real nice to take you boys down—I promise you that." He walked forward and squatted down in front of Aaron. "You make me sickest o' all, though, boy. Your father was th' rock o' our little group, and here you are promotin' th' very thing he fought t' end. I was hopin' you and Oronus's little daughter o' his would go down along with that hoverin' craft!"

Aaron kicked Edgar in the chin, and he fell backward at Simon's feet. "My father was a good man! He was just confused, like the rest of you are confused! Taking lives is a short-term answer! If you would have let Captain Oronus help you with the humanitarian aid and chances for dialogue that he offered, it might have turned out differently! I think *you* are responsible for your family remaining homeless for so long!"

Edgar stood and glared down at Aaron. Unclenching his fists and rationing his breath, Edgar spoke. "Your father killed more men on that ship Oronus sent us than anyone else, so just shut your mouth about that."

He turned and walked back to the chest, feeling the grooves in the wood and the glass with his fingers. "Well, I seem to remember us talkin' about Oronus's daughter, she wouldn't happen to be here too, now would she?"

Aaron started to speak, but Osiris stepped on Aaron's bound hands with one of his heels to stop him. "She's not here. We left her at O.R.T."

Edgar smiled. "I'm sure you did. Well, Captain, this's one o' your own, huh? Why not show me around for old time's sake? Simon."

Edgar motioned for Simon to help Osiris to his feet, and Edgar motioned for Aaron to stand. Aaron looked past Edgar at the hallway. "I wouldn't try anything just now, Aaron," Edgar said calmly as he pulled out his pistol and pointed it at him, pulling back the hammer. "Let's just look at the ship together, shall we? Have you boys been eatin' and sleepin' in this thing? Goodness. Let's go check out the crew members' quarters, Captain. It'll bring back old memories; you did, after all, assign me to help construct the *Manifold*. Remember?"

Osiris smiled as he led them down the hallway to the beds. "Yes, I remember well the skill and effort you exercised in your work, Edgar."

He smiled and patted Osiris on the back as they walked. "Why, thank you, Captain!"

They reached crew members' quarters, and Edgar and Simon pushed them into the room. Edgar began to look around. "Well, if she's here, I don't think she's in this ol' room. We should..." Edgar stopped as he turned to look at the sleeping area. "Tell me, Captain, if there are only two of you boys here, why would ya need *three* bedrolls. That *is* confusing."

Osiris shook his head. "Well, Edgar, you never know when company will arrive."

Edgar and Simon both started laughing. "Well, I guess you're right about that, Captain!"

Osiris and Aaron laughed too. "You just never know, do ya, Captain?" Edgar added.

Osiris smiled as he watched Anna creep up behind Simon at the door. "No, Edgar, you really don't."

Anna kicked Simon in the back of the head with the heel of her riding boot. When Edgar turned to identify the source of the noise, Aaron kicked Edgar in the back with such force that he fell over one of the beds.

Osiris ran to Anna. "Anna, check Simon's jacket pocket!"

She knelt down, and, just as Osiris had expected, she pulled out a pistol. Edgar's pistol had fallen from his hand as he toppled over the bed, and Aaron leapt over the bed, landed on Edgar, and kicked the pistol across the floor. Osiris smiled. "Good. Now, quick, untie our hands and arms!"

Anna did just that, and when Aaron was untied, he ran and picked up Edgar's pistol off of the ground. Aaron looked from Simon to Edgar, who had stood up by now between the beds. "We can't just leave them here, but we can't take them with us either."

"Edgar! Simon! Where are you guys?" Edgar's eyes widened at the sound of Thacker's voice, but Aaron anticipated his urge to call out.

"Not a word," Aaron said as he pointed the gun in Edgar's face. Edgar nodded silently with his eyes shut tight.

Osiris grabbed one of the ropes and kicked the rest under the bed. "Anna, loosely tie my arms together and hide beside the door! Aaron, keep the pistol pointed at Edgar and duck behind that bed!"

Aaron ran to Simon and pulled him back behind a row of beds. He ducked down below Edgar just as Thacker walked into the room. "Ed, I didn't find anyone else in the ship. Where's Simon? Edgar, what's wrong… hey, where did Aaron go?"

Anna walked up behind Thacker and put the pistol to the back of his head. Aaron rose from under the bed and backed away from Edgar, keeping his pistol pointed at him while keeping an eye on the unconscious Simon. Osiris came free from the loosely tied rope and walked forward to bind Thacker's hands and feet.

Anna grabbed some of the rope that Osiris had kicked under a bed and did the same to Simon.

When Osiris was finished, he took the pistol from Anna and turned to Edgar. "Sit down, Edgar."

Edgar sat on the edge of the bed he had recently fallen over and remained silent.

"Aaron, tie his arms, hands, and feet. Edgar, if you attempt to harm that boy in any way, I will not hesitate to kill you. I'm crazy, remember?"

Aaron bound Edgar and pulled him to the floor on his belly to where Simon and Thacker were lying in a similar fashion. "Anna, go get the chest please. Take this with you." He tossed her the pistol, and Aaron tossed him the other one.

Osiris walked up to the three on the ground and looked down at them. "You have two options: you may either promise to remain silent until we have safely left the valley unnoticed, or I can shoot each of your knees to ensure that you cannot follow us. The choice is yours, Edgar."

They were squealing and wriggling on the floor as Edgar pleaded with Osiris. "Captain, don't shoot us! Please, we'll be silent! Just go! Take my pistol, even—just don't shoot us!"

Aaron shook his head. "No, Osiris, they would have killed us just as easily as they tied us up. Also, Edgar's already sent for Graff."

Osiris snapped his head to the side and looked at Aaron. "*What?* Why didn't you tell me that? We have to get out of here, or Graff will kill us! As for you three... as much as I would like to kill you," Osiris said as he checked the chamber (three bullets left) and pulled back the hammer, "there will be none of that for today."

He walked around and grabbed three pillows off beds and set them between their faces and the ground. "Bite these."

He fired three clean and accurate shots into the backs of each of their left knees. Howls of pain and discomfort erupted from them as Osiris tossed the pistol down and motioned to Aaron. "I'm sorry you had to see that, my boy, and I'm sorry, you three; perhaps fortune will smile on you and you'll pass out soon... or perhaps it won't. Let's go, Aaron."

They moved swiftly down the hallway and into the control room, where Anna stood next to the chest.

She tossed her pistol to Aaron, who gave it to Osiris. "I've never shot one; you take it."

He grabbed the Chest of Worlds, and they followed Anna to the entrance. "A ship just lifted from out of the basilica a moment ago. We have to move quickly!"

Osiris shrugged and shook his head. "There's no way out of here! If we go on foot, we'll be overrun, and it would take hours to blow all of the sand, air, and gas pockets out of one of these ship's pipes! We're stuck."

Anna smiled. "No we're not. While you two were beaten up, I went to see the *Ontonus*. Grandfather, there's a hovering craft *inside* of it."

Osiris's eyes widened. "They kept it in there? After all these years... Does it work?"

Anna shrugged. "I don't know. Let's find out!"

They reached the entrance to the *Manifold*, and Aaron peeked outside. "Was it bad out there, Anna? Could we get there unspotted?"

Anna nodded. "Yes, I think so. There are a lot of men out there, but they think Edgar has all of us captive—they're all working on different ships, so there's no one on the ground."

Osiris sighed. "All right, Anna, take us the way you came from. We must be silent and stick to the hulls as best we can."

They all nodded and, instead of walking down the ramp, hung off of the side and dropped down. Anna went last with the chest, falling backward into Aaron and Osiris's linked arms.

Osiris was already heaving. "Let's hurry; I don't know how much longer I can stand up."

They quietly snuck to the end of the *Manifold*, watching the men on the decks they could see from their position. Osiris's mouth dropped. "Those are explosives and cannons from my era as director... My God, what's going on?"

Anna motioned for them to move on with a quick nod in the direction of the *Ontonus*. They passed four ships along the same row as the *Manifold* and finally reached the captain's flagship.

Anna cursed and stomped her foot as they approached. "They weren't this far before."

Sure enough, men had lowered the ramp of the *Ontonus* and were milling about the deck making sundry and violent addendums.

Aaron looked at them both with a frustrated expression. "What are we supposed to do now?" he hissed.

Osiris pointed at the lowered ramp. "The same thing, my boy, steal that hovercraft. It was the first crafted, you know, and—"

"Grandfather! We can discuss this later. Let's go."

Osiris smiled and nodded to Anna, setting his fascination with ship building aside. Anna ran across the aisle first. Aaron and Osiris did the same. They sidled along the edge of the *Ontonus* until they reached the ramp. Aaron and Anna made preparations to pull themselves up, but Osiris stopped them. "No! We shouldn't all go. I know these models better than you two, anyway. You two slide under the ramp with the chest and I'll slow down long enough for you to hop on."

They looked at each other and then at Osiris, nodding in agreement. He smiled and squeezed both of their shoulders, then disappeared from view as he crawled to the base of the ramp.

A group of men were coming around the front of an adjacent ship, and Osiris took refuge in a large, wild fern. They turned and walked up the ramp of the *Ontonus* carrying fist-sized fuse bombs, and Osiris found his chance. When they were far enough ahead, he simply walked in right behind them, and, upon entering the *Ontonus*, he ducked immediately down a side hallway. When they had climbed up the ladder to the hatch and had gone onto the deck, Osiris went back to the main entrance. What would have been the control room in any other ship was a tiny hangar in the *Ontonus,* in which rested the hovering craft.

He checked to make sure that no one was close by and, running up to the hovering craft, hopped into the driver's seat. *"Please, please, please work!"* he whispered to himself.

The control panel of this hovering craft was much simpler that Anna's design. Osiris simply pulled back a lever that opened the port holes, turned a switch that activated the starter-fuel tank, and pressed the on button. The hovering craft sputtered loudly and backfired, shutting off completely.

Osiris repeated the process with much more anxiety as he looked from the ramp to the hallway with the hatch. It started again, sputtered just as loudly, but this time the engine turned over, and air burst through its ten holes. Osiris grabbed hold of the steering device—two levers that allowed for zero degree turning in midair. However, as he prepared to move forward, two men came from the hallway and stopped, staring right at him. Osiris did not hesitate. He drew the pistol and shot them both in between the eyes. They fell backward, and Osiris passed over them and out onto the ramp. The air flowing from the craft's belly created sickeningly fascinating patterns in the blood that was pooling around the two—they were the next to become martyrs in the struggle against the oracle. They did not die for something they believed in, but Osiris knew their deaths affected families at home and friends. He knew that they probably weren't working for Graff because they wanted to, but rather because they wanted comfortable futures for their children.

He stopped at the side of the ramp and shouted over the noise at Aaron and Anna. "Come on, you two! We have to go!"

They rolled out from underneath the ramp as men from the decks on either side of the *Ontonus* began to shout and climb down their hatches. Aaron and Anna jumped into the hovercraft, and Osiris headed for the slope they had used to enter the valley.

Anna pointed up at an airship that was hovering high above the slope. "There it is! It's the ship from the basilica!"

Osiris watched with horror as Melinda Stockstill's airship began to descend in front of the entrance to the valley. He recognized who was there, even from so high above them: Jacques Aevier, Raulph Hartsfield, Graff, and Melinda were standing in a row at the bow of her ship.

"Hurry, Osiris! We can make it!" Aaron shouted as they headed full speed in the direction the ship was landing.

∽

Melinda laughed. "Ha! They are making it simple: crush them, helmsman!"

It seemed as though that would be the case, and Graff made no move to stop the ship from landing.

∽

Osiris was losing his courage and considered sparing them all when he saw Anna with the Chest of Worlds. "Anna! Hold up the chest! Do it, show them we have the chest!"

Anna was extremely confused. "No! That would be stupid!"

Osiris shouted with frustration. "Impertinent youth! If you show the chest, we won't be *crushed!*"

Anna's eyes lit up, and she stood with the chest. Aaron held her waist firm as she hoisted the Chest of Worlds for all to see.

∽

Graff saw the brilliant colors of the spheres and shouted out. "Helmsman! Stop this descent immediately!"

He shook his head. "We're too close, oracle! Halting so abruptly would risk our lives!"

"Fine! I'll do it myself!" Graff struck the deck with the end of his staff, pushing the top of the staff to the right. Blue light enveloped them for a split second, and the ship took an angled dive at the ground in the direction he moved the staff, away from the entrance to the valley. Anna sat back down in the craft and sat the chest on the floor. Osiris laughed with glee as they passed where the ship would have been. Graff kept his feet as the crew and the three directors rolled or fell toward the railings. Aaron looked at Graff, who was gazing at the hovercraft as it sped out of the valley. Without thinking, he pulled the pistol as Graff turned and fired the remaining four bullets in the chamber, screaming as he did so.

Osiris turned angrily to face him. "Fool! We have no more bullets now! Did you really think that would work?" They sped up the slope as those who were running after the hovering craft turned instead for the downed ship. Graff had not gone unscathed, however. One of the bullets struck the wooden staff as he leaned on it, and it snapped immediately.

"It did! I broke his staff!" Aaron shouted in surprise.

Osiris was ecstatic. "Really? Well done, Aaron! This will reach further than you know!"

Eleazer looked down as the bottom half of the serpentine staff rolled to the railings. He shook with silent rage. He raised a fist in the air, veins bulging from his pale temples, and punched in the air in the direction of the slope. The side of one of the nearby mountains exploded, sending a shower of jagged sandstone pieces onto the slope. "No! The Second Key! No! Stupid child! I am the oracle! I will end you!"

He looked down at the railings. Aevier was holding the hand of a frantic and dangling Melinda Stockstill, and Raulph lay unconscious face first on the railings.

Aevier was red faced and struggling to keep hold of the plump, sweaty woman. "Jacques, sweetheart, pull me up!"

Jacques reached down with his other hand over the railings and grabbed her forearm. As he did, however, the railings creaked and began to give way. "Let go of me! Ve'll all fall if you don't let go!"

She screamed and squeezed his hand. "No! Save me! Save me, Jacques!"

"Let *go* or ve all die!" She shook her head, screaming and crying. The railings creaked again and began to snap. Aevier shook his head and let go of her forearm, grabbing instead his pistol, he pointed it directly at her head. "Let go, Melinda."

She screamed even louder, and Jacques pulled the trigger. Melinda fell to the ground, her white dress and the wild fern she landed in creating a stark contrast of colors. There were now only five members left on the Council of Directors.

He got up and ran to Raulph. "Vake up! Ve need to move!" He hoisted Raulph up and helped him to crawl to a place where they could climb to the hatch.

Graff walked down, perpendicular with the steep deck, to the railings and picked up the end of his staff. He placed the upper half in his belt and held the end that had fallen in his hand. It still glowed softly. Clenching his teeth, Graff jumped down and landed effortlessly. He walked to where Melinda had fallen and stared down at her. "Welcome to the Void, my child."

Jacques, Raulph and the surviving crew, most of whom were *inside* Graff's ship at the time of the crash, came from the half-lowered ramp and stood in front of him.

"Gather everyone at this spot; it is time to engage our common enemy." He closed his eyes and reconnected with Edgar. He shook his head and sighed. "Edgar..."

He snapped at two of the men they had hired. "You there! Go to the *Manifold* and get Edgar and his cronies over here immediately!"

CHAPTER 29

They had gained quite a bit of ground thanks to Graff's crashing of Melinda's airship, but it was not enough to fully escape the deluge of the loosened and fragmented mountainside he had created.

Osiris looked up and winced. "Take cover!"

Aaron threw himself over Anna to shield her from the falling debris, and Osiris screamed as adrenaline coursed through him. He was glad to have the steering system of his design, for he was able to turn, stop, and accelerate rapidly and efficiently. He maneuvered between the larger pieces as they crashed around him, but it was no use when the smaller pieces fell. Those that did not strike the craft in some way rolled under it, causing the craft to wobble and lose control. The levers moved about wildly, and Osiris unstrapped himself. "We need to get off of this thing!"

Using all of the strength he had in him, Osiris steadied the levers and brought the craft to a halt. The tumbling stones began to sweep the hovering craft off of the path and over the edge. They all stood, and Aaron held the chest as they jumped off of the hovering craft and landed on the ground. They watched the craft fall over the edge of a cliff with the wave of broken sandstone.

Osiris lay on the ground, gasping for air and moaning. Aaron rose and ran to him. "Osiris!" The tube had fallen out of his mouth, and water was trickling onto the path from it. He wiped it off and placed it back into Osiris's mouth. "Are you okay?"

Osiris nodded. "I am weak, Aaron. We need to hide... Graff will come to finish us... We need to hide... I can't walk... Leave me, Aaron. Take Anna and the chest and hide in the mountains... I'm sorry."

Aaron shook his head and lifted the old man. Turning around, he wrapped Osiris's arms around his neck and lifted him.

"We're not leaving you, Osiris." Anna picked up the Chest of Worlds and walked to them.

"You two... are amazing... Let's go... need to hide." Aaron and Anna took off, heading for the narrow pass between the two mountains that they had taken to get to the valley.

~

Oronus walked into the office of the third province with council guards on either side of him. One of the guards stepped up to the desk of the senior secretary. "I must speak with Director Addlebrecht immediately."

Johannes's door was open, and he heard the announcement. He stepped outside and shook his head at the sight of Oronus in his office. "What are you doing here, Oronus?"

The other guard spoke to the director. "Director, Captain Bretton knocked out four of our guards in two attempts to contact the outside."

Johannes sighed. "You are dismissed, gentlemen. Oronus, come into my office." Oronus walked in silently and sat down in front of Johannes's desk. "Oronus..." Johannes rubbed his face with his hands and reached for a glass of water. "You do realize that the council is supposed to be deliberating upon your new trial *at this moment*, don't you? You realize, don't you, that you probably possess an artifact that has been promised to the 'oracle' by the council? You do realize that the Council Guard is at Omni Revival Technologies to prevent any of you from *dying* and to protect the power of the council, don't you? Why, then, do I find you here in my custody for a second time?"

Oronus smiled. "Yes, I had realized those things. But, if the council is supposed to be deliberating my fate, why are you *here?*"

Johannes slammed his hands down on his desk. "Because three of them have rendezvoused with the oracle and one of them is dead!" He spun around in his chair and stood with his hands on his hips, facing away from Oronus.

Oronus's eyes widened. "Dead? Who?"

Johannes's hands fell to his sides. "Joseph. He bled to death in his office right after your dismissal. No one knows how or why."

Oronus stood. "Graff."

Johannes laughed and shrugged. "Maybe! Maybe not! We have no way of knowing! Why do you think we're trying to keep you shut down, Oronus? If the council is dissolved, then Graff can claim emergency control over the provinces! If that happens, we'll be thrown into subservience to a tyrant who thinks he is God! If you would just think about others for a hot second, Oronus—"

"My father, my daughter, and my Apprentice are in the Sandstone Mountains hiding with the Chest of Worlds so that Eleazer Graff can't have it! My entire family, Johannes! I *am* thinking of others; everyone, to be exact! If they get in trouble, if someone inside gets hurt, if the first province suddenly decides to act against us again, then we're screwed because we aren't allowed to breathe right now, Johannes!"

Johannes immediately sat down in his chair, mouth agape. "The Chest of Worlds. Oronus, until you said that I really didn't believe it. All this time..."

Oronus put his hands down on Johannes's desk. "Yes, and that is why I need to be able work freely! Lives are at stake!"

"We can't do that, Oronus," Michael said as he entered the room. "Do you realize that by Graff's new orders, even *we* are heretics just for bringing you in? If O.R.T. can't function, then Graff will have to find another way to achieve his power."

Oronus threw his hands in the air. "You too, Michael? Where's Estelle? She will listen to me."

Michael shook his head. "She's with Joseph's family right now, and even if she wasn't it wouldn't matter. The council is scattered, Oronus—there really *isn't* a council right now. If Graff knew that—"

"Emergency rule. I am aware of this." Oronus sat down in his chair. "What are Jacques, Melinda, and Raulph doing in Astonne, then?"

Michael and Johannes looked at each other and back to Oronus. "We don't know, Oronus. That's why we're worried. The people under them here could be listening as we speak—there's no way to tell."

Oronus sighed. "May I please just contact Parrus and check in on everyone?"

Johannes shook his head. "No, Oronus. I'm sorry."

Oronus knocked a picture frame and several papers from Johannes's desk into the floor. "I'll be in a conference room. If the council is 'scattered' for a while, I would think about a search and rescue for that woman you guys banished. She's probably still alive."

Michael laughed. "Gods, Oronus! That's a great idea! I hadn't even thought about it!"

Johannes smiled too. "There would really be no consequence any time soon if we rescued her."

Oronus stopped in the doorway. "If it won't ruin the fate of the provinces, you could send one of my rescue ships. We're running a full-scale preparedness drill right now, so at least one will be ready by now."

He walked out of Johannes's office and into the nearest conference room. He turned off the lights, closed the blinds, and sat in silent darkness, wondering about his family's safety and wondering what he could do next to get out of there.

⌇

Parrus watched with satisfaction from his office; the drill was going so well. The W.A.S.P.s were almost ready, the defensive ships had already taken their positions around the facility, and there were smaller ships and ships with hovering crafts attached for reconnaissance and rescue. Fearing that they might follow in the captain's footsteps, the council guards rounded up all of the O.R.T. guards and sat them together in an unused part of the hangar. The guard who was subdued by Parrus was still so frustrated and confused that Parrus wasn't also taken in that the guard placed in charge by Johannes reassigned him to Dorothea's office in medical.

Parrus stood and paced around. "What do I do now, Oronus? Leave everyone in their positions? Call them back and send them out again? Is this for show or something else, Captain?"

Just then he heard Johannes's voice on his comm panel.

"Parrus! This is Johannes Addlebrecht! Parrus, are you there?"

Parrus walked to the comm panel and sat down. "Just what in the hell are you playing at, Johannes? Keeping business suspended is one thing, but trying to shut down the entire facility? Isn't that a little rash? Where's Oronus? I must speak to him immediately."

"*Michael, get Oronus for me...* Parrus, you need to understand something; the council, such as it is, is not willing to let *anything* assist Eleazer Graff in gaining *any* more power. If O.R.T. can understand that and follow our orders, then we'll all be happier. If you *can't*, and I have to allow the council guard to actually *load* their rifles and be ready to stop you from breaking our orders, I will do it."

"We are running full-scale drills right now to measure our efficiency and accuracy. That is *not* going against your orders, Director, and the first guard I see that gets a bullet into his or her rifle in *my* hangar is going to get one in the chest as well."

"Calm *down*, Parrus, and don't threaten the Council of Directors ever again. That was a mistake on your part, and one that I am only willing to forgive *once*—"

"My statement stands as it is, Johannes, so either state your business or let me talk to Oronus."

"Fine. This little drill of yours is why I called—we want you to send a rescue team to search for Gwen Alden. She's been banished to the ground level of the fifth province, and we want to *covertly* bring her to O.R.T.—"

"Parrus, this is Oronus. I stand by what you said, but if we can help it, let's not spill any blood today. Send three small ships and circle the province, starting at the border and slowly circling inward. Bring Gwen here when you find her, though, and not to O.R.T."

"Oronus! We agreed to a single ship! If they come here in an O.R.T. ship, then Graff can just declare everyone here a heretic!" said Johannes.

"Do it, Parrus..."

"Oronus, you—"

"Yes, Captain." Parrus switched the comm panel to address the hangar. "Everyone! I have orders from the Council of Directors to find Gwen Alden! She has been banished to the ground level, but the council wants her back. Three teams go out and circle the province, working your way in. Whoever finds her should immediately take her to Council Headquarters in CentrePointe. The other two teams should come directly back here. Go now; let's do this as quickly as possible."

No sooner had he said this than four council guards burst into his office and pointed their rifles at him. "Rescind that order, Mr. Vademe!"

Parrus stood angrily and marched forward. "I just got that order from Director Addlebrecht, so if you want it rescinded, I suggest you talk to him about it. Also, there are no bullets in your rifles, so stop waving them around like there are."

He walked through the guards and down to the hangar floor to send off the teams. One of the council guards nudged the head guard. "Call the director! They're about to leave!"

The head guard turned to face the others. "No. That will take too long. We need to stop them *now*. Let's go."

They sprinted down the steps and formed a line in front of Parrus as he walked toward the rescue teams. "Mr. Vademe! If you do this, you will risk jeopardizing the goals of the Council of Directors! I refuse to believe that the director would issue such an order!"

Parrus sighed and pointed up to his office. "He *just* contacted me! Go call him. He will tell you the same. Stop wasting my time."

He made to walk through the guards again, but this time they stopped him. "No, Mr. Vademe! Doing anything that would give the oracle cause for undermining the council is strictly forbidden at this time; those are my orders, and I can't let anyone leave O.R.T. until the director contacts me *personally*."

Parrus laughed and walked around the line. "If you are too lazy to make a simple call, it's not my fault, and it also calls your leadership into question. If you'll excuse me—"

Parrus was tackled to the ground by three council guards. As they turned him over, he shouted, "O.R.T. guards! To arms! They have no bullets in their rifles right now! They are trying to usurp the authority of the council! They have no bullets!"

The council guards surrounding the O.R.T. guards immediately turned to see rifles pointing in their own faces.

"Those could be empty too! Don't surrender!" the head guard yelped.

An O.R.T. guard fired a shot at the ground in front of the

council guard who had said that. Soon O.R.T. guards were running up to every group of council guards they could find and aiming their rifles at them.

One of them ran up to the head guard and put the rifle directly in his face. "Release Parrus Vademe!"

The head guard watched as Parrus struggled on the ground with three guards holding his arms and legs. "Let him go, you idiots!"

The guards released him, and Parrus stood to face the head guard. "Those were their orders, Captain—surely you can appreciate that. How did it feel knowing your orders could have gotten you killed?"

The head guard drew close to Parrus. "Yours could get us killed as well, and if we're not executed for *heresy*, we'll probably be fired!"

"Listen to yourselves! You are letting this man rule you by fear! That is nowhere in the *Book of the Four!* If any of you are religious or educated, you know this! If not, let me say that Eleazer Graff is nothing more than power hungry! Now, back down and let us try to save someone's life!"

"We really don't have a choice, do we?" the head guard asked coldly.

Parrus shook his head. "No, you don't." Parrus turned and walked to the rescue teams. "You have your orders; they come directly from the captain *and* the Council of Directors. Don't come back until you find her."

~

Hundreds of men and boys from the first province stood on the ground and on ship decks facing Eleazer Graff. Jacques and Raulph were on either side of him, and Edgar, Simon, and Thacker were behind him on the ground.

Graff had removed their bullets personally and bandaged the

wounds himself. "Do not worry, simple friends," he had said to them. "The next time I need a divine task brought to pass, I will trust it not to fools."

Now, however, Eleazer Graff had lost all sarcastic pleasantries and his somewhat calm disposition. He was angry and determined, more so, perhaps, than ever before. In his left hand he held the *Codicil,* and in his right he held the bottom half of his staff. "Some of you have already died for the Chest of Worlds alone, and for that I am sorry. I know that the chest is not the concern of most of you. However, I know what is: O.R.T.! Steam power! Poverty! Hunger! Revenge!"

The crowd erupted in roars of applause and approval.

"Oronus Bretton and his line are now a common enemy that we share, my children! Sitting high in his network of towers, Oronus advances his and O.R.T.'s cause while leaving behind those who helped him achieve his success!"

Jacques smiled as he looked at the faces of the men. They were angry, as well as ready to cause pain they assumed would alleviate their own. Graff stepped forward. "You have gone through the worst of times, my children! However, you have worked diligently, prepared for this day with your time and effort, and now it is here! Our common enemy, O.R.T., must be removed from the provinces! They are heretics and traitors! They have wronged you! They have wronged me! Let us show them the meaning of suffering! Let us show them the meaning of pain!"

His hands were raised as he walked through the group on the ground. "I am the oracle and can only take you so far! I am the oracle, whose promises and revelations are only so marvelous! I have promised a release from penance, but I can give you so much more! I believe the Chest of Worlds to be in these mountains as we speak, but it may be somewhere in the bowels of O.R.T.! Find this out for me! My children, I draw near to a celestial transcendence that will bring me into the heavenly light of the Four! My children, whosoever brings me the Chest of Worlds will be made oracle in my place! Whoever storms O.R.T. and ends a life that has caused suffering to their own will be immediately rewarded!"

Eleazer let go of the *Codicil* and pulled the upper half of the staff from his belt. He let go of the pieces, as well, and they remained floating at his side. He reached his hands toward the ground and rose from it, until his feet were level with the eyes of those on the ground.

The crowd erupted in cheers, some bowing, some gaping. "You have sworn your loyalty to me, and for that you will be rewarded! Those of you that give your lives today will be remembered as the first followers of the true God! Together we will bring the new order of our faith to pass! Together we will answer the suffering and pain that O.R.T. has caused with the sounds of thundering cannons and breaking bones! Together we will cleanse the wounds of our past with the blood of traitors and heretics! Make yourselves ready! Climb to your posts! Prepare to wage war!"

The crowds erupted in cheers and shouts, and those on decks loaded cannons and fired *Nitro* into the air. Amidst the cheers and explosions, Graff had seen all of his plans come to pass, and only one step remained in securing his place in the cosmos: the Chest of Worlds. Graff turned to face Jacques, Raulph, Edgar, Simon, and Thacker. He lowered to the ground, returning the upper part of the staff to his belt and the *Codicil* and the remainder of the staff to his hands.

"I must go and see my teacher, my mentor. He has something of mine—something I've been searching for for quite some time now. I may no longer be a part of this assault, for I must obtain the chest before he does anything rash with it or hides it away. You five will now lead the attack. The *Ontonus*, the *Manifold*, the *Regalus*, and *One* through *Seven* will constitute the head of this little brigade. Poor Melinda. She never quite understood. Make the *Ontonus* the first ship that fires at O.R.T., and there will be a hefty bonus for each of you. I must go. Be swift, my children, and be terrible."

They bowed as Graff walked passed them, heading for the slope and for the Chest of Worlds. He bent down and ripped the bandages from Edgar's knee. Edgar shouted in pain as Graff used them to bind the two halves of his staff back together. Placing his hands on the bandages and muttering under his breath, the bandages solidified under a flash of bright, blue light. Raising the staff in the air, he swung the bottom end in the direction of the downed ship with tremendous force. The ship raised, as if to straighten, then fell back to the ground. The light at the bottom of the staff faded and regained the color of the rest of the staff.

"Stupid child!" He turned and sped for the mountains at a pace that surprised them.

~

Anna, Aaron, and Osiris had made it off the mountain pass where they had once almost lost Osiris and the chest. They knew it better on the return, and their pace was much quicker. They turned to see explosions in the air. The sound of the blasts and the cheering of men reverberated into the mountain range.

"What is that?" Anna asked.

Osiris closed his eyes and rubbed his face with his hands. "A send-off."

Aaron's eyes widened. "To where, Osiris?"

"I don't know. But I do know that we need to hide. Graff could come after us. They could bomb the mountains. Who knows what else they are capable of. We need a hiding place."

Anna shrugged. "There were several other paths in that clearing."

"Yes," Osiris said, "but if they pass over while we are in the clearing, we are done. No, our refuge will be somewhere nearby, if we are lucky."

Osiris looked around him and back down the pass between

the mountains. "Aaron, Anna, he is coming. We need to hide right now. If he catches us, then all is lost."

Aaron walked up to Osiris and looked down the pass. "Oh no! We have to hide!"

Anna looked terrified. "Where?"

Aaron looked up. "We can climb. If we're fast, we can reach one of those large holes in the mountainside."

Osiris nodded. "You two take the chest and *hurry* up there. I will stall Eleazer."

Anna shook her head. "No, Grandfather! I won't allow it! We can't risk losing you again! Climb up with us!"

Osiris shook his head and sat down on the ground. "I barely made it here, child. Let me do this. Hide the chest. If Graff gets the Chest of Worlds, it won't matter whether or not I lived. If he doesn't, then at least I died for something. Go now!"

She embraced Osiris on the ground, sobbing quietly. "I love you, Grandfather."

He patted her head gently. "I love you, Granddaughter. Aaron," he said while shaking his hand, "take care of Anna. You two have my blessing, for what it's worth. You will be a fine leader for Omni Revival Technologies."

Aaron fought back a flow of tears. "Thank you, Osiris. It was an honor to meet you."

He smiled and waved them off. "Go! Go now, or it will all be in vain!"

They ran off of the path together toward the wall of the mountain. As Anna and Aaron climbed to safety with the Chest of Worlds, Osiris watched the fleet of ships rise from the valley and take formation.

As they began their flight, Osiris heard a single word fly from Graff's lips as he ran along the pass: "O.R.T.!"

Osiris gasped with horror as he realized where the weapons-laden ships were headed. Shame and sadness washed over him as he spotted the ship leading the flight: the *Ontonus*.

Tears ran from his face as he slumped, and his hands scraped the ground. "Irony of ironies—I have failed the goals and squelched the desires of our line, Son. I am sorry."

Anna and Aaron found a steep path that had been dug into the side of the mountain, perhaps by a flow of water long since dried. They climbed on all fours, Aaron tucking the chest under one arm. They soon came to a shallow cave in the mountain and ducked in. They sat down and watched as the ships flew over the range heading west. Aaron got down on his stomach and crawled to the mouth of the cave. He watched as Graff drew closer, and he heard Osiris call out.

~

"Oronus! Victoria! Brevard! A fleet of ships armed to the teeth is headed for O.R.T.! They'll be there soon! Graff is orchestrating the attack! Oronus, I have the chest! I am about to face Graff! Oronus!" Osiris's voice floated to the walls of Victoria's dark office from Logan and died. "Oronus! Oronus!"

~

Osiris sighed and closed his eyes. He then began drawing in the sand around him. Anna had crawled to the mouth of the cave by now, as well, and watched with Aaron as Osiris began to draw hieroglyphs around him.

Anna started to shout down at him, but Aaron put his hand over her mouth and pulled her to the back of the cave. "If you shout, Osiris will break his concentration! You will also give away our hiding place," he whispered into her ear. She nodded as tears rolled down her face and onto Aaron's hand.

CHAPTER 30

Graff approached his old, weakened mentor on the path. "Hello, Osiris, teacher. I have come to learn some new information and to leave with more... knowledge."

Osiris remained seated. "Hello, Eleazer. It has been quite some time. I believe the last time we saw each other, you gave me these." Osiris lifted his shirt to expose the multiple stab wounds.

Eleazer nodded and smiled and then sat down in front of him. "Didn't you hear, teacher? They're calling me the oracle now. Oh my, that is a magnificent contraption you have there, teacher. You must really be thirsty to have a whole tank of water on your person at all times."

Osiris winked at him. "You would know, Eleazer."

Graff left the *Codicil* floating beside him and gripped the staff with both hands. "I see you grow weary of pleasantries, teacher. Tell me, where is it? Where is the Chest of Worlds? I would so love to see it."

Osiris cocked his head sideways and pointed at the awkward bulge in the serpentine staff. "Eleazer, have you been so careless as to break the second Key? I thought you needed the chest to open if you were to become, who was it? Ah, yes—God."

Graff gripped the staff tightly, clenching his teeth and phasing out his grimace with a smile. "A minor setback, teacher, and one that the brat will pay for, no doubt. Speaking of the brat and the twit—where are they? We could have a wonderful little getaway in the mountains."

The smile left Osiris's face. "Leave them out of it, Eleazer. I've sent them away."

Graff stood and dusted off his robes.

~

Jacques and Edgar stood at the bow of the *Ontonus* as they approached the eastern border of the fifth province. They were slowly decreasing in altitude, and he looked down at one of Harrah's surrounding cities. He was tossing a wrapped ball of *Nitro* with a very long fuse as he awaited the coming attack. Looking down again, he lit the fuse on one of the brightly burning fuel barrels that were dispersed throughout the ships. He leaned over the edge, smiling, and dropped the bomb.

Edgar hit Jacques and stared him in the face. "What did ya do that for?"

Jacques knocked Edgar's arm away and straightened his jacket. "Zis is var," he said, shrugging.

~

As Graff walked away, the ground around him began to shine out a pale blue light as it rose from the ground, spinning around him. Osiris leapt up, thinking he had caught Graff by surprise, but Graff simply turned to face him.

"*Hieroglyphs? Idiot!*" With a swoop of his hand, Graff blew the sand forward and broke the power Osiris had placed in the ground.

Osiris was shocked. "But, how can you do this? How?"

Graff sighed and struck Osiris with the staff, bringing him to his knees. "You were director of O.R.T. for years, teacher! Surely in your time there and as you taught me, you came across the theory that the Raujj evolves! Surely you have noticed, teacher, that things happen around me—things that are achieved without your methods of meditation or writing children's symbols in the sand! I am bringing in a new age of its use, teacher!"

Osiris struggled under the pressure of the staff. "It is a perverted age, then, an age raped of divine approval and of meaning. The old methods were given for a reason, Eleazer. You are nothing more than a blasphemer."

With a shout Graff hammered Osiris in the chest with his staff.

~

Parrus stood in the hangar, awaiting news of the search party's success. It was quiet in the hangar; teams of all kinds stood ready for tasks they would never carry out. He thought that Oronus would be back by then, to take over and to guide them. The council guard had gone into their ship and loaded their rifles, assuring him that they would not hesitate to shoot.

"Good," he had said to the head guard, "we won't either."

He continued looking through the open portholes for a time. As he turned to walk back to his office, however, Kline Stephens came sprinting through the hangar.

"Parrus! Parrus! Ready the ships! Ready the W.A.S.P.s! Parrus!" He stopped, catching his breath, in front of Parrus.

"Kline, what in the name of the Four are you talking about?"

"Sir, our radar imaging has picked up a fleet of ships on a collision course with O.R.T.!"

"Where did they come from, Kline; was it the facility in Restivar?"

"No, sir. They came from the east." Parrus closed his eyes. "Then, the chest...oh, no..."

"Sir, the men out on the defensive ships can see them coming. They said the *Ontonus* and the *Regalus* are two of the ships in the lead. They are equipped with cannons."

Parrus's eyes widened, and he sprinted for his office. He addressed the entire facility. "Attention! We are about to be under attack! Every department needs to go to the area of their building designated for such. Everyone in the hangar, we were lucky today! Fly the W.A.S.P.s! Begin prepping more ships with explosives! I want those W.A.S.P.s ready to meet this fleet!"

∽

Jacques looked over at Edgar. "You have had dealings in zhese things, Edgar—are ve close enough?"

He nodded. "I'm sure we could hit those floatin' ships, if we wanted."

Jacques smiled. "Good. Fire! Fire at vill! Break formation as you see fit! Fire at vill!"

∽

Parrus saw the first ship get hit. He heard the men on deck shouting as the Nitro exploded on the deck, sending splinters and bodies flying. He ran forward and stood in shock as the W.A.S.P.s turned to face the direction the bomb had come from. "This is really happening...Hurry, men! Your fellow crew needs you right now! O.R.T. needs you! Fire! Fire at will!"

It had begun. Over the skies of Harrah, W.A.S.P.s began their flight through the fleet as it broke ranks and swarmed the buildings of O.R.T. The defensive ships engaged and fired their massive cannons into the approaching ships. Two of the fuel ships exploded from the engine room in the belly of the ship and sunk slowly.

Above the battle, Jacques looked down at the ships lining O.R.T. "Get ozher ships up here! Ve need to break through zhose ships!" Jacques pushed one of the men out of the way and pointed a cannon downward at the blimp of one of the defensive ships. He fired the cannon, and when the *Nitro* struck the blimp, it ripped open. As the ship began to sink, the men on deck turned all of their cannons in the direction of the fighting going on above them and fired. Simon and Thacker were on the *Regalus*, and it flew between two W.A.S.P.s without being targeted. To the employees of O.R.T., the ship looked like one of theirs. Simon flew the ship into one of the portholes and docked.

Parrus saw that it was the *Regalus*. "Guards, take them down!"

The head of the council guard watched as the O.R.T. guards sprinted at the ship. He yelled at his men. "You too! Go, go, go!"

He slapped Parrus on the back as he ran toward the ship. Parrus nodded solemnly.

"Thank you."

Thacker lit one of the bombs and ran to the edge of the deck. "For the first province!"

He was shot twice in the chest before the bomb had left his hands. Simon sprinted over, picked it up and threw it at the guards. It blew up midair, sending shrapnel down on them. The ramp of the *Regalus* came down and revealed a group of men with two cannons. They were immediately dropped by a wave of bullets. One of the O.R.T. guards ran up the ramp, lit a couple of the bombs that were lying by the cannons, and shut the ramp.

"Retreat!" The guards fell back as an explosion ripped through the deck, killing everyone on it. Simon was thrown from O.R.T. with an enormous splinter through his chest. He landed on one of the fuel ships at a lower altitude, rolled down the blimp, and plummeted to the ground below.

By this time, two more ships had taken the *Ontonus*'s lead and were dropping bombs on the blimps of the defensive ships from above. From Jacques's vantage point, however, it was clear that their casualties were much worse. They hadn't counted on the ships lining O.R.T. or on the quick response to their presence. However, something caught his eye down below—a fuel ship was speeding away from the battle and directly for one of the buildings in O.R.T.s connectional framework. Parrus was standing in his office and surveying the battle when Kline called.

"Parrus! There's a ship headed straight for Navigation!"

Parrus gasped. "Find someone close to take it down, Kline! Hurry!"

"We're trying, sir!" Parrus closed his eyes and gripped the table he stood at as the impact of the blast shook the hangar with a violent force.

The building stood firm for a few minutes, but a second explosion from the hull of the ruined ship finished the job. The top half of Navigation broke from the rest of the building and plummeted to the ground. Parrus stood patiently by the comm panel.

"Sir... we lost Navigation."

"Lost it? What do you mean, Stephens?"

"They've destroyed the building, sir... it's gone."

Parrus reached blindly for the nearest chair and fell into it. "Murderers."

∽

Jacques laughed hysterically from his place on the *Ontonus*. "Yes! Vat an advantage! Zis is marvelous!"

∽

Navigation wasn't the only building affected. The ships that had been destroyed were falling all over the place, and some crashed into Harrah's Residential and Market buildings. Smoke filled the air, fires raged, and O.R.T. was breaking. Despite their efforts, however, the superior numbers and firepower utilized by O.R.T. were proving too great for the fuel-powered fleet. Ships that were not hit were beginning to turn away and fly for the mountains to the north or back east to the seventh province.

Aevier was outraged. "*Traitors! Stand and fight!*"

Edgar laughed. "Easy for you t' say; we've been floatin' up here the whole time."

Jacques turned and struck him across the face. "*Ve* may have to pick ze oracle up soon, you little brat, so don't lecture me!"

Edgar scowled and reached into his jacket. Aevier drew his pistol as Edgar remembered he lost his. "Do you really want to do zis? No? Zhen shut up and go below deck!"

Edgar stood and hobbled to the hatch. "I *will* kill him before I die."

∽

With his staff pressing into Osiris's chest, Graff spoke. "You may practice this art's primitive application with some small measure of success, teacher, but I have discovered its true meaning and power! I will decide if it is used as a disease, a blight upon my enemies, or as the very hand of salvation for my people! Not you, not Oronus, not God or the Four, not any of the other peons at O.R.T.! I will! Me."

Osiris chuckled through coughs and gasps for air. "You're right about that, Eleazer. There is a great difference between us and you."

He smiled. "Oh? And what is that?"

∽

"Johannes! Michael! Anyone!"

Johannes shouted back through the speakers. "Parrus, you leave me with no choice! By the authority of the Council of—"

"Shut up, will you! We're under attack!"

"Attack? Who is? By whom?"

"O.R.T. was just ambushed by a fleet of ships from the first province *and* from the airship reserve in the Sandstone Mountains. They were orchestrated by Graff, but I'm guessing they had the help of Jacques, Melinda, and Raulph as well."

"Parrus, are you okay?"

"I am fine, and many of their ships are starting to turn back; Oronus's drill saved us all. However, we are reporting extensive damage to O.R.T. and to parts of Harrah. We will need all the immediate aid you can muster. It's not over yet, but it's clear we have the upper hand."

"Parrus, this is Oronus. Do you know anything about my family?"

"No, Oronus. I only know that if they aren't still hiding on one of these ships. They're somewhere in the mountains. I pray that they are, though—we exercised no mercy on the fleet."

"I have to go, Parrus. I'm going to get them. If I find them, I'll be coming to O.R.T., so be ready for communication from a council ship."

"Yes, Captain."

※

Graff looked intently into Osiris's eyes. "What is it, teacher? What is so different?"

Osiris smiled. "We have gained our power through community, Eleazer. Banding together in an expression of love allowed us to stand against you, and we use our strength to hold each other up."

Graff smiled. "How touching. And?"

The smile left Osiris's face, and he removed the tube of the nutrient water from his mouth. "You gained your power alone, and you use it only for yourself. That is why you will lose, Eleazer. That is why you are going to lose."

Osiris did the only thing he could. He turned his head to the west and shouted down the path from which they entered the range. "Run, children! Run! Hide the chest!" He then turned back and grabbed the end of the staff. Throwing it off of him, and embracing that familiar madness that came from a lack of water, he dove into the mind of the oracle. Graff dropped the staff and reached for his head; they were both screaming in pain.

Osiris saw many things: his time spent with Eleazer so many years ago; Jacques's first run-in with the Raujj at the basilica and his transformation; Gwen's horrific experience in Jacques's mansion; Victoria's smiling face as their son was born; the maiden voyage of the *Ontonus;* his father's hands; Logan's contorted face; the fall of the Navigation building and the deaths of many of his friends; and, finally, Anna and Aaron, smiling and holding each other as they watched the sun rise over the Sandstone Mountains.

Running forward and tackling Eleazer, Captain Osiris Bretton passed into the Void as they fell together over the edge of the path and into the blackness of the canyon.

CHAPTER 31

"Fall back! Fall back to ze mountains!" Aevier commanded.

The remaining ships followed their flagship away from O.R.T. and toward the mountains. Kline reached Parrus on the comm panel.

"Sir, they are retreating!"

"Do *not* pursue under *any* circumstances! Let's keep the damage as contained as possible! Do *not* pursue!"

"Yes, sir!"

Parrus stood and watched as the remaining ships returned. One by one, the ramps slowly lowered and battle-weary crew members stepped out, some carrying injured allies, and some carrying dead ones. They instinctively laid the fallen in sickeningly neat rows in the center of the hangar, and Parrus hated Jacques and Eleazer for this instinct.

When the ships had been emptied, the men and women of O.R.T. stood in silence. Explosions were still ringing in their ears, and the smell of hot blood and visions of lost friends still invaded their senses. He went to the comm panel and contacted Johannes, telling him that the battle had ended and aid was needed in the city of Harrah. Rescue ships were already flying amidst a *real* airship graveyard, for these ships would never see the skies again.

～

Oronus flew past O.R.T. and joined the fleeing and broken armada. He shouted out in anguish at the site of his facility and his city: broken buildings, ruined ships, lives lost. It took all of his strength to continue flying for Astonne.

～

Aaron held Anna in the blackness of the cave as her hysteric cries echoed off of its walls. He hadn't made a sound; he was still in disbelief. Was Osiris dead? Was Graff dead? How deep was the drop?

He pondered these things with numbed emotion as Anna clung to him. "Anna, I need to go see … Anna, I have to go for a second."

She loosened her grip and lay down as Aaron left the cave. "Grandfather…"

Aaron slid on his backside down the steep path and rolled as he reached the bottom. He stood and dusted himself off, then ran in the direction of where Osiris and Graff were standing. He got there and knelt at Osiris's water tank; it was still on. He reached for the valve and turned off the tank. This proved to be the closure Aaron needed, for as he took his hand from the valve, tears ran down his face. He had watched Osiris intently and knew what he was doing when he removed the water, thinking back to that day in the safe room when water had been denied him.

He reached for the *Codicil*, which had fallen to the ground when Osiris entered Graff's mind. Osiris was right; he knew just enough about the Raujj to be dangerous. He dusted off the cover and started to open it but decided not to as he sat it down and reached for the staff. How proud Aaron had been when he broke the staff and Osiris praised him. He wondered what the far-reaching effects Osiris talked about would be. Aaron grabbed the staff and the *Codicil* and stood to return to the cave.

"I would like those back please. They are very dear to me—I can't be separated from them for long."

Aaron turned as the staff and the *Codicil* were ripped from his hands. "Here! Take this instead!"

Graff hurled Osiris's body at Aaron as he floated in the air above the drop. "Oh my, Aaron. It seems as though your little friend's pathetic attempt failed. It's really a shame that you have only seen that idiot's use of the Raujj. It is rather...limited. Here, let me show you mine!"

Slashing the staff in the air, Aaron watched in horror as the ground began to break and rippled toward him. He picked up Osiris and turned to run, diving up the path to the cave to avoid being crushed and swallowed by the earth. Graff landed on the path and continued talking.

"Would you like to know what I have seen, heretic? I have seen one of O.R.T.'s buildings collapse and fall to the ground! It was Navigation—any friends there, heretic? No? Well, would you like to know how I know it was Navigation? I went there several times secretly when you were a child. Brevard and Victoria let me in." Graff stretched his neck and strained to see if his provocations were having any effect. "Would you like to know who told them to let me in? Why, it was Captain Osiris Bretton, Director of O.R.T.!"

He heard Aaron's voice from behind some large rocks.

"That's not true! You're lying!"

Graff smiled and laughed. "I am God, My child! Nothing I say is a lie anymore! Isn't that magnificent? No, he did, Aaron—those three taught me everything I know."

Graff swung the staff in the direction of the rocks. They exploded, and Aaron screamed as he climbed for more cover.

"You broke this staff, you know! It is technically beyond

repair! Would you like to know why I think it is working, heretic? I think it is working because it is near the Chest of Worlds!"

With a swoop of the staff, the broken pieces of the rocks were lifted in the air, and with another they were thrown in his direction. By that time, however, he had reached the cave.

"Where is it, you heretic? Where is the Divine Artifact? Tell me! I am so close! Tell me, curse you!"

Graff raised his staff again, but as he looked up he saw the fleet returning quickly east. Graff set down the *Codicil* and the staff and ran in the direction that Aaron had fled. He found the path and glided up with ease.

Aaron and Anna were frozen with fear as Graff appeared in the mouth of the cave. Immediately, as if triggered by his presence or immersion in the Raujj, the spheres in the chest lit up and began to spin rapidly, as Aaron had seen in the Source House. Graff walked in without saying a word. Anna covered the chest with her body and Aaron covered her with his own.

"How touching," he said, and, pinning them both painfully to the wall, Graff picked up the Chest of Worlds. His face was hauntingly colorful in the light of the spheres. "It is done, my children. I have the divine artifact—I am God."

He released them from the wall and rushed forward. "Don't go too far, my children. You two will be the first to be judged by the true God! You should feel honored! I will return shortly to collect your souls for the Void, for I now hold its keys. Good-bye, for now."

Graff glided down the path and quickly collected the staff and the *Codicil*. He walked back toward the valley, where he would gather news from Jacques. Aaron and Anna stood and ran to the mouth of the cave.

"What do we do, Aaron? Grandfather is gone! Graff has the chest! We're stuck in the mountains without food!"

Aaron lifted Osiris from the corner of the cave. "We run."

They made it carefully down the steep path and headed west,

looking for the path where they had fallen. They reached it after a time, and the going was slow and labored as they crept carefully down the steep, narrow corridor. They reached the clearing and Aaron sat Osiris on the ground, breathing heavily.

Anna looked around. "We can take one of these other paths now and hide out."

Aaron shook his head. "We'll starve to death or be killed, Anna. No, we need to continue west."

～

Oronus had been slowly pulling back as the fleet entered the sixth province. By the time he reached Astonne, they had left him behind. He dropped low and walked from the helm, peering over the railings as the ship inched along. After passing over the foothills, he spotted something in a great clearing. Two people were running carrying a third.

"It's them!" he cried.

Oronus ran to the helm and steadied the ship, then ran down to the control room and lowered the airship down into the clearing.

～

Anna and Aaron stopped in their tracks. "Aaron, who is that

The ramp lowered, and Oronus ran down the ramp. "Daddy!" Anna ran forward and jumped into her father's arms.

He swung her around and kissed her on the forehead. "My daughter! Oh, you are safe!" Aaron slowly walked forward carrying Osiris. "Aaron! My boy, you've made it!"

He walked forward to hug Aaron and stopped as he saw his father. Osiris was pale and overly thin; his final use of the Raujj had removed all color from his skin and had made his face gaunt and his eye sockets shallow. Aaron handed him his father and walked to stand by Anna.

Oronus embraced his father and held his head to his shoulder. "Did you know that I thought our world was ending, Dad? I thought all of our time was done. Did you know that I always kept a picture of you in my pocket? All those years that I spent working against you and hating you for dying, I kept a picture of you."

Anna began to weep, and Aaron led her onto the ship.

"I held the picture of you during the end, Dad. I sat there with you at the end." He turned and faced the west, looking up as the stars began to peer out from the cosmos.

"And as I sat with you there, at the end of all things, I realized something: I love you; I always have. Our inadequacies and failures that plagued my consciousness at the world's closing became bereft of meaning. But then it was the end of all things, and I was unable to tell you."

Oronus wept there, embracing his father, and eventually returned to the ship with Osiris in his arms. He found Anna and Aaron in the control room. He laid Osiris on one of the tables and turned to face them.

"Graff has the chest?"

They both nodded.

He sighed. "It is no longer safe for us here. Graff will have unimaginable power if he can manage to open that chest."

Anna spoke amidst sobs. "Where will we go, Daddy?"

Oronus put his hand on Aaron's shoulder. "Aaron, I need you at the controls."

Aaron nodded and silently sat in front of the systems panels.

Oronus took his daughter's hand and motioned for her to go with him. "We fly west."

Anna looked up at him. "To the first province?"

Oronus shook his head as they climbed the ladder to the deck. "No, Anna. We can't hide here in the provinces. We have to leave."

"Leave? To where, Daddy? Where could we possibly go?"

Oronus walked to the helm. "Across the waters to the west, Anna. I refuse to believe that this is the only mass of land in these waters. We will search for a place to land and collect our thoughts. When we have been gone for a long enough time, we will return and attempt to gather allies against Graff."

Anna closed her eyes. "I'm scared, Daddy." He nodded as a tear rolled down his cheek.

"Me too, sweetheart."

～

Graff sat around a table in the control room of the Ontonus with Jacques, Raulph, and Edgar. In the center of the table were the Chest of Worlds, the Serpentine Staff, and the *Codicil*.

"High Priest Aevier, High Priest Hartsfield... Edgar, let's collect the brat and the twit and go to O.R.T. We can end the Bretton line tonight! Also, there are some documents there that my remaining teachers possess. I don't need them really, but I don't want anyone to have them, either. We'll work from O.R.T. for a while; there is quite a bit of reading to be done, a great many heretics to execute in my name."

He pulled the Chest of Worlds to him, caressing it and basking in the glow of the steadily spinning spheres.

～

Oronus, Anna and Aaron flew for two days, passing by O.R.T. and saying a painful good-bye. Oronus had given Aaron the helm and had left Anna on deck.

"Kline, this is Oronus."

"Captain!"

"Kline, I need to speak to Parrus, but before I do you should know that you are doing a wonderful job."

"Thank you, Captain! Wait for Parrus..."

"Oronus!"

"Hello, Parrus. How bad is it?"

"Captain, we've lost a few ships and several lives were taken, but the worst part is Navigation."

"Yes, Parrus, I saw it on my way to pick up Aaron and Anna."

"So they are safe? Excellent! And your father?"

"He died facing Graff, Parrus."

"Captain! I am so sorry for your loss! Captain Osiris was a good man."

"Thank you very much; it means a lot me. Listen, Parrus, Graff is in possession of the Chest of Worlds as we speak. O.R.T. has to respond to this; who knows what he will do."

"Yes, Captain. When will you be back so we can discuss a strategy?"

"Well, Parrus, that's why I contacted you. It's too dangerous for us now, and Graff wants to personally execute the three of us, so we're leaving the provinces."

"*Leaving* the provinces? Oronus, where will you go?"

"We don't know, Parrus. The plan is to find more land and hide until we can come back and help mount a resistance."

"Oronus, what about O.R.T.? Who will lead us?"

"You will, Parrus."

"Captain!"

"Listen to me, Parrus. As director of O.R.T., I hereby turn over to you the title of director and all of the benefits and responsibilities thereof. I am also giving you O.R.T. The property is yours now. If you wish, the Vademe line may become the protectors of the secret knowledge of the Ancients.

"Parrus?"

"It is an honor, Captain. Thank you."

"You are welcome, Captain Vademe. Listen, we are about to be out of range. If for some reason we are unable to return, give my regards to everyone and know that it was an honor working with you. Also, tell Gwen that I love her like she was my own sister."

"Yes, Captain. It was an honor working with you."

"Good-bye, Parrus."

Oronus, Anna, and Aaron flew over the western edge of the first province in the glow of the setting sun, not knowing what awaited them on the coming horizon.